D0768680

Alberta and Jacob

Cora Sandel / Alberta & Jacob

Translated by Elizabeth Rokkan
Introduced by Solveig Nellinge
Afterword by Linda Hunt

DISCARD

Ohio University Press
Athens, Ohio

First published in English by Peter Owen Limited 1962
Original title, *Alberte og Jakob*
English translation copyright © Elizabeth Rokkan 1962
All rights reserved

Library of Congress Cataloging in Publication Data

Sandel, Cora, 1880-1974.
  Alberta and Jacob.

  Translation of: Alberte og Jakob.
  Vol. 1 of a triology; v. 2, Alberta and freedom;
v. 3, Alberta alone.
  Reprint. Originally published: London: Women's
Press, 1980, c1962.
  I. Title.
PT8950.F2A813   1983   839.8'2372   83-19324
ISBN 0-8214-0756-2
ISBN 0-8214-0757-0 (pbk.)

Ohio University Press edition 1984
Printed in the United States of America.

INTRODUCTION
A personal memoir by Solveig Nellinge

Cora Sandel's real name, Sara Fabricus, did not become known until several years after her first book was published. She was born in Oslo, in 1880. Her father was a naval officer and when she was twelve her family moved to Tromsø, in the most northern part of Norway, which is where *Alberta and Jacob* is set.

She decided early to become a painter and around the turn of the century left for Oslo, then called Kristiania, to become a pupil in Harriet Backer's Art School. When she was twenty-five, in 1905, Sara Fabricus left for Paris, taking with her 800 Norwegian Crowns. Her plan was to stay for six months but her visit was to last for fifteen years. She was determined to earn her living as a painter and worked hard at it until 1918 when she put down her brush, having finished her last painting, a landscape from Bretagne. In the spring of 1970, when she was nearly ninety, an exhibition was arranged in Stockholm of as many of her paintings as could be gathered together. She found it very strange to have her first exhibition so late, especially as she had given up painting so long before.

While in Paris Sara Fabricus had sent home a few sketches, articles and short stories in order to survive. She also admitted to having written down ideas, sentences and words on pieces of paper which she threw into a large suitcase. Writing never came easily to her and that she was for so long torn between her two major talents – writing and painting – was a continuous source of conflict for her until she decided to give up painting. She would never admit that both her talents were far above average but she chose to write – or, rather, writing chose her.

Her first novel, *Alberta and Jacob*, was published in 1926. By then she had left Paris: 'It felt like having one's heart torn out.' Those fifteen years left their stamp for life on Cora Sandel's personality. French taste and French ésprit always characterised her.

She was married in 1913, while still in Paris, to the Swedish sculptor Anders Jönsson and together they had one son, Erik.

1

For his sake they tried to save their marriage but in the summer of 1926, as she wrote the last chapters of *Alberta and Jacob*, their divorce became a fact.

Cora Sandel had Swedish citizenship through her marriage and lived in Sweden before the war, moving there permanently in 1939. For several years she lived in Stockholm in the home of a good friend, a Swedish woman doctor, but later, in 1945, moved to Uppsala. She was sixty-five by then and for the first time had an apartment of her own. She lived there almost to her last years.

She was never keen to acquire lots of possessions. Cora Sandel and her character Alberta are alike in this: 'in their fear of dying of surfeit they'd rather die of starvation and are capable of running away from everything – even pension benefits.'

There is one fairly complete biography of Cora Sandel, written by her countryman Odd Solumsmoen. In this book (*A Writer of Spirit and Truth*) there is a typical footnote added by Cora Sandel who had read the book herself and approved of it before its publication in 1957. Towards its end Solumsmoen writes that Cora Sandel always followed the example of Alberta in not having too many belongings to worry about: 'Everything she owns is packed in trunks and deposited in various attics here and there.' Cora Sandel's comment (the *only* one in the whole book) states in three words: 'Not *quite* everything'. This reservation is characteristic of Cora Sandel, who always kept a certain distance. Although she was prepared to part with a certain amount of information about her private life she would never tell everything. 'I have always been of the opinion that no more needs to be expected of an author than that they should write books', she once said in a sentence which has become a classic. When asked by a literary magazine which was the most important experience in her life Cora Sandel replied: 'That I prefer to keep to myself.' The biographical data she once gave to her publisher could hardly be more concise: 'I was a child in Oslo, a young girl in Northern Norway, a grown woman in France and Sweden. I grew old during the Second World War; I had a son during the First and I live in fear that he will be sacrificed during the Second.'

When I first met Cora Sandel she was eighty-five years old. She was living in her apartment in Uppsala and made very few new acquaintances. There was a myth about her reserve, many stories were told at the university among the students who studied her

2

work of how she always refused to see people. It is still easy to remember the calm sitting room with beautiful, beloved belongings – the stillness of the room and the things themselves in such contrast to the heavy traffic in the busy street outside. She used to sit on a blue sofa, above which hung a painting of Tromsø. She cut ice cold grapes: 'Grapes, like chocolate, should be kept in the fridge.' On the small table next to an easy chair were many of the new novels or collections of poetry which authors had sent her, or new novels and books of poetry which she had bought herself. In her bookshelves were many French books in beautiful leather bindings, several by Colette, her twinsoul, whose books she translated into Norwegian but whom she never met in person. 'I considered it too presumptuous to have friends arrange a meeting – Colette was forced to meet so many people anyway – although it could have been done while I lived in Paris.'

She had no television set and when, in 1963, *Krane's Café* was adapted for television, her Swedish publisher brought a television set to her flat in Uppsala so that she could see it at home. All her life she refused to be interviewed for television or the Swedish Broadcasting Corporation. When she was over ninety her Swedish publisher and I were allowed to make a long radio interview with her. Out of respect we hid the technician in the bathroom but she immediately caught on when she saw the wires and asked him in and gave him a glass of sherry.

Animals were always most important in her life. She even called one of her books *Animals I have known*. In her study all the animals from *Winnie the Pooh* sat in a row and it was, of course, Piglet, the small and frightened one, who had most of her sympathy. One of the paintings in her small breakfast room where we used to have tea is dominated by the green colour so characteristic of her style. It shows a garden in summer and in the lush grass a black and white cat is arching its back. If one looks closely one discovers that it is a wooden toy cat. 'I don't find it all that good,' she said, 'I would have liked a real cat for a model.'

To all those who even late in life feel that they have an unborn novel inside them, Cora Sandel may represent a certain hope. She was forty-six when she published her first novel in Norway, under her pen name, Cora Sandel. Her real name was not known and no photo was to be had of the author. Her uncle wrote to her from Tromsø: 'I have just read a book by a woman who calls herself Cora Sandel. Everyone here says that it is you.' And he

3

went on to tell her how he liked the book and how he always thought she would do something quite exceptional one day.

Alberta and Jacob is indeed an unusual book and with it she made a real breakthrough. It was to be followed five years later, in 1931, by *Alberta and Freedom* and the final volume in the trilogy, *Alberta Alone*, was published in 1939. It didn't come easily. Proofs were read and sent back to the publisher together with the next chapter – and all the time cables and letters were arriving imploring her to send more of the manuscript.

'One of the truly great woman characters in contemporary Scandinavian fiction' was how Alberta was described by the critics. The trilogy is partly autobiographical but, one wonders, can such a perfect whole be 'partly'? Cora Sandel herself says: 'In everything one writes there is woven in a thread from one's own life. It can be so hidden that nobody notices it, but it *is* there and it must be there, I suppose, if it is to be seen as a piece of living writing.'

Although the trilogy was a feat in itself several collections of short stories were written and published while Cora Sandel was grappling with her Alberta character. In 1927 came *A Blue Sofa*, followed by three more books of short stories. Her last novel, *Köp inte Dondi*, was published in 1958 and translated into English under the title *The Leech*. She did not publish much after that, only a last collection of short stories with the symbolic title *Our Complicated Life*.

Cora Sandel's own life was long. She was ninety-four when she died and she left an impressive legacy, perhaps above all, she had created Alberta. Cora Sandel said about the writing of *Alberta Alone*, the last volume in the trilogy: 'Every word came floating up from the unknown depths whence it rises anew, transformed, unrecognisable, like a dream, impossible to refute.'

Solveig Nellinge
Stockholm, 1980

ALBERTA AND JACOB

PART ONE

THE church clock shone like a moon in the night sky.

It struck, and weak little lights took shape out in the darkness and burned dully, lost in its infinity, scattered and lonely.

The clock struck again, and the lights multiplied, grouped themselves, formed lines and squares. Life stirred between them, a sleigh-bell tinkled, what might have been an empty sled could be heard jolting from side to side behind a horse on the hard-packed surface of the road. Something fell with a splash into the sea, a chain rattled. The sound of oars and creaking rowlocks came up out of the darkness, a boat thudded against timber, heavy feet in sea-boots clattered along a quay, someone shouted.

Out on the western fjord a ship's siren hooted. Red and green lights slid slowly out of the dusk. People were running with hawsers on the New Quay; at the Old Quay the bell of the Southfjord steamer was ringing, impatient to be gone at six o'clock. The eight arc-lamps in Fjord Street shone weakly in line, except for the one outside Louisa-round-the-bend, which was always broken. And windows, lit up in a flash, bright, strongly shining rectangles, joined ranks and fell into fresh lines and squares.

The clock struck one heavy chime on the quarters, four on the hour, and then, very rapidly, the hour itself. And Kvandal the tailor, who played the trombone in the Temperance Orchestra, was practising before opening his shop. At long intervals he would produce a single, tremulous note. These were a part of the regular early morning sounds, and a favourable wind could carry them all the way to Upper Town.

If there had been a snowfall during the night, the plough would fuss from one end of the town to the other with a great to-do, with six horses, shouts and a cracking of whips, and Ola Paradise in charge. The roads were then officially open to traffic, and you could throng wherever you wished.

7

Theodorsen the baker appeared at the top of his steps. You couldn't see it in the twilight, but you knew he had flour in his beard and floury trousers. He looked up at the weather. Inside the shop Mrs. Theodorsen was taking the loaves passed in to her through the hatch from the bakery, and stacking them slantwise on the shelves. Baker Theodorsen shivered a little and said Brrrr! Then he buttoned up his cardigan, took the snow shovel from the corner by the door, and set to work clearing a path out to the street for his customers.

Tailor Kvandal's music died away. Shadows came gliding between the houses, and shop doorbells tinkled. Hands moved in the Misses Kremer's window arranging coloured ribbons, hats on stands, christening robes, bridal and funeral trimmings. And there was Miss Liberg taking a hurried morning airing, and old Stoppenbrink taking his time, and Bjerkem on his way to school with a pile of exercise books under his arm, and Nurse Jullum the midwife on her way home. A new day was beginning, and no mistake.

It might be dark, with northern lights and swarming stars, and so cold that the snow squeaked under your footsteps. There might be a south-westerly gale damp with rain, and overcast, black streets; then the weathercock creaked on top of the church tower and the gilt signs outside the two bakeries rattled alarmingly. There might be moonlight too.

But mostly there would be thick snow, rounding off, smothering, muffling everything; shapes, colours and sounds.

When Alberta woke up in the morning she was always warm. It was the only time of day when she was not cold. Her limbs were snug and relaxed, physically at peace. Nothing could be better.

She would lie full length, her legs straight out.

The whole bed was warm, and her body felt as if it had uncurled, as if a shell surrounding it had been broken.

She stretched herself, feeling agile and supple, able to treat her warmth lightly. Sometimes in her arrogance she would stick one foot out into the cold simply in order to feel it warming up again as soon as she drew it back.

At night she would lie huddled and trembling beneath the blanket for hours, chilled to the marrow. She made herself as small as she could, drawing her legs up under her and hugging herself. The cold would sit between her shoulder-blades gnawing like pain. She carried it in her body all day, and it accompanied her to bed. Her feet, like blocks of ice, seemed not to belong to her, and she became cramped and sore from her huddled position.

After a while she would fall into a kind of waking doze. Her body slept, ice-cold, but numb and unfeeling. Up in her head her brain sat spinning, engrossed in its own affairs.

Time passed, hours went by. Through a thin web of half-waking dreams she would hear the church clock.

Then suddenly the warmth would come. It came like fever. She stretched her legs, and it was release from an instrument of torture; she relaxed her muscles as if after vigorous effort. She lay intoxicated and drifted into sleep.

When she woke she listened. Something ought to happen, the church clock strike, Tailor Kvandal begin, the Southfjord steamer ring its bell. She had to find out where she was in time, and how long she could stay comfortably in bed. But the Southfjord steamer rang three times, the church clock had the annoying habit of striking only once whether it was the first, second or third quarter, and Tailor Kvandal was subject to his human nature – he was not absolutely punctual. There were even mornings when he failed her altogether.

Eventually something happened on which she could rely. The stairs creaked beneath Jensine, who was going down them. Then she heard the door to the office, and a distant rumbling of coal. Jensine was lighting the stoves, first in there and then in the dining-room.

Alberta thought about all the stoves that were lighted every morning. The red glow from a stove door, the crackle of fire, were they not symbols of life's happiness? Warmth was life, cold was death. Alberta was a fire-worshipper in the full, primitive sense of the word.

Warmth made anything possible.

Warmth, and the cold gnawing in her back surrendered.

9

Hands and feet came alive. She became more cheerful, more lively. Her limbs freed themselves from her body in unrestricted, beautiful movements; it was like putting on a well-fitting dress. She had a desire to talk and laugh, and a desire to sit still, busy with something.

Her face was no longer blue. She was a new person.

The stairs creaked again. It was Mrs. Selmer.

She paused once or twice to do up the remaining buttons on her dressing-gown. The door downstairs opened and shut. And Alberta had stayed in bed too long again, and there was only one thing to do: get up with the greatest possible speed and the least possible loss of warmth, dressing herself more or less inside her nightdress, only slipping it over her head when all her underclothes were on.

As for the rest of her toilet, she hated the ice-cold water as much as the sight of her thin arms and sharp collar-bones. But neither were to be avoided. The mirror hung over the washstand, and Mrs. Selmer was Argus-eyed. Not the slightest shadow on Alberta's neck had ever remained unnoticed the whole day through. While she washed she scrutinized her appearance with pessimism.

Oh to be different, in colouring and shape and dress, different in every way. That face in the mirror, was it really hers, the one she was to have all her life? Its features were so vague, she never really got to grips with it. Her hair hung smooth and unattractive round it, revealing far too much of her forehead; her complexion was blue and muddy.

And her eyes – yes, her eyes had a cast in them. Mrs. Selmer sometimes called it a squint.

Alberta put up her hair in a curious manner, in a way that, without being either what Mrs. Selmer liked and Alberta disliked, was nevertheless a compromise and a step towards reconciliation. Then she put on her dress. There were always a few eyes missing, and she hooked it shamelessly into the lining. This took some time. A disagreeable day of reckoning, when the holes and the crooked hooks would be exposed, was inevitable. But it was no use thinking about it.

Before she went into the dining-room she paused outside the

door, just for a moment, a few seconds. She conquered something, and braced herself.

Then she went in to Mrs. Selmer and the new day.

Inside the room the stove was crackling and the opening was bright. The fire could be heard and seen and would have given warmth had not the door to the sitting-rooms been open. It was supposed to warm up in there as well. But the sitting-rooms resembled the lean kine of Egypt, devouring all the warmth and becoming no warmer.

Mrs. Selmer was sitting at table. Over her dressing-gown she wore her large check shawl. A novel from the lending library lay open beside her plate.

'Good morning, Mama,' said Alberta.

'Good morning, Alberta,' replied Mrs. Selmer wearily and curtly, without looking up. Alberta sat down. The joyless still life of the breakfast table was immutable. The goat's cheese, the sour-milk cheese under one dome and the clove cheese under another, the bread basket. Two butter dishes, with dairy butter for the older generation and margarine for the younger, cream, sugar. But by Mrs. Selmer's place was the coffee pot under its cosy. When the cosy was removed the coffee pot stood there like a revelation, its brass well polished, warm, steaming, aromatic, giving life and hope, a sun among dead worlds.

Alberta helped herself to bread and margarine with as little noise as possible. Cheese she took if the atmosphere seemed favourable. She cautiously handed over her cup, and Mrs. Selmer filled it without looking at her. Not until the cosy was back in place over the pot once more did they glance up at each other, Mrs. Selmer with a resigned look that crushed Alberta completely. She blushed and stiffened, her hands shook. Disarmed in the first round, she dared not ask for more coffee. If only Jacob would come.

Jacob had to be at school at half-past eight. At twenty past he clattered downstairs, arriving out of breath with a 'Good morning, Mama. Good morning, Alberta.'

He tossed his books, strapped together, on to a chair, dragged his sleeves, which were far too short and which immediately crept up again, over his blue wrists, and looked from Mrs.

Selmer to Alberta and from Alberta to Mrs. Selmer. He was sounding the terrain. Everyone did so in Jacob's and Alberta's home; it had become a well-developed instinct, an extra faculty.

'Jacob, Jacob, you'll be late,' said Mrs. Selmer, putting aside her book. And Jacob assured her afresh each morning: 'No, I won't, Mama, I'll manage all right. I've got ten minutes.'

She cut thick slices of cheese and piled them on to his plate: 'Here you are, hurry up and get something inside you. You never eat properly – you get *up* too late, Jacob, my dear.'

Alberta left the table quietly, thankful for anything that drew attention away from herself. She sat by the dresser where the sewing basket stood – where the sewing basket always stood – took out a stocking and began to darn it. Sometimes this was not the right tactic, and she should have started on something else. But the basket was there, providing a kind of haven and a chance of salvation.

Frozen to the marrow, she twined her legs round each other. Her fingers were white and numb. If only Papa had eaten, if only Mama had gone upstairs, so that she could get hold of the coffee pot!

Jacob clattered out with a final: 'It's all right, Mama, I'll be there in time,' and disappeared.

Mrs. Selmer sighed. And if it was one of the days when Alberta appeared in a slightly better light than usual, one of those unreal days of clemency which at any rate began well, she would be allowed to share in her concern for Jacob and his schooling. He was not likely to move up into the second year at *gymnasium*.

But if it was the kind of day – and this was most frequent – when Alberta was a cross and a burden from early morning onwards, Mrs. Selmer would sigh without addressing her. She would sigh many times and not only on account of Jacob, not by any means only on account of Jacob. Alberta would cringe. She longed for Papa's arrival and feared it.

The stairs creaked heavily. Magistrate Selmer was on his way. He was large, and heavily built, the door seemed too small for his tall, broad figure, powerful in all its dimensions. His small grey eyes were tired and strained in his red face; the veins in them were like delicate tracks of blood. He carried the news-papers under his arm.

Now one of two things would happen. Either he said good morning, sounded the terrain, concluded with a 'Well, well—' and sat down; and then said something in a tone of voice im-plying that he wanted – wanted most decidedly – to be good-natured and frank, a tone of voice that was doing its best. Then peace or strife would depend on Mrs. Selmer.

Or he did not say good morning, he said nothing at all. He sat down, was given his coffee, helped himself to bread and butter, unfolded his newspaper and still said nothing. But an inner struggle was taking place in his huge body. Something or other gave warning of it: a growl under his breath, a bitter mumble. Even the way he helped himself, even the set of his shoulders, seen by Alberta from behind, were full of ill omen.

Mrs. Selmer trembled, looking at him sideways. Alberta trembled even more.

Then it came. He threw down his napkin, he threw down the paper. He pushed his plate away from him and moved something angrily, putting it down again with a clatter. And the storm broke. Strongly and with conviction and by no means under his breath he invoked the Prince of Darkness in several variants.

Nothing had happened necessarily. It need not have been a bill that had arrived by way of the office, nor did it have to be Jacob.

Magistrate Selmer's wrath piled up inside him for obscure and unknown reasons, and when the pressure became too strong there was, in accordance with the laws of nature, an explosion.

Mrs. Selmer cried. She cried childishly and helplessly over her coffee cup, looking small and shrunken in her faded dress-ing-gown.

Alberta was also permitted to cry. Her tears, which unhap-pily welled up with ease, normally gave rise to vexation. On either side of the table she and Mama dabbed at their eyes with wringing wet handkerchiefs. The Magistrate had gone into the office.

Mrs. Selmer pulled herself together and said jerkily: 'It

helps me so much, Alberta my dear, that at any rate *you* understand – it's a great comfort to me.'

Alberta tried to say something, but had to give up. Racking sobs overcame her afresh.

Mrs. Selmer rose, went round the table, patted her on the back and said soothingly: 'There, there, my child. We must remember that Papa is kind after all. He has many worries and difficulties, we mustn't forget that. But I do hope he'll control himself a little in there, so that the Chief Clerk won't hear anything – or Leonardsen. It's a perpetual anxiety to me, Alberta.'

But Alberta was already breathing more easily. Deep in her heart, beneath a chaos of evil and warring emotions, she had great sympathy for Papa, a great weakness for him. She knew that where the Clerk and Leonardsen were concerned there also existed a Magistrate-in-office, buttoned up, correct, his features tightly controlled. In fact, his mouth was slightly twisted. He could expunge the raging Papa of everyday life and put himself in his place, just as when one picture follows another in a magic lantern. She had an unreasoning faith that the Magistrate-in-office would always know when to appear at the call of respectability, cost what it might.

Mrs. Selmer went to fetch a pail of hot water from the kitchen, and wandered upstairs to dress, red-eyed and resigned.

And the moment came for which Alberta had been watching and waiting. She forced herself to calm the last waves of tears, fanning herself with a rolled-up napkin until the worst traces had disappeared. Then she seized the coffee pot, carried it out to the cooking stove and put it on to heat. She kept her hands round it to warm them and to test the temperature. A blissful, torturing glow travelled through them up to her armpits and into her shoulders. When she could stand it no longer, when the palms of her hands began to burn so that she almost cried out, she fetched a slop-basin from the pantry, poured coffee into it and gulped it down through a lump of sugar held in her mouth.

I shan't have a tooth left in my head by the time I'm thirty, she thought, imagining she could hear them crack, while the scalding-hot waves of coffee washed through her, making her back ache. She drank it almost boiling, three or four cupfuls one after the other.

Jensine, who would have to cook more coffee for herself with the grounds and polish the pot into the bargain, muttered sourly: 'I'll tell the Madam, Alberta, and that's a certainty. I'll be glad when she comes in one of these days and catches you.'

Alberta turned, still drinking, and looked at Jensine with distended eyes over the rim of the bowl: 'I must have it, Jensine,' she managed to get out between two gulps.

Jensine went on muttering, but she never gave her away.

And Alberta was warm for a while, warm right down to her fingertips. Her blood beat strong and fast, and her blue face turned bright red.

Alberta was dusting. Grey with cold she pottered about in an apron and an old pair of gloves, armed with a knitted rag. She wore gloves more for their warmth than to protect her sadly neglected hands.

The grey light seeped slowly in through the ice-covered panes. There were six sets of windows altogether in the two sitting-rooms, all of them iced over. The little warmth from the dining-room had no effect on them. When Alberta started dusting she could only just see well enough to walk round.

Objects came to light in the same order each day, this year as last year. First the table in the middle with its plush cloth and small piles of illustrated leather-bound books. *Buch der Lieder* on top of *The Princess's Bridal Procession, The English Pilot* on top of Doré's Bible, the Norse Sagas on top of *The Arabian Nights*, Asbjørnsen's *Folk Tales* on top of Holberg's plays. In the centre of the table stood epergnes with visiting cards in them, and framed photographs.

Along the walls between the windows, behind the groups of plants, behind the ivy on its trellis and behind the big armchairs, pools of night still lay. Around them objects rose to the surface like skerries in the ocean: the sofa with all its cushions, the bureau with the clock on it, occasional tables with knick-knacks and books, the bookcase with rich colours and gilt edgings behind the glass.

Footstools emerged, and the pattern on the carpet. More and still more objects were touched by the grudging light of the dark season. Knick-knacks everywhere, knick-knacks and photographs, on Mrs. Selmer's writing table, on the piano, on étagères. Small tables set aslant, small cushions of every size and shape, small pieces of fur. And a multitude of plant pots. Pots with palms and aspidistras or simply a dry stick, pots with crinkled tissue paper round them, majolica pots, pots large and small. They stood in jardinières, on steps, on pillars and on window ledges. In severe cold they were moved into the centre of the room at night and back again in the morning. Alberta hated them.

She also hated most of the countless little objects she had to lift and put back in place every day. It was a quiet hate, expressed in her intense loathing at having to see the things, touch them, have them in front of her like a thicket through which she had to pick her way each morning – and in her tendency to put them down roughly and angrily.

As long as she still went to school and had nothing to do with them they had seemed like a magic world. There they were, either pretty or curious, if not the one, then most certainly the other. Ever since she was small she had wandered among them on silent voyages of exploration – loving some of them, and admiring the rest.

But during the years she had spent at home she had learned to recognize their true nature: they were merely a nuisance and an encumbrance. She had already made one rule of life: to have few possessions, as few as possible, to look after and care for.

There were only one or two things against which she had acquired no grudge. First, the two little Dresden china figures, a shepherd and shepherdess each under a rose bush. The bushes had red, yellow and blue roses. The shepherd played his flute to the shepherdess, a dog lay at his feet. The shepherdess held her hat by its knotted ribbons in one hand, laying the other on her curving china breast, which burgeoned out of her delicate, slender waist as if from a flower vase. A lamb lay at her feet.

There was something about the smooth, shining forms of

the tiny figures, their dancing-school grace and the colours of their clothes, that ensnared Alberta afresh each day, so that she paused when she reached them, held them in her hand for a while and looked at them more attentively.

She would never really be fond of the rose bushes; they were knobbly and uncomfortable to the touch. But the shepherd and shepherdess were smooth and good to hold, and they had something indefinable about them that made her happy. They were beautiful.

Then there was the red lacquer box from China. A curious world was carved in the lacquer and peopled its sides: men, trees, houses with balconies, people on the balconies, clouds, animals, all swarming mysteriously together. Somewhere on it there was a magnificent and terrifying dragon.

If you opened the box it was gold inside, a dark, deep golden lustre, beautiful and sinister. The box was a fairy tale, an unfathomable realm of mystery. Alberta opened it every morning and stood looking into its golden interior, where her face could be glimpsed at the bottom, faint and veiled as if seen through fantastic, costly hangings.

The Chinese box, the shepherd, shepherdess and bureau had all come from Grandpapa's house. A vague memory of a large low-ceilinged room with mahogany furniture and old portraits, where the light was green and cool from the foliage in the garden outside, lay about them like a faded halo.

When she was quite small Alberta had visited Grandpapa in the little town in South Norway to which he had retired.

The Magistrate was in the office, Mrs. Selmer was dressing, Jacob was at school. For the moment nobody was asking for Alberta.

She put on the altered jacket, inherited from Mama, placed an unbecoming hat on her unbecoming hair, looked at herself despondently for an instant in the mirror, and went out.

The arc lamps hung in the falling snow like pale moons. But a warm, red glow fell on the snow from windows and shops, making it bluer round the patches of light.

Alberta gathered up her skirt and followed in Jacob's tracks. Ewart, whose business it was to hold a passage open to the middle of the street, was probably still on the office side of the house. Ewart came late, later and later every day, whatever the reason might be.

Kvandal the tailor was standing in the doorway of his shop in a fur cap and thick woollen cardigan. He did an old-fashioned kind of scrape towards Alberta. He had the family's custom in so far as he altered Papa's old clothes for Jacob. Alberta greeted him, stiff and tongue-tied as always, and hurried past. If he had called at the kitchen door with a bill recently she would turn red and hot.

But it probably could not be seen in the twilight. She blushed easily, it was one of her misfortunes, and she was thankful each time it went unnoticed. Invariably she blushed because of people, merely because for some unaccountable reason she had done so once. If she had the chance she unhesitatingly took any roundabout way in order to avoid them.

Quickly and quietly she glided down the street, a shadow among other shadows. Alberta always made herself as small as she could, shrinking inside her clothes, as if that would help. She held her hands clenched inside her cuffs, out of the cold, and had turned her collar up round her ears. With her stiff little nod, looking straight in front of her, she greeted Schmitt the butcher; Vogel the café proprietor; and Beda Buck, who worked in the Recorder's office and who shook her fist through the window at Alberta, because she was wandering about in freedom, while Beda had to sit indoors. Alberta smiled a half-smile at this, but hurriedly resumed her normal expression.

She caught her breath. A little way down the street Bergan the lawyer had come into view. His large, thick-set, slightly swaying figure was easily recognizable. He was one of the people who made her blush most, who made her helpless, crimson and tense.

For what reason God and Mrs. Selmer alone knew. For Alberta was not in the least in love with Bergan, indeed, she would have been more than horrified were he to present himself as a suitor. But the thought that people might perhaps suspect her of being in love with him, and that Mrs. Selmer might perhaps get an encouraging look in her eye if she were so suspected, was enough, more than enough.

Now he was coming towards her, he was coming closer, she felt tense already. What was he doing out of doors at this time of day, why wasn't he in his office? Oh, why did this have to happen?

And then Bergan went into the pharmacy, into the 'Polar Bear'. He moved calmly up the steps, and disappeared. Alberta's blush, which had already flamed up, faded away, her heart was released and started beating normally again, she was saved. But when she turned into the Market Square the tenseness was still in her body and prevented her from moving her head for a while, even though there was no-one there.

Here there was no traffic. The square was deserted right up to Peter on the Hill's house. Not a soul was in sight besides Schmitt the butcher's shaggy dog, lifting its leg by the bandstand.

Alberta ran. Past the fire station, past Peter on the Hill, from Lower Town to Upper Town, upwards, upwards, until she reached the main road into the countryside above the last houses. She stopped and turned, panting.

Her face glowed and her heart beat like a hammer. She breathed as if she had cramp. But her blood thrust warmly through her body, she felt it tingling in the palms of her hands and in her finger tips. It was some time before she got her breath again.

She was away from home, she was warm, she was alone. Priceless blessings, that might lead to undreamt-of opportunities. Every day she rushed up the hill at the same furious speed in order to win them.

She stood for a while and looked about her. The snowfall was slung like grey draperies about the light-abandoned world. It hung over the mountains, partly obscuring them; it stood like a black wall above the fjord to the west, like a grey one to the south above inner Southfjord. It shut out the view in every direction, and the river, which flowed dark and rapid at the very bottom of it all, seemed to come from nowhere, to be going nowhere.

The town lay below on the slopes running down to the river. With so much fresh snow on the roofs it looked as if a white fur coverlet had been drawn over it, with the lights that shone down there all day blinking out of slits and holes like cunning, drowsy little eyes. There was a large rent here and there: a spire, and a gable or house-wall of importance, where the bank, the school and the Lutheran meeting-house stood out. The sharp needle of the church tower had bored right through, and stood triumphantly up in the sky with pieces of the pierced coverlet hanging down about the pinnacle and gables.

The church tower was strange. It was an ordinary, ugly, yellow church tower built of wood. Alberta could see perfectly well that it looked like two excessively long, narrow boxes piled up on end, the one above the other, with an ice-cream cone on top. Nevertheless there was something distinctive about it. It stood straight up and down to good effect against the many horizontal lines drawn by the river and the main streets of the town; it changed and was new with every season. In summer it shone brightly against the grass-covered mountains and the river, which was then green, deep and opaque. Now it was grey in all the rest of the greyness. Only a shadow of yellow remained, a faint wash of colour.

But to turn one's back on the town and the tower was like bidding farewell to this world and its glories. Although Alberta had done so time and again, year out and year in, she was still seized by the same uneasiness.

No snow-plough had gone inland across the bog. Only a few sleds from the farms had driven here early this morning, painstakingly marking where the road went, the road through emptiness out to nowhere.

In clear weather rounded, solid mountains, blue and distant, formed a wall in the far north of the province. Now there was nothing there, less than nothing, a colourless infinity.

Scattered across the foreground, half buried in snow, lay tiny summer cottages, their shutters closed, witnessing that people had been there once upon a time. A suggestion, a shadow of low, snow-clad birch thicket hinted at a line of hills; a steaming patch of horse dung, that organic life was still to be found on earth. There was no other focus for the eye. And a great feeling of desolation, something of what the lone survivor of a catastrophe at sea might be imagined to feel, chilled Alberta, shrinking her heart into a hard little whimpering lump. But she braced herself and advanced purposefully into the deep snow, into the eeriness, her skirt held high, her face flushed and hot. She was fleeing from her permanent conviction that she was a malefactor, from the painful self-knowledge which never left her – and there was nowhere else she could flee.

Her heart hammered so that she could feel it in her neck, and when a crow suddenly fluttered up from the ground she started so that she lost her breath and had to stop. But after a while a giddy audacity rose in her, and she opened the door a little to her dream world. Only a little – not wide open, without anxiety, as when she wandered about in the summer. Here in all this eeriness it was important to keep her wits about her. Her own terror was lurking in the air, it might grip her at any moment. She had to be on her guard against it and not allow it to get the upper hand. And not run, above all not run. She set herself reprieves and goals. The next curve of the sled tracks, the next piece of horse dung – and she would stop and get her breath and start back, as calmly as if nothing were the matter. But she kept on walking. Of the joys that could not be taken from her, walking was one of the greatest. To feel her muscles working, feel the healthy, wholesome warmth spreading over her body, while awkwardness and tenseness slipped away like a sloughed skin, leaving her body free, supple and relaxed as if after a bout of gymnastics. It was a resource from which she could gain fresh courage, the only resource Alberta had at her disposal for the time being, besides the coffee pot.

She walked, sank down into the snow, struggled up again and almost forgot she was frightened.

Then a flock of crows came flying straight towards her out of the driving snow. They screeched, screeched, and a gust of eeriness accompanied them and settled on the earth.

And the terror gripped Alberta. She gave in to it, turned and, seized with panic, ran, tripped, fell flat on her face, struggled up and ran again. Only when she saw the lights of the town did she stop. Her heart beat as if it would knock her down, and her hands shook too much to open the neck of her jacket.

Where shall I go, she thought: there is nowhere to go any

more. On the other roads there are people, and up here the eeriness. I am trapped – this year as last year.

*   *   *

The lamplight fell on the table from under a red shade. In its circle there stood generous plates of cake and two dishes of jam, the silver basket with the teaspoons in it, the blue cups. Beyond, in the shadow, the tea-urn shimmered on a little table by itself, together with the Japanese tea-caddy and the slop basin with the curious, old-fashioned tea strainer on top of it. The faces were also in shadow, but hands moved under the light.

It was warm from the glowing coke fire and three lamps. 'Much too warm,' said Mrs. Buck, getting up and fanning herself with a folded newspaper. She opened a window, and a cool stream of air was let into the living-room.

Alberta wrapped herself in the heat as if it were material one could pick up and feel. It was never too warm for her. Her hands and body and face felt different, and she sewed Mama's table runner quickly, not quite sure whether she was enjoying it, or whether it was merely the warmth and the cosiness of the lamp-light that made her feel like this. She laughed unselfconsciously at something Beda was telling her, and Mrs. Buck cried: 'Just look at Alberta, she's so attractive when she laughs. Why are you always so serious, Alberta? Laugh, my girl.'

Alberta blushed, but was comforted by the fact that the light was red too. She withdrew into herself again for a while. One of her sore spots had been touched. She often heard the same thing at home, although the choice of words was different.

Beda never sat still for long. She threw down her embroidery, stood up, and wandered about with a lighted cigarette in her hand. She paused in front of the table, standing crookedly and daringly with her hip jutting out and her arm akimbo, making provocative remarks and gesticulating with the cigarette. Then she tossed it out of the open window, sat down and made a few stitches in her embroidery, while Mrs. Buck cried, horrified: 'Darling Beda, are you crazy – throwing cigarettes out of the window!'

22

And Beda replied: 'Darling Mrs. Buck, why do you think we have such a lot of snow up here? We can throw cigarettes out of the window without any danger of fire, my poor dear.'

'Yes, but my sweet little Beda, it might fall on somebody's head.'

'I'd love it to fall on Mrs. Governor Lossius's head, when she's wearing her tulle hat – or on Lotten Kremer, when she's out in her finery.'

'Darling Beda, how you do go on.'

Mrs. Buck laughed, but looked anxiously in the direction of the Archdeacon's Christina and Harriet Pram, who were so correct. They smiled and exchanged glances. But Gudrun Pram leaned back in her chair and laughed riotously.

Alberta sat wondering what was really wrong with Beda. Both she and her mother were the bugbear of Mama and all the other ladies. They agreed that if Beda were not an old school friend and if it were not so embarrassing to break off the connection, there would be no question of their daughters frequenting that house. Beda was held up as an example of how a young girl should never behave. Her language, her manners, her clothes, her walk, everything was wrong. And yet the men were attracted to her like moths to a flame. In adolescence it had been the boys, now it was chemists and editors, mining engineers from Southfjord, and the new dentist; in other words, all young, presentable males.

She was hung about with skirts that dipped at the back. Small, slanting eyes, that could turn into narrow slits, a large mobile mouth with white, even teeth in a broad, flattened little Mongol face. Encircling the face were clusters of natural dark curls, which would turn snow-white early like Mrs. Buck's. She had inherited her mother's deep dimples in her chin.

Beda said crude and vulgar things and made faces like a girl from Rivermouth. She was not afraid of dreadful words, and her language was almost like that of the country folk.

'Beda, my child, do watch your language a little,' sighed Mrs. Buck; it was one of her refrains. But Beda did not watch her language. She put on an act and said frightful things just for the sake of it.

23

She dared the incredible. When tea was over, for instance, she would say: 'Now Mrs. Buck, you must be tactful and disappear, my poor dear. We're going to talk about things that aren't good for an elderly lady's ears,' leading Mrs. Buck to the door as if under arrest. Mrs. Buck would laugh resignedly and say: 'What will become of the child?'

Beda followed people on the street, mimicking them in broad daylight. She followed Lotten Kremer one Sunday, waddling her behind and mincing along; she had even gone so far as to follow the Governor's wife all the way from the bathhouse to the brewery, holding up a furled umbrella like a lorgnette. She used to follow the Recorder too, singing 'Adam in Paradise'. That was before she went to work at his office.

It was Beda who once pinned old Mrs. Klykken's and Nurse Jullum's skirts together with a safety-pin in the crush when the congregation was coming out of church, so that old Mrs. Klykken's trimming was torn off all the way round; Beda who set fire to the splendid midsummer bonfire that had ten tar barrels in it, on the Flemmings' summer property, so that it burned up in the middle of the afternoon, long before the guests arrived; Beda who fastened the outside hook on the door when Bjerkem the school-teacher was out in the privy, so that he was stuck there for an hour in the middle of the winter and had had chronic catarrh ever since. Her skirts aswing round her long legs, she had been the ringleader in boats and on skis, climbing on board the Russian trading ships to beg for sweets, and going to old Kamke to beg for delicacies.

She knew amazing things and was familiar with all that was mysterious and hidden. Beda read whatever she liked, without hindrance.

Mrs. Selmer said: 'That terrible Beda Buck'; the Magistrate: 'If only she'd walk more prettily and use a different kind of language.' Then they both would trace the misfortune back to Mrs. Buck, saying: 'One couldn't expect anything else, poor child.'

But the Recorder said in his quiet way: 'The most efficient person in my office.'

Headmaster Bremer pursed his lips and declared: 'Without comparison the best brain I have ever had in my class.'

And Mrs. Buck herself would ask at every opportunity: 'Can you tell me what I should do without Beda, desperately impractical as I am?'

Harriet Pram leaned forward, looked at the photograph on the piano for a long time, and asked politely: 'Which rôle was this one, Mrs. Buck?'

Mrs. Buck screwed up her eyes short-sightedly: 'Oh, my dearest Harriet, that was in the journey to China, it was taken at the time I met Mr. Buck, my dear, in Malmø. He sat in the stalls one evening and his face was as brown as an Indian's. He had put in with the *Augusta Amalie*.'

And Mrs. Buck drew up her chair and recounted yet again, with alacrity, the story of how that brown man sat in the same seat in the stalls for a fortnight. Then she gave in, left the stage, and went off with him to sea. 'Everyone thought it was a pity, of course, but he was a dashing fellow at any rate. Can you remember Victor Buck, girls?'

She looked up at the enlargement hanging above the piano in an oval frame, and nodded to it. 'Dashing,' she repeated lingeringly. And she threw back her shoulders, stuck out her bosom, and concluded: 'Dignified – and a real *man*, nothing of the sissy about him. Practically all the girls were after him.'

Scattered about under the light from the variegated lampshades there stood and hung pictures of Mrs. Buck in different stage rôles, and of Mrs. Buck as the captain's wife on the *Augusta Amalie* – with and without Beda in her arms. Beda was born in Hull.

A reek of adventure and experience filled the room and lay about Mrs. Buck's corpulent, white-haired, but lively and youthful person – something not quite proper, but amusing and enticing. She had been on the stage, she spoke Swedish in spite of all the years she had spent up here in North Norway, and she had seen a good deal of the world before Buck gave up sailing the high seas and transferred to the coastal service at home. Odessa 12.5.86 was written on one photograph, New Orleans on another, Port Said on a third.

'Damn it,' Beda would say. 'Why did you have to go ashore

up here, when I was only a year old? You must have been bewitched.'

Mrs. Buck had the same slit eyes as Beda, and there was a hole in her chin as deep as a scar. No-one had ever seen a similar chin-hole. It was difficult to keep one's eyes off it when talking to her.

The people she mixed with kept themselves afloat a couple of fathoms below the surface of society. They were Mrs. Dorum the jeweller's wife, Mrs. Kilde the clock-mender's wife, Mrs. Lebesby the dyer's wife, Mrs. Julius Elmholz, novelties and hardware. Well-situated, genial women, who travelled to Kristiania once a year, and abroad now and again, who were more expensively and better dressed than the officials' wives, the Governor's lady excepted. And young Mrs. Klykken of course, who trumped everyone where clothes were concerned.

Mrs. Selmer and her circle greeted them, chatted with animation and familiarity across counters with them, manned bazaar stalls with them, but never invited them to tea in any circumstances, and talked about them in a particular tone of voice and with a particular expression. Especially where Mrs. Buck was concerned, they would drop their voices a little and cough warningly to each other when the young people were present. It was rumoured that she had a relationship with the Russian consul in one of the towns to the east. There must have been something in it, for why should Mrs. Buck, who was Swedish and had sisters still living, stay up here years after Captain Buck's death, and what business took her eastwards three years ago? 'Well, don't tell anyone I told you, but there are all sorts, and poor Beda, that's what I say . . .'

And the ladies would raise their voices and remark: 'She is supposed to have been quite mediocre as an actress.'

But old Consul Stoppenbrink, who saw her on the stage twenty-five years ago in Gothenburg, when she was still called Ulla Liljekvist, would assure them: 'She was a lovely girl – a lovely girl – such a tiny waist,' and blow a kiss with two fingers.

Tea had been drunk, and Mrs. Buck had sung various numbers from her repertoire: 'Nitouche' and 'The Grand Duke of

26

Geroldstein'. She retired, pursued by Beda. 'Very well, very well Beda, my dear. I'm going like a good girl,' she laughed. 'But don't say anything too shocking.'

Beda drew the portière after her. 'There, now we can be as indecent as we like. Christina, you're worse than any of us, you can begin.'

Christina smiled virtuously and cryptically over her embroidery: 'My poor Beda, you had better begin yourself.'

'No, since you came home from Germany, Christina, you're definitely the worst of all of us.'

In fact Christina had come home from Germany primmer and more embroidered, richer in domestic virtue, more admirable than ever. She fidgeted on her chair and smiled with embarrassment and scorn: 'Oh, Beda,' she said.

But Beda was merciless. 'My poor Christina, I told Bergan yesterday that if he wanted you, he'd better grab you now, for you're getting more depraved each day. Christina is going terribly downhill, I said to Bergan, no one knows how terrible Christina is.'

Christina took offence, pursed up her mouth and sewed for dear life. 'If you did say that, Beda, Lawyer Bergan is sure to understand where the depravity lies,' she said with dignity without looking up.

Beda stood beside and a little behind her, and from time to time nudged her teasingly: 'Listen Christina. Christina, don't you think he's a lovely man, Christina? They say he has two of everything already, beds and bedside tables and – well, I won't go into details – it's only the proposal that's lacking. If only he could get round to it.'

Christina was furious. She sat with her back to the company and sewed like one possessed. The general opinion was that she doted on Bergan. 'Oh!' she exclaimed once, crimson with vexation.

Harriet Pram sewed in silence. She was cold and clearheaded, calm and correct, a little older than the others. She had been to Kristiania to take a course in massage and was far too refined for the tone adopted by Beda. She demonstratively started a cultured conversation with Christina across the table: 'Have you read Blicher-Clausen's latest, *Violin*?'

Christina grasped at the straw thus offered. 'No, but it's supposed to be wonderful. It was out when I asked for it, unfortunately.'

But Beda was not dismayed. She struck her breast: 'My God, how cultured they are! But Harriet, it's time you took pity on that assistant of yours, Dr. Mo, for he's going with Palmine Flor. Someone saw them coming out of the Flors' summer cottage at midnight, so there's not much time to lose. The two of you could get more pleasure out of that money after you're married, my poor Harriet. They say Palmine's none too cheap – she likes fox-fur boas and feather hats.'

Harriet was well-bred and self-controlled: 'I'm quite sure that if Dr. Mo has been seen with Palmine he must have been sent for as a doctor to the Flors. Besides, if your friends Kirkeby and Lett saw them, they'd do better minding their own business.

'—Or perhaps that's the sort of thing you discuss at the Recorder's office when Mr. Jaeger is out,' she added coldly, with polite scorn.

'Of course, and when he's in for that matter,' replied Beda defiantly. 'We don't inhabit the higher spheres in our office, let me tell you. We take life as it comes – and after all, it is a cesspool. Besides, nobody would be ill up at the Flors' cottage – they do that down in town at this time of year.'

'Stop laughing so improperly, Gudrun,' said Harriet in sharp reproof. Gudrun Pram was weak with laughter.

'Oh, kiss my bottom!' remarked Beda scornfully under her breath.

And Gudrun wailed: 'I can't – I shall die . . .'

The warmth and well-being enfolded Alberta like a narcotic, half stupefying her, lulling her into a vague, bright, undefined world of fantasty, where nothing but enjoyable sensations flowed one into the other as in a pleasant dream.

She let her sewing fall and sat looking at her hands. They were no longer hers. Hers were purple everyday hands, on which Mama cast resigned glances, asking her to keep them under the table. These were a pair of hands out of a novel, white and slender, a little large, a little scrubbed, but beautiful.

She could not stop thinking that they were beautiful, lying there in her lap, the skin transparent, with blue veins and pale pink knuckles. They belonged to a friend whom only Alberta knew – a happy, beautiful, carefree girl, who walked invisibly beside her, whom no-one saw but herself, but who lived a more intense life than any visible creature. Who knew everything, dared everything, hoped for everything and feared no-one and nothing, not even Mama – and to whom everything was granted: freedom, happiness, beautiful clothes. On Alberta's lonely walks it sometimes happened that the carefree girl blotted her out, materialized in her stead, became Alberta, but it was a miracle that brooked no witnesses. As soon as anyone appeared the transformation was over. There was the old Alberta, just as if nothing had happened, shrinking inside her clothes to make herself as unnoticeable as possible.

The girl's hands were lying now in Alberta's lap, white and warm, looking as if they were never dead from cold; and life was straightforward with small cosy worries of the kind the others had – dresses that would never be ready in time for a party, embroidery that would never be finished in time for Christmas. For what troubles other than these did they have, Harriet, Christina and Gudrun? Beda – perhaps she had more important ones and more of them, perhaps not – but neither she nor the others had the cold, and a guilty conscience waiting for them outside the door. These waited only for Alberta, accompanying her home like two bodyguards, not leaving her until she slept, standing ready at her bedside when she opened her eyes again.

But now they were outside at least. They were never so completely outside as at the Bucks'. In the first place Mama did not frequent the house, and this gave an invaluable feeling of security. And then nowhere else was so warm, so snug and so generous in every way.

Beda and her mother suffered from a chronic lack of ready money. They would turn their purses inside out when bills arrived, to demonstrate that there was nothing there. But they always had full cake boxes, and an unparalleled supper table, a glowing coke fire, flowers, sweets and new music, fashion magazines and theatre journals. And Mrs. Buck's little copper kettle,

29

Coffee-Peter by name, stood permanently on the stove. 'You drink your tea,' Mrs. Buck would say. 'I much prefer my little cup of coffee.'

'My dear, this is nothing by comparison with what we'd call an ordinary *smörgasbord* in Sweden,' she was in the habit of saying with an apologetic gesture towards the numerous dishes on the supper table. And she sent her delicious little sauces and yellow omelettes round the table with a: 'Just something warm' – which caused Alberta to think bitterly of the gruel and milk and the fried egg for Papa served in her own home.

Going home with Beda for supper was an oasis in life's desert. To be sure it felt deceitful. Out in the desert sat those nearest her, consuming grey gruel frigidly and with ill-humour. It was her duty to share these things with them. Once she had been seized with such a strong feeling of anxiety for everyone at home that she suddenly found an excuse for leaving. Dreadful scenes presented themselves to her imagination: Papa in full outburst, Mama small and shrunken, the tears trickling down her cheeks, Jacob cold, defiant, with set mouth. She rushed home – to find everything comparatively peaceful and idyllic. Since then she had stayed, and let herself be lulled to rest by the warmth and the well-being, forgetting for a while her travelling companions in the vale of misery.

It was at the Bucks' that she would become bold and say: 'Do you know, I almost think I'd like another cup of coffee.' And Mrs. Buck would pour it out at once: 'Now that's sensible of you, Alberta, I like that. We know what's good for us, you and I.'

But the others were talking about the south, about going south. That most burning of all questions. Alberta was jerked back to reality again. It seemed to help a little to talk about certain things, as if it brought them a little nearer.

'All I need are some fine relatives down south like the rest of you – and no Mrs. Buck to look after.' Beda said it in that quiet, introspective tone of voice she very occasionally adopted, as if talking to herself.

'But my dear, you have relatives too – and in Sweden into the bargain.' Harriet looked so innocent as she said it, although everyone knew Beda's aunts were only so-so. One of them was married to a station-master on a small local line, and the other was said to support herself by dress-making.

'I said *fine* relatives, my poor Harriet. You heard, and you know what I meant. Don't try to seem more naïve than you are.' Beda's tone was no longer introspective.

But Harriet was correct and ladylike: 'I really don't know what you call fine and not fine.'

'You know all right. When I talk to you, for instance, I mean what you mean, I run with the hare . . . And as for what you mean, my poor Harriet, if we couldn't tell by your appearance, we only need hear you say, "My aunt, the General's wife".'

Harriet sighed resignedly and let it be known that she considered it beneath her dignity to reply. She adopted the same attitude as Christina and sewed in silence. They glanced up at each other and smiled in complete sympathy.

But Beda had started on Gudrun. 'I suppose you'll be going to stay with your aunt, the General's wife, too, Gudrun, unless you take Stensett the schoolmaster, of course. They say he dotes on you so that he daren't hear you in class any more, he blushes furiously if he so much as talks to you. You won't get your matric., my poor Gudrun, but you'll get Stensett.'

'I don't want Stensett,' groaned Gudrun, gesturing away from herself with her hands. 'He has egg in his beard every morning and a patch on the seat of his trousers.'

Harriet coughed disapprovingly, and Alberta was afraid her turn was coming. They teased her about her father's Chief Clerk now and again, and it offended her, because he was the sort of person nobody would fall in love with, awkward, with clammy hands. Besides, she reacted to certain kinds of jokes like an innocent person under attack, becoming tense, incapable of adopting the same tone. Her future would never be in question. But beneath the knowledge that she was ugly, boring, hopeless and impossible, something fluttered – a yearning unrest. She carried it, as one might carry a secret hurt, an invisible injury of which one is ashamed, not daring even to touch it.

Fortunately her schoolgirl crush on Peter, the chemist's son, seemed to have been forgotten. It had been an unfortunate youthful aberration, a time full of anxiety, of much blushing and walking in back streets, her heart in her mouth. Meeting her heart's desire on the public highway had been more than she could bear. Peter Bloch was apparently completely unaffected, however, and the whole thing came to an end abruptly when he began wearing a bowler. It was immediately obvious that he was not the right one after all.

'And what about you, Beda, who will you have?' she threw out deprecatingly. 'Lett or Kirkeby or Bengtson the engineer?'

'Me!' Beda threw herself full length on to the couch and folded her arms behind her head. 'Do you think anyone will marry Beda Buck? No, I'm the sort of poor wretch men confide in and kiss to console themselves – I'm not the sort they marry. I expect I shall go the same way as Caroline Kamke. She had a child by a Lapp, so they all found themselves put to the necessity of marrying her off to old Isaac Hwass out east in Berlevaag. For you needn't think I shall end up like Jeanette Evensen, who's half crazy, all because she's never had anything to do with men.

'But you—' continued Beda, sitting upright on the couch, drowning the indignation of the others and prophesying with outstretched index finger towards Harriet and Christina: 'I'm telling you now, consider getting yourselves a man before the grey hairs and wrinkles come, for if you don't marry you'll not get so much as a kiss all your lives. Your sort have to do their sinning inside marriage – there'll be nothing for you outside, believe you me and Beda Buck.'

An hour later Alberta sat struggling with the lukewarm, grey gruel that had been standing in the oven and was now covered with skin. She had been late for supper. She always was when she had been out to tea, but it was overlooked because Alberta did what was expected of her in other respects, and because there had to be moderation in all things.

'I have plenty to scold about as it is,' Mrs. Selmer had said once. 'If I were to scold her about that as well, it would be too much for me.'

Jacob sat at the other side of the table with *The Prisoner of Zenda.* He would look up now and again and make a face, and when Alberta had swallowed a spoonful of gruel he would pretend to belch.

But Alberta swallowed manfully.

Mama was in the large sitting-room playing the piano. She stopped for a moment when Alberta arrived, called, 'Is that you, Alberta my dear? – and went on playing.

And Alberta, who always felt when she had been at some-one else's home, and most of all at Beda's, as if her home-coming was a rude awakening to bleak reality, and whose conscience troubled her because of it, understood at once that this evening there was a truce, this evening there was a fine, calm spell on life's voyage. Papa had gone to play cards with the Chief of Police. So Mama would go on playing for a long time, and she would be gay and talkative when she had finished, and tease Alberta and Jacob. Their sins would be as if blotted out.

Maybe she would even fetch jam and cakes. Worse things had happened.

*   *   *

Dinner, and the hanging lamp was lit. Mrs. Selmer was at table. She did everything first: got up first in the morning, sat down first at table, finished her meals first and went first to bed.

Now she sat in her check shawl getting more and more tense round the mouth.

The Magistrate, on the other hand, was always late. He got up last and went last to bed, was always the last to be ready on every occasion and added greatly to Mrs. Selmer's burdens, which were heavy and numerous enough as it was.

Jacob was like him. As a rule they both arrived long after they had been summoned, their eyebrows raised as if in apology. But Alberta, who had troubles enough in other respects, had adopted punctuality at mealtimes as a propitiatory act. Now she was standing behind her chair, happy as long as Mrs. Selmer's glance rested on the steaming beef collops and not in her direction.

The door opened, Papa arrived.

If he had exploded recently, this was now a thing of the

33

past. He wished in fact to make up for his behaviour, and would therefore begin by apologizing for his tardiness.

But to Mama it was by no means a thing of the past. Besides, he had kept her waiting yet again. What with the one thing and the other there was no reason why she should be pleasant.

Alberta sent silent cries to heaven to make Mama pleasant all the same, but Mama was not. She replied curtly and coldly with pursed lips, and Papa said, 'Oh, so that's how it is, is it?' and went red in the face. He, too, pursed his lips. He looked at the beef with disfavour, turning over the slices contemptuously with his fork, while Alberta had palpitations and her hands turned clammy.

Papa chewed his meat demonstratively in order to make it clear to everyone how tough it was, and pessimistically contemplated his portion several times from various angles. Now and again he looked darkly at Jacob's empty chair.

Jacob arrived. He pulled down his inadequate sleeves and gave some explanation about a message concerning homework that for some obscure reason he had had to get from another boy, and the boy was not at home and Jacob had had to wait. This was believed by nobody and nobody replied.

'Sit down and eat,' said Papa roughly.

Jacob stopped mumbling and sat down. An oppressive silence fell.

Then Mama began. She began in the tone of voice that always spoiled everything – a cold, injured tone: 'Mightn't it quite possibly have happened as Jacob says?'

Papa flared up: 'I don't care a brass farthing for what Jacob says. It's his business to be home at a certain time, regardless of this, that and the other. I demand – do you hear – I *demand* that the boy keep up to the mark.'

Papa thumped hard on the table with his fist and went very red. Mama went white, her mouth a thin line. Alberta felt herself beginning to tremble, and Jacob put on his bad face, the cold obstinate face that always frightened Alberta.

For a while only the forks could be heard. Alberta looked sideways at her father's hands; they were shaking. He mumbled with twisted mouth. All of a sudden he put down his knife, pointed at the door and said roughly to Jacob: 'Go upstairs, get out of my sight.'

'Very well,' said Jacob, and got up.

But Jacob should not have said that. Papa struck the table and thundered: 'There's no need to answer me, boy, when I speak to you, all you have to do is obey and look sharp about it. Or I'll – now – out you go.'

He pointed again. And Jacob disappeared.

Mrs. Selmer collapsed, a crushed, tiny figure, the tears trickling down her cheeks. Her entire appearance implied that both she and Jacob were being trampled under foot, the maltreated wife and child of a coarse brute. Unable to defend themselves against superior force, all they could do was submit.

The coarse brute was already fighting his anger. He looked crossly and questioningly over at Mrs. Selmer, who did not return his glance, but looked straight in front of her in utter despair. The tears rolled down her cheeks, one after the other.

So he muttered a lot of bad words about environment, that caused him to lose control again, and yet again. Then he rose abruptly, pushing his chair noisily away from him, and left – closing the door behind him in such a way that everything in the room trembled and clinked.

Mrs. Selmer sobbed for a while with her handkerchief pressed against her mouth, and Alberta wept silently on her side of the table. She wept for everything, for life in general.

Mrs. Selmer wiped her eyes, arranged her shawl and ordered Alberta to open the window, ring for Jensine and explain that no one wanted dessert so there was no need to bring it in. She went upstairs.

After a little while Alberta went upstairs as well. On the way she paused for a moment outside the closed office door. She could hear Papa behind it, and seized with sudden rage she shook her fists at the door and whispered devout administrations at it, of the kind she had heard issuing from his own mouth: 'God damn you to hell,' she whispered. 'Curse you.'

She repeated them several times and it made her feel better.

And she went on up to her room, sobbed violently for a time, her fists clenched against her face, became calmer, wrapped herself in the travelling-rug Aunt Marianne had given her for her confirmation, and sat listening, waiting for Mrs. Selmer to go downstairs again.

When the coast was clear, Alberta went in to Jacob.

He was sitting at the table leaning his head on one blue-grazed fist, playing with a penknife. His school books lay beside him, still strapped together.

The light from the lamp fell sharply on his face. He sat looking at the knife, and his mouth wore the expression Alberta feared most of all. Behind it lay all the dangerous thoughts that could lead Jacob astray, in wild directions that she was only vaguely able to imagine.

It was ice-cold in the room as it was everywhere else in the house. She could see her own breath, and Jacob's.

At first she found nothing to say, and remained standing in front of the table. Jacob looked up and asked with hostility: 'What do you want?'

Alberta did not reply immediately. There was no point in being too quick. She had to find a point of departure without worsening the situation. She sat down on Jacob's bed, hid her frozen hands in the blanket, and said nothing.

'What do you want?' repeated Jacob crossly.

Bitterness towards Jacob flared up in Alberta, and she replied, 'Nothing.'

'Huh – What do you want to come in for, then? Besides, Mama was here just now.'

'I know she was.'

'All right, so you don't have to come too. You're both after the same thing.'

Alberta was silent again. She got up and screwed the lamp to stop it smoking.

'Don't you want me to help you with your homework?' she said after a while.

Jacob made no reply. Then he flicked his knife; it stood upright, quivering in the table. 'I'll sign up for the Arctic,' he said roughly.

'No Jacob, you won't,' said Alberta vehemently. Something snapped inside her, and she began to sob. Jacob looked up, went across to her and patted her clumsily on the shoulder with

36

a large, blue hand. His voice had altered: 'Come on, don't cry Alberta – do you hear me Alberta, you mustn't cry.

'Proper old leaking tap, that's what you are,' he added with an indulgent little laugh, his voice strangled.

But Alberta clutched his hand, for now he was close to her in every way. 'Jacob, can't you be a bit more punctual, for Mama's sake?'

'Punctual!' Jacob tried to free his hand. 'Huh – if only Mama hadn't started up in that tone of voice, Papa would never have got so furious, you know that. It's only because they quarrel so.'

'Yes Jacob, but at any rate we can try not to give them the chance,' answered Alberta philosophically. 'And you *must* see to it that you matriculate, Jacob,' she hastened to add, making the most of her chance, for it was not always so easy to get hold of Jacob's hand. She could see that he was trying to free it in earnest now.

'Come on Jacob, let's begin.'

For the moment Alberta felt strongly the drive that Jacob lacked. Jacob *must* matriculate, he *must* become an educated person – not a mere sailor and a dissipated character.

But the result of Jacob's examination on leaving secondary school had been worse than wretched and had cost much private tuition. Her own education had been sacrificed to it, for she had been taken out of *gymnasium* the previous year. His weekly reports left more and more to be desired, and the Magistrate prophesied the worst every Saturday: 'You'll grow up into an uneducated ruffian, my boy, mark my words. No one will be able to tell that you come of a decent family.'

Now Alberta had yet another of her attacks of desperate optimism. They came upon her from time to time. It would be all right, it must be all right, in spite of everything, in spite of Jacob's own embittered aversion to school and everything that had to do with it.

'Wouldn't it be nice if you got a good report on Saturday, Jacob,' she said, in a different tone of voice. 'Hurry up and find me the books.'

'Ugh!' said Jacob, finally twisting his hand out of hers. He sat down on the edge of the bed with a morose expression.

But Alberta was on her feet unstrapping the books on the table.

She read the time-table above the chest of drawers: 'German, History, Maths, Norwegian – you must have homework, Jacob, come along.'

Jacob rose unwillingly to his feet and brought pen and ink. He grumbled: 'If you think I'll get better marks because my homework's right, you're mistaken. Huh, I get delta however well I've learned it. The Head—'

Alberta was already struggling with x and y. She knew what Jacob would say about the Head and the masters, things it was best to ignore. For although they might be a little unfair and spoken at random, they were not entirely so, and it would be dangerous to embark on a debate.

Jacob had been completely at odds with society and the powers-that-be for a long time. Rebellion smouldered within him. Alberta still had an inherited respect for the mysterious and immense machinery in which Papa, the Head, the teachers and other officials were the cogs. It worried her that Jacob should have lost respect for it. It was these thoughts that would lead both of them astray, perhaps into real wrong-doing. It almost seemed as if Jacob was a somewhat wayward character already. Nothing ought to be neglected that might get him back on an even keel, and she energetically attempted to rouse his interest in an equation which she herself found thoroughly confusing.

After a while the equations lay there looking fairly plausible. It was better than a blank sheet of paper, at any rate. The German grammar was placed open in front of Jacob: 'I'll hear you after supper, and in Old Norse as well,' announced Alberta, standing with her hand on the door knob.

She opened the door. And she hesitated again for a moment, before saying rapidly and a little uncertainly: 'Don't be too late for supper, Jacob.'

And Jacob replied in the voice that made Alberta happy, and secure, and full of hope: 'I'll be on time, Alberta.'

In the kitchen with Jensine it was cosy and warm and smelling of coffee. Alberta hurried to fetch a cup from the pantry and served herself from the boiling kettle so that the grounds poured thickly out into the cup.

'It's not ready yet,' called Jensine, who was cleaning knives at the kitchen bench. 'Will you please leave the kettle alone Alberta, or I'll tell the Madam.'

Alberta drank it all. She was so cold after sitting still in Jacob's room that she could not feel her fingers. They were white and numb, and the cup she held seemed extraneous to them. Now the waves of coffee washed through her, scalding hot, paining her body and rousing it to life again. She picked coffee grounds out of her mouth, turned over the lump of sugar on her tongue and replied: 'If you knew how cold I am, Jensine.'

Jensine muttered over her knives. Not everything could be heard clearly, but cream, sugar and the Madam were repeated over and over again like a refrain.

'I take such a little, Jensine,' Alberta assured her, drinking quickly. And when Jensine turned her back for a moment and made a noise with the tap, Alberta poured herself yet another cupful and filled up the kettle from the water kettle beside it. She was in the pantry helping herself to cream when Jensine saw what was going on and rushed over. 'No, poor dear, now that's going too far. The Madam will think it's me – and if you've filled up the kettle with water again Alberta—'

'Only a little, only a little, just a tiny drop. Just let it boil a little longer, Jensine.'

She pushed Jensine in front of her out of the pantry. It was not wise to linger in there longer than necessary. Sometimes Mrs. Selmer would get up in the middle of her after-dinner nap, driven by foreboding, and descend on the kitchen like Nemesis.

'All right Alberta, poor dear, I'll leave in the summer, and that's for sure and certain,' Jensine assured her, really angry now. 'If it were not for embarrassing the Madam, I'd leave this very minute.'

Alberta slunk away. Jensine made her feel a little ashamed and scared, but she was also thawed-out and warm. She stretched herself secretly. Jensine had threatened to leave for many years.

At the wood-box Alberta bent down as if by chance and collected sticks and bark into her skirt. Jensine said nothing to this, merely looking at her sideways and coughing significantly. She coughed again when Alberta moved off with her booty.

An undertaking full of danger, even for one expert at passing doors noiselessly. It was dark, and an accident might easily happen. Once a piece of firewood had fallen on the way through the dining-room, with highly unpleasant consequences. But nothing venture, nothing win.

Up in her room she lighted the stove. And when the birch bark began to crackle and curl the world was transformed. One after the other Alberta added the pieces of firewood, feeling a wild, intense joy at the sight of the flames leaping up round them. Then she crept on tiptoe down to Papa's office to steal coal.

Once there she moved like a mouse, feeling her way to the coal scuttle, fumbling and groping with her hands to find it. One might think Jensine had put it purposely outside the pool of light falling from the stove.

With every pore Alberta breathed in the stifling warmth, the permanent, pervasive smell of Papa's tobacco, that belonged to the inner office, while she picked up the coal piece by piece and put it in the shovel, making sure that nothing would spill and give her away afterwards, nothing fall and make a clatter. Papa was asleep on the other side of the wall, and in the outer office sat the Chief Clerk and Leonardsen, she could tell by the strip of light under the door.

In a little while she sat wrapped in the travelling-rug in front of her stove. She put her feet up on top, the fire roared, light flickered through the ventilating hole and fell on the floor. And a sheltered enclave, a place where it was good to be, slowly but surely came into being, spread, took over the whole room. A happy indolence pervaded her body and soon deadened the uneasy gnawing of her conscience.

She was acting meanly and she knew it. When the wood and coal in the cellar came to an end, it would provide an occasion for tragic scenes.

In the afternoon Mrs. Selmer went out. She went out to tea or to one of her charities or to the lending library. It was important to manoeuvre so that she left the house without discovering Alberta's criminal intentions.

First of all Alberta must be in the dining-room when the after-dinner nap was over and coffee was served. She must look innocent, the soul of honour. After that the programme could be varied a little. She might sit with a stocking from the mending basket, imbued with domestic zeal, or she might take out the red and white table cloth. She might also be deep in something or other for Jacob, an essay, some arithmetic. In any case her alibi was in order, and Mrs. Selmer would not feel impelled to reconnoitre upstairs, even though from principle she would contemplate Alberta's hang-dog appearance with suspicion and sarcasm.

The moment when the front door slammed behind her finally arrived. Alberta packed up again in order to return to her ill-gotten warmth. Then someone came through the office door, the flooring in the passage creaked beneath heavy footsteps, the dining-room door opened. It was the Magistrate.

'Hullo, are you here?' he said, obviously surprised to find Alberta.

She explained why she was there. And she wished, she wished to heaven Papa would not go over to the sideboard, but he did go. He bent down and took out the whisky decanter, poured himself a wine-glass full – so full that he had difficulty guiding it to his mouth – and emptied it in one draught. 'Ah,' he said. And he turned to Alberta and patted her on the head good-naturedly. 'Well, what are you going to do with yourself now, my lass?'

'I don't know,' replied Alberta. She drew slightly away from him but Papa did not seem to notice. 'All right, my darling,' he said, and left again.

Sick at heart Alberta wandered upstairs. She lighted the lamp and took out various things. A book she had borrowed, perhaps, or one of the poetry books from the sitting-room. Or maybe a little notebook, that led a secret existence beneath the woollen vests to the left in the chest of drawers. Sometimes she would not light the lamp, but would curl up on a chair in the comfortable darkness and sit looking out at the lights scattered along the river.

But if she knew for certain that Mrs. Selmer would be away until supper-time, she might go down into the corner parlour, lighting her way with a match, and look for one of the forbidden books in the bookcase: *La Dame aux Camélias, Belami, A Mother's First Duties*—

—And creep upstairs with it hidden in her skirt.

*   *   *

From time to time Olefine the dressmaker would come and install herself for two or three days upstairs in Jacob's room. She sewed blouses for Mrs. Selmer and altered her old dresses for Alberta.

Olefine the dressmaker was pale, small and black-haired, and had a child by Isaksen the editor. Everybody knew about it.

When she had a fitting Alberta was always dismayed by the touch of Olefine's ice-cold, anaemic hands, which made her start and shrink away. But she liked to be in there with Olefine. It was warm, and coffee was served twice a day, coffee in a pot. When Olefine had drunk her two cups and pushed the tray away, Alberta would say: 'If you don't want any more, Olefine, I think I'll have a drop.' And she would pour it into Jacob's tooth mug and lose no time rinsing it clean again.

She was supposed to be helping. When Mrs. Selmer came up now and again she would look sceptically at whatever Alberta had in her hands: 'Is Alberta of any use to you, Olefine?'

And Olefine would reply with her pale, tight little smile: 'Oh yes, to be sure she is.' And not a word more. Neither Mama nor Alberta were ever sure what Olefine really thought about it.

But when Mama had gone again, Alberta would lean over the table, rest her chin in her hand and watch Olefine's operations. Or she would stand at the window and look down into the street, tentatively leading the conversation on to various topics.

Olefine was not talkative. She answered with a brief: 'No, poor dear – thank you I'm sure – yes indeed, that's so.'

But Alberta, who was affected by the cosiness of the room as if by a stimulating drink, became good-humoured, chatty and bold, and attempted to broaden her knowledge of the mysteries of the town and of life in general.

Look, there were the two prostitutes going by. They were sisters, a little plump and getting on in years, and they wrapped up their heads and shoulders in large, brown shawls, which made them look as if they were wearing some kind of penitential costume. They would look out shyly or invitingly from behind their shawls, whichever happened to be appropriate, and they would often draw down one corner of their mouths at the same time. They lived on the west bank of the river near the distillery in a tumbledown little house, and had no permanent, official competitors, for Palmine Flor and Lilly Vogel did not consider themselves to be in the same class at all.

Another girl came to town occasionally, however. She was called Fanny and followed the fishing. When there was fishing to the south in Lofoten, she was there, and when the boats went eastwards to Finnmark, Fanny went with them.

She was tall, loose-limbed and blonde, and wore a large, furry, black hat on the back of her head. A dishevelled ostrich feather trailed from it. She was always laughing and had a vague look about her eyes; to tell the truth she usually looked a little drunk. And she was not afraid to appear in Fjord Street, surrounded by a positive thunder of sea-boots, arm in arm with her favourite. That was typical of Fanny. She didn't go round in penitential dress.

Fanny and the two sisters occupied Alberta's imagination now and again, just as they occupied the imaginations of Beda, and the Archdeacon's Christina, and Mama, and all the other women, although none of them would admit it. Mrs. Selmer said of them: 'Poor miserable creatures,' as if she were referring to the lowest form of animal life.

The Archdeacon's Christina said: 'I can't see why you bother your heads about those disgusting individuals.'

Beda whistled significantly and pretended to know a lot about them.

Olefine lived on the way to Rivermouth and, it stood to

reason, must have possessed a good deal of information. If only one could get it out of her.

'There are those awful girls.'

Olefine stopped the sewing machine and broke off the thread. She rose half-way out of her chair and looked down into the street. 'Yes, poor dear, I see,' she said. She smiled a little half smile and added: 'They have the day to themselves for walking.'

'They say it's dreadful in Rivermouth in the evenings.'

'Yes, so I've heard them say,' answered Olefine slowly, as if considering something privately. Then suddenly she declared curtly: 'But I'm not their keeper.'

The sewing machine droned on, and the subject of the two sisters was exhausted for the time being.

Alberta remembered that perhaps Olefine thought it embarrassing to talk about them, because she had a child herself. Once, a couple of years ago, Alberta had drawn her attention to Isaksen, who was passing by. After all, one wasn't bound to know that Olefine had a child by him, and it would be fun to see how she took it. She had replied in almost the same way: 'Yes, poor dear, I see.'

'Do you know anything about a girl called Fanny, Olefine?'

'Fanny – yes, I know there is a girl they call Fanny.'

'She's supposed to be a dreadful girl.'

'She's the same sort as those two.'

'Yes, but Olefine—'

'Oh – I know nothing about it.' Olefine bent over the sewing machine, pale and stubborn.

But Jensine, who had arrived with the coffee tray and had stood for a while listening, joined in the conversation: 'It's not always them you'd expect it of as is the worst. It may be the very ones you'd least expect it of.'

Jensine did not say it with indignation, rather with a kind of inner satisfaction. She chuckled a little inside, nodding prophetically at her own words.

'But nobody could be worse than Fanny, surely?' Alberta was full of expectancy, this was obviously a thread. She must grasp it tightly and draw it out in its entirety. 'Well, Dirty Katrine maybe, but she's so old.'

44

'I don't mean that sort, for that's the sort they be, and one can't expect more of them,' declared Jensine. 'I mean them as one can expect more of.'

Olefine nodded and helped herself to cream. 'Oh yes, it certainly takes all kinds, that's for sure.' She looked initiated, but she did not appear scandalized either. With her raised eyebrows and pensive eyes she almost seemed to adopt a waiting attitude, and it was impossible to tell whether she would smile or grimace.

'You mean Palmine Flor and Lilly Vogel.'

'Oh yes, them too. Of course I'm not saying they're among God's chosen children, but then they're not our betters' children neither.'

There was triumph in Jensine's voice. Olefine nodded, her mouth full of coffee, and made a small throaty noise in affirmation.

'Who do you mean?' Alberta had waited before firing her question. Her diplomacy seemed to be getting her nowhere, so she moved to the attack.

But Jensine and Olefine were prudent, and distressingly prone to talking in riddles.

Jensine put her hand over her mouth, tittered and said: 'Silence is golden.'

And Olefine looked vaguely over the machine into thin air and had obviously been thinking about something else for a long time. 'How's it going with Marie at the Flemmings,' she said. 'I heard them say she wants to go south. That young Mrs. Klykken has a situation for her in Trondheim.'

Alberta pressed her nose resignedly against the pane. It was not easy to unravel mysteries. No one spoke straight out, neither books nor people. All those who were in the know were like members of a secret society, a freemasonry, in agreement that their shared knowledge should be kept to themselves. They tittered, they joked, they knew so much and took pleasure in knowing it. All about her the town was full of secrets. Behind all that she saw with her own eyes there lay a reality about which no one would speak out loud. It lured and frightened, attracted and disgusted her simultaneously. In it unheard of, unthought of, and dreadful things were done, but people had a smile in their eyes and a chuckle in their laughter when they thought of them and hinted at them.

* * *

Between seven and eight o'clock the traffic in Fjord Street was considerable, particularly on the stretch between Theodorsen the baker and Louisa-round-the-bend. Beyond these two poles went only the energetic, the lonely, and those in love, people who deviated from the normal in one way or another. They walked to the east end of the wharf or out along Rivermouth, where the last of the street lights ended and the blackness of the winter night began.

Life collected in Fjord Street as in a canal, indeed it was channelled down the very middle of the street, for the pavements were full of snow. For this reason, and because the same people walked back and forth many times, the movement of the crowd was especially lively, almost intense – an incessant black stream under the eight arc-lamps.

The Magistrate and his daughter Alberta did not walk along Fjord Street as far as Louisa-round-the-bend like other folk. They had their own route and went along River Street, which was very dark and deserted in the evenings.

Young Klykken's living-room windows shone red, and a yellow border round a blind showed where the Catholic priest had his office in the Badendück building. But the other old houses with their wharves lay quite black, their dimensions unnaturally large in the darkness. You could see they were haunted.

Down on the Old Quay there was a circle of light under the lamp. There Papa and Alberta stood still, looking out at the dark river, where the current eddied cold and comfortless in the reflections from land. They discussed what kind of craft were lying out there, and contemplated the government dredging apparatus that could only be glimpsed in dark silhouette, freshly fallen snow along all its contours. Papa pointed outwards with his stick: 'They haul pretty large amounts up from the bottom here, by Jove. You get some idea of how much when you see the tip growing. It's a big undertaking. But we pay for it, it's the taxpayers who pay for it. All they have to do is squeeze.'

46

'I suppose it's necessary,' said Alberta. She said the same thing every time.

'Necessary, necessary, should damn well think not. I'd willingly go on taking a boat to board the steamer, as I have done all these years, to avoid giving them all that money.

'Now then, you know I don't mean it literally, Alberta, but God knows there's no sense in it, the sort of taxes we have now – they fleece folk, they fleece folk, the country's in a sad state of affairs.'

Alberta stifled a sigh. She had heard about taxes and the country's state of affairs as long as she could remember, had heard about it in the family circle and elsewhere, until it had seemed to turn into an unspeakably disconsolate little melody, endlessly repeated. It *was* so. In some place known only to God, far south in Kristiania, there sat an assemblage of inhuman, merciless people – peasant Members of the Storting, Radicals, heartless, uneducated persons – plotting the incredible in order to plunder and impoverish Papa, Uncle the Colonel, Aunt Marianne in Grimstad, and all their relations, friends and acquaintances. 'They' had their hand-picked men planted all over the place, in local government and town councils; gruesome, blood-smeared individuals like Ryan the butcher, who was terribly radical, and sinister, cunning people like Hannestad the schoolmaster, who was quiet, hollow-eyed and hollow-chested, and so radical that he even had a wife who was too.

But it was no use talking about it? As long as Alberta could remember it had never been any use. Besides, it was an obscure and far from attractive subject.

'Imagine being the captain of a dredging barge,' she said apropos of nothing, in order to get away from it.

'Yes, by Jove, it's not a proud vessel exactly, and they send old-fashioned ones up north, but they do good service. We must be glad as long as no one decides we're to have our own dredging apparatus here in town – God knows they're capable of it. One fine day someone who wants to call attention to himself will discover we need something more modern, and the ball will start rolling. Just squeeze the taxpayers a little, it's so simple.'

47

Alberta stifled another sigh. But now they were turning up into River Street again. And Papa halted and planted his stick deep in the ground. He did it exactly where he always did it, and he said exactly what he always said: 'You know, Alberta, I'd like to go round by the New Quay to see how things are getting on there. I enjoy looking at the new buildings.'

So, at their accustomed pace they went their accustomed way round the big Stoppenbrink wharves, the Magistrate large and heavy on his feet, slow of movement, Alberta thin as a shadow, her chin jutting out and her hands drawn up inside her sleeves. Still they met nobody. Who would go down to the quay on a snow-dark winter evening, when no steamer was expected? No one but Papa and Alberta.

The desolation on the New Quay was oppressive and complete. In the light from the arc-lamp down below the snowed-in heaps of barrels and crates looked like the last surviving witness of a dead world. In spite of the cold a rank smell of cod-liver-oil and fish came from them and mingled with the smell of the filth left by the ebb tide. Like a pale arm the new stone quay could be glimpsed seawards in the darkness. Along its landward side lay small coastal trading vessels and heavy ten-oared rowing boats, their outlines drawn up in wool out of the new-fallen snow. There were river boats too, that had brought wood and kindling from the east. Furthest out, the harbour light glowed like a red full-stop.

A little path had been trampled in the snow by people going to and from the various craft, and Papa's and Alberta's programme included going as far out as the light reached from land. Wherever there was a mooring the snow had been swept into the sea, and the stone body of the quay showed through, smooth, iced over, treacherous to walk on.

Papa went first, feeling his way with his stick. Now and again he would halt and prod at a stone: 'Good work this,' he said. And he turned and pointed, today as on other days, out towards the harbour light and in towards the unfinished office buildings which rose blackly on land: 'That'll be a big installation when it's finished, by Jove.'

He pounded his stick against several stones: 'There are some fine pieces for you.'

Alberta mechanically placed her feet precisely where she always placed them. She knew every block and every juncture. If she departed from the ritual she did so with mature deliberation. The lights up on the river bend were not visible in the snow haze, and she drew Papa's attention to it. He agreed that she was right, it must be snowing over there: 'It never stops, by Jove.' – 'No,' said Alberta.

She fought against the exhausting, dizzy feeling she always got when one of her wanderings with Papa was drawing to a close, and they had to go back amongst people again – a painful, almost physical sensation of time creeping by.

Every time they turned the corner into River Street, and it became dark and silent round them, a feeling of expectation came over her. Something must happen; some decisive words, bringing clarity and giving hope, must fall. It must happen some time, perhaps today, why not? Papa must have some confidence to make to her, everything couldn't possibly be meant to continue for ever in the same way.

She remembered an occasion a couple of years ago. Papa had pounded once more with his stick, and said: 'Back we go, Alberta. We must keep at it – no use being down-hearted, by Jove.' It had been full of significance, rich in inner meaning and unspoken promises for the future. It was at the very least an admission that all was not as one might wish. Much could be deduced from it, and Alberta had done so and lived on it for a good while. But the need for something fresh had become pressing and acute a long time ago.

She longed, too, for him to talk to her as he did when she was small. He had talked about the stars and pointed them out to her, spoken of the bottomless depth of the universe and a god, more strange and fascinating than the God of school or of church, a god who was one with creation, a hidden flame that burned in everything: 'Well, well, Alberta, that's how we can imagine it to be, but none of us holds a patent in knowledge, by Jove, and I'm blowed if a priest in a pulpit understands any more than the rest of us.'

It became so easy to breathe – heaven and earth seemed aired when Papa talked like that. The old, strict, pernickety and punishing God, who kept such a sharp eye on people and

49

boasted unceasingly of retribution, dwindled and disappeared. The smell of corpses, the horrible odour of churchyards and rotting bones, that hung round death, were no longer anything to worry about. She had never really been able to accept that the soul floated off somewhere else, how could anyone know? Suppose it did lie in the earth with all the others, writhing for air and waiting for Judgement Day? Her face turned hot and dry at the thought, as if the coffin lid were already pressing down on it; her hair rose up in dread. When Papa talked it was as if a fresh wind from heaven blew the horror away. One became nothing, a mere breath – but a breath that had nothing to fear.

But all that had been long ago. Nothing happened any more. She and Papa repeated the same words that they had repeated countless times before. They would turn back and go home, nothing had changed, everything was just as hopeless and just as oppressive.

'We ought to go home now, Papa.'

'How right you are, by Jove, we ought.' He pounded with his stick, and they went.

In silent agreement they always chose the streets where there were fewest people. They could go back the same way, they could also make a detour through shabby old Strand Street. But unless they were to appear downright laughable by wandering right round Upper Town, they would end up in Fjord Street just the same. This crowded thoroughfare could not be avoided in the long run.

Before they turned into it the Magistrate drew himself up slightly, threw back his shoulders, stuck out his chest, and brushed down his coat with his hand. Then he saluted those they met courteously and with extreme cordiality.

'You must tell me if there's anyone we know, Alberta.'

Alberta greeted them formally and diffidently. Her teeth chattered slightly, as always when she did not walk fast enough; her fingers and toes smarted with cold. But she was not afraid of blushing in this light, and there was a certain agreeable excitement in walking along, meeting all these people and feeling safe. It did not matter so much if the worst happened, and they were spoken to and stopped, when Papa was there.

The shops were still open. They shone in competition with the arc-lamps. Where there were large plate-glass windows all of a piece, as at Holst's and the Gentlemen's Outfitters, there was a city atmosphere, an atmosphere of the south, thought Alberta. You had to try to plan your way through the throng, to walk into it and out again as in great, milling capitals. You could pretend you were walking in one.

There was Beda with the chemists from the 'Polar Bear' pharmacy, and the new dentist. She laughed loudly and unselfconsciously, and sauntered carelessly along, swinging her muff. She put herself completely beyond the unwritten law that demanded of young girls in this town that they must walk stiff and straight as soldiers, their elbows at their sides, eyes front, with every sign of tremendous haste; and that they must greet others looking into space, almost without moving their heads – certainly not in the way Beda did it. She nodded so that her fur cap hopped forward on to her nose and had to be pushed back into position again.

'Our worthy Beda has no *tenue*,' remarked the Magistrate. 'It is quite distressing to see. She walks so appallingly—'

'Harriet Pram, Papa.'

Harriet had a new winter coat. It had come from the south and was trimmed with fur. You could see at once that it had not been bought at F. O. Yenning's. She walked like a soldier, but smiled when she greeted people and said good evening in passing. She had learned that in the south.

'Remarkably pretty girl,' commented Papa. 'You should apply yourself to becoming more like her, Alberta.'

'Mrs. Lossius,' warned Alberta, glad to get away from the subject, and Papa prepared himself for a fresh greeting.

The Governor's lady had a lorgnette, the only one in town, which dangled outside all her furs at the end of a long gold chain. It was, so to speak, a sign of her rank. Indignation would have been roused far and wide if anyone else had taken the liberty of wearing one. When you were not the Governor's wife elementary tact required you to wear ordinary pince-nez – at least in town. As she passed she swivelled it towards Papa and Alberta and called: 'Greetings from my little girls,' smiling with a narrow, tight little mouth.

'Thank you very much,' replied Alberta with an evil pang.

'The Archdeacon's wife – the Weyers—'

Mrs. and Miss Weyer approached slowly, arm in arm. Mrs. Weyer was gradually getting deafer and more difficult, and Otilie's beautiful, kind, faded face gradually more patient. It was generally accepted in the town that she had been the loveliest woman anyone had ever seen. It was incomprehensible that she should still be unmarried, such a fine, sweet girl, a pearl of great price. She was in her thirties now, terribly old, and everyone had given up, except Mrs. Weyer, who was often deceived by renewed hope. They were with the Archdeacon's wife, who was small and transparent and had such crystal-clear eyes that you could look right through them to the bottom of her pure soul.

The Magistrate saluted the three ladies genially.

'Miss Liberg!'

'Oh, confound it!'

Miss Liberg bustled officiously past, righting her pince-nez to satisfy herself as to who was saluting her, and called out exuberantly: 'Good evening, Mr. Magistrate, good evening.' One more glance and she would have stopped, but Papa resolutely quickened his pace, unrelenting as stone.

She was one of the energetic walkers and a teacher at the girls' school, feared for her talkativeness and for her declamation of 'The Ode to the Polish Republic'. On festive occasions both were seldom to be avoided.

'The Pastor and Mrs. Pio.'

'Poor souls,' muttered Papa sorrowfully. 'It can't be so confoundedly easy.'

Mr. Pio, Perpetual Curate, and his wife passed them slowly. They adopted the same speed as at a respectable funeral. Pastor Pio had thick lips in a small, bristling beard, and heavy eyes under heavy lids. Everyone knew that he had moved up to the attic last spring, and that it had not helped. Mrs. Pio was having yet another baby and she looked tired and despairing, dragging a little on her husband's arm. Six children in eight years was a lot. The town conceded it and disapproved of Pio.

'Mr. Bergan.'

In the lamplight and among so many people this was not

such a great catastrophe. Alberta noted with pride that she only trembled a little when he went past. But when she discovered that Mama and a number of other ladies were standing below the steps of the 'Polar Bear' looking after him, the blood flooded into her face.

Mr. Bergan the lawyer had bought a piano recently, and his home was said to be complete in every way. Surely he would have to make up his mind soon, but on whom would the choice fall? Since the arrival of the piano it had been a burning question.

He had light blue, slightly indolent eyes and increasing corpulence, topped with colourless hair which stood up straight like a brush. He greeted no one person more vivaciously than another, so it was difficult to make any prediction. If only he would decide on Christina it would be a great relief, thought Alberta.

Now she and Papa were passing the ladies outside the 'Polar Bear'. Papa saluted them with a broad sweep of his hat, turning deferentially towards the group; while Mama radiantly returned his greeting in a manner that differed from the others. It was clear that they had both lived in other, more gracious circumstances.

Immediately afterwards Alberta caught sight of Jacob a short distance ahead. He popped up, was lost in the crowd, and popped up again. Now he was saying good-bye to another boy, who turned and came back.

And Alberta saw with dismay that it was Cedolf Kjeldsen. He raised his cloth cap as he went by. It seemed to her that a smile passed over his strikingly handsome, aggressive face.

'Who was that, Alberta?'

'I can't imagine – someone who has been to the office probably.'

Thank heaven Papa was trusting and unsuspicious, short-sighted and easy to deceive – much easier than Mama.

Jacob could still be seen further down the street. Now he was turning in to the front door, and taking the steps in one bound, as he always did. He would be at home when they arrived, sitting in the dining-room with *The Prisoner of Zenda*. Papa's face would brighten and he would be kind to Jacob, and relapse into the hope that it might still be possible to make a man of him.

But Jacob would have that set of the mouth against which she was helpless. He would not see Alberta when she begged him with her eyes. He would not bother about his homework, but ask permission to go out after supper, explaining it away with a lie. Papa, thanks to his relapse and possibly for other reasons too, would give him permission.

Then Jacob would go to mysterious, hidden places – in the alleys and at Rivermouth – with Cedolf, who had come home from sea. And early tomorrow morning there would perhaps be a smell of drink, she knew where.

Alberta's thoughts distracted her, and something unheard-of occurred. She forgot to stamp the snow from her feet.

'Your feet,' called Papa in despair and resignation. 'Your feet, Alberta. When will you learn——?'

Alberta turned obediently and, with preoccupied expression, executed a step on the door mat.

Immediately afterwards they heard Mama. She was bidding exhilarated farewells to several ladies outside the front door. They could hear her witty and amusing remarks from well inside the hall. She was standing talking through the half-open door.

'Humph!' said Papa quietly, hanging up his coat and hat. 'Humph!' he said once more, and kicked off his galoshes.

Mrs. Selmer arrived.

The cold made her look healthy and young, but her mouth, which had just been talking and laughing, had a sad, tired droop. She wandered round taking off her outdoor things without seeming to see Alberta and Papa. Then she stood in front of the mirror, arranging her hair and sighing deeply.

'Well?' said Papa tentatively. 'You all seemed to be in good humour. What was so amusing?'

'Amusing? I don't know that anything was amusing,' replied Mama wearily and coldly, as if from a long way off – still seeing nobody. 'I talked to the others a little, I'm sure I don't know what for—'

'What on earth are you standing about here for?' she exclaimed with sudden sharpness, inspecting Alberta and Papa as if she had just caught sight of them.

Alberta's heart sank. She made a cowardly movement towards the door, but happened to look at the Magistrate at the same time. His mouth twisted a little, very very slightly. Then he opened the door, clicked his heels, bowed lightly towards Mama, and said in a voice that in a curious way warmed Alberta: 'We're waiting for you, my dear.' And he stood holding the door open for her, his whole attitude one of respectful chivalry.

Alberta's heart swelled painfully with affection.

*   *   *

Snow, storm, delayed packet boats. Day-long, tense listening for the ship's siren, watching for Larsen, the postman, through the icy panes that had first to be breathed on for a while. Snow and still more snow.

'Isn't Larsen coming yet, Alberta?' asked Mrs. Selmer, who was eaten up with anxious waiting on post days. She paced the floor, stopped at the windows, breathed on the panes and looked out, and when two hours had passed since the arrival of the packet boat and still Larsen had not appeared, she sent Alberta out to catch him at Kilde's, before he turned into River Street. 'And then come back with the post this way,' she called after her down the steps.

And she would search feverishly through the bundle of official circulars and newspapers. Her letters were easily recognizable from the backs of the envelopes, even if only a fraction was showing. They were so different from the Magistrate's.

What was Mrs. Selmer waiting for, and what was Alberta waiting for? Mama's anxiety and excitement pulsed in her blood too. It was through the post that something wonderful must come, something that would bring to an end everything as it was at present, turn life upside down, open wide the future – the letter from Uncle the Colonel, who would invite Alberta to come south; or the discreet hint from good friends that some splendid post, Aker and Follo for instance, was free, and that Papa had every expectation, if he would apply . . . Or the unexpected announcement of a large inheritance, why not? It must come some day, this whatever-it-was – and it could not come otherwise than by post.

The living rooms were like an icy sea and the world outside a swirl of white and grey. The snow stood up like smoke from the roofs and was whipped into high crests round the corners, torturing the face and blinding the sight. It settled, packed and hard, on projections and ledges, closed up afresh each day the windows laboriously kept free of frost, filled cracks and grooves, entered like a cloud whenever a door was opened. Snow in the entrance in the morning, snow piled up against the street door, snow down one's neck and up one's sleeves as soon as one stepped outside. When the gale quietened now and again the snow went on sifting down from the thick sky like feathers from an inexhaustible grey quilt.

The houses became tiny, dwindled, and disappeared. Only the top half of Kvandal the tailor's house was left. The Telegraph Station, so impressive in summer with its long flight of steps, could soon be entered straight from the street.

The butchers' windows were covered with snow flowers. Karla Schmitt and Signora Ryan, who served in their fathers' shops, both had chilblains as in previous years. And, as in previous years, they became clumsy, cut themselves and were bound up with rags here and there. Alberta, who had been sent to fetch sliced meat, could not stop herself thinking of the moment when the knife had slipped and cut into the swollen, mauve-coloured fingers. Pressed meat and smoked sausage lost their appeal for her.

There was not much to see in the street any more. The few pedestrians were grey, unrecognizable bundles, who crossed in the teeth of the wind and snow with their faces hidden. But there came Kwasnikow stamping, and livened it all up. He was not grey, he was red, and the colour was most obvious in winter. His worn top hat, the joy of the street urchins, was not lording it as usual on his head. Kwasnikow was wearing a sheepskin cap with red ribbons hanging down the back, and a sheepskin coat with red edging to it. The snow powdered his red hair and his red beard, making both burn a little less brightly than in summer, but to make up for it his face, with its round, blue eyes, was more highly coloured than ever. It was full of tiny, red veins, broken by the wind and the weather and brandy; on his nose and cheekbones they clustered into three flaming roses. And he sang to himself, as was his habit when walking; a melancholy, monotonous, never-ending melody. Once, long ago, no one quite knew when, Kwasnikow had come from Murmansk with a Russian ship and been left behind, lying ill at the hospital. So he had found work with old Kamke and stayed for good.

Some distance behind him came the prostitutes in their shawls, snow on their heads, shoulders and other horizontal planes, like wandering monuments.

Every day the stifling dark nibbled a little more of the weak twilight.

The lights were on all day. It was almost Christmas. Mrs. Selmer's breakfast novel had disappeared. Her almanac, a pencil and a notebook had taken its place. Mrs. Selmer leafed through the almanac, wrote notes, and made marks with the pencil, muttering to herself and drumming on the table with her fingers: 'Madam Svendsen says we shall be having *vol-au-vent* at the Archdeaconry on the first day of Christmas, so we can't have it on the third, it's out of the question. Otherwise I had thought of having it this year before the roast – last year we had tongue and green peas, so that's no good either. Oh bother, whatever shall I choose?'

She read her notes to herself and Alberta: 'Washing sixteenth and seventeenth, flead cakes eighteenth, wafers and Berlin rings nineteenth, boil ham in the evening, clean house twentieth, polish silver twenty-first, hang up curtains in the evening. Gingernuts, raisin bread twenty-second – no, I see we shall have to do them early too, Alberta, otherwise we shan't get out the plants and the carpets – scrub kitchen twenty-third – you'll have to decorate the tree, Alberta—'

Mrs. Selmer speculated, drummed, muttered and scribbled more notes. And Alberta made the most of it, helping herself to cheese with her bread, and more coffee, while she replied, 'Yes, of course – yes, I expect that would be best,' in the tone of voice that by experience had shown itself to be most expedient when domestic affairs were under discussion. An

57

interested, calm, friendly tone, which tolerably hid the black-ness of her soul.

She was colder than ever. The curtains were at the wash, and the windows stared blackly at her from all directions like empty eye-sockets. On the outer sills the snow lay piled high against the panes, the darkness and cold grimaced in without mercy. The dining-room stove seemed to burn to even less purpose than usual; the warmth was no longer devoured by the living-rooms alone, it seemed to be swallowed up in the universe.

Mrs. Selmer drew her shawl tightly about her: 'Last year the flead cakes came to so and so much, but this year butter and eggs are dearer – and I sent something to your Aunt the Colonel last week, I thought I should – I daren't tell Papa – I don't see how I shall make the money go round, Alberta.'

She wrote a number of quick, small figures on a clean page in the almanac, added, subtracted, and counted on her fingers.

Alberta added and subtracted as well. All the prosiness and tedium of life was piling up ahead like bad weather forecasts. Her lonely walks, those fixed points of her existence, her in-numerable secret visits to the coffee pot, her vice and stimulant, disappeared from view as lights are extinguished for the sea-farer. The daily storms might turn into hurricanes and the approaching festival into a catastrophe, it had happened before. The cold, the dark, and the shortage of money, these three, these invincible three, each of whom alone could kill all joy, now concluded a terrible pre-Christmas pact to ravage life and lay it waste. Scrubbing and polishing days were gloomy and full of traps and dangers; the day when the one thousand and three potted plants had to be carried out and in again, washed and sprinkled, even worse – but it's an ill wind ... Alberta's un-fortunate person was generally put in the shade by the flead cakes and wafers, by burning financial problems, by Madam Svendsen who helped with the baking, and old Oleanna who helped with the wash. Besides, a couple of days in the kitchen rolling out flead cakes or laying Berlin rings on the hot plate would not be too bad. It would be warm in the kitchen, so warm that she could wear an open-necked summer blouse with the sleeves rolled up. Her skin would turn smooth and white, her hands beautiful and plump. Once in a while she would be able to fill up on a left-over piece of dough or some burned or otherwise unsuccessful cake, and there was no lack of coffee. On the other hand Madam Svendsen had red, running eyes, the sight of which ruined the appetite. She groaned from time to time and had to sit down and explain over and over again that it was the sores on her legs. Alberta was filled with horror at the thought of these legs full of sores, they obsessed her. She imagined them to be pale and bloody, could not get them out of her mind for long periods, and dreaded them every time Madam Svendsen came. What with one thing and another, there was a good deal to be taken into consideration.

But Mama was more conciliatory towards Papa. Her voice no longer turned cold and bitter, but she would explain patiently and pleasantly why such and such were necessary and why they cost so and so much. She did not emerge, as she normally did from her skirmishes concerning money, small and crushed, fighting her tears, the notes crumpled convulsively in her hand. And Papa did not hand them over in a fury, but merely sighed a little and said: 'Well, well, if it's necessary' – or, 'You understand these things better than I, my dear.'

They discussed the party for the third day of Christmas at the breakfast table. There were even mornings when Papa, in high spirits, threw bank notes across the table to Mama, saying: 'If we're to have Christmas, then let's have a proper one – *après nous le déluge*'.

And Alberta at her mending basket felt her spirits rise, and it seemed as if everything could be borne if only Mama and Papa would behave like this to each other. But then she remembered that it had been like this last Christmas too. For some mysterious reason it was like this once in a while.

It never lasted long.

* * *

'Are you up, Alberta?'

'I'm getting dressed. What do you want, Jacob?'

'I must talk to you, Alberta – you must let me in.' Jacob's voice was low and urgent. He grasped the door handle.

'No Jacob, do wait a bit – you are mean!'

59

Jacob was already in the room. 'I'm sorry Alberta, don't be cross,' he said quickly, short of breath.

Alberta groped for something with which to cover herself. Since Jacob's confirmation, when he began to wear long trousers, she had been shy of him, and it embarrassed her to have to display her arms and collar-bone. Perhaps it was also a little because of Cedolf Kjeldsen, Jacob's evil genius, who had been to sea and whom Alberta dimly suspected to be a man of experience, capable of opening Jacob's eyes to all manner of things.

But there was nothing within reach. Not for the world would she cross the floor, so she remained standing in front of him, a little hunched, knock-kneed, her elbows pressed in to her sides, her hands crossed over her breast and the compromising collar-bone – trembling with cold and modesty.

Jacob did not even see her. He spoke quickly in the same low, urgent voice, and Alberta realized that her sensitivity was for the moment of no ·importance whatever. This was one of those situations in which the barriers of everyday life fall, when people act without regard for trivialities, when one only made oneself ridiculous and insignificant by insisting on formalities.

'I say Alberta,' said Jacob. 'You've got to help me.'

'What is it, Jacob, what is it?'

Jacob waited for a second. It is no joke dealing someone a blow, even if you are in a hurry and action must be taken.

'Can you lend me twenty *kroner*?' he said, looking fixedly at Alberta. There was no other way out and he was beyond all scruple.

'Are you out of your mind, Jacob?'

'I must have it, Alberta, I must have it this afternoon, or else—'

'Or else?'

'Or else they'll send a bill for forty *kroner* to Papa.'

'Jacob!'

'Yes, you see, Alberta, it was a marble table – we sat on it, you understand, another fellow and myself, one on each side, and it cracked right across – and Krane won't wait. You see, Alberta, we each have to find twenty *kroner* by this afternoon. He'd wait until then, he said.'

'It was you and Cedolf.'

'I haven't time for so many explanations – Mama may come any minute and find me here. And you know how it'll be if she gets to know, she'll lie about on the sofa and all that. You see, I *must* have the money, you *must* help me – I have to dash now – good-bye.'

And Jacob was gone.

Alberta stood there alone and tried to plumb the depths of this catastrophe. Her head whirled with one-legged pale pink marble café tables. Cedolf Kjeldsen's cheeky, handsome face, and Krane the hotel keeper's sour, pursed-up little one span past against a background of the horribly vulgar drinking-parties that went on in the small back rooms at the Grand, behind the banqueting hall. She had had a glimpse of one once when she was up at the hotel on an errand and took the wrong turning. The memory had remained with her in a reek of squalor. A disgusting, airless stench of stale, cold tobacco and drunkenness, slops on the tables, boisterous laughter. A hoarse voice, incessantly repeating damn, damn, damn from the centre of a group, one of the chambermaids on the lap of a man in shirt-sleeves. A commercial traveller in a state of dissolution, collarless, his waistcoat unbuttoned, who, glass in hand, had come to the door and called to Alberta: 'Come on in Missy, we were waiting for you. No, no, come on in' – and had made after her down the stairs calling pssst! The chambermaid had twisted herself off the lap on which she was sitting, had come and taken the man by the arm and brought him to order, whispering: 'Be quiet, Pettersen, she's one of the Magistrate's family – so be quiet now, do you hear?' – And it had been only the middle of the afternoon. People said it got worse later in the evening. Then Krane was said to hang dark blankets over the windows, and Palmine Flor and Lilly Vogel were there.

But it must not happen, it must not happen. The thought of what might come about, of Papa's fury and Mama's lamentations, made her feel physically ill. Cedolf had always been Papa's red rag and one of Mama's countless crosses, Cedolf alone was more than enough. The Grand, Krane, and forty *kroner*'s extra expenditure in the middle of the Christmas preparations was too much by far, and would bring about something very similar to Domesday. Papa might throw Jacob out of the house, give him up completely, beat him to death, kill Mama.

Alberta already felt that terrible giddiness that comes of enduring something, dreading something. It was an old acquaintance. When she had told Mama lies, done school work badly, stolen cakes from the sideboard, it had been there – and when she had had to take an exam or have a tooth pulled out – and the time she and Jacob had been out rowing on the river, were carried away by the current and came home in the middle of the night. It was like a sickness breaking out, a malignant fever.

Now she could hear Mama going downstairs. She pulled herself together, finished dressing and went down after her. As she entered the dining-room the street door slammed behind Jacob. She wilted and shrank under Mrs. Selmer's gaze which, sharp with suspicion, was directed at her across the almanac.

'Strange that Jacob should be out so early today,' commented Mama, as she handed Alberta her cup. 'He had disappeared by the time I came down, and it's not more than eight o'clock. I can't understand why he should leave so early.'

'No, I can't either,' answered Alberta, blushing to the roots of her hair.

'It is also strange that you should be blushing,' continued Mrs. Selmer. Her eyes never left Alberta, her mouth was sarcastic. 'Are you hiding something from me?'

Mrs. Selmer was by no means trusting or easy to lead by the nose, and Alberta did not possess the saving grace of audacity.

'Of course not, Mama,' she said, but her hand trembled so that she had to put down her cup, and her eyes were wooden as they avoided Mama's.

'Take care,' said Mama. And Alberta felt the same anxiety grip her as when Mama had said take care to her when she was small: 'Take care, if I find you've been making a fool of me – you'll pay dearly for it, Alberta, my dear.'

Mrs. Selmer's voice was pregnant with misfortune. There was a cold composure in it that froze Alberta. She tottered over to the mending basket and concentrated on rummaging amongst the stockings without bringing herself to begin darning them.

'Don't sit there rummaging,' exclaimed Mama irritably. 'Get out the silver and take it into the kitchen. My adult daughter should know that we clean the silver today.'

Alberta got up again, weak at the knees, opened drawers and cupboards and began to wander in and out, butter-fingered and clumsy, relieved each time she slipped past without being assailed afresh. But no one avoids his fate for long: 'When did Jacob come home last night?'

'I don't know,' replied Alberta, feeling as if she were plunging headlong into the abyss. With any luck she was the only one in the house who did know when Jacob had come home. At any rate she was the only one who knew what he did with himself. The alleys, Rivermouth, the Grand – all that lay outside Papa's and Mama's range of vision.

She had lain listening as he crept up the stairs. It had sounded as if he was steady on his feet.

Now she was piling lie upon lie. Where would it end? If she were found out retribution was certain. Everything gave warning of it, Mrs. Selmer's eyes, her icy voice. Oh – if only something would happen, anything, a catastrophe if necessary, as long as it put an end to this situation. It took nerve to deny anything consistently to Mama. Alberta felt with dismay that she had none. And now she would have to sit face to face with her the whole morning and polish silver.

If she had had the saving grace of audacity she would have asked with innocent voice and expression if Jacob had not come home at eleven o'clock, as he had said he would – but she did not possess it and was incapable of touching on the subject. Inwardly, she felt something give way. The moment when the sinner breaks down, and can maintain his stubbornness no longer, but prostrates himself and confesses all, seemed not so very far away for Alberta.

Mrs. Selmer was speaking again. With the confidence of one who knows his time will come, she said: 'I don't know when he came home either, I was asleep. I don't even know where he was. I have my doubts as to whether he was with the rest of his class, as he said he would be. But I shall see to it that I find out, and I shall also see to it that I find out whether you have told me the truth today, Alberta.'

Then the stairs creaked. Papa was on his way, and Alberta was given a breathing-space. It was in everyone's interest to keep him out of it as long as possible, at any rate until Mama had discovered what was really going on.

The morning was endless. Alberta sat as if on live coals, scarcely daring to move so as to avoid attracting any more attention to herself than was necessary. She breathed more easily every time Jensine's many duties brought her out to the kitchen. She prayed to heaven that Jensine might stay there, but Jensine did not stay; she merely emptied her bucket in the sink, filled it with clean water, exchanged a few words with Mama and disappeared again. And the atmosphere remained as oppressive as before.

Once Alberta took courage and tried to begin a conversation on a neutral subject: the silver they were polishing, the abundance of silver that derived from Papa's and Mama's palmy days, a fairy-tale time from before Alberta could remember.

It was a complete fiasco. Mrs. Selmer answered yes and no, all the while looking at Alberta like a detective who knows he has caught the criminal, and that it is only a matter of time before all is confessed.

Alberta went under again and surfaced no more.

Twice she got up and pretended to go to a certain place, simply to get out of Mama's atmosphere and think a little. In the fateful silence that prevailed it was impossible to follow the slightest strand of thought. She stood outside on the steps for a suitable length of time, twisting and rubbing her ice-cold hands and trying to find a solution. Faces whirled in her brain, popped up and vanished.

Beda? Beda would probably bring out a couple of ten *kroner* notes if she had them, but she never had any money except at the beginning of the month. And she would despise Alberta and say: 'You're a proper fool, Alberta, poor dear, to waste your time helping Jacob with a thing like this – don't bother Alberta.' Beda did not understand how things were. She had a mother who would say: 'But my dearest, darling, sweet little

64

Beda, how could you do such a thing?' when Beda had done something terrible. A mother who was not in the least like Nemesis, but who was only a little extraordinary, a little scandalous – and a father framed behind glass on the wall. It was easy for Beda to be fearless and happy-go-lucky.

Christina? Impossible. Gudrun? No, none of her friends. The Chief Clerk – reveal to the Clerk that his superior's children could not find twenty *kroner* on their own – no! Leonardsen? His worn, obliging, little person, always suffering from a cold, appeared before her against the background of two small crowded rooms, stuffy with wet napkins, coffee and paraffin vapour – no, not Leonardsen.

Nor Jensine.

But then there was nobody else – then there was only one way out, a highly embarrassing solution, one that opened new depths for Alberta. She had resorted to it once before when money had to be raised. Now it almost felt like a compulsion. She knew it existed and could be turned to account, and that she would be unable to avoid it.

After dinner she waylaid Jacob in the hall. They whispered out there together.

'Can't Cedolf lend it you – he has his wages, hasn't he?'

Jacob looked away. 'He was treating me,' he replied evasively.

'I suppose he always treats you,' said Alberta bitterly, with some scorn.

'Mm-yes – I never have any money, you know that.'

'Yes, but you don't have to go to the Grand.'

'Don't have to go to the Grand?' Jacob's expression was suddenly helpless. 'We don't usually go to the Grand, it was only yesterday evening – and besides, I must be allowed to go somewhere. It's always so loathsome here at home. Papa can scarcely bear the sight of me.

'I know Alberta, but it's no good preaching morals at me now,' he added deprecatingly when Alberta opened her mouth. 'If you can't help, never mind. I'll be leaving home soon anyway. Now or later, it makes no difference. And whether I leave on my own or get sent away makes no difference either.

If it weren't for Mama, Krane could bring his bill – she suspects something already, by the way.'

Jacob turned up his collar and prepared to leave the house.

'You shall have the money, Jacob – I think – in a little while. Go upstairs and read, I'll come up later.'

'But can you manage it, Alberta?'

'I don't know, I'm going to try. Go on up, Jacob!'

The street was deserted immediately after dinner. That was as it should be, otherwise the expedition would have been unthinkable. But it also increased her feeling of being out on an unlawful errand, of this being a special time for deeds of darkness.

It was clearing up. A whiff of colder weather was in the air, and the snowfall had lightened towards the north. A star was visible through it; it twinkled weakly. Alberta remembered distractedly that the moon would soon be full. Perhaps it would shine the bad weather away until Christmas.

She felt as if her body were unreal, non-existent. If Mama or Papa had any inkling of what she was doing now, the day of judgement would probably have the same dimensions as if Krane were to come with the bill. One misdeed leads to another. Alberta and Jacob were on the slippery slope, rolling downwards at top speed. The next link in the chain would be to begin telling lies with audacity and cold-bloodedness, those two good and necessary weapons in life's struggle. Those such as Alberta who did not possess them by nature were ill-equipped, but it served no purpose to think of that now. A dangerous course had presented itself and had to be followed to its conclusion without hesitation.

There was Kvandal the tailor standing at his door. Was he not wondering where Alberta was going in the middle of the after-dinner nap enjoyed by officialdom and the higher business echelons? Could he not see it written all over her – did he not scent scandal through that flattened little nose of his?

Kvandal the tailor was one of the people who, she was certain, knew something positive about Papa's money matters. There might be some point in taking in the Archdeaconry and the Governor's family, the Prams and the Pios. Perhaps they went home from Papa's and Mama's parties after fine wine and plenty of food, thinking: 'Perhaps they're not so badly off after all.'

But Kvandal the tailor – he would smile derisively if he saw the spread. And Lian the shoemaker and Schmitt the butcher.

You see your home from one side, the inside. But it has an outside facing the town as well, in fact it has two, a front side and a back side. You yourself swing with it in its course and never see either the front, that faces towards the gentry and has a door on to the street, or the back, that faces Kvandal the tailor, Lian the shoemaker and Schmitt the butcher, and has a kitchen entrance. You can only guess how it looks.

The people who come to the kitchen door *know* everything that, with much care and sacrifice, is concealed from the rest of the world. You carry your head high in front of them, as high as you can – but unfortunately Alberta could do no more than that. And now she was making an admission to them. It is difficult to conceal facts – if you succeed in one quarter they will leak out in another.

Dorum the goldsmith – he had looked at her so craftily last time. He would look even more crafty now, most likely. And yet Alberta would lie to him, lie although she would blush to the roots of her hair. It was natural to lie to Dorum – if only it were equally natural to lie to Mrs. Selmer.

It could be seen from a distance that Dorum the goldsmith kept warm and comfortable in his business. There was no ice on the large plate-glass window, and you could see into the shop from a long way down River Street. A couple of country folk were inside trying on rings. Behind them Dorum's bald head shone like a moon under the lamp.

Alberta walked quickly past, as if she were going somewhere quite different. She went round the block at a speed suggesting haste and purpose. The next time she passed, the country folk were still there. The third time they were gone, but Mrs. Dorum was in the shop, helping her husband to tidy up after them.

Alberta went past once more. She met Kwasnikow. He was drunk. He stood in her way, took off his top hat, bowed deeply, and placed the hat in front of her in the snow.

Afraid, Alberta started to one side and hurried on. She heard Kwasnikow speaking Russian in a threatening tone and stumbling after her. Was Kwasnikow going to stop her now? When he was angry as well as drunk, there was no getting rid of him. If he were to see her going into Dorum's, he would be capable of gathering a crowd outside.

Perhaps it had been stupid of her not to go in the last time. Mrs. Dorum would hear about it just the same. It would have been best to go in and behave as if it did not matter, to take it easily and without concern. But again, for that sort of thing audacity and cold-bloodedness were necessary, those two stout weapons that Alberta did not possess.

She came out into River Street for the fourth time. Now the coast was clear. Mrs. Dorum had gone, Kwasnikow made harmless. He had fallen into the clutches of P.C. Olsen, who was going his rounds. They disappeared from sight under old Kamke's doorway.

Alberta braced herself. What must be, must be. People had even gone to the guillotine. She grasped the doorknob, feeling as giddy as if she were doing it in a dream. The little bell above rang out as if disturbed.

'It's terrifically kind of you, Alberta.'

Jacob's voice was deep and rough with emotion. He looked alternately at Alberta and at the two ten *kroner* notes she had placed in front of him.

'Put them in your pocket, Jacob, hurry, Mama might come – and you'd better be quick and get it settled.'

Alberta was out of breath, and spoke in gasps. She sat down on Jacob's bed and watched her breath; it rose like white smoke each time she opened her mouth. She felt ill at ease, for the deed was only half finished. For several reasons she ought to have gone herself, but could not bring herself to do so.

Jacob stretched two blue, grazed fists out of his shrunken sleeves, picked up the notes and stowed them away. He said without looking at her: 'How did you manage, Alberta – you haven't sold something again, have you?'

'I sold the bracelet.'

'The chain?' His face was full of dismay.

68

'The chain.'

'Oh, but Alberta – now it's you who are out of your mind – the chain from Uncle the Colonel! What will you say when Mama . . . ?'

'I suppose I'll have to say I've lost it.'

'But then she'll be terribly angry, Alberta – and what about Papa?'

. . . 'But Alberta, surely you could have taken some other trinket, a ring or a brooch, you got such a lot for your confirmation.'

'It wouldn't have brought in enough, Jacob. And then Mama might have recognized them if Dorum had put them in the window. There are a couple of chain bracelets there already.'

'But neither of them is as heavy as yours, Alberta. Anyway, you must have got a lot of money for it, my goodness, you must have got at least a hundred *kroner*.'

'I got twenty-five.'

'Then he's cheated you, the scoundrel, you should never have let it go for that. Was it Dorum himself?'

'You get so little for jewellery, Jacob,' answered Alberta in an experienced tone of voice. Deep down she was bitterly disappointed at the pecuniary result of her expedition. If one were going to turn criminal, the rewards ought in principle to be greater.

'You should have gone to Vik as well – he might have given you more,' said Jacob, talking nonsense just like a man. He did not really know what he was talking about.

But he must have had an inkling all the same, for he added: 'But of course it was bad enough having to go to that fellow Dorum.'

And suddenly he took a couple of large strides across the floor, threw his arms round Alberta and thumped her hard on the back several times with the palm of his hand, knocking her backwards and forwards. In a choked voice, his cheek against hers, he muttered: 'It was terribly nice of you, Alberta – you'll get it back – when I start to earn money you shall have a much heavier bracelet, you can count on that, Alberta.'

'Jacob,' began Alberta, groping for his head. Her heart was

overflowing, there was such a tremendous amount she wanted to say—

But Jacob saved himself, retreating into the middle of the room. He picked up his cap and turned up his collar. 'Well, I'd better sprint over to Krane, he might easily take it into his head to come here.'

He was already at the door when Alberta stopped him. She was going to find out about one thing at any rate, and the moment might never come again. 'Jacob, tell me, were there girls there?'

'Girls? Where?' Jacob opened his eyes unnecessarily wide.

'You know what I mean. They say Palmine Flor and Lilly Vogel are there in the evenings.'

'Phooey—' Jacob's voice was not in the least tearful any more, but full of scorn. 'I didn't see any Palmine or any Lilly either. You'll believe anything. But I must hurry. Good-bye Alberta.'

And Jacob was gone. Alberta heard him go out through the office door.

She stood at the window in his cold room, breathed on the pane, and saw him come out into the falling snow under the arc lamp at the corner, lift his cap to Kvandal, and be swallowed up by the darkness.

She had not had time to think of it before, but it had been lurking in the shadows, and now it emerged. She had disposed of a piece of property of real value, of the kind that only falls to one's lot at life's turning-points, given her by Uncle the Colonel 'not without sacrifice' – disposed of it for twenty-five *kroner*. The little ring last spring had been nothing, a mere trifle. Besides, Mrs. Selmer had decided that Alberta was not to wear rings: 'Hands like yours should not be emphasized; on the contrary, they should be hidden, my child.'

But the bracelet!

'. . . We wish to give Alberta a memento for life on this solemn occasion, we do so not without sacrifice,' the letter from Aunt the Colonel had said. Alberta felt dimly that she had sinned against the class instinct for collection and preservation. The kind of people who went out and sold their possessions had sunk very low. She was one of them. The ground opened up beneath her . . .

Downstairs in the living-rooms Mama and Papa were asleep, each on a sofa, suspecting nothing of life's bitter realities. Jacob was impossible at school and sought out acquaintances from lower down the social scale; Alberta was unfortunate in appearance, incompetent in the house and not very presentable; that was as far as their knowledge and their anxieties went. If they had only known a little more they would probably have given up Alberta and Jacob altogether.

She was seized by great weakness and exhaustion – an overwhelming desire to lie down, to put herself at the mercy of darkness, cold and fatigue, to surrender herself. Was life really so bad, were she, Jacob, Mama and Papa really unhappy, or was it only something she imagined, and were they really like other people? Did everyone live like this behind their closed doors – was it only Alberta who was unreasonable and dissatisfied and who strained after impossibilities? Would there never come a time when anxiety and vague longing were quietened, when lies and evasions and all kinds of small, hidden irons in the fire would no longer be necessary – when life was enjoyable and straightforward? Suppose it did not come, suppose this were all.

A short while ago she had been standing in Dorum's shop. It was not an unpleasant dream. He had leaned ten fat fingers on the counter, given her quick, sharp looks over his spectacles and asked again and again whether she really wanted to sell. It was more reasonable to exchange it for something, she would get more for it – he couldn't give much in cash, it would scarcely amount to the value of the gold. He had brought out boxes with brooches and rings and said jokingly that a young lady could never have too many of them.

He had said exactly the same thing last spring, when she had gone to him with the little ring. That time it had been gloves for Jacob, who had been invited to a dance. Papa had said Jacob could go with a pair of his. If they were too big, it ought to be possible to sew up the finger tips on the inside. It was pay day and payment was due on the bank loan. He had forbidden, absolutely forbidden, the purchase of new gloves for Jacob.

71

Mama lay on the sofa in despair and said: 'I am powerless, children – you see I am powerless.'

But Jacob got his new gloves, handed to him outside Kilde the watchmaker's, on the way to the party.

Dorum had said today as he had said then: 'Have you thought it over, Miss?'

Disgust for the whole business, the desire to give it up, had crept over Alberta like an infirmity. Anxiety that someone might come in, dread at the thought of finding herself outside again without having concluded her business, had come and gone like waves of fever.

When finally the whole transaction was over, and she stood watching Dorum unlock the drawer with the banknotes and take out two tens and a five-*kroner* bill, she felt physically exhausted.

And Jacob – he was on his way to the Grand on an honest errand in a sense, to protect Mama and stave off catastrophe. He would meet Cedolf, and in the back room some of the travelling salesmen were probably sitting drinking, the kind who were willing to offer anybody a drink. Besides, Jacob was not anybody – he was the Magistrate's son and by no means unwelcome there or in the alleys.

If she were the least bit brave she would have gone herself. Straight from Dorum's at that. She would have settled the affair for Jacob and made it unnecessary for him to set foot in the dens of vice any more.

But Alberta was incapable of settling matters. She had an ingrained fear of the spoken word, an irreparable horror of argument and explanation. She blushed, was prostrated, lost the thread and might well say something quite different from what she had intended. The mere thought of explaining to Krane why she was there made her go hot and cold.

Life is immodest in its demands and makes no allowance for individuals' differing powers of expression. Alberta was insignificant, that had been decided long ago.

A bitter feeling of impotence and of general doom came over her. She leaned her head against the window frame and sobbed.

A door opened below and Mrs. Selmer called loudly and sharply up the stairs: 'Alberta!'

Alberta started like a dozing horse at the word of command. She went towards the door, hastily assuming her defensive mask on the way – that innocent, unsuspecting face, which so easily dissolved and was reduced to impotence at the first attack.

When she appeared in the light from the little lamp in the passage outside Jacob's door, the enemy assailed her without hesitation from the foot of the stairs: 'Oh, so that's where you are, and here I sit toiling in the kitchen, polishing and polishing, without it ever occurring to my adult daughter to lend me a helping hand. Will it please you to put in an appearance in the kitchen immediately?'

*   *   *

The moon had shone the bad weather away. A miracle had taken place. The world was no longer a grey and white swirl, a confused and formless chaos. It had crystallized into an open, generous landscape, firm and still. It seemed endless. The moon shone upon it without setting, hanging low in the small hours, turning white and losing strength later in the morning. But it recovered and changed to yellow, wheeled up into the bowl of the sky and shone huge, recreating and expanding the kingdoms of the earth. Distant mountain ranges, swathed in mist by the sun and the daylight, were pointed up and exhibited by the moon. Everything caressed by the sun and the daylight was drowned by the moon in oceans of blue shadow.

Alberta woke earlier than usual and saw a shining stripe between the curtain and the window pane. She struggled with herself, then abandoned her warm bed, was up on her bare feet and let the blind shoot upwards.

The cross made by the window was thrown far into the room along the floor, and outside the world lay like a new sphere, untrodden, unspotted, shining clean, full of enormous, fantastic forms.

Everything was thick and soft and generous. The coverlet of snow had spread everywhere, above and below, and was only slightly lifted by the houses beneath it. It hung and poured from roofs and eaves and filled the courtyard like a swelling eider-down.

Behind Flemming's warehouse, which looked as if it were built of blue shadow and secrets, ran the river like flowing, streaming light. Beyond, the mountains raised up on their shadowed frames wide, shining plateaux towards the moon.

Above them stood Orion alone in infinity.

Alberta curled up on the chair with her legs under her. New snow and moonlight – the loveliest and worst of all – an experience each time. The world became still and open, nothing was frightening any more. She journeyed in a landscape without anxiety, and the mild, intense light fell protectively round her, recreating her appearance as it recreated everything else. She moved in it boldly, and even her face was easier to bear.

But a wound opened inside. Delight and melancholy welled up simultaneously from the depths of her mind. She could not understand why nor protect herself from them. They streamed over her together with the light, making her shrink with painful impatience. Tears came, God knows how. One moment she was crushed to the ground by life's misery, the next, new strength coursed exulting through her – it was like madness.

If she could go out on skis now – or stay sitting here long enough under the moon, quite still – the sounds would begin inside her. Small stanzas would come fluttering, small webs of words with rhythm to them, and join up with other small webs that had come fluttering before, when she was alone and quiet and everything was beautiful. Or they might not join up with anything – they might just conceal themselves in her mind. You never knew.

Did they come from within or from the wide, mysterious landscape outside? They were there all of a sudden, demanding to be written down in the secret book under the woollen vests in the chest of drawers. The book was full of small, fluttering stanzas scattered among its pages. Some belonged together naturally and had become verses, others stood apart, waiting. Some seemed to wait in vain, while others found company when she least expected it.

A large number of them were useless, she had to choose and sift. Often a word was wrong, and it might take months to

74

listen her way to the right one. Generally it was less a matter of searching than of listening – listening inwards. Taking pains seldom got her anywhere, the word so easily became false and failed to fit in. The stanza must be stored in her brain and come to fruition on its own. When that happened, the same wonderful and troublesome state of mind followed, the same happy intoxication and bitter disgust. Nothing was more painful than to tumble from the fluttering stanzas' airy regions down into Mrs. Selmer's storm-laden atmosphere, a predicament that often befell Alberta.

When Mrs. Selmer wandered upstairs after breakfast with her jug of warm water, Alberta saw her opportunity and stole out of the front door, in spite of the gingernuts and Madam Svendsen, whose eyes had been watering since eight o'clock over a large piece of dough, which she was belabouring in the wonderfully warm kitchen.

Already when Alberta was dusting she had seen through the ice-covered panes a new sky, a suspicion of fire and colour. Now she ran up the hillside without looking about her, careful not to catch a glimpse too early and shatter the experience into small pieces. She was even cunning enough to wait while she got her breath and calmed down before turning round to find it all before her eyes like a revelation.

The landscape shone of itself, with a blue, cold, dead and muted light, under a sky that was kindled. In the lowest quarter to the south it was a delicate, crisp shade of gold, and the fjord had captured it in layer upon layer of answering reflections.

Soon the sky would look like a glowing bell of light above the earth. It would glow with all the colours of the rainbow from flaming red to deep violet, and the river would flow through the cold kingdoms of snow like a precious band woven of purple and green, gold and rose.

But to the north the moon hung white in an opaque infinity. The thin, crooked birch trees tentatively planted along the roadside stood bent beneath their furs of snow, sober as in a woodcut, against the dead background. A bird took wing from one of them, a fleeting ruffle of feathers and a slow scattering of snow

75

broke the silence. The air had a cool, bitter taste, as fortifying and refreshing as a drink.

And look, now the earth was visible in all directions, as far as the eye could see: in the middle the river flowing out into the fjord, with Southfjord, looking like an estuary, straight to the south; on the one side of the river the town, wrapped up in cotton-wool, like a collection of dolls' houses ready for packing, the warehouses outermost like a bulwark; it looked as if they were holding on to the town to prevent it from sliding out into the water. On the other side the steep, barren range rose straight up from the shore; on the sandbank at Rivermouth the cod-liver-oil factory like a snuffed-out volcano under its snow hat. Far, far out in all directions the landscape held up the sky like a cupola upon a wreath of rounded mountains. To the south they raised themselves higher and became peaks. To the east was the range from which the river came, cold and impenetrable as a fortress jutting from the wreath.

Somewhere below the edge of the bell of light the sun was shining on other lands and other people. That was where one longed to go, that was where one travelled, that was where life was lived and events took place.

Alberta sighed. She was tempted to stay up on the plateau; to walk on in the deep snow and go far inland across the bog before the snow-plough and the energetic walkers made the roads unsafe; to see the miracle accomplished; to see the glow turn blood-red and then fade, the mountains darken against a green sky, the moon be lit.

A star would blaze up from the depths of space. Only Orion's belt would be visible. It would go eastwards above the bend in the river and move slowly south. The northern lights would look like airy, tangled veils, would be rolled up, coil together, frolic and disappear. A breath from the universe, from all that is great, elemental and limitless, would fill nature. The peace of infinity would pervade everything, restless human organisms as well.

Look, the mouth of the river was already stained with purple.

But down there under the big roof north of Flemming's warehouse, Mrs. Selmer was going to and fro in Christmas busyness, certain to have been dressed and ready long ago. She could not be seen, but Alberta knew she was there, she felt it instinctively. A mysterious force, strange currents against which opposition was both useless and unthinkable, compelled her back at a respectable speed, to all that she longed to escape from with all her heart.

*   *   *

Christmas came and went. It was what it usually was, what it had been as long as Alberta and Jacob could remember: a shining hope – and a flat, embarrassed wonder that yet again they could have been so trusting and naïve.

Hope is a frugal plant, that puts out new shoots in obscurity every time it is plundered. To stamp out hope would be a long undertaking, perhaps an impossible one. It lives on nothing, like yellow lichen on a stone, it lives in spite of everything – even in spite of the Chief Clerk, who was to celebrate Christmas with his superior.

'Do you think the Chief Clerk will leave early this year, too, Jacob?'

'I expect so. I wish he wouldn't come at all.'

'So do I, but I suppose we have to invite him – and I expect he feels he can't say no. That's how it is, you know.'

'Ugh!'

'I wish I knew why he leaves. After all it is warm here on Christmas Eve, so it can't be because he's cold. What do you think it is, Jacob?'

'I don't suppose he thinks it's much fun here. That's not surprising.'

'No – as long as he doesn't notice that Mama and Papa—'

'He would have to be a complete idiot not to notice.'

'Oh but this Christmas we'll have a nice time, you'll see, Jacob.'

'Do you think so, Alberta?'

'Yes, of course – we'll do our best at any rate.'

Naturally the Chief Clerk would notice. He had always noticed, whatever his name and whoever he might be. Alberta could remember it ever since the time when she had found no

77

other expression for her own troubled uneasiness than 'it's all so boring'.

Kvam was the only one who had noticed nothing. He remained talkative, riding his hobby-horses undaunted and unaffected by the shifting pressures of atmosphere around him. But after Kvam had come Bolling. An uneasy expression came into his eyes and already at tea he began to be careful. And the present incumbent was quiet and shy, excessively polite and excessively attentive, but he left before supper. He was determined to go, and stood firm in the teeth of Mrs. Selmer's entreaties and the Magistrate's regrets, embarrassed but resolute. Bergan the lawyer was having a few friends in for goose and a bachelor party, it had become quite a tradition. He had promised to be there a long time ago. He was sorry not to be able to come on New Year's Eve either.

His brief attendance tortured Alberta, who was on guard against every word that was spoken. She was incapable of taking part in the conversation, and would sit on the extreme edge of her chair, only half-sitting, as if that would help.

Every Christmas she hoped afresh that things would go well, that they might get through it unscathed.

Christmas Eve was approached as if it were the moment of a visitation, when miracles could be expected. Everything presaged them: the closed doors of the corner parlour, the scents of the tree – a pine from inner Southfjord – of baking, and clean curtains. The arrival of wine and food in the kitchen, of mail and parcels to be hidden away, and of the annual bowl of bulbs – tulips and hyacinths – for Mrs. Selmer from the Chief Clerk. It had pink and white crêpe paper crinkled and crumpled round the pot, and was one of the masterpieces from the Sisters Kremer's hat shop. Every year Mrs. Selmer would say: 'Oh, how delicious! I heard Lotten Kremer say they were expecting a great deal by the packet boat – they really are good at getting hold of flowers.'

And the bowl would be placed on the coffee table, from where it sent out an intoxicating scent of luxury and festivity.

But when tea had been drunk and the parcels opened, when

the candles on the tree began to threaten the pine needles, and Mama had sung her carols and wept in a corner over her letters; when Jensine had been in to see the tree and drink A Merry Christmas and for the last time the Chief Clerk had put down the Christmas magazines, in which he had repeatedly sought refuge, and taken his leave; then the artificial atmosphere, towards which everyone had attempted to contribute to the best of his ability, and which had been in greater danger than ever before, immediately deflated. Mama opened a window to let out the tobacco smoke and the tension seemed to relax. No one exerted himself any longer except for Alberta, who was always ready to indulge in naïve and hopeless endeavour.

The Christmas candles were extinguished, and with them the Christmas hopes. Everything was back to where it was a couple of hours ago. Ordinary life was back, in Mama's aggrieved voice, in Papa's muttering over the ham which was too fat, and the roast pork which had other defects. Danger lurked once more, and all kinds of mischief might occur.

Alberta went out into the kitchen to Jensine. To see her sitting there celebrating Christmas all alone, at a table spread with cakes and nuts, with her Christmas magazine and her package containing the annual dress length, gave her the same feeling of embarrassment as the sight of the burnt-out candles with their smoking wicks – as the sight of the parcels, which had only contained useful things they had needed for a long time. That was all, for us as for Jensine, this year as last.

'So Christmas is over once more, Jensine.'

'Yes, Alberta poor dear, he comes and goes as fast as he can. I'll be happy when the party's over too.'

'So shall I, Jensine.'

Alberta pressed her nose flat against the window pane. The moonlit evening was clear without a breath of wind, lights shone peacefully from all the windows. Not a soul to be seen besides Nurse Jullum's black cat, cautiously testing the surface of the snow on the roof of the porch.

The houses looked as if they held entertaining secrets. Behind the red blinds over at Doctor Pram's shadows moved in similar, even rhythm. They were going round the tree once more before blowing out the candles.

79

And Alberta abandoned herself to her hunger. It came like a severe, long-drawn-out stitch and remained gnawing at her body and limbs. Hunger for peace, joy, warmth – for God knows what, for God knows what.

It was strange, but it seemed as if it could be satisfied out there in the broad landscape that lay shining and enticing under the moon. Something was to be found out there at any rate: freedom – the beginning of all things. And did not the roads out to life lie hidden under the snow like strands in a ball of yarn? If only she could find one of them and follow it.

But much had to happen first. Everything had to be changed, for Mama and Papa too. To know that they were at home, still living in exactly the same way as now – no, in that case it would be better—

And Alberta realized that she was almost wishing her own parents were dead. She stiffened with contrition and horror. She felt as if she had looked down into an abyss and almost lost her balance. What sort of a person can I be? she thought with distress.

'Do come back, Alberta,' whispered Jacob from behind her, tapping her on the shoulder. 'It's terrible in there again, they're not saying a word to each other now. It's a bit better when we're there.'

Alberta rose from the chair in which she had been crouching on her knees. In Jensine's presence no discussion was possible, there was nothing for it but to go. So she went in with Jacob to the burnt-out Christmas tree and the burnt-out stove.

*   *   *

'Well,' said Mrs. Selmer, casually putting her napkin down on the table, 'I'm afraid I have nothing more to offer you.'

Every glass was raised towards her, everyone smiled and leaned forward to catch her eye. Several waited, glass in hand, until she had time to look in their direction: 'Thank you. An excellent dinner.'

The Magistrate's turn came, and then the scraping of chairs.

Alberta rose and took the Chief Clerk's arm with a serious nod. She looked straight in front of her, thankful for the hub-

bub made by the chairs. All speech became useless and unnecessary, she could safely limit herself to a nod.

They parted in the sitting-room once inside the door, the
Clerk with an indistinct mumble and a bow, Alberta still
silent. Thank heaven Mrs. Selmer was busy shaking hands.

Alberta fetched the flower vases from the dining table and
distributed them in the sitting-rooms. Then she sat down under
the potted palm with her hands in her lap, looking straight in
front of her.

That terrible neckband!

It was made of green tulle, caught up in loops of frilled ruch-
ing over a stiff base which cut into the hollow of her throat and
under her ears. It was much too high, and Alberta discovered to
her sorrow that the colour in her face, which normally rose and
fell, had stayed up there for good, kept in place by this new
instrument of torture.

It was her Christmas present from Aunt the Colonel. It had
arrived, yesterday, the second day of Christmas, by the packet
boat. It was a characteristic of Aunt the Colonel's despatches
that they were always a little late.

When it was unpacked, Mrs. Selmer had said with a sombre
look at Alberta's hair: 'Hm, if you were pretty and soignée like
other young girls, it might have suited you – but still, it is fearfully chic and the latest fashion, according to your Aunt.'

And Alberta knew her fate was sealed.

She moved her head neither to right nor left. When anyone
spoke to her she turned the whole of the upper half of her body,
and her overheated face became even redder. When she had
the opportunity Mrs. Selmer found time to direct a look of
aggrieved and complete despair in her direction, even closing
her eyes as if to avoid the sight. Alberta was even more hopeless, even further beneath all criticism than ever.

She sat under the palm tree, apart and to one side, as usual.

Round the circular centre table the conversation went back
and forth between the ladies. It was as if they were playing
ball with words, but slackly and without animation. Now and
again the ball dropped to the ground and stayed there until

someone made an effort and sent it on its way again. They had been in each other's company yesterday and the day before, which did not make matters any easier.

From inside the corner parlour the men's voices could be heard. They were talking about the war in East Asia and Port Arthur's prospects. Magistrate Selmer had everyone against him, he was the only one supporting the Russians. Now he was speaking quite alone in that deep voice he assumed now and again, and which never failed to make an impression on Alberta. It gave matters more weight, more moment.

The ladies fell silent and listened to the conversation. One or other of them nodded appreciatively at what was being said. The gentlemen's words were full of superior insight – a little too superior after a time, to be honest. One enterprising soul introduced a new subject.

Mrs. Selmer was an excellent hostess. No-one could catch the ball as she did, send it on its way, keep it moving. She was inexhaustible, and it was only when she was occupied elsewhere that it really fell to the ground.

She came and went, settled cushions behind the backs of her guests, had eyes in the back of her head, took out photographs, pointed, explained. She said a great many witty and amusing things that made the ladies laugh, and showed herself to be superior to them all in the ways of the world and in light conversation.

On the piano there stood a youthful portrait of her in party dress with bare arms and bare neck, a fan in her hands. Her arms were incomparably slender, supple and beautiful, the position of the hands holding the fan full of grace. The large eyes in the small, short face had a frank, pure, childlike expression that one never tired of looking at. The mouth was so soft and young with small, innocent corners that curved a little upwards. And it looked as if the same tender modelling-hand had pressed in the two small dimples in the cheeks and the little dimple in the chin. She held herself erect looking almost as if turned on a lathe; narrow-waisted, not beautiful, but unspeakably charming and captivating all the same. Alberta knew it, and she knew that she would never be anything like Mama. It was her biggest and most obvious failing.

Mrs. Selmer had kept her figure from that day to this, a little plumper, a little heavier, but with more or less the same outline. Her corpulence was evenly distributed over her body and had not accumulated in one place, as was the case with many of the other ladies. Her stomach did not stick out uncontrolled, or her arms burst out of the silk. She moved differently from the others too, with great lightness and assurance, and her skin was fair and smooth, almost without wrinkles under the blonde, frizzed hair that hid her own greyness.

The young Mama of the photograph was recognizable in everything except the expression and lines of the mouth. That small, pinched mouth, that could turn into a furrow in her face, was it really the same as the one she had had then? And the eyes, those Argus eyes, had they once looked so unsuspicious? Was it from having to live up here, enduring the cold and longing to go back to the south, from having insufficient money and disappointing children, that Mama had acquired a different mouth and another pair of eyes, or were there other, more obscure reasons? Beside Mama's portrait stood Grandmama's. Her eye-sockets were so deep. It was difficult to make out her expression, it seemed to have sunk back into the thin face. Her mouth was a firm-willed line. And Alberta suddenly shivered in spite of the heat of the room, her heart became small and afraid. Was it so, that generation after generation coerced the next, desiring only to fashion and form their lives in accordance with their own? Involuntarily she looked away from Grandmama down at the little drawer in the bureau where Mrs. Selmer hid old letters.

It was not the first time Alberta had sat here under the palm tree puzzling about these things. This had become her permanent seat, her fortress, as the result of years of experience. A little nearer, and she would be indiscreet and obtrusive, pushing and forward, and might very well find herself playing a rôle that did not suit her – a little farther away and she would be trying to make herself appear interesting and odd, different from other people. No, the palm tree was the correct strategic position for one lacking social talent and all external advantages.

In the corner parlour with the gentlemen sat Jacob. His

situation was less critical. For a while he kept resolutely to a corner without anyone finding anything to comment about; for a while, later on in the evening, Papa became good-humoured, forgetting old scores against him. He would nod to him with raised glass and call: 'Wake up, my boy—' or: 'Cheer up, Jacob, you look so serious.'

Jacob was wearing his best confirmation clothes, and they suited him. When he wore them it seemed as if Papa felt affection and a renewed interest towards him.

Was Jacob looking serious? He sat with his arms crossed over his chest, surveying the assembly in silence. But the expression on his face, was it irony or hostility? Alberta did not like it, it disturbed her. She could see him through the door every time she leaned forward.

The Archdeacon's wife got her butter from Southfjord. She assured everyone, her eyes crystal-clear, that of course it was so much cheaper than buying it from Holst. The Governor's lady swivelled her lorgnette towards her and could not quite understand that, for Holst's butter definitely went farther. It came from the dairy in Flatangen and naturally was handled better than the country butter, there was less water in it. Her experience had been that it paid to buy from Holst, even if it did cost a little more.

The Archdeacon's wife, who was without guile and not quite of this world, assured them open-heartedly, her eyes just as clear, that really the butter from her butter man was every bit as good as the dairy butter. Mrs. Bakke, the lawyer's wife, young, recently arrived from the south, and in her seventh month, looked about her innocently and said: 'My dears, I *must* find out which is better and most practical.'

The Governor's lady fell silent and pursed her lips. She had many good qualities, the Governor's lady, but did not brook contradiction; she had that little weakness. Mrs. Selmer scented danger and interjected gaily: 'To tell you the truth, *I* use margarine for everyday' – betraying herself and throwing herself into the breach. And Mrs. Pio righted her prostrate and encumbered form, revealed her enormous set of false teeth in a smile and found the courage to declare: 'So do I – so do I.'

84

The Governor's lady let it be known that she considered the subject exhausted. Demonstratively she picked up a book from the table, leaned back in her chair and leafed through the book. But Mrs. Selmer was at her post. 'Have you heard what Professor Werenskjold said about Rikke?' she threw out, and a wave of excited interest travelled through the group. 'No, what has Werenskjold said – is it possible, has Werenskjold said something?'

Mrs. Selmer nodded knowingly. She had sat next to the Governor's lady at dinner at the Archdeaconry. Mrs. Lossius put down the book and resolved to let bygones be bygones. She righted herself in her chair and reported what Werenskjold had said, but with reserve and not at all exuberantly, for the sting still rankled a little.

'Oh, how wonderful, how simply wonderful! So Rikke will become an artist, I suppose, Mrs. Lossius?' The ladies all spoke at once. The Governor's lady shrugged her shoulders: 'It is a very serious matter, and we would really prefer Rikke to use the gifts she has in some other way. After all, there are so many different fields. Applied art, for example, is the coming thing these days. But of course – if she decides after trying it out that she must take that course, we shall have to defer to her wishes.' Mrs. Lossius was self-sacrificing and motherly, re-signed in advance. And now she had got over her little ill-humour: 'Rikke draws night and day, writes Gertrude. She goes round with a sketch book all the time, literally all the time. You see, it was her drawing Werenskjold commented on. "Draw, draw, my child," he said. "That's the best thing for you".'

The unpleasantness over the butter forgotten, the tone was gay and sociable. Mrs. Selmer, who did not intend to let any shadow of disagreement creep back, asked after Gertrude.

'Very well, thank you. Gertrude is practising hard. Both of them seem to be enjoying themselves too. Aunt Honoria writes that it's nothing but balls and parties, so I'm afraid there is sometimes too much of both fun and work. But we're only young once, Mama, writes Rikke.'

Mrs. Lossius quoted amusing passages from her letters, and

then swivelled her lorgnette towards Alberta: 'I suppose you hear from them now and again too?'

'Now and again, yes.' Alberta went even redder than she was already. It was a misfortune to be the object of everybody's attention. She replied curtly and with embarrassment to a couple of questions, looking as if hypnotized at Mama, whose eyes rested on her with undisguised displeasure. The knowledge that she was not gifted, not pretty, not amusing and sweet, not in Kristiania, nothing, paralysed her. It seemed to be her own fault.

Besides, her conscience was far from clear. In the first place there was the chain. It usually went with her party regalia, and it was miraculous that heaven and earth had not been shaken some time ago. She was prepared to bear almost anything as long as Mrs. Selmer did not discover that it was missing. At the dinner table she had been silent and impossible. The Clerk had looked helpless more than once and had finally given up. She did not smile, she was serious all the time, an unforgiveable thing in company. Her condition was aggravated by the neck-band, which she knew was just as irrelevant on her person as Mama's toque from Kristiania would be on Jensine. And it had been no better yesterday at the Archdeaconry or the day before at the Prams', even though Harriet, Christina and Gudrun had all been away on a visit to Southfjord, and had not, as in other years, blackened Alberta even more with all their virtues.

Mrs. Lossius turned towards her yet again and asked a terrible question: 'And what are you doing these days?' she said with especial kindness, surveying her through the lorgnette.

Mrs. Lossius had touched on a sore point, and Alberta suspected that such was her intention.

'Nothing,' she replied curtly. It was true that she did nothing. She simply existed, did nothing and became nothing, while life rolled past somewhere far away, to the south.

But that was the wrong answer. Mrs. Selmer turned pale with anger and hastened to interrupt: 'Alberta helps me in the house, it's very necessary. I get tired sometimes, Mrs. Lossius. And then she coaches Jacob in some of his subjects.'

Alberta hated them all. They were fond of their own children and satisfied with them, but where others' were concerned their tact was cunning, their silence deceitful and their speech an open trap. She looked at young Mrs. Bakke, who sat there newly arrived, looking round her with happy eyes, and thought: 'You simpleton, you innocent. You'll get like all of them in time, fat and heavy, with double chin and uncontrolled stomach, false in mouth and eyes – perhaps your face will collapse and get hollow-cheeked and almost vanish round a large set of false teeth, like Mrs. Pio.'

To live here amongst them, sitting round the coffee table embroidering, while they nodded knowingly to right and left and sent quick little side glances to see if it was true that you were expecting; and asked about one thing, while spying out another; and confided in each other when you had gone: 'Oh yes, no doubt about it, my dear. It can't be so very long now, when was it they married?'

To grow like them – to grow finally like the old ladies who could remember nothing but confinements.

Or to go round half old like Otilie Weyer, the Sisters Kremer, Jeanette Evensen, like something life had rejected and had no use for; to have been here for ever and to continue to be here always, while the days passed by, each one like the next, and Mama like old Mrs. Weyer perhaps.

No, neither course, better to die, better to—

Alberta contracted her thin, wiry body inside her clothes and felt with relish that she had control of her muscles, that she held them in her hand like well-disciplined troops. She clenched her strong, even teeth, the only things about her person that could not be faulted, in a resolve that never, never should any of this happen to her. The thought of belonging here for ever gave her the same constricted feeling in her breast as when she was sent as a little girl to old Miss Myre, who lived by taking in repairs. In the little room with its stuffy atmosphere, where one could scarcely move between the chest of drawers and the bed, and where Miss Myre pottered about, small and yellow, short-sighted and finicking, wrapped in knitted shawls and smelling nasty, Alberta would always imagine how it might be if, for some reason, she was left with nobody but Miss Myre, and had to live with her, just like her. It had made her sick to think of it, and the day Miss Myre died

87

Alberta had felt a secret relief. Because whatever happened, Miss Myre, at any rate, would be out of the question.

But the others might be in question, unless a miracle happened. It *must* happen, it *must* happen.

The Magistrate's voice could be heard among the gentlemen: 'Now listen to me, my dear Mr. Archdeacon—' He continued in a low voice, and laughter rang out. Glasses clinked, toasts were drunk, and Alberta saw Jacob was laughing. She wished she were sitting in there, but it was unthinkable.

In there the talk was more interesting. Distant countries, world affairs, politics. Even politics were interesting, although Alberta knew nothing about them. She would learn by sitting in there. Here she was only told things she knew, on which she had already formed an opinion. And besides, ladies were stupid. Heaven knows what they learned at school. It couldn't have been much, they said the silliest things.

Through the door she could see Governor Lossius. His small, twinkling eyes under the grey, bushy eyebrows looked good-natured. So did Papa's and the others', good-natured and guileless. Men's eyes had something innocent about them. Men did not go in for quick side-glances at each other, as women did, averting their eyes again, and pretending they had been thinking about something quite different. They let them wander openly and honestly about the room and rest in the eyes of those with whom they spoke.

But both Papa and the Governor were very red in the face, more so than usual. Was it simply because of the warmth and because they were big, heavy men, or—?

There was the Archdeacon leaning forward. He was big and heavy too, but he had kept his natural colouring; so had Mr. Jaeger, the Recorder. The Chief of Police, on the other hand, who was small and thin, was redder than any of them.

Unpleasantly agitated, Alberta shifted her position, so that she could see no one but the Recorder. He was clean-shaven, tall, a little angular, a little nonchalant, with searching eyes and a calm smile beneath greying hair, hair that tended to fall over his forehead whenever he leaned forward. To see him sitting there seemed to be some kind of guarantee that everything would proceed properly. There was something reassuring in seeing him sitting looking just as usual.

He enjoyed a certain reserved respect because he was a man with unusual interests. The Recorder put a lot of his money into books and was interested in art. He subscribed to a large and expensive series of reproductions, *Les Musées d'Europe*, and old masters covered the walls of his rooms.

The gentlemen said of the Recorder: 'Good heavens, an uncommonly well-educated and cultured man.' The ladies: 'Gracious me, he's a splendid fellow, of course; they say he's wonderful to Beda and her mother, for instance, but somehow you never know quite how to take him, do you?' – They did not much like this reticent man, who was unfortunately a radical and probably something of a freethinker, since he never darkened the church door. They also had a number of comments to make on his appearance. His trousers had baggy knees, and his tie was usually a little crooked, yes, even a button might be missing from his person here and there. They had given him up as a candidate for matrimony after ten years of alternating hope and disappointment. It was now accepted that the Recorder would never marry.

But Beda would not tolerate any criticism of her superior. 'Jaeger's a poppet. Since I started working for him I've bitterly regretted singing "Adam in Paradise" after him.'

He lent Beda books, and she often displayed knowledge of surprising subjects. 'I got that from Jaeger,' she would say in explanation.

Alberta was becoming drowsy. The air was heavy from the numerous lamps, from Mrs. Selmer's incense, and from the tobacco smoke that invaded the room from the corner parlour. Dully she followed the ladies' conversation. They were talking about Madam Svendsen's ability. Mrs. Pram could not understand how everything was always excellent at Mrs. Selmer's, for she herself was so often unfortunate with Svendsen. The goose last year, for instance, she simply burnt it, and once there was salt in the ice-cream instead of sugar. Very vexatious. 'But I really haven't the courage to give her notice – may I inquire whether anyone else has?'

They talked about the Archdeacon's Christmas sermon, about

poor relief, about the weather, about the scandal of Mad Petra, who was expecting a baby, and of Beda Buck, who had gone visiting the mining engineers in Southfjord with a party of gentlemen. 'Yes, really, it's a fact. First the idea was that Lett the dentist's sister was to come by the packet boat, but she didn't arrive, so Beda left just the same. What is one to say about a mother like that? I'm really sorry for Beda.'

Mrs. Pram spoke her mind: 'Yes, her language is said to be so incredibly vulgar. Harriet says it gets worse and worse. The last time the girls were at the Bucks' it was so bad they thought of leaving – Alberta was there too, of course.'

'Is it true, Alberta, that Beda is so vulgar?' It was Mrs. Lossius speaking, and she was swivelling her lorgnette towards Alberta.

But Alberta, who felt something snap inside when Beda's name was brought into the discussion, turned giddy. Her blood streamed to her head and she could no longer see clearly. 'Beda is certainly not vulgar,' she answered curtly and furiously. The blood sank back again, and she saw with horror the extent to which she had forgotten herself.

Oh – Mrs. Selmer's expression!

Nobody said a word. There was an awkward little pause, in which Alberta felt like an outcast, beyond the pale.

Then Mrs. Lossius rose and went uninvited to the piano. She really was kind, Mrs. Lossius, and generous beyond all doubt, prepared to help Mrs. Selmer over this quickly. She played *Marche Hongroise* by Schubert and a Liszt rhapsody. Afterwards the Archdeacon's wife sang 'The Great White Flock' and 'Hymn to the Fatherland' and 'The Seter Girl's Sunday', and then Mrs. Pio felt ill and had to leave. Pio accompanied her, a little embarrassed and guilty. The ladies shook their heads and confided to each other that they had noticed it a long time ago.

The conversation flagged and seemed to be past saving. Then Mrs. Selmer ordered tea, and the talk flared up again. Depraved Alberta was forced to run the gauntlet with the cream and the sugar.

*   *   *

The New Year came and went.

On New Year's Eve tradition and a certain feeling for propriety decreed that everyone should sit up until twelve o'clock. In silence, Mrs. Selmer had brought out wine, nuts, apples, cakes, the remains of Christmas joys. They were eaten without a word. One and all were reading something. Now and again the Magistrate took out his watch and looked at it. When the stroke of twelve approached, he kept it in his hand, stuffing it back in his pocket the moment the church clock began, and as the last stroke died away he raised his glass and said: 'Well, a Happy New Year, and thank you for the old one.' – He raised his glass especially towards Mrs. Selmer and said: 'Henrietta!'

Mrs. Selmer's eyes filled with tears, this year as last year – as every year. Alberta's did too, the solemnity of the hour affected her strongly.

Then Papa made a speech. 'You, Alberta, I would ask to try to behave a little more in accordance with your Mother's wishes in the new year. I expect you know what I am referring to. And to you, Jacob, I need scarcely say in what direction all our wishes go. A Happy New Year, Alberta – A Happy New Year, my boy!'

Papa looked across at Mama, to see if he had done right. But whether he had or not, nobody ever discovered. Mrs. Selmer put down her glass and said coldly: 'I for my part have no more wishes – I know it's no use.'

She sighed, picked up her book and her keys, said, 'Good night' – and disappeared.

The ritual was over and everything was as before.

*   *   *

'I am astonished to see that you have given up wearing your chain, Alberta.'

'I suppose this is another of your bright ideas? Yet another way of being peculiar. You have to be different from everyone else so you mustn't wear jewellery – in fact, you must care for your appearance as little as possible.'

'You needn't think I haven't noticed that you have been hiding a good deal from me recently. I am not nourishing the hope of being allowed to know why our young Miss is so sober in her dress – I don't enjoy my daughter's confidence, unfortunately.'

'But the day may come, my dear Alberta, when you will regret that you didn't do more to make yourself attractive and that you had no desire to please your Mother, believe me.'

Mrs. Selmer's voice was lost in a whisper. She sobbed.

Alberta knew from bitter experience that this was the prelude. Sooner or later the matter would come to a head, and she would simply be ordered to go upstairs, put on the chain, and come down again.

She carried on imaginary conversations with Mrs. Selmer, saying, for example: 'I can't tell you now, Mama, the reason why I am not wearing my chain. It is best for us all that it should remain hidden for the time being. In a few years, perhaps—'

And she immediately felt dizzy at the thought of the consequences should she really express herself in such a manner.

She could not bring herself to say she had lost the chain, as she had first thought of doing. Mrs. Selmer paralysed her.

There it was in Dorum's window. Alberta, who had been scrupulously keeping watch, saw it at once. So did Jacob. Now all that remained was for Mrs. Selmer to notice that there were three chains there and connect the fact with Alberta's sobriety. She was quite capable of it. Her powers of discernment in unmasking crime were unparalleled. She might almost have been Sherlock Holmes.

Every time Mrs. Selmer came home from town Alberta went hot and cold.

A misdeed, once perpetrated, is like a sickness. At night, when you lie awake, it rages in you like fever. When you wake up in the morning, you only remember at first that something is wrong, that something prevents you from breathing freely. It takes a little time before you realize what it is. It has sunk to the bottom of your consciousness and lies there like a weight.

But it floats up again. You recognize it with dismay and it remains with you all day long. And then again the fever attacks.

Beneath all Alberta's anxiety lay the longing to throw her arms round Mama and tell her everything, to unburden all her distress; a longing that was like an inborn infirmity which she had never learned to bear.

Besides – a bracelet, a heavy chain, was a beautiful thing to own and to feel round one's wrist. When her friends had leaned forward and fingered it and said: 'Goodness, how lovely!' it had made her happy.

Now it was gone.

PART TWO

It was getting lighter. When Alberta dusted a strange, pale light lay across the room, arriving earlier as the days went by. The darkness that had flooded in until only a blur of twilight was left, ebbed back. The blur took hold and grew.

The glow in the southern sky became brighter; the clouds took on a golden tinge. One day a lone mountain peak in the far distance was rose red, and the next day another.

One day the upper part of the mountain above the town was alight, as if from the reflection of a fire. The day after Alberta went up to Jacob's room a little before twelve o'clock.

Immediately afterwards Mrs. Selmer arrived, as if by accident. They stood silently looking at Lake Peak far to the south. A halo grew round it, and became blinding. A sickle of intense light slid into view at the side of the peak.

'There it is, Alberta,' said Mrs. Selmer breathlessly. 'Hurry – fetch Papa, Jensine, the Chief Clerk – they must come at once. I'm sure they've all forgotten the time.'

Alberta ran, called down the stairs for Jensine, and, out of breath, knocked on Papa's office door.

When she came back she had to shut her eyes for a moment. A miracle, a revelation, something beyond anything she had remembered or could imagine was there in the cut between Lake Peak and Flatang Peak shining straight into Jacob's room. And the room was illuminated slantwise from below, with long shadows falling upwards on to the walls – as strange and as wonderful as the décor in a theatre. The world was no longer cold and solid, complete and finite. It had dissolved into gold and blue.

Behind her she heard Papa, the Clerk and Jensine streaming into the room. Last of all came Leonardsen.

'Come along, Leonardsen, come right in,' said the Magistrate. And Mrs. Selmer chimed in: 'Yes indeed, my dear Leonardsen, do come in. Then you can say you've seen the sun. It will be some time before it will be visible from the ground floor, as you know.'

There was a pause. Nobody found anything to say. Everyone stared at the phenomenon. And whether because of the unfamiliar light or for some other reason, Mrs. Selmer's eyes filled with tears, this year as last year, as every year.

The Chief Clerk closed his mouth abruptly over something he had decided to say. Alberta noticed it, saw Mama's tears, and was embarrassed too. The Magistrate stood, watch in hand, examining it and the sun in turn, oblivious of the others.

In a moment of self-forgetfulness Alberta suddenly lifted her hands to the light to test its warmth. The Clerk was happy to find something to say. He smiled and shook his head: 'Oh no, Miss Alberta, it's too early yet.' Alberta blushed as if she had done wrong.

Now the sun was disappearing behind Flatang Peak, which was dark blue. When its last crescent had vanished, Leonardsen remarked timidly but sincerely: 'That was a fine sight to be sure.' The ice was broken. Everyone smiled and said something. Mrs. Selmer assured him: 'How very true, Leonardsen.'

The Magistrate put his watch into his waistcoat pocket and announced: 'Three minutes, three minutes precisely, just as I said. You insisted it was four last year, Mr. Chief Clerk, but you see you were wrong.'

*   *   *

Nothing could be bluer than the sky to the east of the river bend, thought Alberta. Nothing could be bluer, southern skies, the Mediterranean, nothing. And yet it seemed to grow bluer every day. Blue and bottomless. To look into it for long was like sailing out and sinking into infinity. You lost the feeling of solid ground under your feet, turned giddy, had to sit down in the snow so as not to fall.

Against the sky stood the range of mountains from which the river came, sparkling with light as long as the sun was up, rose red when it had disappeared behind the peaks at the end of Southfjord, ghostly dead, cold and white when it had gone for good.

The brief day was ending. The blue thickened, seeming to

turn into solid material behind the light-abandoned mountains, until the light of the first stars penetrated it like a trembling, hesitating message from somewhere forgotten.

Since the sun and the daylight had come back, life had changed. The roads were not snowed under again as soon as the snow plough had cleared them. They lay solid and frozen and screeched under foot. Ski-tracks led inland across the bog, numerous, hard and confused near the town, fewer and easier to follow the further you went away from it; solitary, buoyant, when you went any distance. Through the clear, still air the clatter and gliding of skis could be heard continually.

Alberta was trapped no longer. She followed the tracks, conquered the landscape afresh, this year as last, made new conquests daily, she and her companion, that other invisible, bold girl. Out of consideration for Alberta's old ski clothes, lengthened once by Olefine and patched under the arms, they went along the back streets in order to slip out of town unseen. Her companion was better equipped. She moved so lightly and gracefully in her becoming modern ski suit that Alberta actually felt it in her own body. And when they had crossed the open space just outside the town and come to Peter Aasen's birch thicket, they glided together and became one person. After that nothing was impossible.

After that, imperfections no longer existed. Jacob was a model of righteousness, Papa and Mama had overcome all their difficulties and lived for ever in peace and understanding. They treated each other as once one summer day a couple of years ago, a day Alberta would never forget. The weather had been warm and still, several windows were open. There was red currant jam in a dish on the table, mirrored beautifully in the water carafe. And a calm, happy conversation, in which she and Jacob joined, coursed back and forth and created an inimitable atmosphere of security that Alberta could recapture at will. In this she would install her family before turning her attention to herself.

Herself – oh, she was far away, heaven knows where, out in the wide world. The sun was shining – perhaps palm trees were swaying too. But one thing was certain, she was as free and as light as a bird. She was the bold girl who had no need to hide her face, her hands or her thoughts, who was not afraid of people and who did what she wanted – But what did she want?

The Archdeacon's Christina wanted to learn lace-making, weaving, elaborate embroidery. Harriet Pram talked about the Central Institute in Stockholm as if it were a place of salvation. Gudrun wanted to be an actress, Rikke Lossius an artist. Gertrude played the piano. Beda explained that if she were to do something she really liked, she would be a sailor. Sometimes they might add: 'If I don't get married, of course.'

But Alberta?

The truth was Alberta only knew what she did not want. She had no idea what she did want. And not knowing brought unrest and a giddy sensation under her heart. She existed like a negative of herself, and this flaw was added to all the others.

To get away, out into the world! Beyond this all details were blurred. She imagined somewhere open, free, bathed in sunshine. And a throng of people, none of them her relatives, none of whom could criticize her appearance and character, and to whom she was not responsible for being other than herself.

On Sundays she went to the Gronli farms with Harriet, Christina and Gudrun, and was simply and squarely Alberta. They took with them Danish pastries and oranges, ground coffee and lumps of sugar. The bad-tempered woman at Gronli made their coffee, gave them cream, and lighted the stove in one of the large, deserted rooms full of stale air, all for fifty øre. They danced with each other to keep warm, humming *The Blue Danube* in unison until the fire began to take effect. And sometimes a desperate gaiety would take possession of Alberta. Something would be unleashed, a sudden laughter, and she laughed simply to release it. It lay in wait for everything and nothing and infected Gudrun. In the end they could not stop. Harriet and Christina became annoyed and called them idiots.

Other parties arrived and were shut into other rooms. It might be a gay, fur-clad group that had come in sleds: Mrs. Buck, Mrs. Elmholz, Mrs. Lebesby and Mrs. Kilde – Mrs. Selmer and her circle never went to the Gronli farms. It might be Beda with the chemists, the dentist and Dr. Mo, in which case they might join them and indulge in a kind of circumspect gaiety, with Beda the life and soul of the party. It might also be Bergan and the Chief Clerk, in which case there would only be distant exchanges of greetings in the passage, for neither of them displayed any initiative where women were concerned.

But sometimes Palmine Flor and Lilly Vogel came with their men friends. Then the echoing house was filled with scandal. Corks popped, shrieks and laughter followed each other in waves, cigarette-smoke lay thick and cold in the corridors, doors slammed interminably. Palmine and Lilly rushed in and out in Lapp costume, their eyes dulled, curls wet with snow hanging about their overheated faces. Yelling, they tumbled on top of each other in the snowdrifts outside with the men in pursuit.

If Alberta's luck was out, Jacob and Cedolf came. They mixed with nobody, sat by themselves listening to the din, smiled faintly, said nothing and looked furtive. But a secret exchange took place. Alberta felt it and would become ill at ease and restless. Nothing could be proved, but anything guessed at. The air was full of secrets.

Harriet and Christina became tense round the mouth, and wanted to pay and go, saying that this was dreadful, they refused to listen to it any longer. Gudrun suggested staying for a little to see whether Lilly and Palmine really were drunk. Alberta was so restless on account of Jacob that she forgot her interest in the mysteries of life. She had to leave with the others, while Jacob stayed, and she dragged herself home, paralysed by the warmth at Gronli, preoccupied and aloof out of anxiety as to what might happen. The others gave her to understand that, without any doubt, they considered the situation to be critical. The way home in the cold twilight seemed endless.

The fact that Alberta went skiing in the middle of the morning was to nobody's credit. Mrs. Selmer was quite aware of it. But she seemed to have given way on certain points, as if she could not be bothered any more. She said as much, too: 'It is not within my power to make a useful person out of my daughter. I shall have to give up the attempt.' She contented herself with sighing resignedly when Alberta sneaked guiltily out of the house in ski clothes after finishing the dusting, making herself as small and invisible as possible, but stubbornly resolved to accept any indignity provided she might finally get away.

The fact of the matter was, of course, that Alberta had too much time on her hands. It was not really proper, and it was embarrassing and difficult to explain away. Gudrun went to school, Beda worked in an office, Harriet and Christina helped at home, ironing, using the sewing-machine, making clothes, embroidering, baking; both of them patterns of virtue, pearls of great price.

Alberta dusted, cleaned silver and mended stockings. None of these activities was worth mentioning as a domestic achievement. She did them without any enthusiasm whatsoever, and there was nothing of the pearl about her – on the contrary, she was an affliction and a disappointment. She read, but what did she read? If only it were languages, if only it were the cookery book. But no, in addition to Mama's novels, which she skimmed quickly when they were left lying about, and devoured when they were hidden from her, she read learned tomes, 'Alberta's tomes'; Mrs. Selmer could find no other way of describing such abnormal reading-matter for a young girl. Her friends were astonished and a little scornful when Alberta came staggering out of the library with them. 'How *can* you be bothered?' they said.

There was Lübke's *History of Art,* an old yellowed edition with poor woodcuts. There were twenty- and thirty-year-old works on the Stone Age, the migrations, Indian cave temples. She went haphazardly through the catalogue. And bad-tempered old Miss Jensen, who looked after the lending library as well as her books and stationery, had to climb the step-ladder to find them, tripped over her skirts, got dust up her nose, sneezed, and explained in an injured tone that this kind of book was never out.

Once it was Professor Monrad on aesthetics, a work that nearly took away Alberta's taste for further research, and which she very soon gave up.

The result was a flimsy, patchy knowledge about all sorts of things that no-one else wanted to know. She could for instance unexpectedly explain what a swastika was. What was the point of knowing that sort of thing? It was almost unseemly, and gave the impression that she was correcting other people. The ladies looked at her coldly and with astonishment, and Mrs. Selmer felt no pride at all, quite the reverse. She pointed out on every possible occasion that reading learned tomes was a pure waste of time and no better than wandering about the streets. A way of making oneself unusual and eccentric, that was all it was, like straight hair and stiff-necked silence.

But Papa might pat Alberta on the head when he found her deep in a tome and remark, 'You're an odd child, I must say.'

She followed a blue, lonely track. It led her away from every-day and reality. Unfortunately it also led her back again, but then she had at any rate been away. She skied until she was buoyant and warm, losing herself in dreams and in the satisfy-ing give of her body when she coasted downhill.

The sunset moved further and further towards the west, glowing behind new peaks. They stood deep blue, boring into the flaming sky, which gradually turned golden and then green behind them. – Eastwards above the river bend the first star had already appeared in the solid expanse of blue, and there was a new sound under her skis, that came with the evening – the sound of thin crust breaking.

And the painful, wonderful moment arrived, when the long-ing for something to happen – something, anything – almost anything at all – turned into an ache that could no longer be borne.

But when Alberta came clattering on her skis down the hard, much-trafficked streets from Upper Town – when she swung round and stopped as had been her habit ever since childhood, at the very moment when it looked as if she would shoot out on to the market place and into the clutches of P.C. Olsen – her conscience gripped her again. It thrived in the cold down here in town, between the houses where the lamps were being lit.

And when, a little later, she sat on the bench in the kitchen over the dinner which had been waiting for her in the oven, it was all over. She was the old, constrained, guilt-ridden Alberta, and the good, tired feeling of relaxation in her body had given way to troubling anxiety.

She lost no time pouring herself some coffee and adding water to the pot, to get the scalding hot drink inside her before Mrs. Selmer, her after-dinner nap over, entered the kitchen like Nemesis.

* * *

'Well, well,' said the Magistrate with resignation, putting his large pile of newspapers down on the dining-room table; 'Well, well, you can go this time then, but you know I am not normally in favour of any running about after supper. It will please you to come home at the proper time.'

He sat down and ordered his newspapers for reading. They arrived in bundles twice a week, and he never succeeded in keeping up to date. He looked tired.

In the perpetual warfare waged with alternating success, which was his and Mrs. Selmer's married life, he would on occasion capitulate, surrendering positions about which no open fight had as yet taken place, withdrawing from them quietly. This happened particularly if he had recently crushed his opponent in one way or another by brute force, with his heavy artillery. For his opponent invariably recovered and erected against him an icy wall of revenge against which he had so far been defenceless; whereupon he fell into uncertainty and tried to repair his erroneous strategy with an ignominious retreat.

Now he looked searchingly across at Mrs. Selmer, but not the slightest expression betrayed her thoughts. Only when Jacob got up to go did she raise her eyes from her book and say: 'If your father has given you permission, naturally I have nothing to say. Good evening, my child.'

Jacob looked perplexed, but started to make for the door nevertheless. He paused for a second before opening it, and it seemed as if everyone was waiting to see what he would do next. Then he left.

Papa glanced quickly at Mama over his pince-nez, pursed his mouth and muttered: 'Wrong manoeuvre, futile sacrifice. Womenfolk – devils, the lot of them.'

Alberta ducked. Now for the storm. But Papa said no more and buried himself in his newspaper.

A wave of sympathy so strong as to be painful went through Alberta. Papa might be heavily armed with a great broadsword, he might be able to crush all that stood in his way; but he lacked those poisoned arrows that came whistling treacherously from behind the icy wall and remained quivering in the wound long afterwards. He was defenceless against them. They wounded him, and his perplexity was worse than any amount of Mama's tears.

As a contribution towards preserving the peace Alberta decided to take out her embroidery. Mrs. Selmer then rose and disappeared into the darkness of the sitting-rooms. Shortly afterwards they heard her light matches, open the piano and strike a few chords.

An astonished 'Whatever next!' came from the Magistrate. He raised his eyebrows high up his forehead in increasing incomprehension of the female psyche. And he definitely gave it up for the evening, sucked at his pipe, and again bent over his newspaper.

But Alberta hastily fetched her confirmation-rug and seated herself quietly in a corner of the cold, dark sitting-room.

Far away in the opposite corner, beyond the black silhouettes of the centre table, the armchairs, the phoenix palm and the ivy, Mama sat playing. Two candles on the piano were alight. She looked so small and so inexpressibly lonely out there in the darkness, her shawl over her shoulders, sitting between her two candles, that something in Alberta melted and she was overcome by great tenderness for Mama. She wrapped the rug round her tightly and listened with a sob in her throat.

Mrs. Selmer played the repertoire she had had in the time of her youth, old, well-practised pieces that her fingers never forgot, even though she never practised any more. Picturesque, tender, tuneful little melodies that conjured up visions before Alberta's eyes: *Scenes from Childhood*, *Carnival*. And then something unnerving and disintegrating, stealing in like an insidious and dangerous potion, making her weak, impotent and anxious: Rubinstein's *Night*. When Mama had played it to the end she sat still for a while looking down into her lap. Then she raised her head with a sigh. She raised her hands as well, and Alberta hoped she was going to leaf through the music and play more. But she clasped them together, closed the piano and snuffed out the candles.

An unreasonable desire to approach Mama, to give her a caress, came over Alberta. If she had dared, she would have gone over in the darkness and put her arms round her. But that sort of thing was not done. Mrs. Selmer wandered past as if enclosed in an impenetrable aura, lighting her way with a match and taking a book from the bookshelf.

She said good night at once, a distant, cold good night, that did not appear to be addressed to Alberta and Papa. Then she wandered upstairs. She always went to bed earlier than anyone else in the house.

It was when the Magistrate was on circuit that the piano really quickened to life. No sooner had his heavy footsteps in the tall, furry travelling boots died away, no sooner were his and the Chief Clerk's bulging brief-cases and despatch boxes and the important package with the supply of bottles, carried down by Leonardsen, out of the house, than the piano lid stood open as if of its own accord, and the music was propped up, open and ready: Heyse's songs and Grieg's.

Mrs. Selmer's somewhat slight, neglected voice resounded perpetually through the sitting-rooms: 'The princess sat high in her virgin bower' – 'I scarcely dare speak'. – The voice would break a little at the verse: 'I think of days gone by—'

She also sang Schubert and mischievous little modern songs. She could sit for hours at the piano, and when she got up she would go round humming for a long time afterwards, while she attended to her innumerable flower pots and remarked thoughtfully from time to time: 'I see I shall have to transplant this one.'

She would send Alberta for some extra little delicatessen for supper and ignore her frailties. Cedolf and Beda were mentioned without the epithet frightful. A spirit of forbearance hovered over the house.

It was when the Magistrate was away that Mrs. Selmer

would put down the leaf of the bureau and sit at it. She sat there with many letters and faded photographs in front of her. There were withered flowers too that had to be handled carefully. If someone came in she would hurriedly put it all into a little drawer and push the drawer back into place; she would brush her hand across her eyes, as if to bring her thoughts back to this world. She might sigh. And she would rise with a tired, preoccupied expression. That was all.

A few faded pictures, a few letters, a few mummified flowers that crumbled into dust between the fingers, were nothing. But they were fraught with destiny, sinister, deceitful and treacherous. The feeling hung about oppressively in an atmosphere which was otherwise fresh and cloudless.

Alberta bore a grudge against the little drawer in the bureau.

* * *

The Civic Ball took place at the end of March.

'No, we are not thinking of going this time,' said Mrs. Selmer when the subject was raised at tea parties and soirées. 'Neither Alberta nor I have anything to wear. We shall stay at home this year.'

A few days before the ball she had a discussion with Papa in the office. They came in to dinner together, and Mrs. Selmer said with finality as she entered the dining-room: 'As I said, the Governor's family is going, and the Klykken Juniors and the Prams. Mainly for the sake of the young people. The gentlemen will probably arrive later.'

Papa looked resigned, his eyebrows raised high. He ate in silence. Mama was conciliatory, almost friendly, not even taking offence when he pessimistically turned his steak over several times and called it a piece of leather, admitting that Jensine was undeniably careless now and again, the beef really was tough.

Towards the end of the meal Papa said: 'Very well, if you think we ought to go, then in heaven's name I suppose we must. It's so desperately expensive, that's all. But if you will get hold of the tickets, then – you know I—'

He shrugged his shoulders helplessly to indicate that he was a man overburdened with business and duties, and went in to his sofa and his newspapers.

Mrs. Selmer opened the window: 'Oh Alberta, just run over and say I'll take the tickets they promised to keep for me.'

Alberta ran. The bracelet, she thought desperately, the bracelet. But Mrs. Selmer opened another window and called after her: 'And then go to Olefine's and say she *must* give us a couple of days as soon as she can, it's to do with the Ball. Whether she's free or not.'

Olefine came. She hadn't time really, but Mrs. Selmer generally got what she wanted.

Olefine explained her position in whispers. She was really supposed to be going to Ryan the butcher's, she had promised. To make a new dress for Signora. But as long as it didn't get about that she was at the Selmers' she would have to make some excuse to Mrs. Ryan. Olefine whispered and looked about her anxiously as if the walls had eyes and ears. She fluttered her hand to emphasize how quietly and carefully the matter should be discussed.

Alberta's ball dress from last year was to be let down; once again she had grown. In addition it was to have new sleeves out of the material that, thank heaven, had been left over – short little puff sleeves. The old ones had come to her elbow.

'Short sleeves are pretty and young,' said Mrs. Selmer, turning up the old ones to see how Alberta would look. 'You're shockingly thin, my child,' she added doubtfully.

Then she made up her mind. 'We'll have them short just the same, Olefine, it makes a change.'

Alberta stood in front of the mirror trying on the altered dress. She dragged and pulled at it, folded it up and let it down again, searching breathlessly and vainly for something in it that suited her. If she managed to make it pass muster in one place, it failed all the more lamentably in another.

She turned this way and that, lowered and raised her face, wondered whether she really was so plain, and thought: suppose it were sorcery, like the fairy tale. One fine day the spell would be broken, and an Alberta no one had ever dreamed could exist would stand there, as beautiful as the princess.

Every time she had something new she locked herself in alone, trembling with excitement. Was it not so that a garment could work miracles? It was cast over the changeling, and hey presto, the spell was broken. He stood there in his true shape, young, beautiful, powerful, and had merely to pluck the joys of life like golden apples from the trees.

But it was not easy to find the magic garment. It was doubtful whether Olefine was even capable of producing it. Certainly it was not this altered dress. Alberta gazed at herself dispiritedly, by no means looking forward to the festivities.

*   *   *

The cold, grey half-light of the March evening fell across the ballroom of the Grand. Krane was economizing on the lighting now that winter was so far advanced.

Alberta sat in the row of ladies along the window wall. One of the tall windows was behind her. She could feel the draught from it. If she turned she could look straight across Market Square to Rivermouth, where the mountains were standing on their heads in the dead calm. The reflections of snow and scree reached the sea-bed through infinite depths in a fantastic grey-on-grey pattern, and on the surface the current flowed in light little rings, dimples and whorls that never altered. There was a curious feeling of unreality in the fact that everything was going on its way quite unchanged, while in here there was a ball.

Up on the platform on the short side of the hall Mrs. Selmer and her circle sat enthroned. Harriet and Christina were sitting there too; they had as it were withdrawn from the public eye. The time was approaching when the company would become somewhat mixed, when elements debarred from arriving at six o'clock would put in an appearance and take over the floor, and officialdom would retreat to its established positions. If you stayed sitting down in the hall you simply risked being asked to dance by any Tom, Dick or Harry. You could leave, to be sure. But nobody did.

For the moment there were only three or four couples on the floor and the music lacked ardour. In one of the back rooms, reserved for the occasion, the gentlemen had gathered for brandy and soda.

Alberta knew that Mrs. Selmer had signalled to her several times to come and sit among her equals. She stubbornly pretended not to see. To walk up the long, now almost empty floor, alone, to arrive up there a target for everyone's eyes and the lorgnette – no, decidedly no. She felt plucked and bare in the white dress, which was too small, Mama and Olefine could say what they liked. She felt as if her unfortunate person was bursting through its splitting sheath under the public eye. Nervously she pulled at her gloves. They inched down over her sharp elbows all the time.

Pure chance, a stumble on the part of the Chief Clerk, who was no dancer, had washed her up here under the windows beside Lotten Kremer. It had not been the first time the Clerk had stumbled and lost the rhythm, it was perhaps the tenth. It became clear to him and to Alberta that they might as well give up, and she found herself sitting there. Lotten, who had not yet had one dance, but kept herself going by talking and laughing and behaving as if she were having a marvellous time all the same, had willingly made room. It was uphill work preserving this mood of gaiety with her sister Maria, who never said a word on her own initiative; besides, she was so old, certainly more than thirty, that it was no wonder she didn't even pretend to be enjoying herself any more.

Lotten was in sky blue with swansdown and long, white gloves. In her hair was the big, pink artificial rose that had been on a stand in the window of her hat shop a long time before the ball. Look, *this* is how it's supposed to be, with the stalk up and the flower down. Lotten knew how a rose should be worn, and serve you all right, she thought, referring to the ladies of the town.

She chattered ceaselessly and laughed strenuously at everything Alberta said. Alberta too became chatty, feeling a sudden sympathy for Lotten, with whom she normally only talked across the counter. As long as they were engaged in this animated conversation, Alberta had an excuse for not noticing Mrs. Selmer's small signals and curious behaviour. Besides, she imagined what Lotten's position was like. If Papa were not the Magistrate, holding office in the town, his daughter Alberta would probably have been a wall-flower too.

Now they had all done their duty, those who were invited home now and again, and those whose parents were. She had danced twice with the Chief Clerk, who made her feel even more hopeless than she was already. She had danced with Bergan, who seemed not to advance at all, but simply turned on his own axis, taking his partner with him at arm's length like a distant satellite; with Dr. Mo, who was from the south and indulged in unknown tricks; with the Archdeacon's Henrik, who was out of step from first to last; and with the Pram twins, who danced like the social lions they were, and imitated Dr. Mo.

She had also danced with Jacob. He was the most fun to dance with. But Alberta was a little shocked to see him on the floor. For Jacob danced with a self-confidence and conviction that would not be quite fitting in a drawing-room. He danced like a sailor, although he had never been to sea. Indeed, when Jacob took the floor in his confirmation clothes, he seemed like a stranger to Alberta. He looked attractive in a way that appalled her. It dawned on her that strange girls in strange countries would like Jacob, if he were ever to find himself among them. The girls here liked him. That was why she was afraid of Palmine and Lilly.

Then she had danced opposite Papa in the quadrille. Papa went through the figures and bowed to her, gallant and chivalrous as only he could be. In the chain she saw Mama a little way ahead of her weaving in and out among the gentlemen, light-footed, gay and radiant, carrying herself like no one else in her old, much altered lilac silk. Now she was sitting up there on the platform, a bright, festive speck among the black silk dresses. Even the Governor's lady, who was dressed in the very latest fashion from Steen and Strom in Kristiania, looked less festive than Mama, so brittle, blonde, elegant and petite. There was something about her that had nothing to do with clothes, something that gave her whole personality brilliance. Young Mrs. Klykken was really the only one who could outdo her; she got all her clothes from abroad and was in light green silk, dark and slender as a heroine in a novel.

But young Mrs. Klykken stayed outside with the gentlemen. She did not sit putting anyone in the shade, but shone quite alone among black tails, white dress shirts, and red, animated faces. Alberta had seen her through a doorway. She was sitting on the arm of her husband's chair, with a hand on his shoulder. She had pushed her gloves back over her wrists so that her diamond rings were flashing – they said young Mrs. Klykken got one for each child – and she tossed witticisms at the red faces and laughed, tilting her head backwards to show her long, white throat.

And all the red faces had the same, almost idiotically blissful expression when they turned towards her, even Papa's and the Governor's. Alberta felt rather sorry for them. It was embarrassing to see, as if they were being made fools of by young Mrs. Klykken.

In the other back rooms refreshments were being served. The Kranes themselves stood behind a trestle table handing out ginger ale and beer, wine, coffee and hot chocolate. The hotel waitresses swayed in and out with loaded trays. The engineers kept open table with Beda as the centre of attraction and Mrs. Buck and Mrs. Elmholz as chaperones. Gudrun Pram had a tendency to disappear out there, and Harriet became anxious up on her platform, stretching out her neck and looking as if at any minute she might shoot up out of her chair.

There was a pause. The music stopped. The couples disappeared from the floor. There was nothing more to watch and discuss with Lotten, and the coast was alarmingly clear between Mrs. Selmer and Alberta, who nevertheless stuck temporarily to her position with her eyes turned in another direction. Then Lotten said: 'What's going to become of Rikke Lossius? They say she's going to be a painter.'

Alberta spied land again. Lotten was clearly just as interested as she was in keeping the conversation going. To this extent they were allies. Eagerly she squeezed out all she knew about Rikke and stubbornly kept her eyes away from Mrs. Selmer.

It was getting crowded down at the door. Young Theodorsen, who had recently opened his own barber's shop, arrived at the head of a whole party. There were Elmholz's shop assistants and Weydemann the telegraphist, Karla Schmitt and Signora Ryan, Palmine Flor and Lilly Vogel. A number of strange young men who looked like commercial travellers were with them.

Suddenly Lotten Kremer gripped Alberta's arm, then just as suddenly let it go. 'No, it was nothing,' she said shame-facedly, when Alberta stared at her. Perhaps she had forgotten that all the ladies in the party were her customers. At any rate she remembered in time – she had said nothing.

The new arrivals seemed to breathe new life into the festivities. Young Theodorsen had gone up to talk quietly to the band. It struck up *The Blue Danube* with dash and vigour. He danced out with Signora, and now in a trice the floor was packed with dancers. Krane became even busier. He brought small tables to put along the window wall, now that it had become impossible for all those wanting refreshments to have them in the back rooms. A gust of something new swept through the hall, something frightening and tempting. Alberta could see Mrs. Selmer no longer. New arrivals streamed in through the door incessantly and joined the mêlée. The air thickened with tobacco smoke. It was now so dusky that faces and dresses appeared to be pale smudges, except near the windows where details were still visible.

The dancers formed a compact mass composed of revolving particles. The mass surged over towards the window wall, and a table lurched so that the people sitting at it had to defend themselves against bottles and cake dishes. It surged over towards the inner wall, and Maria Kremer opened her mouth at last: 'Let's try to get out now, Lotten, while there's still room.'

Immediately the floor was packed in front of them again, and Lotten laughed: 'No, my poor dear, it's no use trying. Besides, the fun's beginning now, that's what I think anyway.' Alberta did not like the ring in Lotten's laughter. It sounded so strange, as if in league with the half-dusk and the bewilder-ing, underhand atmosphere. She felt uneasy and wished she were sitting up with Mama after all as she usually did at this time of the evening. It was impossible to get there now.

There was young Theodorsen with Palmine. There was Lilly with a commercial traveller. There was Beda spinning past with a mining engineer, and Gudrun with another. There was Jacob – my God! Jacob was dancing with the fair little girl who served in Holst's. What would Papa and Mama say? And there was Cedolf. Cedolf, brown as a gipsy, with blue eyes and black hair, impudent and strikingly handsome in his shore-leave clothes. He was dancing with the new shop-girl from Haabjorn's, the one who was supposed to be from Kristiania and looked like it too.

Were not the young men holding their partners closer than before – were not the girls putting their arms round the men's necks with more abandon? There was Palmine – simply hanging on young Theodorsen.

Smiles and short phrases were exchanged in passing. The two engineers from Southfjord changed partners in the middle of the dance; they exchanged Beda and Gudrun. All four laughed and were lost in the mêlée.

All of a sudden somebody was pushed almost into Alberta's lap, and in trying to recover his balance stepped forcefully on her toes.

'Pardon me, Miss, I couldn't help it,' said an embarrassed voice. Alberta looked up. It was Weydemann the telegraphist. He had blushed to the roots of his thin, fair hair, and his large hands in their white cotton gloves twitched nervously.

'Not at all,' replied Alberta with as good a grace as she could muster, and blushed too.

Telegraphist Weydemann looked at a loss. Then he bowed.

And perhaps he did so merely in order to retire gracefully. But Alberta was disconcerted and did not quite know how to interpret it. She stood up in front of him, felt Lotten nudge her and imagined she heard a suppressed titter. Weydemann appeared to be even more at a loss and bowed once more. Then they were dancing.

Alberta had always felt sorry for Weydemann, as one does feel sorry for people for whom nothing turns out as it should in this world. For he came of a good family really, his mother was a Jaeger. She hoped Mama and Papa would consider it from this aspect when they in all probability caught sight of her. But she was far from being at ease when she did in fact pass the Magistrate, who was standing watching from one of the doors. Did he not readjust his pince-nez to make certain his eyes were not deceiving him? And when she and Weydemann were pressed forward below the platform and waltzed round a couple of times right in front of Mama and all the ladies, her reputation was not worth a sou. Beyond all doubt there was quite a stir up there. She caught a glimpse of Mrs. Selmer, who rose to her feet just as Alberta and Weydemann were swallowed up again in the throng. She slumped down apprehensively beside Lotten, inclining her head dumbly in thanks for the dance. An expedition to fetch her was presumably on its way.

'Well, what sort of a dancer is that fellow Weydemann? That wasn't what he meant at all, poor thing,' tittered Lotten.

'Wasn't it?' said Alberta unhappily.

But Lotten nudged her again. For someone else was standing before her bowing, a tall, strong fellow. Alberta looked up. It was Cedolf.

It was Cedolf! Looking down at her and smiling and bowing once more, blue-eyed and brown and impudently handsome.

The blood rushed to Alberta's head. This was an insult. But she had danced with Weydemann. And a compelling power seemed to emanate from Cedolf – she felt as if he were coercing her with his smile. Here, beside Lotten, among all these people, she was defenceless. There was no chance of turning her back on him and running. Trembling she rose to her feet.

Dancing with him was not at all disagreeable, it had to be admitted. On the contrary – it was miraculous, a suspension of the law of gravity. A suspension of the will and of responsibility too; a feeling of being disembodied and at one with the rhythm. Whatever else might be said about him, he could dance.

Now they were turning in front of Papa. And Papa wrinkled his forehead. It occurred to Alberta that he was saying something. Now they were dancing in front of the platform, and she caught a glimpse of the Governor's lady raising her lorgnette, and of Mama, who had been standing ever since

113

the last time she saw her, and who now sat down. Mrs. Pram leaned over towards Harriet. They spoke to each other. Then they were all gone, and Cedolf was guiding her down towards the dark corner of the hall again.

Couples must have had a tendency to stay down there. There was a perpetual crush. Now the music changed abruptly to a gallopade and a wildness entered into the dance. A great knot formed, of couples colliding into each other in the dimness. Before Alberta knew what was happening she and Cedolf were in the middle of the knot, stamping on one spot without moving, shut in by a living barricade. On the outside young Theodorsen, the commercial travellers and the engineers with their partners blocked the way. They were laughing and singing in time with the music.

Alberta felt Cedolf take firmer hold of her. The others pressed her close against him. His large brown fist with the anchors on was no longer in her right hand, but was holding her arm above the elbow. She heard him say in her ear: 'Don't you be afraid.' And there was something in his voice, a dark purring, that made her afraid in earnest. Mortified too. What right had Cedolf to talk to her in such a voice?

His neck was close to her face, and thick, short, curly hair suddenly tickled her nose. Did she not almost press her mouth into Cedolf's neck, in the middle of the curls? Heavens, she must be out of her mind!

They were almost knocked over in the crush, and Cedolf lifted her up, smiling down at her as he did so. And something new and strange flowed through Alberta's body. It was like a deep call, a sweet, strong sigh in the blood. It passed through her and died away, leaving her behind, amazed, as if newly awakened from a dream and still listening after it.

At the same moment she caught sight of Beda in the dimness, Beda and Lett the dentist. And Beda and Lett were dancing cheek to cheek, Beda smiled as Alberta had never seen her smile before, and shut her eyes – it lasted for only a second, then it was over, and Beda and Lett were like other people again. Alberta asked herself: 'Is it real, is all this reality?'

Suddenly she was on the brink of tears of shame and anger. The tumult, Cedolf's body against hers, Beda's smile, the wantonness about her, were violence and shock, mortifying and degrading.

'I won't dance any more,' she cried. 'I want to get out, we must try to get out.' She attempted to free herself from Cedolf, and saw his mouth curl up.

Now he was thrusting people to one side as if they were pawns, pushing and shoving to clear a way: 'Out of the way, fellows, we're not staying here stamping any longer.' And he galloped off with Alberta so that she scarcely touched the floor.

'I think you really were frightened,' he smiled, when she had been brought back to her seat beside Lotten. 'They were only kicking up a row,' he said.

Alberta, who normally blushed on every occasion, was pale for once, so pale that she felt it herself. She was crushed. She was miserable and disgraced.

Above her she heard Cedolf explaining to Lotten: 'They're crazy. It's that fellow Theodorsen and the commercial travellers that's the worst. You don't feel ill, do you?' he asked Alberta. 'You look so seedy.'

'No,' answered Alberta briefly, and now she blushed.

'Well, thanks for the dance then.' Cedolf bowed urbanely. She could hear that he was smiling, that he was talking with his mouth curled up.

'Thank you,' she muttered without looking up. Lotten remarked: 'Somebody's popular, I must say. The one partner more dashing than the last.' She laughed ambiguously: 'That Cedolf Kjeldsen's a nice fellow too.'

'Ugh – he's horrid,' said Alberta.

And she jumped, for someone had touched her on the shoulder. It was Jacob. He was in his overcoat, cap in hand. 'You must come now, Alberta,' he said. 'We're going home, we're all waiting for you.'

They walked home through the quiet, empty streets in the half-light. The short, transparent March night was over, the day was approaching. But it was neither dark nor light, it was pearl grey. Everything was pearl grey, the snow, the air, the mountains. They were still standing on their heads in the calm water, and a fishing smack was inching its way out of

Rivermouth on the tide, mirrored blackly and distinctly. A long, light stripe followed it in the water like a line drawn beneath it all. The landscape seemed to be in light, half-waking slumber, and the houses slumbered with it. The blinds looked like closed eyelids. The crisp, frozen snow crunched like granulated sugar, making a jarring, disproportionate noise beneath the feet of the returning ball guests.

Her luck was out, Papa's and Mama's faces bore set expressions when they looked at Alberta and Jacob. They even turned away again quickly, as if they might be harmed by catching sight of something they did not want to see. Once Mama muttered to Papa: 'There are various matters I have to discuss with Alberta,' and Alberta felt a stab. 'The chain!' said the little stab inside her. As long as she was with somebody else nothing would happen. Perhaps nothing would happen until they were home in the cold, empty living-rooms.

She imagined Mama's icy voice: 'I cannot tell you how astonished I am. Weydemann perhaps, after all he comes of a good family really and I'm sure he's a nice boy – but that fearful Cedolf—' And Papa: 'You must remember that you are a young lady, my child.' And Jacob: 'I say, it really was nice of you to dance with Cedolf, Alberta. He's a good fellow, you know.'

Behind her Mrs. Pram was talking about young Mrs. Klykken: 'Sitting in there with the gentlemen all evening – for my husband's sake I'd never do such a thing. But you may be sure the gentlemen think their own thoughts, Mrs. Lossius.'

The Governor's lady was airing much suppressed indignation: 'We should have left long ago. The tone always degenerates later in the evening, it's scarcely right to allow the young people to witness all that goes on. But it was impossible to get the gentlemen away.' Harriet had been sent in time and again to remind them, and even Mrs. Lossius had gone in once, all to no avail. She herself, praise be, had neither of her daughters there, but she was thinking of the others. As for young Mrs. Klykken, she ought not to forget her origins so quickly. She might be married to one of the town's leading businessmen, but after all she was still simply Sigfrida Flemming. There could be no one who didn't remember her serving in her father's shop, looking like a simple little country girl with a gold cross round her neck and her hair parted in the middle. But then she came home from Kristiania and had grown into such a beauty – gracious me, she *is* beautiful – and young Klykken was completely stunned by her. She supposed that sort of thing went to the head when you came from simpler circumstances. It looked very like it. It was sad for the old Klykkens. Mrs. Lossius tightened her mouth so that it disappeared into her face completely.

Harriet Pram assured everyone that she for her part had attended the Civic Ball for the last time, but Gudrun was loud in protest: 'Gracious, it was so much fun—'

She was frozen into silence. The others laughed a little and talked about something else, but no one was vexed. Gudrun was pretty, with dark eyes, radiantly pretty. Then it's not so dangerous to be a bit glib, thought Alberta bitterly, as she walked along, eaten up by her various anxieties.

Under cover of the leave-taking with the Prams and the Lossiuses, Jacob whispered to her: 'Now for it, Alberta. But I'll go to sea. I'll not stay here to be nursemaided like a girl.'

After which the Selmer family continued its progress across the market place in ominous silence. Were Papa and Mama both waiting for the other to begin? Papa gave a preliminary cough—

Then someone appeared in the deserted square, someone in a hurry. It was Nurse Jullum carrying her worn, black bag, the one for which Alberta felt a secret terror.

'Heavens!' exclaimed Mrs. Selmer. 'Go on, the rest of you. I must hear whether anything has happened at the Pios' or the Bakkes'.'

She stopped and spoke quietly to Nurse Jullum, who, looking in need of sleep, put down her bag and wiped her forehead up under her hat with her handkerchief. Papa said nothing. He would probably wait until the family was together again.

Mrs. Selmer caught them up. She was both shocked and animated and had completely forgotten Alberta and Jacob. 'A big boy at the Pios',' she announced. 'Over eight pounds. But it was a hard struggle. Nurse has not been out of her clothes since yesterday evening. Now she's on her way to Mrs. Bakke, who has been ill since yesterday and does nothing but cry for her mother. I'll go up there, I'll change and go straight up. Mr. Bakke is quite beside himself, walking in and out of the house with his hat on in utter bewilderment, poor man.'

Mrs. Selmer was so kind in that way, absolutely wonderful. In a crisis there was no limit to her friendliness. You could always rely on her.

'Hm—' said Papa. 'It's not so easy, by Jove.'

Alberta dawdled about in her room, taking off her finery, still weak with anxiety. Sometimes it did turn out like that. Mama had actually forgotten, for the time being at any rate. She had gone straight up to her bedroom, changed, and disappeared. And Papa? Was he not really quite pleased to have the opportunity to forget? Papa, who underneath had the same soft spot for Alberta as she for him, and who never willingly scolded her for anything. No doubt the matter would be brought up again, but in milder form.

The sun of a new day shone on the upper part of the mountain from quite the wrong direction, contributing to the general feeling of unreality.

A night outside existence, yet giving her a glimpse into it; an intense and confusing glimpse, as if seen in a flash of lightning. All this unreality, it was real. This astringent taste of antipathy and sweetness, of alarm and longing, of wanting and not wanting, was that of life itself, Alberta knew that already. Even Nurse Jullum had not been omitted from the fantastic events of the night, she who was always there in the background with her terrible bag and her quiescent, know-all smile. Tall, thin, dressed in black, she appeared and conjured up the gathering storm like a sinister, supernatural figure.

Alberta was free to give herself up to her conflicting feelings and to a new anxiety, a new fear, born in her that night.

* * *

One evening Jacob raised his head from his plate of gruel and remarked: 'Skipper Danielsen is leaving for the Arctic on the twentieth. He'll hire me, if I want.'

Alberta dropped her spoon. Her whole being stood still. She

118

glanced over at Mrs. Selmer, who looked as if someone had given her such a cruel blow that she could not open her eyes after it. She dared not look at Papa. What was going to happen?

The Magistrate did not answer immediately. When he finally did so, he said something quite unexpected. He described a careful circle round his plate and announced: 'I'm expecting by every post an answer to a letter I have written to my old friend, Shipowner Bjorn, in Flekkefjord. In it I asked him to keep you in mind, should he need an apprentice seaman. I have no doubt that he will do what he can.'

'That would be long-distance shipping,' said Jacob.

'Good gracious, yes. They carry freight all over the world.'

But Mrs. Selmer collapsed in a heap. With her hand to her breast as if to stop her heart beating – or to keep it going, it was difficult to say which – she said in a weak, dying voice: 'And what about me! Nobody thinks about me. Nobody thinks of my feelings.'

'My dear Henrietta, nobody sympathizes with your feelings more than I,' began Papa, 'but the boy must go out into the world some time, after all, and since he—

'God knows I'd rather have sent him south to the University or to the Military Academy,' he added. 'Then he could have counted on living with my brother Thomas, and he would have had the chance to become an educated lad and make a career – but unfortunately, it is some time since I gave up that idea. I have talked to the Headmaster on several occasions recently, and he has given me to understand that – well ... And since Jacob himself desires to make a new start, I think we ought to consider—'

But Mrs. Selmer had recovered from her relapse. She was white with fury. 'And here you all go making decisions and arrangements without so much as mentioning the matter to me. I am *quantité négligeable* – of no account – the boy's mother is of no account.'

'My dear Henrietta, we have decided nothing. I have consulted my old friend Bjorn as to how the matter might be arranged. I have, as I said, talked to Bremer, and he considers—'

Mrs. Selmer girded herself in her armour of mortification. She stopped eating, leaned back and stared into thin air with a fateful expression in her eyes and with pinched lips.

The Magistrate surveyed her angrily above his pince-nez. He muttered: 'So that's how it is!' His mouth twisted, and he kept the Headmaster's remarks to himself for the time being.

Tears began to roll down Mrs. Selmer's stricken face.

Alberta saw clearly that this was the end. Papa was letting Jacob go, giving him up for ever. From now on Jacob would be wandering alone, a poor sailor. He would travel to far-away ports, terrible ports full of squalor and girls. When he was not out on the savage sea his environment would permanently resemble the back room at the Grand. And suddenly Alberta quite distinctly saw a wave washing over Jacob. He was ship-wrecked, sitting on a piece of wreckage, cold and frozen, clinging fast with his blue hands – and at home they knew nothing about it, nobody knew about it. He was alone and helpless out on the Atlantic, far from everyone, abandoned by God and his fellow men. All he owned in the world was a miserable sea-chest, which was also floating in the ocean.

Alberta hid her face in her hands just as she gave way to tears. She felt Jacob's hand on her arm, heard him say: 'Oh no, Alberta, don't cry – there's nothing to cry about.'

She heard Mama say bitterly: 'Alberta, my dear – of what use are our tears, yours or mine?'

She heard Papa mutter something about preposterous, over-excited females, and fled out through the door and up the stairs.

'Don't take it like this, Alberta. It's nothing to cry so terribly about.

'But other boys leave home. I can't stay here for ever, having money wasted on me.

'I *must* get away, Alberta, I can't stand it any longer. I'll never be any good here – it's no use *my* going to school – I'm too stupid, you see. Oh no, don't cry like that, Alberta, it's so awful when you cry.

'Besides, all the teachers hate me, they're as beastly to me as they can be. It doesn't matter how hard I try. You said your-self yesterday, I *knew* my German, but Stensett gave me gamma just the same – he can't stand me, you see—

'And it's so miserable here at home – and cold and every-thing.

'Listen Alberta. After all, I'll come home again. I'll go ashore pretty soon, you see – Cedolf and I, we've thought of getting a piece of land in Canada, that's the sort of place for fellows like us. If only I can get started on something like that I'll come home prosperous – just you wait and see, Alberta.

'Cedolf *is* a good fellow, take my word for it – but he says that when he's home he gets so that he has to drink – and be-sides he never gets drunk, if that's what you're thinking.

'When he's at sea he never touches a drop.

'Don't you see, Alberta, everything will get much better if only I can get started on something and begin to earn money – I'll help Papa with the bank loan, I promise you – And you'll get back your jewellery and a lot more besides – are you listen-ing, Alberta? Oh no, do stop it! Can't you stop crying—

'I'll go teetotal if you want me to. Stop crying and I promise I'll go teetotal – If I stay here I'll never amount to anything – And you really must try to cheer up Mama a little. Can't you try to be a bit like she wants, it would be much better for you too.

'If I had to stay here I don't know what would become of me – I'd probably get like Kornelius Kamke in the end. Oh, Alberta – if I could only—'

Jacob struck the air with clenched fists, as if clearing away obstacles. He would have liked to say more, but got no further and finished somewhat self-consciously and in confusion: 'Oh, I don't know.'

'Oh Jacob!' Alberta sobbed in the darkness and called his name. She cowered in bed, rearranging the blanket again and again, unable to get warm. And she thought and thought about him, shaking with sobs.

It seemed as if Jacob had led a lop-sided existence, never really fitting into the circumstances in which he was born – never living up to Papa's expectations.

She remembered him as a little boy. He had been slender-limbed, with large grey eyes and fair curls that were a sorrow to him because they were girlish. And he had had a tender, courageous little heart, that went out warmly to people and animals and never kept account of its gifts.

He had gone for Ola Paradise with his fists because he whipped his horse – and cried himself to sleep at night in desperation for the poor horse, who was driven every day by that terrible Ola, and could not be saved from his clutches.

He had gone for big boys who were unkind to the little ones, and got a thrashing and forgot it and did the same again.

He had come home one day leading a shabby little snotty-nosed boy from the street. The boy was wearing Jacob's overcoat, and Jacob's intention had been to install him in the nursery and load him with things from the middle drawer in the chest, his own drawer. But as luck would have it they met Papa on the way.

Papa was not angry with the little boy. He explained to him kindly and quietly that he had to go away again. But afterwards Jacob was caned in the bedroom by Mama because he had taken his coat off and put it on a stranger – a boy who might have all kinds of diseases and about whom she knew nothing.

Did Papa begin even then to suspect that Jacob did not have the right instincts – or was it later? When he was very small Jacob had been the pride and joy of Papa and Mama and everyone.

It was really when he started secondary school that matters became tragic. He had managed somehow to get through elementary school. It was then that he began to grow so enormously fast, and everything went wrong: his Saturday reports, the boots he wore out, the boys he was seen with on the street, the clothes he continually outgrew. He became big and tall, with arms and legs that always stuck out too far, and eyes that gradually turned shy and hid themselves.

Everything Jacob wanted Papa did not want, and everything Papa wanted Jacob did not – or could not – want.

Jacob wanted to be a Boy Scout. Papa called it nonsense, and after brief consideration refused to give him any money for that sort of twaddle. In his childhood boys had played Indians without it costing anything.

Jacob and another boy wanted to build a hut beyond the river bend and spend Sundays there during the holidays. When Papa learned that the other boy was Julius, the son of Karen the fish shop, the whole scheme fell flat.

'If only it had been one of the nice boys in the class,' said Papa.

After all, there was the Archdeacon's Henrik, a bookworm, admirable in every respect. There were the Pram twins, a little less admirable, but proper social lions with beautiful manners. There were boys from good homes all over the province. And there were the Headmaster's boys, notoriously perfect specimens, though somewhat reserved and self-sufficient. Suitable friends were by no means lacking – but Jacob spent his time with Julius and with Cedolf, with Klaus Kilde and George Ryan. He did not go collecting specimens on the mountainside in summer like the Archdeacon's Henrik, but frequented the quarries to the east of the town, the wharves, every kind of craft, and Badendück's quay, among the Lapps and Russians. He had an unfortunate tendency to make his acquaintances among the lower ranks of society; to come home in the evening tattered, dirty and guilty, his clothes reeking of fish and tar, too late to do his homework which was set for six o'clock – too late for supper, when it was arranged that he must work first and go out afterwards – always with some misdeed on his conscience. Papa thundered and prophesied the worst, could not fathom what would become of the boy, and again came to the conclusion that he would be an ill-mannered guttersnipe. Mama wept and wailed, lay on the sofa, had little talks with Jacob in private. Alberta energetically put all her diplomacy into the service of a good cause. Jacob remained Jacob.

Schoolmasters came home to interview Papa, Papa went to interview the Headmaster. When Jacob moved up into the fifth form by the skin of his teeth, Alberta was in her second year at *gymnasium*. At Christmas she was taken out of school. Jacob had to be coached in several subjects – by Bremer and Stensett and Alberta.

And everything became worse than ever.

'I want to go to sea, Alberta, I don't want to stay at home,' grumbled Jacob.

A year later, when he once more slipped – or rather, was squeezed – through the needle's eye, he snarled: 'I'm not going to be a sabre-rattler or a clerk.'

'A clerk?'

'Yes, what else is Papa? He sits wearing out the seat of his trousers on an office chair. But I can't stand that sort of life, I'd have you know. I don't care whether I'm a gentleman or not, don't you understand. If only I could get to America.'

Alberta did not understand. Naturally, to ride round throwing a lasso on the Pampas or in Texas, to wear high boots, a highwayman's hat and a multi-coloured scarf loosely knotted round your neck and look for gold in Alaska, would be a wonderful sort of life, frightfully dashing. That she understood. But Jacob must not become anything like that all the same.

And definitely not a sailor.

Now and again a distant relative of Papa's, a captain on one of the Hamburg boats, would come visiting. He was well, nay, warmly, received. He and Papa drank toddy and chatted until late at night, and Mrs. Selmer would join them with her knitting.

There was no apparent difference between him and the Magistrate. Nevertheless since Alberta was small she had known that he was not nearly as much of a gentleman as Papa – knew it without being told.

Jacob was not going to struggle and toil, only to become like that in the end, less of a gentleman and of a slightly lower class.

But Jacob became more and more at cross purposes with it all.

'Bjerkem hates me,' said Jacob. 'If he can do me a bad turn, he's glad. If that fellow Stensett can find an opportunity to crack down on me, he will. However well I've prepared my lessons they take it for granted I don't know them, just because it's me. The Head takes real pleasure in giving me delta.'

There were also occasions when he announced rebelliously: 'I'll sign on for the Arctic – I'll fail on purpose, then they can all go to hell.' And others when he explained earnestly to Alberta: 'You see, Alberta, digging in the earth, working with your hands, that's the sort of thing I can do, and going to sea and things like that. If only I could do something like that I'd be all right. But you see, I hate school more than anything. It stinks.' And Jacob shook his clenched fists at the sky in helpless rage.

Those of Jacob's companions who had gone to sea after their school-leaving examination came home again. They walked the streets with clay pipes, the beginnings of sea legs, and cloth caps; had tanned faces, spat far and spoke English. An insolent strength radiated from them and was apparent in their walk and their looks.

'I feel like a girl,' said Jacob furiously. 'All I need is spectacles on my nose like the Archdeacon's Henrik. I'm ashamed of myself.'

He accompanied them on board, was with them in the evenings, heaven knows where, and came home late, his eyes shining and his cheeks flushed, carelessly loud-voiced and noisy. Sometimes Alberta, who lay awake listening, would creep down in her nightdress as soon as she heard the distant sound of the front door, to shush Jacob and make him go quietly.

She confiscated the pipes and the quids of tobacco, packs of cards and photographs of ladies in tights, that she found in his pockets, so that Mama should not find them. She lied and covered up for him as best she could, and scolded him.

And Jacob assured her: 'I don't get drunk, Alberta, but I can't refuse when I'm offered a glass. Besides, if there were something else to do here, none of us would drink a drop, the others say that too. In places where there are theatres and things like that, out in the world, they don't drink. And a grown fellow must learn to hold it a little, you know.'

And Julius went off to sea again, but George came home. And George travelled south to the Seamen's School, but Cedolf turned up instead. Cedolf had had particular influence on Jacob from schooldays on. He was a little older and had stayed down a couple of years. If the masters really had a down on Jacob, it was perhaps mainly on account of his friendship with Cedolf.

Bjorn, the shipowner, had use for Jacob. Quite by chance he needed an apprentice seaman immediately. His S/S *Aurora* would be docking at Liverpool during the second half of the month to take on freight for Pernambuco. Jacob must make up his mind at once and leave as soon as possible.

It was like a bad dream.

Papa and Jacob talked at table about registered tons and deplacement. Papa seemed to see Jacob in a better light now that he had given him up. He talked to him in friendly fashion about the little town in South Norway: 'That was where your grandfather lived during his last years. You wouldn't remember him, my boy, but your sister should. You were almost five, Alberta, when you were down there with me. And it was at your grandfather's house, my dear Jacob, that I used to meet the old man, the present shipowner Bjorn's father.'

And Papa continued to talk about people and conditions in the south. He revived old memories, became animated by them, and ended up genial and good-humoured: 'As you see, I've spent some time among seafaring folk too. I'm not completely ignorant of navigation, and can talk about leeward and windward with the best of them.'

Light was cast deep down into the darkness of Alberta's childhood. It fell strongly and suddenly on unexpected things: on a bush with small, round sulphur-yellow roses. They smelt nasty, but attracted her hands, which stretched out towards them.

Jacob laughed. He and Papa were good friends. It almost seemed as if it were not so terribly tragic any more that Jacob was becoming a sailor, instead of a government official or an army officer. If it had not been for Mama, she might perhaps have begun to see the bright side. But a glance at her was enough for the abyss to yawn once more. Her face was swollen with weeping and she said nothing, but looked straight in front of her with hopeless eyes. She sat shrunken into her shawl, the personification of misery. Nobody would have recognized the elegant, vivacious Mama of social life. Every time her eyes met Alberta's a lump rose in Alberta's throat.

'Pernambuco – where's that, Alberta?' asked Mrs. Selmer in a weak, almost inaudible voice.

'Brazil,' answered Alberta, feeling as if she were pronouncing sentence of death.

'Brazil,' repeated Mrs. Selmer in an even weaker voice, scarcely more than a breath. She leaned her head against the back of her chair and shut her eyes.

'Now look here,' said Papa, red in the face. 'You're behaving, so help me, as if the boy were being sent to the devil. Of course we had other plans for Jacob's future, for many reasons – but we shall have to bear the disappointment. Apart from that I can't see that Jacob is in a worse position than any other boy who chooses the sea. On the contrary – he's joining a good shipping company from the start, an excellent company known to us, where they will most certainly keep an eye on him. If he behaves himself and makes progress, there's every chance that he may be able to work his way up in the same company. I think that, considering the circumstances, we have every reason to be pleased, and the boy himself looks forward to it with hope and optimism—'

Papa came no further in his speech. Mama rose and tottered towards the door, clearly summoning her last remaining strength. A groan escaped her, and she disappeared.

Papa struck the table, making everything on it jump. His mouth twisted violently. He addressed himself to his plate and was silent for a while, but his clenched fist, which still lay on the table, continued to tremble.

Alberta's desire for Papa to be right warred with a painful suspicion that perhaps he would just as soon be rid of Jacob, since he despaired of him anyway, and would therefore let him sink with deliberate intent. Judging by Mama, Jacob must be on the way to the bottom.

A memory surfaced, filling her cup of pain and anxiety to the brim. When Cedolf came home from sea the last time – it must have been last summer – she had confiscated among much else in Jacob's pockets a mysterious little piece of pink card with a printed inscription. '*Kommen Sie doch die schönen Damen zu sehen,*' it had said – and a street and house number below.

'It's something I got from Cedolf, something he got in Hamburg,' replied Jacob when questioned. He reddened, snatched

the card, tore it up and said: 'Besides, you've no business looking in my pockets.'

'Well, if you prefer Mama to find everything you keep in
them, I don't mind,' said Alberta crossly, not attaching any
further significance to the matter. '*Schönen Damen*' had probably meant dancers or something like that. But Jacob had
looked so odd that she went on thinking about it later. And the
light suddenly dawned.

It was showing the way to girls, to wicked girls, who lived
in wicked houses, that little pink card. So it was true. Such
places did exist, and as soon as a seaman came ashore he was
probably handed a little message. Cedolf had no doubt been
to see the beautiful ladies – he was capable of it.

At that time she had made up her mind more strongly than
ever to save Jacob for an orderly life.

And now it had all been in vain. Now he was going out on
the savage sea just the same, and down into all kinds of human
filth. He would go ashore in ports, and everything horrid and
bad and dreadful would happen to him.

Oh God! Oh God!

In the middle of the floor in Jacob's room there stood an
open sea-chest. Inside, it had curious little sections along one
end, and it was broader at the base than at the top. It was
clearly meant to stand as long as there could be any question
of anything standing. And there were handles made of thick
rope for lifting it.

For Alberta it was a symbol of the seaman's tragic life, the
sailor's rootless wandering, his poverty, his toil and depriva-
tion, his struggle against the raging sea, all of which she could
picture only too clearly. Perhaps it represented much the same
for Mrs. Selmer who, pale, with set face, was packing Jacob's
outfit into it.

It all seemed to take on an entirely different complexion
where Jacob was concerned, however. Whistling, he lifted first
the one handle, then the other, rearranged the things Mama had
put into it, and stood looking at the chest, swaying from his
knees with his hands in his trouser pockets. He walked round
it, bent down and inspected it intently from every angle,

experimented with the locks and hinges, and behaved almost as if it were a fellow-creature of whom he was fond, but whose reliability he nevertheless desired to test.

Jacob had changed. He no longer avoided people's gaze, but looked straight at them. And Jacob's eyes were dark grey under the fair hair that curled thickly over his forehead. He smiled with a broad, frank smile that Alberta seemed never to have seen before.

He tried on the new, thick monkey-jacket he would wear in future instead of a waistcoat and shirt. It had a high neck and long sleeves – and the frozen schoolboy with the large blue fists sticking out of his short sleeves disappeared as if by magic. A broad-shouldered sailor with a smile in his eyes stood there instead, looking at Alberta from under his fair hair. 'Look Alberta, now the slavery is over,' he said.

To Mama Jacob talked in that voice of his that gave confidence. He sat with her a great deal. Often, if Alberta came in, she would find him leaning over Mama hurriedly withdrawing his hand, as if he had just patted her on the back.

His attitude towards Papa was that of one grown man to another. They looked at each other directly when they spoke; Papa even drew himself erect, smote Jacob on the shoulder and said: 'By Jove, you're not a child any longer, my boy.' Or he would talk half jokingly to Jacob, using sailors' expressions: 'It's up to you to do the navigating, Jacob, and keep a steady course.'

And Jacob answered in the same tone: 'Aye, aye, sir!'

But with Alberta he bubbled over with all kinds of things. 'I've finished with hanging about and being no use to anybody, don't you see, Alberta? Now I'll try to get Cedolf into the same company, and when we've saved as much as we need we'll go ashore. In Canada, you know, that's where there's money for hard-working fellows to earn. It won't be long before I can help with the bank loan and everything. On the other hand, if I had *studied*—' Jacob's voice was full of scorn, he pronounced the word with boundless disdain '—I'd have stayed here simply eating up money. Besides, I'd never have matriculated, however much you all coached me. No Alberta – I'm not stupid, you see, it would be no use for someone like me. But I'll do well all the same, you'll see – oh no, don't cry again, for heaven's sake. I'll go teetotal. I've told you, I'll go teetotal.'

And Jacob put his arms round her and shook her, but in a different way now, as if less embarrassed at giving way to such weakness. 'I'm not the kind of fellow you think I am,' he said.

'And then you must be kind to Mama, Alberta – can't you be kind to her? She has such a bad time, don't you see, she's not happy, and when a little thing like you frizzing your hair could please her—'

A little devil was roused in Alberta and she turned Jacob's weapon back against him: 'It's no use, Jacob, I'm too plain. It would be no use for someone like me. I'd only look silly, like those small dogs with thin, fair, crinkly hair. Don't you remember the one old Mrs. Klykken had?'

Jacob stared at her uncomprehendingly. 'Good Lord, surely it doesn't matter as much as all that? The other girls all curl their hair after all,' he said, talking nonsense, just like a man. 'And you mustn't be upset, Alberta,' he continued, coming closer. 'Listen! You shall go to Kristiania. Just wait until I've saved a little. Now I can start earning my own living I feel as if there's hope about all sorts of things. Simply getting away from that feeling of being a criminal all the time—'

He stopped. Perhaps he realized he was harping on a sore point. 'And I'm jolly glad I don't have to go by way of Kristiania,' he said, changing the subject. 'Uncle the Colonel wouldn't want to meet a black sheep like me, Aunt even less.'

Alberta altered her route. She no longer walked uphill, where the roads were infested with people on foot as long as the sun was up, nor did she ski. The latter would have seemed like unforgiveable indifference at this time, when Jacob's departure was imminent, and would have taken her far from the focus of events.

She walked along River Street, along the quays, and in poky Strand Street, where small green hovels, their windows full of fuchsias and geraniums, stood crookedly supporting each other, and where nobody else walked.

She lived in an unreal world of fantasies about Jacob, and the good or evil that might befall him. Visions of colourful life in foreign ports flickered before her eyes: the tropics, Negroes, piles of pineapples and oranges. Then suddenly there was a storm at sea, the waves washed over Jacob, who was the last one left on the upturned hull, blue with cold and alone and struggling vainly for his life – sobs choked her. She also saw him coming out of taverns, a little unsteady on his feet, in the company of girls like Fanny, and she felt as if the ground were sinking beneath her. Under it all she nursed a hope; now and again it floated to the surface and pushed Jacob aside. A hope that now, somehow or other, it must surely be her turn. For the time being, Jacob was provided for, at any rate until he entered the school of navigation.

In glimpses she saw herself, free and unselfconscious, released from all that was unpleasant, out in the world. At the very least in Kristiania, perhaps in other places, preferably as far away as possible. She was cheerful and active, like the people who came home in the summer.

But then the realization of what it would be like to know that Papa and Mama were left here at home with all their problems, crept across the vision like a mist. She felt again that dizzying feeling of treachery, which gnawed at her night and day every time she was away from home, even during the week she used to spend in Inner Southfjord in the summer as a child.

One day Alberta was passing the spot where you could see right up Fjord Street and into Dorum's jewellery shop. Her heart missed a beat and her legs turned weak. For up in Fjord Street Dorum's door had opened, and out of the door had come Mrs. Selmer.

She looked about her for a moment, up and down the street. Without noticing Alberta she gathered up her skirt and went down the steps, holding her muff out a little with one hand, as was her habit. Inside the window, between silver-plated jugs and trays, Dorum's bald head appeared. He craned his neck – indeed, he was quite clearly standing on tip-toe – to watch her go.

Alberta went home in a fever of anxiety, with pulsing blood and dizzy head. Now the hour of reckoning was near. How readily she would have directed her steps in a different direction! But the mysterious currents that emanated from Mama were as potent as ever. Alberta went straight home, certain of being unmasked as one who lent a helping hand to criminals, compromised her family, and squandered its possessions.

She presented herself in the dining-room more dead than alive. Mrs. Selmer was sitting at the mending basket, without her shawl, still warm from her excursion in the fresh air.

'Oh, Alberta my dear, do help me to mark these socks for Jacob,' she said in a friendly, straightforward tone.

Alberta sat on the edge of the chair and prepared to mark the socks with trembling fingers. This must be a trap, and there was nothing for it but to walk into it with her eyes open.

But Mrs. Selmer talked about Jacob's socks and his other things as if there was nothing the matter. Then she talked about Jacob himself and all the dangers he was likely to meet with. 'But I believe God will hear my prayers and hold His hand over him,' she said.

There was an air of mild resignation about her, a quiet, slightly hollow-eyed pallor as if after illness. Mama behaved like one who has concentrated his whole being on a decision – to bear her cross. Alberta, with her misdeeds and her bracelet, did not seem to exist.

Alberta's reason stood still.

The evening before Jacob's departure she and Jacob said good night to each other across the open sea-chest. They stood exchanging a few words, and Jacob leaned over from acquired habit and arranged the things in the chest, loosening one, packing another in more tightly. He had been living in it for some time. It contained everything in the world that was his, and it could not be tidied too often. Suddenly he raised his eyebrows: 'What on earth?' he said, and he hauled up from the depths an unknown object, a splendid new leather wallet. 'What on earth?' he said again, turning it over and over, his eyes large with amazement. Then he opened it.

Inside the wallet was a dizzy, unheard-of sum of money. Five ten-*kroner* notes, fifty *kroner*. And a small white card, on which it said: 'To turn to in a tight corner. From Mother, who loves you and will always be thinking of you.'

'Damn!' said Jacob.

'Damn!' he said again, and his eyes filled with tears. He had to turn away and dry them with the back of his hand.

'Where on earth could she have got it from?' he asked after a while. 'It's so unnecessary too, I'll get travel money from Papa. But I can't understand where it's come from. Fifty *kroner* – have you ever seen anything to equal it?'

Alberta shook her head. She had no words for what she felt – a great, painful tenderness for Mama.

The moment of departure had arrived.

Jacob's chest had been taken down. Ewart was already driving away with it on a sled. Mrs. Selmer and the Magistrate in their outdoor clothes were waiting for Alberta, who was up in her room, making a last attempt to master her tears. They had been bubbling in her throat all through dinner. Now they threatened to overcome her.

There was Jacob behind her in the doorway. He threw his arms round her, thumped her on the back harder than ever and said in a husky voice: 'Good-bye Alberta, good-bye. I shan't forget what you've done for me – don't worry about me, Alberta, I'll turn out all right, you'll see. And look, take it – you should have had it before now, but . . .'

Jacob pushed something into Alberta's hand, at the same time kissing her roughly, first on one cheek and then on the other.

Bewildered, she looked down at what was in her hand. It felt so familiar. Through the thin tissue paper covering it she saw the bracelet, the very same bracelet from Uncle the Colonel.

'But Jacob!'

'It's all right, Alberta, I only exchanged my gold watch-chain for it. Now I'm wearing this—' Jacob pulled at his sea-man's vest '—nobody can see that I haven't got a watch chain. I'll buy a new one when I get my wages if I can get ashore somewhere. I couldn't do anything about it earlier, because Papa would have found out, you see, and you know what would have happened then.

'And you must forget about the whole thing now. I've told

Mama all about it, so you won't be bothered with it. Well, good-bye, we'll have to go now – promise me you won't cry on the quay. And Alberta – Papa and Mama – they have such a rotten time.'

Alberta had been speechless for some time from suppressed tears. She gave Jacob her hand and he squeezed it so that her fingers cracked.

Jensine was standing at the front door. She dried her hands on her apron, extended one of them and said: 'Here's wishing you well, Jacob.'

And so they went.

Jacob was to travel second class. This alone was inexpressibly tragic. It so clearly marked the step he was taking out of his own environment. With his matriculation in his pocket he would without any doubt have travelled first class south to the University or the Military College, and been a gentleman. Now he was travelling second and was only an ordinary fellow. It was beyond measure distressing and pathetic. Neither Mrs. Selmer nor Alberta went down below with the luggage. Papa and Jacob dived down unaccompanied, like the courageous men they were, into the murky regions of the second class. When they came up again the Magistrate declared: 'By Jove, it wasn't so bad. On the contrary, it looked quite decent down there.'

But Mrs. Selmer peered anxiously after someone who straddled a coil of rope and disappeared in the same direction. He had a celluloid collar and a carpet bag made out of a blanket and was decidedly suspicious in appearance. 'God knows what sort of company you'll be thrown into, my boy,' she sighed.

'Hm,' said Jacob. 'You don't think I could have made a fool of myself and travelled first, do you? The others who go to sea often sleep on deck. I'd have preferred to do that really.'

Every now and again somebody would come on board, shake Jacob's hand, exchange a few words with him, and leave again. Some of them were old class-mates, and some of them were people with whom Alberta had no idea he was on friendly terms: young Theodorsen, Signora Ryan, Karla Schmitt. Jacob seemed to have enjoyed wide popularity. And there was

Cedolf! He stayed waiting for the boat to leave. He and Jacob exchanged a few words over the rails now and again. Mama, Papa and Alberta replied to his greeting very curtly, and then looked as far as possible in another direction.

There was Beda pushing her way over: 'Can't you get me signed on too, Jacob?' she called gaily. 'Here am I longing to get out into the world. Tell them that if they need a first class apprentice, all they have to do is send for Beda Buck. It's no joke, I mean every word of it.'

Jacob answered her in the same tone, assuring her that he would get her hired. 'Many thanks and good luck to you,' said Beda, shaking his hand like a man.

There was the little fair girl who served in Holst's. She was coming up the gangplank, probably going to say good-bye to someone. And there she suddenly was, standing in front of Jacob, very red in the face: 'I just wanted to say good-bye and wish you a good journey.' Jacob was also remarkably flushed. He bowed repeatedly: 'Thank you, that was really too kind.' The little girl from Holst's handed him a paper bag: 'Just something for the journey.' She went redder still. So did Jacob, who bowed several times more and replied: 'Thank you very much indeed, you really shouldn't have bothered.' Then the fair girl left and Jacob's colour gradually faded away.

Alberta was on tenterhooks. Whatever were Mama and Papa thinking, what would they say? But they did not refer to the occurrence – perhaps they thought it didn't matter, now that Jacob was going away. They prepared to go ashore. The terrible moment had come when Mama hugged him for the last time, released him, turned away and left, her handkerchief pressed hard to her mouth, her eyes almost closed, all her strength concentrated on holding back an eruption of pain and anguish. As if in a dream Alberta heard Papa, who seldom mentioned the name of God except to curse, say quietly and seriously to Jacob: 'God be with you, my son.' Then she felt Jacob's hands, hard and warm in hers, and she was down on the quay again. The ship put out from land.

Blind with tears she glimpsed him aft. The propeller whipped up a whirlpool of froth and bubbling water between him and the quay. It grew, became broader, was impassable. She saw him wave. She heard Papa say: 'I must go home with your mother, Alberta, she's very upset. You stay as long as you can see each other.'

Now the ship was out in the middle of the river, now it set its course westwards. Jacob was only a small, black figure waving something white.

Alberta stood until it was just a dark speck with a streamer of smoke, far out on the fjord. She turned to go home. There was no one left on the quay besides Cedolf, sitting on a barrel, swinging his legs. When Alberta went past he lifted his cap and said: 'We'll miss Jacob. Too bad he had to leave so soon.'

Alberta did not reply.

Up on the hill the fair girl from Holst's stood staring out to sea. She suddenly started, turned and disappeared down River Street.

At home it was dismally empty. No one in the dining-room, no one in the sitting-rooms. In the kitchen Jensine was polishing copper, looking as if she for her part was prepared for the worst, but did not wish to express an opinion. Alberta wandered upstairs. The Magistrate's voice could be heard through a closed door, matter-of-factly explaining something. Someone was in the office. Life went on, in spite of tragedy.

She knocked hesitantly on the door of the bedroom. Nobody answered. So she went into Jacob's room.

Mama was standing at the window, her complexion blotched, swollen, unrecognizable. And at this moment Alberta longed so much for tenderness and warmth, perhaps simply for Mama, that in a kind of delirium she went across and put her arms round her, and there they stood. Mrs. Selmer leaned her head against Alberta and whispered: 'We must think of him, we must be with him in our thoughts, wherever he goes. I have had to admit today that it's best for him to go away.'

She sobbed, still leaning her head against Alberta; she was clearly not herself.

But she became so, bracing herself. Everyday life took hold

136

again, it had to be so. She dabbed at her eyes: 'We shall have to sort the washing this afternoon. Oleanna is coming to-morrow.'

She dabbed at her eyes once more and went towards the door. Then she remembered something: 'I take it that you will do your mother the pleasure of wearing your bracelet again, my dear Alberta, now that you have it back.' Her tone was not entirely free of sarcasm: 'You are clever at hiding things from your mother. My compliments,' she said.

Alberta was crimson and tense. Her heart sank to her boots, as usual.

'I must say I am overwhelmed,' continued Mrs. Selmer. 'Really, the most incredible things have been going on behind my back.' She meditated a moment, as if not entirely sure of herself. But she soon recovered. 'I must be quite a monster, if my children cannot come to me with such a matter,' she said coldly. 'And heaven knows what Dorum thinks of us,' she concluded, as she left the room.

*   *   *

Sunshine every day. Vigorous trickles of melted snow under the hard crust – a strong, pungent smell of wet earth and mould. The slopes and mountainsides looked like speckled cows, white and yellow-grey – and in the yellow-grey there had sprung up small living, glistening shoots, thick, and red as meat, and already bursting here and there into luminous green. Children were carrying pussy willow and golden dandelions, playing hopscotch and pitch-and-toss round the church, where the snow always melted first. But the snow still slid off the roofs, and water trickled and flowed from Upper Town down to Lower Town, where the slush in some places reached over the tops of one's fur boots. In the Market Square last year's horse dung was revealed.

At Gronli farms the cattle lowed restlessly in their stalls, the sheep were bleating. The chickens had been let out on to the sunny slope, and all kinds of strange bird songs had woken to life. After sunset the pungent odour of the earth rose up more strongly, and at night, which was almost as light as day, the speckled mountains stood unmoving, upside-down on the fjord and the river. Above them to the west hung a delicate shimmer of light.

People became restless and swarmed out of doors, later and later in the evening. They could be seen as black silhouettes against the green evening sky, bright with spring; the hard surface of the snow crunched beneath their feet. They walked two by two, looking for solitude. Even Bergan the lawyer and the Archdeacon's Christina would meet as if quite by chance and wander out along Rivermouth, for this was the way to go in the early spring, straight into the sunset. If they met anyone, Christina would shrink and almost disappear from coquettish modesty, but Bergan would look just the same. They were being talked about – to be sure people were talking.

Harriet met Dr. Mo at Louisa-round-the-bend, and Dr. Mo turned and walked out of town again with Harriet. She did not shrink in the least, but said good-day loudly and with a smile, as usual, and if anyone looked as if caught red-handed it was Dr. Mo.

Gudrun accompanied her brothers, the Archdeacon's Henrik, and the chemists from the 'Polar Bear'. She admitted openly that she hooked on to anybody to avoid the company of Stensett the schoolmaster. She would stop people and ask them: 'Have you noticed whether Stensett has been this way, for if so I'll turn back at once.'

Beda walked with each and everyone. And she still skied to Gronli farms on the snow-crust that formed in the evenings, although the stone walls had reappeared a long time ago and on all the southern slopes you had to take off your skis and carry them. One evening when Alberta was wandering across the bog she saw Lett the dentist lifting Beda over a fence. He held her up against him for a moment before putting her down again. They disappeared into Peter's wood.

Alberta walked with no one. This was in the nature of things, and Alberta's fate. With whom should she walk? Now and again she would meet the Chief Clerk, who also walked by himself, and this seemed equally natural whatever the reason. They would greet each other guiltily and continue their separate ways. Alberta blushed as usual when she was confronted in broad daylight, and wished that the Clerk would choose another way.

There was one person she would not meet under any circumstances, someone she took devious routes to avoid; whom she hid from, turned her back on and ran away from if there was no other way out: Cedolf.

If only he would go away. What was he doing at home all the time? Wasn't he going to sign on again, go away to the navigation school, to Canada, to Timbuktu?

She would not think about Cedolf. She loathed him. He was horrid. But she could not rid herself of the memory of his arm round her, of the new, strange feeling it had given her. If she had to pass him she trembled and turned crimson, and she saw Cedolf's mouth curl up as he greeted her.

She walked along the ice-crusted roads composing verses. It was a stupid weakness of hers, and it got worse at this time of year. The poems were about the mountains, the spring and yearning, the scent of the earth and the new moon, and came to her idly and easily out of the yellow-green air. So idly and easily that Alberta looked on them with suspicion and did not always grant them admission to the book under the woollen vests.

She found the first small leaf of lady's mantle with a dew-drop in it, heard a new bird song, and was intoxicated by such obvious trifles. But she took care not to mention them to anybody. The sunset, yes – but a leaf of lady's mantle! It would show lack of judgement and a rather simple turn of mind, another defect to add to all the others. Mrs. Selmer would call it affectation.

Uneasily Alberta noted how little she thought about Jacob. She had imagined she would be tormented with loss night and day, that she would never have a moment's peace. But now it all sank back into her consciousness, disappearing for long stretches of time, and then reappearing in the guise of a guilty conscience.

At home Mama stood in front of the window looking at the pale sky behind the dark roofs, and said: 'Heavens, summer is on its way again.' She sighed and drew her shawl round her: 'I'm so tired of being cold, Alberta, and of being lonely. But that's my lot in life I suppose.

Alberta did not know what to say. She wondered whether she should embrace Mama, but was afraid that perhaps it would be the wrong thing to do. For the sake of propriety she stayed in the room for a while, and then went upstairs and sat looking at the river and the mountains. And she declaimed to herself verses by the Norwegian poets, taken from the selection in the bookcases downstairs, until she was warm and had a different face, one that she discovered with astonishment in the mirror. A face she did not recognize, a face that was more than plain.

*   *   *

It was summer in the south, said the newspaper. Mrs. Selmer read out loud the number of degrees they had in the shade. She went across to the window, driving with wet and spattered with sleet, and dabbed at her eyes. The Magistrate remained seated, muttering irritably that well, in heaven's name, we must make some allowance for the latitude. 'Things are comparatively early this year,' he continued. 'I heard the Headmaster say that the Archdeacon's Henrik is supposed to have found a saxifrage. If we get a little sun things will come along quickly.'

Mrs. Selmer shrugged her shoulders without replying.

Outside the turf roof on Flemming's barn was greening, and so was Peter on the Hill's slice of ground that was visible between the houses. In the Sisters Kremer's window the first straw hats were displayed on stands, and the Lapps had arrived at Badendück's quay. They lived down there under the piles of planks and strolled in the streets, hugging themselves in their reindeer skin jackets, their hands stuck into the arms as if into a muff. The street music had arrived too, five Germans blue with cold, wearing woollen scarves round their necks. They stood on the pavement surrounded by a faithful public of boys and Lapps, an infallible sign of summer.

But on the north side of the houses there still lay hard, grey patches of snow. And the south-wester hurled itself violently between the wharves, carrying the Germans' brassy notes in disconnected blasts across the town.

Alberta froze in body and soul. She struggled desperately with her umbrella when she was out on expeditions to the post office, but to no avail; the Magistrate's official documents got damp and sticky. Each time he objected afresh that there was absolutely nothing to be gained by fetching the post. It was much better to let Larsen bring it, as he should, then it would arrive dry and in proper condition. He would thank her not to do it any more, he had said so many times, but by God, you could evidently talk yourself blue in the face where some things were concerned. Could not Alberta, grown girl as she was, understand this clearly once and for all?

Alberta promised that of course she could, and next time the weather was bad the same thing happened, although she hid the big envelopes under her jacket. There was always a corner that stuck out and got wet. It was not easy to please everyone. Alberta was grateful to Papa for not flying into a rage about it. He had some patience, in spite of his hot temper.

Jacob's letters had arrived as they should, one from Bergen, one from Flekkefjord, one from Liverpool. They did not contain much except that Jacob was quite well. 'There's so much on my mind that I would like to have known about,' complained Mrs. Selmer as she folded them up again.

'The important thing is that the boy is well and happy,' said the Magistrate. – Now it was the bad period when nothing would be heard of Jacob for a long, long time – when anything could be expected, anything imagined. Mrs. Selmer sighed frequently and heavily, and Alberta felt more guilty than ever because she was as she was, adding to Mama's burdens. One of the greatest burdens was that Alberta never willingly accompanied her to church.

Mrs. Selmer went every Sunday now. Previously she had gone every other Sunday. It was no small sorrow to her that the Magistrate never set foot in the place, and that it was so difficult to get Alberta to go. Alberta employed the utmost cunning to avoid it: she was not ready dressed, had a pain in her stomach, a headache, had lost a button at the last minute. Mrs. Selmer had to give up and leave, with pinched mouth and tragic eyes.

For Alberta could not stand going to church. She did not like it when Beda mocked the sacrament, sharing out cake at tea-time and saying, 'Take, eat, this is my body'. It offended something traditional in her and seemed to her unnecessary and vulgar. But she froze at the thought of going to church, being unmoved by it and thoroughly bored.

Before her confirmation she had honestly tried to get to grips with it and understand it all. Two afternoons a week throughout the winter her eyes had hung on Pastor Pio's thick lips, and she had listened intently to his slow, monotonous, slightly bleating voice, talking about sin and grace, perdition and rebirth in Christ. The class was held in the old girls' school, in a low-ceilinged room, where the air became thick and heavy from the smoking lamps and the breath of many people. After a while the voice seemed to be issuing from a cloud. However tensely Alberta listened, to her they were merely words, words, empty meaningless words. She would lose the thread for long periods at a time, and find her attention caught by something worldly: the velvet ribbon, for instance, that Signora Ryan never managed to tie tightly enough in her shock of hair, and with which she incessantly fiddled.

She received the sacrament and experienced nothing. Over at the other side of the curved altar rail she had caught sight of that nice girl, Ellen Ovre, who was now training to be a deaconess, her face tilted upwards, a remote expression in her eyes, completely ecstatic. Alberta had felt a prick of envy and inferiority. But just before the chalice came to her, Fina Zakariassen, who had a cold, snuffled lengthily and emphatically over it. Although Pastor Pio turned it a little and dried the rim with a napkin, Alberta was unable to think about anything in the great moment besides putting her lips elsewhere than Fina's.

Then confirmation class was over and it all slid backwards in her consciousness, to become something over which she had exerted herself to no purpose.

Alberta found moral support in Papa. He might lapse and say: 'If it means so much to your mother, surely you might—', but that was as far as it went. And after all, he never went to church himself. He had never been. There had been times in Alberta's life when she was ashamed that Papa was not to be found in the front row in the chancel on Sundays, beside Dr. Pram, the Governor, the Chief of Police, and all the other regular churchgoers. She had prayed for him at night, that he might be converted and become like them. But it was no use, and she gradually forgot about it.

An occasional Sunday would come along, however, when it was impossible to get out of it. Pressure of opinion, unfortunate circumstances, made it unavoidable. Then Alberta would sit as if on tenterhooks on the little bench facing the congregation where Mrs. Selmer had selected for herself a permanent seat. The voice of the preacher above their heads rose and fell. Each time it fell Alberta hoped it would be for good. But no, it rose again in new, monotonous, incomprehensible turns of phrase, speaking of sin and guilt, grace and hard-won redemption, words that gave her the same feeling of pressure on her breast as Miss Myre had given her, as Nurse Jullum and all the married ladies gave her. In church Alberta longed more than ever for Papa's god, who only filled up empty space and was content with mere existence; who left people alone and pursued no-one, either with punishment or love.

If it was the Archdeacon, she would listen to him for a while. He had such a kind face and talked in his natural speaking voice. There was something simple and trustworthy about him that made her think he wouldn't bother with it if it were nonsense. Her old wish to understand was aroused. But she discovered that ultimately it concerned all the same incomprehensible things; her mind became dulled, she lost the thread and failed to find it again. Or she got a frog in her throat so that she had to swallow repeatedly; or her leg went to sleep, or she fidgeted, and Mrs. Selmer would whisper despairingly: 'Sit still!'

When finally the sigh of relief that meant it was over went through the church, and the congregation rose for the blessing, Alberta was numb in body and soul, unable to feel her legs beneath her or to register any more impressions.

Sometimes the hymn could have a strangely liberating effect. One was borne aloft on the crest of a wave and glided out into quiet depths of peace and harmony: 'Praise to the Lord, the Almighty . . .' But the long hymns with countless verses, harsh melodies and old-fashioned turns of phrase, with their talk of the pains of hell, the slough of evil, slaughter, blood and wounds, resembled a heavy, suffocating morass that had to be crossed. Pastor Pio had a deplorable weakness for them.

On the way home from church Alberta was still numb. She would hear the ladies discussing the sermon, hear Harriet and Christina take part in the conversation, expressing their opinions, praising, criticising.

She felt depraved, and outcast, because she had no opinion, except that it was all vastly boring.

One day the post really did bring something. A letter, surprisingly hard and thick, from Aunt the Colonel. Mrs. Selmer seized it with anxious hands. The thick hard object was a photograph of cousin Lydia, in ball dress, with a fan, and flowers on her shoulder and in her hair. And her hair was above reproach, waved, and as well fashioned as if it were moulded round her face. An unspoken reprimand.

It was a three-quarter-length picture. Lydia was standing in half profile holding the fan in front of her, with a little world-weary, disappointed smile at the corners of her mouth, which looked as old and experienced as those of the wives, thought Alberta.

But Mrs. Selmer declared that Lydia had really turned out very pretty, and that she looked so ladylike. Mrs. Selmer sighed and concentrated upon the letter. After a moment she put it down again. She had to collect herself. Cousin Lydia was engaged.

. . . Quite splendidly engaged to an unusually promising young man of particularly good family. He was at the Legation in London, his connections and fortune provided him with the best prospects. Neither Aunt nor Uncle could have desired a more attractive son-in-law. They had to face the fact that they would have to part with Lydia sooner or later. Now they thanked God for putting so noble and sympathic a young man in her path. It was sad that she would have to go so far away, but she herself was radiantly happy.

Mrs. Selmer again put the letter down. When she picked it up again and read on, her tone changed. It said that Uncle would like Lydia to see something of her own country before leaving it for what might be a number of years. So she and

Aunt would probably be coming north this summer. They intended going as far as the North Cape, and it seemed to be a good opportunity for visiting their relatives for a few days. However thin blood might be, it was always thicker than water, wrote Aunt jokingly. Which gave Mrs. Selmer occasion to remark that it was not as thin as all that, since Papa and Uncle the Colonel were brothers. 'But Aunt has the habit of saying things that are not very amusing,' she added, sitting with the letter in her hand, musing. 'That was a great deal all at once,' she remarked, giving Alberta to understand that she was not altogether delighted, that she was, in fact, not really delighted at all.

The first cruise ship of the year was anchored at River-mouth. Small groups of foreign-looking people speaking English were in the streets dressed for rain and carrying umbrellas, looking cold and at a loss. Boys from the alleys gathered and followed at their heels. Forward souls accosted them and offered to show them the way to Badendück's quay, where the Lapps were. But P.C. Olsen was on his rounds and, when the occasion demanded, ordering: 'Get along home with you, lads – break it up.'

All along the street the small signs with 'English spoken', '*Man spricht Deutsch*', had been hung out, along with the reindeer, seal and polar-bear skins. And even the Sisters Kremer had Lapp dolls, horn spoons and reindeer slippers thrust among the hats and the bridal and funeral trimmings.

*   *   *

It was summer, brand new, brought to maturity in a couple of short days. The greenness was immoderately green. It climbed upwards between the mountains' violet screes, was mirrored in the river, making it deep and unfathomable, covered all the slopes up to where the uncultivated land took over with heather and dwarf birch, providing a new, festive backdrop to life. The mountain range to the east hovered blue above all the green, eternal snow in its lap.

A hubbub of cheerful sounds rose up under the tall sky. They were hammering in the shipyard so that the world rang with the sound; they were hammering on board the ships, and singing, slapping their paint brushes, swinging their buckets. An exhilarating smell of tar and paint rose up from the harbour, awakening a desire to travel and thoughts of long journeys.

The planks of the wharves lay bare in the sun, steaming warm, wonderfully easy to walk on. But the last invincible grey snow patches hid away, dirty and sad, in the shade to the north.

The wind was in the east, bringing with it the rushing of the cataracts, a deep, churning hum that made one weak with longing and giddy with unrest. But if it shifted the slightest degree to the west, the smoke from young Klykken's cod-liver-oil factory hung greasy and oppressive above the town. The ladies held their handkerchiefs to their noses, and all flights of fancy were extinguished.

The rowan in shoemaker Schoning's yard, the only rowan in the district that had managed to grow to any height, tossed like a rich green plume above the shoemaker's roof and brought all kinds of colour to life round it. The houses were no longer grey, but red and yellow. The church tower was hung with ochre.

Along the brooks and rills there suddenly appeared luxuriant tussocks of kingcups, their stalks bursting with sap, golden yellow and shining against the black-brown peat. The cow-parsnip had come up, heaven knows when; it was already tropical, heavy and swaying. The ditches were shaggy with lady's mantle and wild chervil. The Archdeacon's Henrik came home with the first *viola biflora* and laid it to rest in his herbarium.

People were moving up to their summer cottages. Harriet and Christina painstakingly carried glassware and other frail objects up the hillside. Palmine Flor and Lilly Vogel did likewise, not to be outdone by their betters. Young Mrs. Klykken worked in gloves, setting shells in place, planting and sowing, while the silver ball in the centre bed mirrored it all.

Windows stood open everywhere. Curtains were carried inwards by the breeze, the hammer blows from the shipyard were echoed in the rooms. When they ceased, the cataracts roared evenly, now closer, now further away. The scents of tar, cod-liver-oil and sea shifted with the wind.

The supper table underwent a metamorphosis. Smoked salmon and gulls' eggs appeared and detracted from the clove cheese. Mrs. Selmer's voice echoed with renewed energy through the sitting-rooms: 'Then I took up the paladin's cap all trimmed with gold and brocade . . . The knight he followed after me with a falcon on his arm.'

Alberta wore cotton dresses, and had new hands and a new face. She went along the back streets, to be sure, but it was summer in the back streets too, with grass in the gutters, warm sun on the grey walls, open windows, light-coloured blouses, the buzz of flies.

And she not only went along the back streets. She went across the bog, past Gronli farms, inland to where the mountains began. Bog-cotton and cloudberry blossom swayed in the wind amongst the heather and dwarf birch. The pale scrubberry flowers formed a thick carpet, alternating with delicate bracken and white lichen. Strange bird cries could be heard above the small lakes and deep bog pools that reflected rich, dark peat and sailing clouds.

Alberta lay down in the heather and plunged into dreams and unreality, while she half-mechanically arranged a posy of bell-heather and small, smooth birch twigs. She got up feeling giddy, as if she had been away for a long time. One day she saw blue smoke coiling above the slopes to the west. The Lapps had come to their camp at Big Gap.

In the evening she would lean out of her window, listening to the dip of oars and the music of accordions, her eyes following the eddies of the river until late into the night. For the days were succeeded by unreal, shining nights, when everything was dissolved into the golden light and long, violet shadows, when the fjord lay like a bright, straining silken sail and the current moved like dimples in the deep green surface at Rivermouth. And a light-hearted summer night's mood full of music and laughter lay over the landscape – a mood that lived and died with the airborne blue smoke from many picnic fires along

147

the shore and up the mountainsides. It was young Theodorsen and his crowd, Beda with her beaux, Mrs. Buck and her circle. Cedolf too, who rowed past in his freshly-painted boat, probably going to fetch someone. He stopped rowing with one hand and raised it to his cap. Alberta pretended not to notice.

Sometimes she was still there at the window when the boats came home in the early hours of the morning with gold in their wake and accordions in the prow. She heard the steps of people returning home echoing clearly through the streets. Did she wish she were with them? Yes and no. Perhaps if everything, if she herself, were different.

The air was so warm and mild. Night and morning she would undress completely and see her body once again in the looking-glass. For in the small pieces of mirror at the bathhouse you could see nothing. And something happened from year to year. A little embarrassed and alarmed, a little ashamed and proud, Alberta stood and took in the fact that in spite of her lean, lithe figure she was a child no longer.

Every boat from the south brought new people. They strolled in the streets and walked differently from the people at home, looking secure and self-assured.

There was Augusta Bremer, who was studying medicine, was fabulously clever, and got distinction in all her examinations.

There was Peter Bloch, with whom Alberta had once been in love. Every year she wondered a little whether she would fall in love with him again. But Peter's face was just as odd this year as it had been last, in a straw hat as in a bowler, the features seemingly much too large. There could be no question of falling in love with him any more, and a good thing too.

There was the dentist's son Rasmus, and Peter on the Hill's daughter Matilda, who was something mysterious in Hamburg and who came home every year and horrified the town with her painted face, incredible waist and incredible bosom.

There was the Russian consul from the east, a short, lively, dark gentleman with olive skin. He spoke in broken Norwegian, paid formal visits on officialdom during the day, and at night went out to enjoy himself with Mrs. Buck and her circle.

There were the new organist and important folk from the cathedral city, the Bishop and the Diocesan Governor. One party to entertain the gentlemen succeeded another. Madam Svendsen soon could not stand on her legs. Certain faces were redder than usual from too much festivity. And soon the most singular, the most exciting of all were expected: Rikke and Gertrude Lossius, with a cousin from Kristiania who was to spend the summer at the Governor's residence, and whom the Governor's lady referred to as Frederick.

Mrs. Selmer stood at the window at midday, lifted the curtain and said: 'I thought I might catch sight of Gertrude and Rikke – they're bound to be out at this time.'

And she was quite right, there they were coming down the street, even more marvellous than when they came home last year, in clothes beyond one's wildest dreams – the kind of clothes in which you could become a different person, thought Alberta. That was probably why they walked with more self-assurance than anyone else. Between them was their cousin, a tall, fair person with pince-nez, swinging a cane. He looked up and down the walls of the houses, adjusted his pince-nez, and wore a satirical expression. Alberta saw immediately that he was a person to be afraid of, and that he would make the streets terribly unsafe.

'Put on your jacket and run down to talk to them, Alberta,' said Mrs. Selmer.

But Alberta had already disappeared in the greatest haste, and had locked herself in a certain place. She had suspected Mama would suggest something of the sort. But to go to meet them, to go entirely on her own initiative and address the person in pince-nez – most decidedly no! It was bad enough having to put up with so much else that was unavoidable, without rushing into misfortune.

Rikke Lossius pottered about in a painter's smock, humming. She had acquired a new way of looking at people – with her head on one side and her eyes narrowed. She was also very much changed in appearance, even more so than last year. Painted canvases lay scattered about her room on chairs and tables. The sofa was covered with them. They had a tendency to roll themselves up again, and they depicted women so naked that Alberta had never imagined anyone could look as intensely naked as they did. There was a man in bathing-trunks too.

Alberta sat on a chair in the midst of it all and looked about her with consternation. The same sight met her eyes where-ever she looked: distressing apparitions in a kind of inert, re-signed at-ease position, with their breasts in, their stomachs out, shoulders drooping, and equipped with such strongly emphasized details that she could scarcely believe her own eyes. Instead of feet and hands they had things resembling mit-tens and bathing shoes. The faces were mere blots.

So this is art, she thought in confusion, knowing only that she would defend it, if only in silence, on the principle that whatever scandalized the ladies must surely be of some value. She was sincerely grateful for the man's bathing-trunks. She had not dabbled about in boats all her childhood, not played about on the wharves and in the warehouses, without acquir-ing ugly memories that had stuck to her mind like revolting slime, memories that perhaps she would never shake off. Thank God for the bathing-trunks.

Rikke gestured with her cigarette towards her *oeuvre*: 'I've captured something of the movement in that one,' she said. 'There's something about the colour that's not at all bad. And this arm – when Ola Moklebust saw it, he said anyone could see that I *had* to paint, that I simply couldn't *help* it.'

'Who is Ola Moklebust?'

'My dear, don't you know? He's one of our very best young artists and an absolute pet. We've been spending quite a lot of time together.

'But you see, it's so hopeless up here,' she continued. 'People don't understand a thing. They're just shocked, as if it were pornography, which it certainly isn't, for heaven's sake. But I suppose this summer will pass too. Then I must see if I can get to Paris in the autumn – you know, Mama and Papa find it rather difficult to understand why that should be necessary. All the art school gang are going, and lots of other amusing people besides.'

'And Moklebust?'

'Oh yes, and Ola Moklebust. Yes, I *am* in love with him, there's nothing to be done about *that*. He *is* so delicious, and if I can't go I don't know what I shall do. I'll be absolutely furious with Mama and Papa.

'Yes, I suppose this summer will pass too,' repeated Rikke, as if implying that she had been through so much already, a little more or less would make no difference. She went backwards and forwards, moving canvases to give them a better light, and humming the stanza that she had been humming ever since she came home: 'Never look ba-a-ack to the time that is gone and the summer's withered flowers, but hope that the re-e-eddest roses may bloom once again in next midsummer's bowers. *I* hope they'll bloom in the winter, I'm so insane,' she declared, lighting another cigarette and extinguishing the match with an accustomed little flick of her hand.

From up in Gertrude's room came the sound of practising, scales up and scales down, resolute blows on the piano and valiant little trills. She had the piano up in her room out of consideration for the office. Now and again the practising would glide over into a quiet melody, and then Rikke would sometimes put her head on one side and say: 'Gertrude does play that beautifully, I must say. I heard Careno play it this spring – he wasn't at all impressive.'

The piano fell silent and Gertrude came into the room, good-looking, elegant and superior. She might stop and point at a study: 'That's delicious, Rikke.' Or she might stand at the window, look down into the street, and say: 'Who's that going by, isn't it little Harriet? What if I stole that Dr. Mo of hers, and made a bit of mischief in this town? For we really must find something to do . . .'

One day when she was standing at the window she put her arms akimbo, drew herself up and asked: 'Now who's that handsome lad?'

'He's a sailor – I think he's called Kjeldsen,' answered Alberta, feeling false and villainous.

'My word, he's handsome.' Gertrude yawned. 'If I lived at home I think I'd make a set at *him*.' She yawned once more, and went.

'That's all right as long as she doesn't make a set at Moklebust,' sighed Rikke. 'When Gertrude makes up her mind she's going to make someone fall in love with her, she can be so terribly attractive that I might as well pack up and go. And I'd even be happy if something could make her forget that man of hers. Oh yes, there's a man who wants to divorce his wife because of her, he has children too. It would be a catastrophe for Mama and Papa of course. I'm scared to death in case they see the letters. As if things weren't complicated enough as they are.'

And she confided to Alberta that Gertrude was having a difficult time because of her opinions: 'Of course Papa and Mama are old-fashioned, you know, and Gertrude is terribly modern and so frantically impulsive, she's incapable of compromising and being a little cautious. We're on tenterhooks, Frederick and I. But just imagine, Gertrude has rejected seven proposals already – seven! And I've had none. I think it's about time someone made me a proposal too.'

Gertrude and Rikke were so secure, taking everything for granted, moving through life like fish in their element, certain of being the first, the prettiest, the cleverest. They would not tolerate contradiction – like Mrs. Lossius their voices quickly became a little curt and peremptory; but they were kind and good-natured, generous with gifts and in giving whatever help they could. Perhaps they appreciated Alberta because she was so silent. Like a sieve, she drank it all in and was never satiated.

Sometimes Frederick would come striding across the threshold with his pipe. Most of the time he sat writing. He was a kind of author, this terrible Frederick with the pince-nez.

'Talented stuff, you know,' said Rikke. 'Quite remarkable things. They'll cause an enormous sensation when they come out.'

He would bow to Alberta and, fortunately, pay her no further attention. She was afraid of him, in fact she was a little afraid of all three of them. They lived on a higher plane, they were so superior, knew so much about the outside world, knew it in a different way than Christina and Gudrun, for instance, who had not been born up here either. They were purposeful and knew what they wanted. They subscribed to the luxury of suffering for their opinions.

Frederick and the Governor's daughters confused her, filling her with a new unrest and a longing for knowledge. She had been looking for different books in the bookcase since they arrived.

*   *   *

The cataracts churned evenly in the golden nights. Blue smoke spiralled lightly up above the dwarf birch trees from the many hearths and bonfires on mountainside and shingle, a pleasant smell of burnt twigs floated on the breeze. Boats with gold in their wake and accordions in the prow, oars at rest, rocked with the current all night long; the sound of voices and creaking rowlocks was carried right across from the other side of the fjord in the stillness.

The whole world was obsessed by the incessant light. Even the powers-that-be and the Church were to be found in the small hours, lying propped up on their elbows somewhere in the heather beside a dying fire, their eyes turned towards the unswerving sun.

No one could equal Mrs. Pram in her ability to take charge of a picnic. She was the one to decide who should be invited, who remembered that Miss Liberg and the Weyers were to bring the coffee kettle and a tablecloth. And she brought the most delicious sandwiches and even waffles as well. She was famous for her powers of organization. But when her health was drunk, she would point proudly at her daughters: 'I have such splendid helpers.' And Gudrun would raise her glass to thank everyone: 'The ones with egg and anchovy are my handiwork.'

Nevertheless the atmosphere among the ladies was not quite as it should be this year, and the reason was the Governor's family. Take Rikke, for instance. She went round with a sketch book all the time, except when she had her painting equipment with her. She would sit to one side on a stone, narrowing her eyes and holding her pencil out in front of her at arm's length, and would be occupied thus for hours. Between themselves the ladies considered that there was too much of it, and that it was poor manners. 'My dear, she surely has time to talk to the rest of us a *little*,' they would murmur, and agree that

153

such behaviour went too far. They discussed her art in whispers: 'Have you seen it? Yes, isn't it fearful? Quite indecent if you ask me. – But it's supposed to be Art,' they concluded as if repudiating all responsibility.

Then there was that fellow Frederick. He was polite and handsome enough, in all conscience, but he was not a congenial young man. The ladies agreed that he looked critical, and that it would be just as pleasant if he were not included. He had the embarrassing habit of not laughing at young Klykken's stories. Young Klykken was really quite amusing, after all. If Frederick laughed, he did so some time afterwards, seemingly on his own account. But then he was probably so much more amusing himself.

Mrs. Lossius was fractious, and as usual took it out a little on the others. Her voice would turn cold and discouraging, so that whoever she was talking to felt almost incriminated. Their agreement was tinged with self-defence. It was an honour, but not an entirely agreeable one, to be numbered amongst her intimates, as she sat in the heather, tapping her lorgnette nervously against her left hand, repeatedly returning to the same subject: 'You see, last year Rikke drew from plastercasts. That was interesting. They were really beautiful things, it was a pleasure to frame them and hang them on the wall; figures from the Parthenon frieze for instance. But these *frightful* nudes.' Mrs. Lossius had to be honest, she did not *understand* why it should be necessary to create ugliness when one's aim was beauty. She herself used to draw and paint in her young days, so she ought to understand a *little*, but she supposed it was true that she understood nothing. She pursed her lips together tightly.

Where Gertrude was concerned, she was such a good pianist, so thoroughly musical, that it was a pleasure to listen to her. But in other respects she had by no means profited by the winter. Mrs. Lossius had observed many sorts of influence. It was not altogether easy when one's daughters were *too* gifted, it really wasn't. Mrs. Lossius nodded in the direction of Harriet, who, well brought up and virtuous, was busy with the coffee kettle. 'You can be glad, Mrs. Pram, that your daughters are not gifted in any particular direction.'

Harriet was appreciated as never before, by her mother and by everyone else. A sweet girl, they would echo after her, wherever she passed. Now and again a discreet conjecture was aired: 'I suppose we shall be hearing some news soon?'

For Dr. Mo was equally helpful on every occasion with branches for the fire. He assured everybody who would lend him an ear, that he thought a fire out of doors was so exceptionally pleasant.

Alberta would lie on her elbow in the heather, listening now to one group, now to another. She selected her place round the cloth with care, preferably a little behind Mrs. Selmer so as not to offend her gaze unnecessarily, taking care to turn to the assembled company the profile in which her squint was least noticeable. Gertrude and Rikke would sometimes pay attention to her and make her sit with them. Then she would listen to their easy, self-assured chatter about art, music, people and conditions in Kristiania with an agonizing mixture of bitterness, excited interest, and anxiety in case they addressed her directly. Frederick also played. Gertrude and he would hum together and nod in rhythm. They used expressions seldom heard in conversation in the town; quoted authors who appeared to be turning the rest of the world upside down, while everybody went about their business up here quite unsuspecting; reminded each other of discussions in the Students' Union; broached subjects that were only mentioned in a whisper with embarrassed sidelong glances here at home. Gertrude talked about everything in the same easy, rounded tone of voice that seemed to touch on the subject from above; her eyes would look far beyond the present topic of discussions. But she was often curt and spoke a little too loudly; her voice would become high-pitched and she would stir her cup of coffee nervously. Sometimes she did not even reply, but would suddenly hum loudly and fall into a state of anxiety. Then Frederick would look at her craftily with a sidelong glance and call her his dearest coz, as he lay tapping his cane against his leg. Rikke would become uneasy and murmur, 'Frederick!' When it was over all three made fun of everything in complete understanding and in an especially knowing way; when, for example, the Archdeacon's wife, full of goodwill, her eyes crystal-clear, went round pouring out rhubarb wine, and Frederick murmured behind her back: 'And behold, she is without sin.'

At times something would erupt in Alberta, an unaccustomed feeling of solidarity with the town's permanent inhabitants. Here one lived outside the world and acted accordingly. What business was it of these travellers from Kristiania? Just because some people had crawled up to a position where they could get a better view, they didn't have to . . . Then the hunger gripped her again, hunger to reach the view-point and see for herself.

One morning she was going home from a picnic with Mama through the silent, sunlit streets of Upper Town, where smoke was already coiling upwards from a few chimneys. They were without masculine protection. Papa and the Chief Clerk were on circuit again.

They met Kjeldsen the smith's cow on its way to pasture. It had a reputation for butting and wore protectors on its horns. Mrs. Selmer retreated hastily into a doorway, while Alberta, as a representative of the younger generation, better equipped for struggle, nervously attempted to change the animal's course. Meanwhile Cedolf appeared. He arrived on the scene looking rested and brown, puffing at his pipe and whistling. 'Don't you be afraid,' he called obligingly. 'I'll hold her, please to come by. Is that your Mama over there?'

Cedolf seized the cow by the horns, leaping and tumbling with it, as resilient as a toreador, and lost his cap. Perhaps he leaped and turned a little more than was strictly necessary, perhaps he panted a little too hard, when they escaped past and he still stood holding the dangerous creature. But he was their rescuer and had the right to be treated accordingly.

'Thank you,' said Mrs. Selmer coldly, 'Thank you, Kjeldsen,' walking on fast. Alberta accompanied her, her face crimson.

'How annoying to have to thank that fellow Cedolf for anything,' commented Mrs. Selmer. 'But goodness knows what would have happened if he hadn't turned up. Cows are such fearful creatures.'

Alberta thought more than she wished about Cedolf's smiling, warm face beneath the untidy dark lock of hair. It remained in her brain as if photographed there. More than usual, she felt as if it had been imposed upon her, a violation and an outrage.

It was the day of the picnic to Big Gap, the event of the summer. The elderly took carrioles or traps as far as was possible, and the provisions were transported on horseback over the last part of the way, across the plateau.

They had pitched camp in the middle of the Gap on the slope towards the sea. Everything was bathed in golden light and violet shadow. A reddish, fairy-tale sun hung low over the horizon, and the sea resembled an immense, brimming bowl of molten metal with a glowing sword plunged into it. A row of porpoises moved along the shoreline, leaving the sea swirling in their wake. Coalfish leapt, gulls circled, birds twittered in the heather, there was a pleasant smell of smoke from the dying fire. Like an enormous respiration the breakers rolled in towards the stones along the shore.

Alberta supported herself on her elbow a little behind Mrs. Selmer and Mrs. Pram, who were discussing the Bucks. The blue smoke rising from behind some large boulders further down was said to belong to Mrs. Buck and the Russian consul. He was on his way through town again. Some other ladies were supposed to be with them. On the other hand Beda was here. What might that mean?

A little further off Harriet was taking advantage of the chance absence of Dr. Mo to explain to Christina how the rumours of his affair with Palmine Flor had come about last winter. Disgraceful slander. Palmine had asked him to accompany her past some drunken Russians who were hanging about in the bend below the Flors' summer cottage, and he had done so, gentleman as he was. 'But you see how people are, vulgar and cheap.'

'Yes, indeed they are,' agreed Christina.

A little puff of wind went through the grass blades among which Alberta was lying. It seemed to waken something in her, to bring the loathing and longing with it. She suddenly got up and walked a little, pretending to pick heather. Then she sat

157

down again a short distance behind Gertrude and Frederick, who were lying a little to one side with their backs to the company, looking out at the sea and talking in subdued voices. Rikke sat near them, sketching. Perhaps they would notice Alberta and ask her over. At intervals, when they raised their voices, she could hear their conversation.

They were again talking about things that were never discussed in the town, except perhaps occasionally by the gentlemen. 'I don't believe in *re*volution, I believe in *e*volution,' said Gertrude, stirring her coffee violently.

'Surely we all believe in *e*volution,' smiled Frederick. 'Each one of us believes we shall evolve splendidly according to his own recipe. I except those thrifty souls who believe in keeping themselves and theirs safe behind the assurance that there is no progress, that humanity is and always will be the same – but the others! Ask Pastor Pio over there, he'll tell you.'

But Gertrude took after Mrs. Lossius, she disliked being contradicted. And she especially disliked her opinions to be the property of everyman, shared by clergymen. She became anxious and hummed.

'Oh, that's enough,' called Rikke, slamming her sketch book shut. '*E*volution and *re*volution. Look round you instead. When something as lovely as colour exists—'

'And Ola Moklebust,' said Frederick.

'Heavens, yes,' cried Rikke. 'I *am* in love with silly old Moklebust, but now I'm forgetting him a bit for the sake of all this.' She flung her arms wide. 'It's exquisite. A little too much Thorolf Holmboe perhaps, but lovely all the same.'

'Wonderful. And you know, Rikke, when the ladies put their heads askew and ask me if it isn't magnificent here, I always reply that it's unique. But I often think how it must look when the storms and the winter darkness set in, and they no longer have this blessed midnight sun as decoration. I'll wager it looks like what it is then – a place of exile.'

'The point is not to be here then.'

'I grant you that. But still I'm sorry for these people. There's something tragic about many of them, something has-been and coagulated. Take their hysterical emphasis of the bright side, there's something embarrassing about it, as if they were trying to hypnotize themselves. These old gentlemen, for instance – it's obvious that the majority of them live on memories and card-playing and alcohol, a little too much alcohol, and it's only human. What have they got besides their toddy? Politics, a little moaning about the lopsided way of the world – oh yes, the Chief Constable is a philatelist, I've heard—

'But any one of us may end up the same way, we who live down south thinking we're going to conquer the world. We may find ourselves sitting up here instead, thickening inside and out. Just imagine, some of them can't afford to apply for positions in the south again on account of the move. Like this Selmer, the Magistrate. I was talking to him the other day and he told me straight out, I can't afford to apply for anything in the south. He hasn't been down there for thirteen years. And then he was in Flekkefjord. Incidentally, he was a fellow student of Uncle Hans in Kristiania. You'd never think so, he looks at least ten years older. He's supposed to have been a very promising jurist once, and what is he now – fat, old before his time, and slightly alcoholic, as far as I can see – it's distressing.'

Alberta's heart had stopped, she was completely tense. Now she could hear every word they said, either because her hearing had become more acute or the breeze carried more to her. She tried to get up and go, but could not even move her head in another direction in order to look interested in something else. She sat there paralysed, like a chicken behind a chalk mark.

'Good Lord, they don't think it's too bad,' said Rikke. 'Many of them have no sooner left than they're homesick.'

'Yes, I suppose they get a sort of exile's mentality in the end, feel like strangers when they return to the world, and that they fit in best in their place of exile. That's what I call coagulation. No, to survive a number of years up here one would have to be either a very simple soul or richly endowed. The average person must find it soul-destroying. The Recorder seems to have his wits about him, by the way, he appreciates art among other things. But possibly he's one of the richly endowed, for all I know. In any case, he was born here in Finnmark.'

'He doesn't understand a thing about modern art, let me tell you. But I think they're rather touching, these old people. They *are* old, after all, and can't help but stay up here.'

'Touching, yes indeed. Good Lord, when they say to me with such happiness in their eyes: We've been brought so close to the world since we got the packet boat, you know, only two and a half days to Trondhjem – I'm touched every time. "Fear God and be content . . ." There's something so incredibly childish and undeveloped about some of them that they give the impression of being crippled and stunted. It can't be natural for young girls to be so desperately awkward and embarrassed as some of these are. This Christina – the Archdeacon's Christina – she squirms like a snake if she has to say yes or no, and Alberta Selmer breaks all records, she doesn't even say as much as that.'

'Yes, they are awkward and strange,' replied Rikke.

Alberta had felt her features harden, felt them knot themselves together into a painful, convulsive quivering. Rough fingers on open wounds . . .

Then it occurred to her that she must not be discovered there. She managed to overcome her paralysis, get to her feet and approach the noisy, laughing group round young Klykken. She went on picking heather, staring down looking for it as if it were of particular importance. Then she sat down a little way behind Mrs. Selmer and pretended to arrange her flowers.

When she looked up again the men were flocking round the flat stone where the bottles were standing. Alberta suddenly crouched as if it might help. It did not. The Magistrate refilled his glass with much whisky and little seltzer – she had seen it happen before, there would be increasingly more whisky and less seltzer in Papa's glass – and skaaled with the Chief Constable, of whom she knew it was said that—

They were both very red in the face and deeply serious.

And the anxiety welled up in Alberta, gripping her coldly and painfully round the heart, making her hands shake. Everything was rolling towards destruction, herself too, and nothing could be done about it. What she herself saw might perhaps not exist, it might only be imagination, an optical illusion. What others saw was given substance, reality – it *was*.

Oh but she had to, she would help, save, guard against it. Notice when Papa was on his way to the sideboard, get him to think about something else, apply herself to it seriously. Pity went through her in a warm wave. Can't afford to move south? Then they must be able to afford it, cut down, save, deny themselves everything, and get away from here, where Papa and all the others were on their way to perdition. She would spread the butter more thinly on her bread, wear Lapp boots in winter to save shoe leather, be the leader and set a good example – encourage and lead.

Then impotence crept over her again. She went on arranging her heather with numb, quivering hands.

Young Klykken was a wit. He always sat with the ladies, entertaining them, and was considered to be indispensable on a picnic. He had just been telling them about the last time he ate nuts, so that you could have died laughing. 'I spent the next few days getting all my teeth filled,' said young Klykken, with a killingly comical expression. My goodness, he can carry it off in style.

But they had finished with the nuts, and the mood was exhausted. Young Klykken had spoiled his audience. He had to be perpetually amusing, it was expected of him, and when he was not in good form the atmosphere round him tended to become a little flat. His wife sometimes came to the rescue and reminded him of one thing or another. Now she leaned forward smiling up in his face with sparkling eyes and flawless teeth: 'Imitate Gronneberg the Chief Clerk, you do that so well,' she said fondly.

A little way off the Clerk had landed himself between Otilie Weyer and Miss Liberg. Otilie was smiling, quiet and embarrassed, faded and lovely, as usual. Miss Liberg was in perpetual motion, continually straightening her pince-nez that had difficulty remaining perched on her agitated face, and leaning forward to look fixedly into the Clerk's eyes, her mouth churning like a mill.

Young Klykken allowed himself to be persuaded. In an undertone he mimicked the Clerk's cautious and elaborate diction, his somewhat over-careful pronunciation and small, self-conscious cough, his habit of pushing back his shirt-sleeves, as if to give his hands something to do. The ladies were helpless with laughter, with the exception of Mrs. Lossius, who was always reserved towards young Klykken, and who merely smiled. Mrs. Selmer also recovered herself quickly, to protest: 'I assure you, he is an exceptionally fine, good-natured young man. We appreciate him highly, and my husband would be lost without him.'

Old Mrs. Weyer, who was vainly trying to follow the conversation, her hand cupped to her ear, persistently nodded encouragement to Otilie across the space between them. Otilie reddened. Mrs. Weyer was equally hopeful every time a man came near her daughter. She seemed to be saying: 'Don't let Miss Liberg put you in the shade, go on, you must talk as well.' But Otilie remained silent. Otilie had withdrawn from the fray once and for all.

Alberta thought a little dully, half mechanically, that from now on she would try to be more friendly towards the Clerk, would try not to look obstinately in another direction to avoid shaking hands with him, try to say a little more than yes and no when he took her in to dinner.

There was Beda throwing herself down in the heather. She seemed restless, preoccupied and fretful. She was not listening to Lett, who followed her and squatted beside her, but looked down all the time to where the blue smoke, now thinner than before and fading, still rose behind the boulders. She nibbled at a stalk of grass.

'Oh, of course you will,' said Lett persuasively, continuing a previous conversation.

'Do be quiet, I've told you, no.' Beda did not seem to be thinking about Lett at all. It looked as if she wanted to shake him off, as if his presence disturbed her. Lett looked insulted, and nibbled a stalk too. Immediately afterwards Beda got to her feet and went over to another group. Lett retired in the opposite direction.

'Tangle in the thread,' remarked Frederick, who had moved nearer, together with Gertrude and Rikke. Rikke turned to Alberta and remarked: 'She is sweet of course, and terribly picturesque – but so hopelessly uncivilized.'

'Beda is certainly not uncivilized,' replied Alberta curtly. She was suddenly filled with enraged bitterness. She had a desire to be rude, to pull a face at Frederick.

She glanced over at him. He was lying looking at Beda, striking at the heather with a twig. His face had the same expression she had often noticed in men's faces when they looked at Beda. They fell silent – and stared – their mouths curled up a little, their nostrils widened, a foot or a hand became restless, and they made a few strokes with a twig or whatever else they might happen to have in their hands. And God knows whether their manner of looking at Beda was complimentary or disparaging.

Then Frederick turned and his eyes met Alberta's. He adjusted his pince-nez as he did so.

Quivering, her expression tense and glazed as if caught doing wrong, Alberta met his gaze for a moment. Her blush engulfed her mercilessly.

On the way home she was walking by herself, looking down into the bog, still collecting heather and unripe cloudberries, when Frederick suddenly appeared at her side. 'Never have I seen anyone so serious,' he said smiling, 'Or so silent. Do you really never say anything at all, Miss Selmer?'

Alberta made no reply. She stood still, as if waiting for some of the others, and turned away, tense and crimson.

'Come and walk with us,' said Frederick. 'Don't keep to yourself. It's not good for you,' he added. He had taken off his pince-nez, and was breathing on the lens and rubbing them. Now he put them on again as if to see her better.

Alberta was silent, bent her head, and contemplated her shoes from every angle. 'Look here,' said Frederick. 'What's the matter? Are you hurt about something?'

Alberta looked up, past him. Her eyes were full of tears and her face was hard and small.

'Very well,' she heard him say, in resignation. He raised his hat and left her. Some time later, when Alberta was pretending to be looking in quite a different direction, he was walking between Gudrun and Mrs. Klykken. They were talking and laughing.

163

Alberta felt a stab. Oh God, to be pretty, to be spontaneous and self-possessed – and wise!

*   *   *

'Good heavens, are they those fearfully superior people from Park Street?' said Rikke, when she heard that Aunt the Colonel and Lydia were about to arrive. 'I know of them from the Association and the Promenade, they're incredibly stiff and starchy.'

And Gertrude exclaimed in her impulsive way: 'Heavens yes, those people who seem so shabby-genteel? Oh, forgive me, Alberta, they may not be in the very least.'

Alberta did not forgive her. She hid the words in her heart and brooded over them.

Aunt the Colonel and cousin Lydia *were* superior.

Even in their best, Mrs. Selmer and Alberta were put wretchedly in the shade beside Aunt's and Lydia's imperturbable correctitude. Alberta miserably smoothed her bristling hair back behind her ears, but it continually came forward again. Her eyes never left Mrs. Selmer's in a frantic attempt to keep up to the mark. Because of Aunt she was wearing the neckband and her chain and felt like a prisoner in irons.

At a little distance Lydia sat with her embroidery, which she would bring out, with a couple of words of excuse, as soon as she sat down. Not a hair was out of place. In fact her hair looked exactly like that of the ladies in the fashion magazines, and a little smile, the same as in the photograph, and which struck Alberta as being strangely wise beyond her years, never left her face. Now and again she would look up and smile more at what was being said, and it seemed as if some mechanism functioned inside her head, so unchanged was her expression in every other respect. She was pale with a completely straight nose and a narrow, oval face, and was considered to be outstandingly beautiful.

Aunt sat upright in the armchair and looked about her with shining eyes: 'I cannot tell you how happy it makes me to see that your home is so attractive and comfortable,' she repeated again and again; and Mrs. Selmer, who had already replied

164

vivaciously and cheerfully a couple of times, laughed somewhat nervously: 'Did you think we lived in a turf hut like
Lapps?'

'No, goodness gracious me,' protested Aunt. 'But it is very
far north, you know, and it's rather difficult for us who live
in the south to imagine that you could live so admirably up
here.'

The sun, pouring in through the open windows, was broken
by prisms, and winked in the glass of the hundreds of photographs. Large vases full of bracken and buttercups, picked by
Alberta for the occasion, stood on the piano and the occasional
tables, giving an effect of luxuriance and richness. Mrs. Selmer's La France had three large roses on it and stood turned
inwards towards the room. The cataracts churned. The day
was warm.

But Mrs. Selmer must nevertheless have felt that Aunt had
emphasized the admirable a little too strongly, for she interrupted her: 'Oh, heavens yes, it might be worse, but it might
be better – the winter is long.' Her voice trembled a little as
she added: 'We don't live here for pleasure.'

She rose and cleared away the books to make room for the
tray Jensine had brought.

The Magistrate, sunburned and animated after his last circuit, asked after his brother Thomas, and Aunt assured him
that he would more than anything have liked to have accompanied them, but his duties – and then the expense, of course,
the confounded expense.

She splayed her hands on the arms of her chair and declared: 'We really couldn't afford this trip. Thomas often has
no idea where the money is to come from, but for Lydia's sake
we felt—'

She looked helplessly about her, although nobody had demanded any reckoning.

Alberta liked neither of them. She became anxious in their
presence, her hands turned clammy. She noticed that they
looked sideways at her when talking of other things, and once
when the Chief Clerk was present, Aunt asked Mrs. Selmer by
means of her eyes and a little toss of the head whether he would
not suit Alberta, whether it might not be conceivable—?

Mrs. Selmer had shaken her head with a brief, sad little smile. Alberta felt their commiseration like a shirt of nettles about her body.

When she and Lydia were alone, Lydia would let her ever-lasting embroidery fall into her lap and talk about herself and the irreproachable young man whose photograph, in cabinet-size, lorded it on her bedside table at Mrs. Korneliussen's private hotel. It had been clear to everyone that the Grand was unthinkable. Alberta could not understand how Lydia could allow the things she said to pass her lips: 'It's difficult being apart you know – almost as difficult as being together and just looking at each other and behaving ourselves. Heaven knows whether we'd have managed it either, if it hadn't been for this trip.'

She sighed, looked at Alberta almost despairingly and allowed her clockwork smile to function. Then she sewed again and said: 'I must finish my trousseau in time, soon I'll have other things to think about.' She leaned forward, touched Alberta's bracelet and assured her: 'I haven't anything as nice as that.' She looked at the red and white table-cloth and said nothing. And she smiled once more and again talked about her fiancé.

Alberta had the feeling that Lydia was thinking: 'You must keep up your spirits, my dear, even though you can never hope to experience anything similar.' She was glad they were not staying longer than between two packet boats, and that they did not intend to come ashore on the return journey south.

In the evenings, when they had been escorted back to their hotel, Mrs. Selmer would lie on the sofa in despair over her daughter. She had kept up her spirits all day, and now her strength failed her. 'It was my hope that Alberta might make a good impression on her Aunt,' she wailed. 'I struggle and strive to do the best for my children, but it is all in vain, in vain, in vain.'

Her voice was lost in a whisper, she sighed: 'Other young girls are happy and gay, they talk and laugh, they don't behave like dumb fish.'

She exploded: 'Look at her, look at her appearance,' drawing the Magistrate's attention to Alberta, pillorying her. He considered her over his spectacles and remarked: 'Unfortunately I have to agree with your mother, Alberta. You do not take sufficient trouble over your appearance.'

Alberta stood in front of them, obstinate and mute as an animal. Only later did she cry in her room.

When Lydia arrived in the morning she had already written to her fiancé and was flourishing a large letter. She had also read some English, and was carrying her embroidery in her hand. She was perfect and a joy to all.

Alberta accompanied her to the Post Office with the letter. Afterwards they strolled in Fjord Street and along the quay. They met various people, and Lydia greeted these unknown persons politely, lady as she was. They met Beda out on an errand for the office, and Beda pulled a face at Alberta and nodded so violently that her hat lurched. Lydia asked: 'Who was that vulgar apparition?'

But later on, when Alberta was waiting for Lydia, who had wanted to go up to her hotel for a moment, Beda passed again. She arrived just as Lydia, trim and *comme-il-faut* with veil, gloves and parasol, was walking across the street. And Beda looked after her with narrowed eyes and said: 'Apple pie.'

What was shabby-genteel? Where did the gentility end and the shabbiness begin, or vice-versa? Were Aunt's words to Lydia, when they were going out walking, shabby-genteel? 'Button up every button on your gloves, Lydia my dear. It makes such a bad impression to do it in the street.' – Was their discussion about how much they ought to give in tips shabby-genteel? Was Lydia shabby-genteel, when she walked the few steps to her hotel and said: 'I feel quite uncomfortable in the street without a veil.' Was Aunt shabby-genteel when she said: 'That's not *comme-il-faut*.' Or when she referred to the family name and smilingly, half jokingly added: '*Noblesse oblige*'?

Are we not all a little shabby-genteel, we who hesitate over a two-*kroner* tip and live in a house we are unable to heat? The thought struck home in Alberta painfully, and she was a qualm the richer.

On the last afternoon but one, she found herself alone with Aunt for a while. And almost at once Aunt broached the subject of Papa. She did so without transition or introduction, as if she had waited for this very moment and was now hastening to avail herself of it. 'Your father had every expectation of making a career for himself, my child,' she said. 'With his origins, his connections, his natural good qualities. But there is one thing he has never understood, Alberta my dear, and that's *money*.' Aunt laid her own particular emphasis on this most important of all words. She added: 'And we've all had to suffer on account of it.

'Yes,' she said in explanation, when Alberta flushed. 'I think I ought to be able to talk to you about it now that you're grown up. Your Uncle Thomas has had to take the risk more than once. It's not more than a couple of years since he had to stand surety again, he and a couple of your father's old friends – and God knows how things are going with that loan, my child, whether it's being paid off properly – for Thomas is so generous that he would never mention such a thing, not even to me. If he has taken responsibility for something, he does so without a murmur.'

'It's being paid off,' replied Alberta furiously. She saw Papa's face on pay-days, a certain expression he had, almost childishly tired and resigned; she saw his broad back in the shiny old coat that he wore when he came in from the office; the twelve cigars she had to run and buy when anyone was coming, because Papa never felt he could afford a whole box. – She felt a little faint.

'You mustn't get excited about it, child,' said Aunt. 'There's no reason for that. I'm talking to you as the grown-up, sensible daughter of the house. You are of an age when you can do a great deal, my dear Alberta, to see that your home gets on its feet again economically. The time has come when, with tact and circumspection, you can put in a word about thrift when necessary.'

'We are thrifty,' answered Alberta curtly.

Aunt ignored the interruption. 'We were all so glad,' she continued, 'not least for the sake of you children, when we persuaded your father to apply for a post up north. Your parents cut quite a dash, you see. Your mother was sweet and charming – a little insignificant, but sweet – it was only natural for your father to be proud of her and to want her to look beautiful. They sent to Paris for one thing after the other – and when one has no independent means ... Then your father started to speculate, my dear, but he's no businessman, and that turned out as one might have expected.' Aunt suddenly struck the table. 'It was like a sieve in the end, my child, a whole lot of holes for the money to run through. Your father has never bothered to learn from life – your mother—'

Alberta's brain reeled. Mama's face over the account book, her miserable little figure in the shawl; the smoked salmon which, after long discussion, it was decided should be bought so that there should be a little in the house when Aunt and Lydia arrived; it all whirled in her head. In imagination she saw the persons who had once opposed Papa, secure, admirable persons with their own affairs in order, condemning him to apply for a post up here, beyond the world, beyond everything. As if in the foreground she saw Aunt's dress with its thousands of stitches.

And the blood streamed to her brain as it had at Christmas time. She was beside herself, wanting to say something, but only able to find one word. It stood out in her consciousness in letters of flame, blotting out everything else: shabby-genteel. She heard her voice hurling it three times at Aunt: 'Shabby-genteel, shabby-genteel, shabby-genteel!'

She covered her face with her hands and left the room sobbing. Behind her she heard Aunt's exclamation: 'Great God and Father of us all!'

On the last afternoon the Magistrate sent for Ola Paradise and the pony carriage to drive the ladies inland across the bog. In the hall, while everyone was preparing for the drive, Aunt seized the opportunity to make her comment: 'Can my brother-in-law really afford this? It's so pleasant here at home – this is quite unnecessary, you know.'

During the drive she several times suggested turning back. 'We've had such a lovely drive now, we ought to be satisfied, it seems to me.'

It was obvious to them all that Aunt wanted to bring the price down. But Ola Paradise had orders to drive past the Gronli farms. He drove and drove, his broad back adamant up on the driver's seat. He did not even look round to reply, merely spitting a notable distance as he spoke: 'Don't you fuss, I'll turn when it's time to turn, I have my orders.' To the general consternation he even drove a little further than had been agreed, and who could tell what he might mean by that? Aunt sat with one foot on the carriage step, ready to throw herself out if things should go too far. She remarked repeatedly: 'This is pure lunacy. Heaven only knows how much my brother-in-law will have to fork out for this little amusement.'

On the back seat beside Lydia sat Alberta, full of contrition. Every time Aunt opened her mouth she was afraid she would refer to yesterday's episode. But Aunt did not mention it and clearly had not mentioned it either, except possibly to Lydia. Did it not seem as if the two of them were sharing something special? As long as they told no tales to Mrs. Selmer, it did not matter.

From time to time Alberta met Mama's tense look and noticed the slight quivering and twitching round her tightly-pinched mouth. Each time it seemed as if yesterday's outburst was not so dangerous after all, but that it had been, on the contrary, justified and necessary, and that it was a good thing she had said it.

On the way home Alberta sat facing Big Gap. There she saw the mist. It lay like a thick, solid coil at the bottom of the gap. A few isolated, airy tufts, amounting to scarcely anything, had come loose and were drifting alongside the mountain. The mist from the sea.

Tonight the coil would swell. In the morning it would be everywhere. Then it would not be so admirable here any more. But by that time Aunt and Lydia would be rocking on the swell off the North Cape.

When the packet boat's pennant of smoke had disappeared westwards out on the fjord that evening, Mrs. Selmer said, still standing looking after it: 'We couldn't have been more fortunate with the weather, but isn't the air a little strange this evening? Do you think there'll be a change?'

'It's the sea-mist,' answered Alberta. Aunt's hurried words, spoken in the moment when they were alone together in the hall, lay like a hard knot in her consciousness. 'I thought you had grown up, my dear Alberta. I see to my great disappointment that such is not the case.'

Fateful words, that were what they seemed – a death warrant.

*   *   *

Raw cold and sleet blew in from the northwest for the third week in succession. The landscape looked soured by too much moisture. The horsetail had ousted everything else in the meadows, the hay hung brown and depressing on the drying fences. The mist enclosed everything like grey felt. People in the know talked about drift-ice in the sea.

At the Governor's they had lighted the stoves, so effeminate and sensual were they. They were lighted elsewhere too, perhaps, but it was at Rikke's that Alberta shared such excessive luxury.

At home Mrs. Selmer went from window to window, moving flower pots and sighing. She sighed over Jacob and over life in general, but over Alberta in particular. At suitable intervals she would glance resignedly at this perverse child, whose face was again blue, muddy and insecure. It came with the cold and could not be concealed. Even her squint seemed to worsen.

To be invited to Rikke's for tea was, in spite of Frederick, in spite of many things, a relief. Of two evils . . .

In Rikke's room the tea table stood in front of the open door of the stove, a tea table with silver, porcelain, golden marmalade. The glow of the fire reached far out over the floor, playing on everything and finding an answering reflection in Rikke's red silk dress, which was lying slung across an armchair. A slight scent of her eau de verveine and of good cigarettes hung in the air. From Frederick's room could be heard the notes of a violin, a couple of bars over and over again.

A weakness crept over Alberta, a drowsiness that permeated

her whole body. She felt paralysed by the warmth, by everything.

She did not become outspoken here as she did at the Bucks'. Nowhere as here did she have such a discouraging sensation of being poor. Not only did Rikke and Gertrude inhabit regions which she had no hope of attaining, regions containing the tree of knowledge and much else besides; they moved therein with such obvious nonchalance, with such inevitability and superiority, that it almost seemed as if she had been invited over to see how clever and practised they were. It had been the same when she was invited, as a child, to play with Rikke's doll's house. Mrs. Lossius helped Rikke a great deal with the doll's house; it gradually became a miracle of studied perfection. Rikke handled the things as if she had known them all her life. Alberta never learned to pick them up, but mostly stood watching, numb, an outsider.

She sat, awkward in speech and gesture, warming her ice-cold hands, while Rikke came and went, seeing to the tea and chattering: 'Heavens, what weather! There's no colour any more, and if you stand outside you freeze to death. I shall have to give up the picture of the Kamke quay. Once the Arctic mist comes in it puts paid to everything. Moklebust and all the others are painting with all their might and main down in the Setesdal valley, having a wonderful time, and of course they'll have heaps of things ready for the Autumn Exhibition, while I—' Rikke gestured with her hands to imply that she was destitute. 'And yesterday that Signora Ryan came to ask whether I taught painting on velvet! What do you think of that? On velvet! They ought to have heard that at the art school. Well, well, it'll be nice to have a cup of tea at any rate.'

She disappeared. Alberta thawed out, settled herself more comfortably in her chair, and attempted to enjoy the interlude as much as she could. Warmth was warmth. And as long as Frederick kept on playing—

At once the violin ceased with a discordant stroke across the strings. She could hear his footsteps crossing the floor, and there stood Frederick in the doorway. Alberta's heart jumped.

But Frederick was so wrapped up in the music that he continued humming from where the violin had left off, smilingly

172

beating time with an outstretched index finger, and peering at her over his pince-nez. Then he sat down, his legs straddled and his elbows on his knees, rubbed his hands together and remarked: 'It's cold, but playing the violin warms you up, it's the only thing that warms you properly. If only it were not so confoundedly difficult.'

He snapped his fingers and bent them backwards and forwards. Alberta sat on the extreme edge of her chair, as if it might help. 'Is that so?' she answered stupidly.

Frederick considered her meditatively above his spectacles. Since the picnic at Big Gap she had noticed him taking a curious interest in her. She had felt his eyes on her, always with the same searching look as if he were trying to find the answer to something. Tense and ill-at-ease, half insulted, she had studiously avoided him, acted deaf and blind when he looked as if he might approach her, found one excuse after another to get away. They had conversed very little.

Now it looked as if Frederick was prepared to·ignore all this and pretend he had not noticed it. Alberta's obstinacy rose.

'Listen,' he said. 'I've asked you this before – do you really never say anything of your own accord?'

'Oh, now and again,' replied Alberta evasively and even more stupidly, feeling quite idiotic. One stupidity presumably gave rise to another.

'Well, that can't be often, so help me.' Frederick laughed and Alberta could not help laughing too, although she hastened to control herself. Frederick took off his pince-nez, breathed on the lenses and polished them, while continuing to regard her with his short-sighted, persistent stare.

'You laughed at any rate,' he said. 'It suited you.'

Alberta flushed crimson.

'Tell me, what do you do in the winter?'

'Oh—'

'In the summer you all seem to exist for the scenery. If one gets into trouble for saying this place is far north, the midnight sun is unanimously invoked. But when that's gone—'

'The light can be beautiful in winter too.'

'Well, all right, that may be possible.' Frederick's voice was impatient, he looked somewhat astounded. 'But you're not going to tell me you can live solely on the light and the memory of a few sun-filled nights and – let us say – tea and a little local gossip and a little handiwork?

'That's not my impression,' he said, more to himself, looking into the fire.

Alberta did not reply. This Frederick had a supreme ability for putting his finger where it hurt most. What right had he to sit here prodding her nerves to the quick? In distress she reacted as those in distress will – with irritation.

Frederick was still looking into the fire. 'All due respect to those who set the tone up here,' he said, 'but what have you got besides the most banal social life?'

The blood mounted to Alberta's head again, and as usual she said the wrong thing and said it coldly and provocatively, with a provocative toss of the head: 'We have cards and toddy.'

'I beg your pardon?'

'Oh, nothing.'

Frederick suddenly slammed shut the book he was holding, threw it on to the table, got up and paced the floor, his fingers in the armholes of his waistcoat. He stopped once and smoothed back his hair.

But Alberta sat there wretchedly. God knows who put the words into her mouth. They were not her own. They were foreign to her, stupid words behind which she hid herself. Her own never saw the light of day, they died unborn or withered on her tongue and were born distorted. She was disabled, she was without the use of speech, she would die of muteness.

Frederick halted in front of her: 'You're not happy,' he said quietly, as if concluding a train of thought.

Alberta's face was suddenly wet with tears. She turned away from the fire to hide them. But Frederick took one of her hands, held it in his and patted it: 'What a great ass I am,' he said in altered voice. Then he released her hand and paced the floor again. The door opened. Rikke and Gertrude arrived in procession bearing tea and toast. A cheerful conversation about the latest news from Kristiania flowed over Alberta's head.

The cold and rain continued. Rikke was forced to move her

easel indoors for good and bring home her half finished work from the Kamke quay. It hung slackly, billowing on its frame. She took up Alberta seriously, fetching her daily and in person: 'You *must* come. You're the only person one can talk to here, you and Beda Buck, but you know *she's* too much for Mama. We scarcely see anything of Frederick; he sits up in the attic writing, when he's not playing or out walking with those teachers of his. My goodness yes, he's taken up with them now. They trudge for miles across the bog in the wet, he and these dried-up schoolmasters. Gertrude practises and writes to that man of hers. I'm left to pine on my own – thank goodness I've got you.'

She made Alberta sit in a comfortable chair, and nestled into another with her legs under her and a pile of reproductions in her lap, holding them out at arm's length, explaining and discoursing about them, knocking the ash from her cigarette and narrowing her eyes.

And Alberta curled up, tried to give herself over to the warmth and the well-being, thawed out a little, feared and hoped that Frederick would appear. She seemed almost to be getting accustomed to being there.

The art she had read about in old, yellowed books, of the period of the worst wood-cuts, was given substance; pictures that had been only printed titles, a few letters, suddenly became a small world of reality. She had seen some of them at the Recorder's house the few times she had been there, but had never dared to go close to them, inspect them and ask questions. Now their secrets were revealed, and at times she forgot herself and her anxieties.

Rembrandt's Polish rider, for instance, what was he riding from, what was he riding to? The four edges of the picture seemed to enclose the wide world itself. He rode through it, released from all that had been, moving untrammelled towards all that might be. An aura of freedom and loneliness surrounded him, making one hot and cold, making the heart beat faster. Alberta put the picture down and then took it up again. 'It's incredibly beautiful,' she said. 'You can have it if you like,' answered Rikke generously.

She brought out Dutch interiors, and Alberta was

encompassed by their neat, cosy comfort as by pleasant warmth. Stillness, a glint of sunlight, practically no people, the perfect place to be—

But Rikke was expatiating about composition, values and perspective, and the pictures fell apart. It was the same when the Archdeacon's Henrik pulled a flower to pieces and added up stamens, germen, petals and calyx – a scented whole disintegrated into nothing. Confused, Alberta looked from what she had in her lap to Rikke's studies on the walls, meditated on the fact that both were supposed to be art, and became even more confused. She listened absent-mindedly to Rikke who, heaven knows how, had started to talk about Moklebust: *'He's* talented, you see, and sweet and naïve. *He's* impulsive. When he meets a pretty girl in the street, he kisses her. He *has* to, he says.'

Rikke raised her eyebrows and stared in front of her with large, dreamy eyes, as if she sank and disappeared in such mysterious depths. But she hauled herself up again and declared encouragingly: 'Well, well, Alberta, your turn will come.'

She narrowed her eyes at Alberta and exclaimed: 'Of *course* you're picturesque. If only you had a little colour. But what Frederick says is true, it comes from inside and only momentarily. He says that when you learn to use that cast in your eye, and make yourself a bit more approachable – you *are* stiff, Alberta. Good Lord, is that something to blush for so dreadfully? I think he's right and you're nervous.'

Frederick's footsteps could be heard in the attic. He was pacing the floor up there. Alberta sat on the edge of her chair, prepared for flight. If he were to come in and sit down she would move even further forward, as she listened anxiously to his and Rikke's chat. Sometimes the atmosphere in the Governor's house was charged on account of Gertrude's opinions. She and Mrs. Lossius each sat behind closed doors, each with her tightly pinched mouth and her irreconcilable opinion of, say, marriage and divorce. Then Frederick would come into Rikke on tip-toe, stretch himself and say: 'Ugh, one daren't breathe here.' And turn to Alberta: 'I must find comfort in your fount of oratory, Miss Selmer.'

He remained sitting with his elbows on his knees, rubbing his pince-nez: 'There really are some lively people in this town, you know, Rikke. I've managed to discover them. Living, un-coagulated tissue in various layers, small colonies of cells – one at the top round Headmaster Bremer, one further down round Hannestad the schoolmaster. People who are not living on what they brought here with them, or on inherited notions, but on new ideas, with their eyes turned outwards towards the present. They keep up with the times, they keep up to an amazing extent. And then there's the Recorder, Jaeger. He's a unicellular organism, he lives alone – That's significant, by the way – the people up here who subscribe to anything beyond the Family Magazine shut themselves in with it.'

'Ugh,' said Rikke. 'These schoolmasters, is there really any-thing more to them besides worn clothes and shortage of money, hurry and scurry and spectacles?'

'Their clothes may be worn and they are short of money, but they don't wear lorgnettes, Rikke.'

'Now that's naughty, you should be ashamed of yourself!'

'Good Lord, but we both agree that it's an apparatus for the hindrance of the sight, more or less.'

'My goodness, yes,' laughed Rikke, without prejudice.

Frederick turned to Alberta again. 'If you persist in this flow of chatter something will happen to your tongue.'

Alberta laughed self-consciously. Her feelings were strangely erratic. This critic from Kristiania, at one moment she felt hostility and bitterness towards him, the next, unexpected con-fidence.

'Seriously, you must overcome this. You must learn to talk, to express your opinions.'

'I have none, I'm stupid.'

'Then say stupid things,' exclaimed Frederick. 'Say them, for heaven's sake, or your words of wisdom will never get a chance to see the light of day, supposing there are any coming to maturity deep down inside you. It's dangerous to keep silent like this.' He leaned forward and looked into her eyes.

At home that evening Alberta put the looking-glass on the window-sill to get a better light. She looked for what was supposed to come from inside her. But she only discovered a small, indistinct face with a squint.

The face became bluer the longer she sat.

*　　　*　　　*

The mist lifted as if a curtain were drawn back. But behind the curtain autumn had been waiting. Now it was present in everything. In the air that was far too clear, the mountains that were far too blue, in the permanent, flat patches of mist that encircled them. It sat red in the rowan tree above the shoemaker's roof, and yellow, brittle and frozen in the dwarf birches on the hill; in the darkening evening and the flaming early evening clouds, in the moon that had reappeared and was turning more and more yellow.

It was also autumn in that everyone was leaving. That stage had arrived, this year as last year. They all left at once, by the same boat. One was forced to accompany them on board, to be left standing on the quay, to see lights and lanterns disappear – to go home again.

It was a quiet, light evening. The moon had made its first serious appearance. It hung warm, round and unnaturally large above the mountains, reminiscent of decorations and autumn festivals. Like an enormous gold ducat its reflection floated and bobbed in the waves at Rivermouth.

The packet boat had all its lights on and looked more European and magnificent than on any other night of the year. On board all was bustle and animation. People bumped into one another in the corridors, no one could find his cabin. The boat was full of people from the further east, and reservations had been made in advance from places further south. Mrs. Lossius was nervous: 'I told you so, children. If Papa had listened to me and spoken to the Captain when he was on his way east, you would have had a cabin to yourselves amidships. Now you'll have to put up with the ladies' saloon at the very best, and I think it's appalling that you should have to sleep in there with the rag tag and bob-tail. But nobody listens to me.'

She urged them to wait until the next boat, called after Frederick and the Governor, who ran from the Captain to the Mate and from the Mate to the Captain: 'It's no use, my dears.

I've spoken to the stewardess, she says it's hopeless.'

'If only someone could make Mama keep quiet,' sighed Rikke. 'I'm *not* going ashore, now this everlasting summer is finally over. Have you ever seen anything so irrelevantly lovely as that moon?'

But in spite of everything Gertrude and Rikke were given a cabin, the Captain's own. Mrs. Lossius thanked him personally, and Frederick mopped perspiration from his brow: 'Heaven help us, what a fuss. Yes, I've found room in the chart-house. Yes thank you, Aunt, it'll be very comfortable.'

The Archdeacon's Henrik and the Pram twins were going south for the first time. The Archdeacon's wife and Mrs. Pram tripped round in a tremendous state. There was nothing to sending one's daughters away; it was much worse with boys, they felt.

And there was young Theodorsen, who was also leaving. He was with a large crowd: Signora Ryan, Karla Schmitt, the fair girl from Holst's, Cedolf, and others. Augusta Bremer was there looking neat and tidy, with everything in order.

Harriet Pram stood with her family group, smiling happily, giving the twins little sisterly pats on the back, and sighing: 'Dear me, you are lucky to be going away.' It was clear to everyone that she really thought she was better off where she was.

The ship's bell rang for the second time, there was sudden crowding and confusion. Hands were shaken, quick kisses exchanged, many small cries crossed in the air. Alberta, following in Mrs. Selmer's wake, fought against a painful feeling of unreality. It was all so bitter that it surely could not be true. It must be a lie, a stupid mistake, that nothing should have happened, that this year as last year, as in all the years past and to come, as far as the human eye could see, she was to be amongst those not going away. An insane notion that something beyond the bounds of reason and possibility might still happen, stirred in her. She smiled mechanically, shook hands, mumbled short phrases of farewell and was shoved hither and thither.

Now everyone was crowding towards the gangway. Gertrude kissed her on the cheek once more, Rikke twice. And there was Frederick. There he stood in front of her, a summer's *bête noir*, someone who put his finger roughly on sore places, someone whom she had gone by back streets to avoid. Now it seemed as if he, more than anyone else, was leaving her behind alone.

She must hide it, she must hide it at all costs.

'Thank you for a pleasant summer,' said Frederick. 'Goodbye. Until we meet again,' he added, and smiled.

But Alberta looked up with the hard, locked little face she could sometimes present, and answered stiffly and coldly: 'Thank you. Pleasant journey.'

Frederick looked somewhat dismayed. He stood for a moment as if expecting her to say something more. Then he released her hand and took that of the Archdeacon's wife, which was held at the ready, extended into the air.

Alberta's heart sank as if with irretrievable loss.

At the last moment Bergan the lawyer arrived, with the intention of going on board to take his leave when all the others had finished. He swayed heavily on the gangway. The ladies on the quay became nervous and slightly irritated, but a fantastic possibility occurred to Alberta: the ship would not leave with Bergan on board. But there he was on land again. And there went the gangway. The ship glided away from the quay, the propeller churned, the water foamed and swirled about the stern. The packet boat was off.

Now it was rocking out at Rivermouth, festive and magical with all its lights shining, a dark silhouette islanded in moonlight, a pleasure boat on Lake Maggiore. It seemed to hesitate a moment, lying quite still before setting course westwards for good. People were waving. Three cheers came concisely and vigorously across the water and were answered by a group of which Cedolf seemed to be the leader. 'Youth,' smiled the Archdeacon's wife. 'Youth.' She looked out across Rivermouth with her crystal-clear eyes full of moonlight. And she put her hand into the Archdeacon's and declared cheerfully: 'Our boys are in the Lord's keeping.' But Mrs. Pram had to be supported by Harriet.

For a moment they all stood silent. The departure of this autumn ship gave rise to many different thoughts. Something came out of hiding in the most hardened.

The Magistrate broke the ice. He pounded with his stick: 'Well, off they go once more. The summer's over. We must hole ourselves up for the winter again – and try to make the best of it,' he added in English, which he sometimes spoke in moments of stress. He looked inquiringly across at Mrs. Selmer, who of course took it tragically, with distant expression and bitter mouth. The moonlight inconsiderately revealed two big tears on her cheeks.

'Hm,' muttered the Magistrate, looking away again. But now the steamer was only a dark patch far out. People were beginning to go home. He pounded again authoritatively and encouragingly, and officialdom marched off in small, conversing groups, with the exception of the Bremer family, who took their leave pleasantly and went their own way. Mrs. Selmer watched them go: 'Just fancy, Mrs. Bremer is supposed to be fearfully clever. She's interested in the rights of women and all sorts of things. With only one maid and all those children I think it's marvellous.'

'Some people are so indescribably capable,' replied Mrs. Lossius icily. She was not in favour of extremes in any direction, and the Bremer family were slightly *too* capable, slightly too good for this world. It sounded like a reprimand: 'I must say I think it's difficult enough to cultivate one's interests with *two* maids. Oh dear, I do hope my little girls will keep warm on deck.'

Dr. Pram reminded them that it was less than two and a half months until the dark period began, and less than four until Christmas. The Archdeacon replied: 'Yes, indeed. Time passes.' Mrs. Pram remarked: 'Soon we shall have to take our winter clothes out again, and we put them away only yesterday.'

Antipathy towards them all erupted in Alberta. She felt utterly paralysed by numbing, inner cold. And suddenly she saw the supper table, illuminated by the hanging lamp, far off in a great darkness; supper tables in an endless row, with their atmosphere of depression, and grey gruel. She shuddered with horror, simulated a headache, and obtained permission from Mrs. Selmer to go for a walk in the moonlight.

In spite of its chill the evening had something of southern

luxuriance about it. It must have been due to the large, warm moon. It was troubling, unseemly, ironic.

Already Rivermouth was a little sinister. Boats were arriving daily with their catch from the Arctic, and the men roared out of them after long hardship and asceticism, to rollick in and out of the taverns, stand loitering on corners with dreadful girls, and shout after the passers-by. Another evening Alberta would scarcely have dared come here. But now she was in flight and noticed nothing. And she was possessed by a fixed, idiotic idea: to go the same way as the steamer.

She had come to Louisa-round-the-bend. The street lay long and gloomy before her, completely deserted. A single soul was visible, a person in skirts, far off. She looked like a working-class woman, an unknown person of no consequence, who in any case was going in the same direction as Alberta, with her back to her.

So she let the tears come, abandoning herself to her anguish and distress. She seemed to see herself from the outside this evening, a failure, ugly, ignorant, full of aversion for everything life had earmarked for her, full of impossible, hopeless, vague longings. They stifled her, they were more than she could bear. She did not go so far as to scream out loud, but she pressed her clenched fist against her mouth to avoid doing so.

Finally she sat on a boulder on the shingle and sobbed openly without hiding her face. It did her good. The tumult within her seemed to melt down and subside. Inertness followed in its place, a great, thoughtless exhaustion. She sat looking out over the water without thinking.

The water rose and flowed round the boulders. When she kept quite still she could hear a swarming in it, a tiny teeming sound of activity and labour. It was full of secrecy, of a mysterious, hidden will to conquer by stealth. The moon had rolled up high in the sky and become small and yellow.

And her mind was rocked into complete peace and became like the sea, without a ripple. All that was painful and trouble-some sank down, and something scattered collected itself and floated to the surface instead. Small stanzas followed one after the other in disorder, without beginning or end.

Then they stopped. No more came. Alberta sat for a while

fumbling and found nothing. But they would come. She would listen her way to them, find a beginning and an end. The poem would be about what it was like to long in desperation and in vain.

Hope was born in her anew. Perhaps something wonderful and impossible might happen one day after all. It was not quite so unthinkable as it had been a short while ago. She made a resolve. She would go back to school, persuade Papa, become knowledgeable and free in spite of everything, become something.

Suddenly someone was standing behind her. She looked round terrified. The woman on the road had been Jeanette Evensen. And although Jeanette had never done harm to a cat, Alberta froze with fear. She had been taken by surprise, and Jeanette's grey, expressionless face with the untidy hair looked so strangely petrified under the moon.

She was queer. Some said a little crazy. Everyone knew it was because she was not married. She always looked unkempt and dishevelled, and dressed below her station in life in old, ugly clothes. But sometimes she would wear a rose in her hat or pinned to her breast.

She was in the habit of lying in bed and getting up late in the afternoon. She did nothing and was no mean burden for old Mrs. Evensen, who was a widow and had a small shop selling sewing things, knitting wool and other oddments. Mrs. Evensen's windows never looked like other people's in the summer; scarcely had a La France blossomed before Jeanette had taken it. She even took the buds.

She could sometimes be seen from the shop, sitting erect on a chair with her hands in her lap in the inner room. Mrs. Evensen would open her heart to the customers sighing deeply.

Now Jeanette was standing there on the shingle, just as if she wanted to remind Alberta of her existence and of how things could turn out, for she said nothing, only stared tensely out across the water. A fresh stab of fear passed through Alberta. She got to her feet and edged away. They said people like that were worse at full moon.

But Jeanette said peaceably: 'I thought I'd go out on the rocks to look for shells, but the tide's coming in.'

183

'Yes.'

'I needed those shells so badly.'

'Oh yes?'

Alberta remembered now that Jeanette was in the habit of embarking on sudden, useless enterprises that she never carried out. She obviously had some plan.

'I didn't even bother to get dressed before I left. I thought I'd come out as quickly as I could.' She smoothed down her skirt, and her hair with her hand and smiled dazedly.

'Oh, never mind.'

Alberta was no longer afraid, but ill-at-ease and uncertain. She had never spoken much to Jeanette and all she wanted to do was to get away. But Jeanette said: 'I'd really appreciate your company. I was quite relieved when I saw you sitting there on that stone, so many bad folk as there are in Rivermouth.'

So they began to walk the long way back to town. Jeanette chatted incessantly, mostly about how she never achieved anything: 'I never sleep, let me tell you, and then you never get anything done, you can't even get up. Just imagine, Mama *chivvies* me out of bed. Would you believe a mother could be so hard-hearted?' She halted and looked anxiously at Alberta.

Alberta answered yes and no more or less as she should. She soon discovered that it was as well to take care to reply correctly, for when Jeanette was displeased with her answer she would stop once more and go into the matter in detail. Exhaustion crept over Alberta. The courage and faith she had found a little while ago seemed to have been blown away. The lines of verse were probably of no value, a poor mimicry of something or other, a bit of jingle she had learned by repetitious reading. It was probably only a delusion that she had been liberated by them. And now they were gliding away from her. She seemed unable to remember them.

Everything was dead, joyless, sickening, without hope.

PART THREE

No ONE saw anything of Beda Buck any more. It was odd. Alberta had been up to ask after her twice, but the doorbell must have been out of order, for she could not hear it, and nobody answered. In Fjord Street, which was re-established as the main traffic artery in the evenings, now that autumn was approaching, Lett, the editors and the chemists promenaded without Beda. It was being talked about.

She did not go home at her usual time any more either. You could still catch sight of a dark knot of hair and a few ungovernable curls now and again above the Civil Service Calendar that lay on the window-sill of the Recorder's office, but not all the time as before. And Beda never looked out of the window, caught sight of you and grimaced or shook her fist. Alberta missed her. There was something worrying about it.

One day, when Alberta was wandering across the bog, she met Beda and the Recorder. They were walking slowly, and stopped from time to time. The Recorder was speaking quietly and urgently, and looked serious. Beda looked down as she walked, with a strangely stony expression. When she raised her head and greeted Alberta her expression was foreign to her, miserable, with something diminished and completely preoccupied about it. Alberta had never seen her so careless in her appearance before; her skirt was shorter than ever in front.

'Goodness,' thought Alberta. 'Beda is being reprimanded by the Recorder.' The thought had something oppressive and heart-sickening about it, as if some evil and inexorable fate was suddenly threatening everything and everyone, not just Beda.

That afternoon Alberta rang the Bucks' doorbell again. Still it did not ring, and she tried the handle. The door opened. She heard voices and went into the hall. The door into the living-room was ajar. Inside voices were raised in sudden, violent exchange.

'You are so utterly unreasonable, Beda. You really are impossible.'

'I'm not asking you for anything. Just let me paddle my own canoe. I shan't be the first.'

That was Beda's voice. New and strange, and yet Beda's. So full of bitter, cutting defiance.

'Dear child, you must let us use our heads a *little*.' Mrs. Buck's voice was no longer shrill and upbraiding. It was deep, and trembled with the suppressed tenderness that rounded and filled it, in contrast to her dry, sensible words.

A third person spoke in support of Mrs. Buck: 'Yes, indeed.' The person sighed.

Alberta was about to leave when Beda appeared in the doorway. 'Oh, it's you, Alberta. I thought I heard someone. No, don't go my poor dear, I'm glad you came.'

'Oh dear, I forgot to lock the front door after me,' said the third person in an undertone from inside the room.

Beda took Alberta and led her into the living-room, where she made her sit down on the couch. 'My poor Alberta, I ought to have been as good at Norwegian composition as you were, then I could have gone abroad and become a writer. Or I ought to have been a boy, then I could have gone to sea. I wouldn't have stayed a day longer in this filthy town.'

Beda's face was flaming with irritation. She kicked at a small footstool so furiously that it shot across the floor.

Mrs. Buck was sitting by the window. Her eyes were red and she looked dishevelled. Mrs. Lebesby, Dyers and Cleaners, sat up high on the piano stool, her travelling coat buttoned, her hat on her head, and a very solemn expression on her face.

Alberta did not know what to make of it. They were all behaving so strangely. There must be something the matter with Beda's job at the Recorder's. It couldn't be anything else.

'If only I had seventy-five *kroner* to get myself to Kristiania.'

'Dearest Beda.'

'If only I had them. You wouldn't need to bother about me any more.'

'Seventy-five *kroner* – oh Beda, you wouldn't get far on seventy-five *kroner*.'

'I'd get far enough,' answered Beda bitterly. She moved towards the door.

'Where are you going, child?'

'To put the kettle on. I suppose we may as well offer them something, since they've come to see us. Since when have we been so mean in this house that we don't offer so much as a cup of tea? Please take off your hat.'

Beda disappeared.

'Good Lord, how could she say I was mean,' sighed Mrs. Buck. She raised her hands from her lap in a helpless gesture and let them fall again, as if to say: 'Am I to sit here and be blamed for that too?'

And she took out a damp, tight little ball of a handkerchief and pressed it to her eyes. A sob escaped her. Mrs. Lebesby's face assumed the fervent expression of sympathy that the situation demanded. 'There, there, Ulla,' she said soothingly.

But Mrs. Buck continued to dab at her eyes with the wet little ball, remarking jerkily: 'Oh Alberta, my dear – life is nothing but sorrow and deception – the world is vile, thoroughly vile—

'And what a fool I am,' she exclaimed suddenly. 'So innocent and so foolish – oh Alberta—'

Alberta prepared to ask a circumspect question. But Mrs. Buck was talking again. 'My little girl, my poor little girl,' she sighed, and suddenly her voice became stronger. 'I'm telling you, Alberta, never trust a man, for they're the vilest of them all – except Victor Buck of course. Oh, if only my darling husband were alive—'

She sat looking at the enlargement above the piano with wet, exhausted eyes.

So Alberta knew that it also had to do with a betrayal on the part of Lett, the dentist. For it must be Lett. She tried to imagine what the situation might be, but asked no questions. Those who truly sympathized were evidently supposed to understand such things automatically.

Besides, Mrs. Buck went on to say: 'You'll hear all about it in time, Alberta, my dear, you'll hear all about it in time.' She sighed, or rather groaned, and disappeared into the kitchen too.

187

Alberta's eyes met those of Mrs. Lebesby. But Mrs. Lebesby closed hers and shook her head resignedly. Her mouth was tragic and fateful. Clearly words were inadequate.

As Alberta passed through the kitchen on arriving home, Jensine, who was standing stirring the porridge for supper, remarked: 'Things are only so-so at the Bucks', I understand.'

'What do you mean, so-so? Besides, I haven't been there.'

'Oh, my poor Alberta, you needn't bother. I was at Theodorsen's getting the bread, and I saw you on the Bucks' steps as clearly as I see you now.'

Alberta was caught out. She did not want to discuss Beda with Jensine, but it had been stupid to lie. Jensine was triumphant. 'Oh yes,' she said with a little laugh, stirring resolutely. 'Soon it won't be any use denying either the one thing or the other. They say that fellow Lett denies everything.'

'How do you mean, everything? That he's going to marry Beda?'

'That too. Oh no, fine folk aren't any better than other people, I've learnt that much in this town,' declared Jensine, who came from the outer islands.

'If what they're saying is true,' she added, 'I'm sorry for Beda. But then she's a flighty one, they all say as much.'

Alberta left the room. She was reluctant to talk about Beda with Jensine, who was partial to riddles besides. There was something disquieting about the whole matter. Alberta dared not admit it, but she began to have her suspicions. She forced them back.

It must not be true!

*　　*　　*

'What is it, my child,' asked Papa, looking up from his work with tired, red-rimmed eyes. 'I'm particularly busy today. What is it?'

'I can wait until later.' At the moment Alberta had no objection to a postponement.

'No, no. Out with it.' The Magistrate let it be known that he was listening, although his pen continued to wander across the paper.

Alberta swallowed. She had sought this interview herself, muddled herself into it entirely of her own accord. For a moment she thought how easy it would be to muddle out of it again, to ask for a couple of *kroner* for something and allow heaven and earth to remain undisturbed. Then she blurted it out: 'May I go back to school again, Papa? Will you allow me to enter *gymnasium*?'

Papa dipped his pen in the ink without looking up. His tone implied honest regret that the suggestion had been made when he said: 'Go back to school again! What sort of an idea is that?'

'I'd like to learn more.'

'Hm. Yes, that's very laudable of course. But after all, you do read, my child, you do have the opportunity to read. And I see with satisfaction that you often choose books from which you can learn something, you don't just read all these preposterous trashy novels that are being written nowadays. I appreciate that. I may not have remarked on it, but it has pleased me. If there is anything you are especially interested in, I could perhaps provide you with more recent books, through the Recorder, for instance. He has an amazingly wide selection, by Jove. Unfortunately I'm quite unable to afford such things myself, much as I would like to.'

'But Papa—'

'All the same, you are not to study, my child. As you know, I have always thought it a lot of nonsense, this matriculation business. After all, there are so many other things for a young lady to do – domestic accomplishments—'

Oh those words! Alberta had heard them before. They had condemned her to dusting and idleness three years ago. If Mrs. Selmer had been present, Papa would most likely have turned to her, as he did then, and said: 'Find Alberta some employment in the house.'

Her completely innocent and unsuspecting Papa had handed her over, lock, stock and barrel, to Mama. Alberta had been disarmed and silenced by a helpless: 'I simply can't manage it,' that had seemed to escape him involuntarily after what had gone before. So she had begun to stay at home.

Now her eyes hung on Papa's lips. Would he say the same

thing again today? For then the matter would be closed. But he did say it, tired and worried: 'I simply can't manage it, my child. It would be too much for me. I have a number of obligations to meet, as you know.'

Alberta knew. It was the bank loan.

The battle was lost for the time being. What argument could be used in the face of Papa's 'I simply can't manage it?' To claim one's rights, to demand anything from such an utterly exhausted and harassed Papa, who could do that? Not Alberta.

But she had not mobilized all her courage, not summoned up her strength over the past two weeks, for nothing. Those who are not bold by nature can be rash, once they have unleashed themselves. Alberta had something in reserve. It would be an exaggeration to say that she directly attempted to exert pressure, but at any rate she came out with it. As considerately as possible she announced: 'In that case, I'll look for a post, Papa.'

'I beg your pardon?' said the Magistrate.

'I'll try to get a post as a governess. I must tell you, Papa, I can't bear simply hanging about here at home.'

Alberta was in deep waters. She had said what for years she had dared only to think. She had to shut her eyes for a moment.

But the Magistrate had put down his pen. 'I've never heard anything to equal it,' he said, in his consternation moving the paper-weight and everything underneath it from one side of his desk to the other. 'You can't bear hanging about in your own home, my child?'

He rose, went to the window, and stood for a moment looking out. His hand jingled in perplexity with the bunch of keys in his trouser pocket.

'Good heavens, is it so difficult for you youngsters,' he said in a different tone of voice. 'You, who have life in front of you,' he added more quietly.

Alberta winced. Out of pity for Papa. Out of irritation. It struck her that the words he had spoken on the Old Quay many years ago, that little encouraging 'back we go', of which she had annexed her share and on which she had based her hopes, had been spoken solely to himself, not to her at all.

'When you're not pretty, you have to try to be something else – a bit clever—'

Now the water was over her head, rushing in her ears. It was not she who had said those last words in a bitter voice, it was someone else.

But Papa had espied land again. He turned, sat down, and crossed one leg hopefully over the other: 'Pretty? Good Lord, my child, if only you'd take a little trouble over your appearance, you'd look really attractive. I must admit your mother is right when she says—'

'I want to travel, Papa, and besides, it would be a good thing if I could earn something on my own. After all, it's almost a necessity.'

'A necessity! Necessity!' The Magistrate tasted the word, and repeated it once more. 'It depends what you mean by necessity. I consider I do what I can to provide you with everything you need, Alberta. I do as much as I possibly can.'

But the last argument had had some sort of effect at any rate, for he changed his mind and declared: 'Well, well, if you really want to I shan't oppose it. I am not in favour of young ladies taking paid positions. It wasn't done in my day, but nowadays everything has been turned upside down. As I said, if you needs must, and if you can find something decent—'

'Though I doubt whether that will be so easy,' he added in a brighter tone of voice.

'The trader on Røst* has advertised for a governess.'

'On Røst! But – I've never heard of such a thing! You have no idea what it would be like, child. Røst!'

Alberta nearly let slip something reckless to the effect that nothing could be worse than here. But she stopped herself in time.

'It's further south,' she said.

'Yes, yes, I suppose so, but—'

'Now then, that's enough. By Jove, I have work to do, my child.' Papa made a gesture towards the desk, obviously considering the subject closed, as long as it concerned the island of Røst.

*Røst: the most remote of the South-West Lofoten Islands, north of the Arctic Circle.

'I'll apply for the post then, Papa.'

Magistrate Selmer looked at his daughter despairingly. Then he said: 'Speak to your mother, then we'll see.'

And he bent over his papers.

Alberta paused in front of the sitting-room door until her heart began to beat more slowly, and her breathing became normal.

Had she hoped for support from Papa, for direct co-operation on his part? Had she simply hoped that, with the island of Røst in prospect, he would have admitted the necessity of sending her back to school again?

In any case she had not envisaged having to confront her mother immediately. Now she stood there, collared by circumstance, trying to screw up her courage. She opened the door, crossed the floor—

'Mama,' she began.

Mrs. Selmer looked up surprised from the stitches she was counting. A direct approach from Alberta was not part of the normal routine.

'Yes, what is it?'

'There's a post I'd like to apply for, Mama.'

The needle with the stitches on it sank down into Mrs. Selmer's lap with the rest of her knitting. 'What did you say?'

'If I can't go to school any more, then I'd prefer to try to find myself a post.'

'I'd prefer to try to find myself a post!' Mrs. Selmer repeated such unprecedented words with incredulity. 'What sort of an idea is this, may I ask?' she said icily.

'I want something to do, I want to earn my own living, not just hang about here.'

'I cannot tell you how astonished I am, my dear Alberta, at the tone you adopt. Just hang about here! As if I did not do my utmost to find you employment. As if it were not your primary duty to help your mother. But of course, it's more amusing to sit hunched up over those useless books of yours.'

Mrs. Selmer was fully armed by now. Surprise had momentarily paralysed her, but that had passed. 'God knows how ashamed I often am when I hear how domestic and practical the other young girls are. They apply themselves, they help, they relieve their mothers of their burdens, while our young miss—'

'Mama—'

'Yes, I'm taking full advantage of the opportunity to broach the subject. You are a great grief to your mother, Alberta. Not satisfied with applying yourself to looking like a common girl – I said a common girl, there is no other expression for it – but you—'

'Mama—'

'May I ask whether you have spoken to your father about this?'

'I said I wanted to apply for a post.'

'Did you? And what did he say to that?'

'He said I should speak to you. He said he had no objection.'

'Did he? In other words you went there to get his approval first.'

'Mama—'

'May I ask what sort of a post you have in mind? Perhaps the whole thing is cut and dried, without my knowing anything about it. It wouldn't surprise me.'

'I haven't applied for it yet, but the trader on Røst has advertised for a governess.'

'On Røst!' Mrs. Selmer looked dazedly at Alberta. Then she leaned her head against the back of her chair and shut her eyes. 'Røst!' she breathed. Her strength had clearly abandoned her.

It was incredible, but Alberta really had sent off her application. After innumerable drafts the document was ready. Now it was on its way to those wild, strange people, the household of the trader on Røst, who required a young lady, with school-leaving certificate, willing to help with a little office work, music not necessary.

She went round in a fever. What had she embarked upon? If she had not had time to think the matter over properly beforehand, she did so all the more thoroughly now. It oppressed her like a nightmare day and night.

She saw herself sitting at a school table with children round her, children who had to be taught something, and kept respectful. She saw her squint, saw the children making faces at each other, saw bills that did not add up, office books in confusion, ink blots, erasures. The sickening giddiness that followed her misdeeds gripped her.

The situation at home was unbearable. Alberta sought refuge in the bog, which lay bright and luxuriant with colour in the thin, clear autumn air. She ran between the tussocks for a while, lay down in the heather, absent-mindedly ate the over-ripe crowberries, and collected heather and birch twigs into a bouquet. And her anxiety subsided. A hot wave of boldness came over her. Why not, why not she just as much as anyone else?

Pictures of life on this island in the middle of the sea presented themselves to her imagination. Naked cliffs, screaming, circling sea birds, long rollers, were what she glimpsed. And a house. Not sheltered by trees, not enclosed by a garden. A house all by itself. A few waving grasses in a crevice in the rock. People – of few words and reserved, as she had seen them at the trading posts deep in the fjords, with kind, slightly wondering faces.

Then suddenly she saw shoemaker Schoning's rowan tree swaying, green and luxuriant, with thick blue shadows beneath it, like a plume above the shoemaker's roof – the fullness of summer; the lush flora of the roadsides, reeking of warmth; round, yellow, nodding buttercups. The magnificence of the bog's autumnal carpet, spread out at this moment before her eyes, impressed her as never before. Her heart dwindled with loss. But it expanded again. The infinity above and around her out there on the island in the ocean beat against her, a breath from space, from simplicity and boundlessness. Immediately she longed to be there, to have the untrammelled, open horizon round her, to be a speck at the centre of its immense circle, to be receptive and to listen. New verses, new dreams awaited her there.

She would send money home every month—

Then Jacob's face appeared. She heard him say: 'Mama and Papa – they have such a rotten time . . .'

She rose abruptly to her feet and hurried back. The currents from home had reached her.

Mrs. Selmer lay on the sofa. She lay there as never before, crushed, all her strength gone. She dragged herself in to meals, her look was distant, her mouth bitter. Now and again a solitary tear would trickle down her cheek.

The Magistrate periodically muttered to himself, his eyes testing the terrain. Then he would turn to Alberta and embark on a conversation of no consequence in an unnaturally lively tone of voice. The island of Røst was not mentioned. The atmosphere was deathly oppressive.

This went on for a week. By that time Alberta was almost ready for anything, capitulation, an oath devoting herself to the domestic virtues. Then the Magistrate unexpectedly came out of his office with the reply in his hand. Somehow Larsen had stolen a march on her. 'I took the liberty of opening it,' said Papa. 'Here you are, my child, read it yourself.'

Quivering, Alberta ran through the short missive and handed it in silence to Mrs. Selmer. Mrs. Selmer read it. Then she sat upright on the sofa. 'Heaven has heard my prayers,' she murmured.

Papa patted Alberta on the head: 'I'm sure it was for the best, my child, for you and for all of us. Your chance will come in one way or another, you can be sure of that.'

The position on Røst was already filled.

Was Alberta disappointed or relieved?

She was empty. After a week brimful of hope and fear, she had nothing to hope or to fear for. She went about feeling embarrassed, less certain than ever of how she should occupy herself.

Beda was still not to be seen. And now everyone was silent about her. A mysterious, ominous silence one did not dare to break or to puncture with questions. Alberta often went past the Recorder's office, but nothing happened, and she wandered aimlessly.

In shabby Strand Street the sun still shone between the grey walls. It seemed as if all the old, unpainted wood down there had stored the warmth and was giving it back, now that the air had turned cold and autumnal. Here grass grew in the gutters. Framed by all the grey it looked greener than ordinary grass. Behind the small window panes fuchsia and calceolaria glowed. A lapful of summer had hidden away down here and been left behind.

No-one walked there. And the Kjeldsens, who once lived there, had moved to Upper Town long ago. When Alberta was small, they had lived in the little corner house, that was so old that the inside walls were of timber. She had gone inside once, and still remembered the timbered walls that were painted blue and on which nothing hung straight. The pictures and the clock hung stiffly outwards at an angle from the nails on which they were suspended. She remembered a chest of drawers with two china dogs on it, a sofa covered with imitation leather, a shut-in smell. And Kjeldsen the smith, who sat drinking coffee out of a saucer, with a completely black face.

The sight of this innocent house was suddenly disagreeable to her. Was it not in some strange manner in league with everything that was trying to hold her back, with everything that was treacherous and oppressive – Nurse Jullum and other dark powers? She imagined how it would feel to be tied, to live for ever between a chest of drawers and an imitation leather sofa with two china dogs and the old Kjeldsens. A stupid thought, which nevertheless caused Alberta to quicken her pace, as if fleeing from it.

She turned down on to the old Stoppenbrink quay that once, long ago, before Consul Stoppenbrink built the two big new wharves, had been busy and full of traffic. Alberta used to play here sometimes as a child. Here she and Beda had once stolen a big piece of candied sugar from an open sack, kept it for two contrite days, and then crept down again and left it on an empty barrel, for in the meantime the sack had disappeared. The Archdeaconery boat used to be tied up here, and there had been much coming and going of wharf hands and country folk.

Now the quay was abandoned and desolate, all its doors shut. Alberta's footsteps rang empty and hollow as she went through the dim, roofed-in passageway. The sun was hot on the little bench right at the end by the landing stairs. It was warm and quiet. She could look right across Rivermouth, where there were no autumn colours, only boats and water and sun-warmed wood. Not a soul was in sight besides an old man in a boat a little way out. He stood scratching the back of his neck. Alberta sat down and sank into vacancy. Beneath her the sea busied itself, lapping round the posts with gentle little gurgles. The tide was coming in.

She started. There were footsteps on the quay. Someone was coming, a black shadow in the darkness under the wharf. Alberta looked involuntarily for the old man who had been scratching his neck, but he had disappeared. Oh well, it was probably someone coming to hail the boat. But something about the footsteps made her uneasy.

The figure came out into the sunshine. It was Cedolf.

She was petrified. She had no desire to meet Cedolf down here alone. He would talk to her—

She looked about her, down into the water, out after the boat, trembling and paralysed. Then she arrived at a desperate decision, broke the spell and began to hurry up the quay, towards Cedolf and past him, crimson, staring straight in front of her, as if he did not exist. He stopped, lifted his cap, she sensed that he was saying: 'Excuse me—'

She hurried on as if blind and deaf. Her heart pounded. It pounded wildly. For Cedolf was coming after her, coming with long strides. She began to run, knowing as she did so that this was one of the most stupid things she had ever done.

The old Stoppenbrink quay was long. Today it was endless. If only she were out of the shadow and in the steep little square between crooked houses that led up to the street.

Suddenly she stopped. For flight was useless. Cedolf towered in front of her in the dimness, unnaturally tall. She looked in all directions to avoid meeting his eyes. Eventually she could do so no longer. They both stood for a little, looking at each other, still out of breath from running. And now Alberta's fright melted away. Outraged dignity had the upper hand. Even the anxiety in Cedolf's hands, which alternately clenched and unclenched themselves, left her unaffected. Just let him try—

'Will you be so kind as to let me pass,' she said from the superiority of her position as Alberta Selmer.

Cedolf did not reply. He stood his ground. 'What did you want to run away for?' he asked, his voice quivering and outraged.

Alberta was silent. She walked round him, saying nothing. But there was Cedolf in front of her again, and this time he openly barred her way. He was highly insulted and held her to blame: 'What did you want to run for, I'm only asking. What have I done to you? When you set eyes on me, you might be seeing the devil himself,' he said, emphasizing 'devil', as if to make sure of conjuring up that unsympathetic character.

Was Alberta afraid again? She replied curtly, but more meekly: 'I didn't see who it was.'

'Oh, so that's it, you didn't see who it was?' Cedolf's voice was full of scorn. 'No, you never see. All you see is that it's not one of your grand folk, so he must be a dangerous scoundrel.'

'I told you, I didn't see who it was, Kjeldsen.'

'Grand folks' little girls,' said Cedolf ambiguously and without answering, apparently to himself. 'What do you think we want of you?' he said, suddenly including vague masses of humanity in the question. 'What do you ruddy well think we want? Do you think we'd bother to run after you only to—'

Alberta interrupted him. Outraged dignity was again uppermost: 'You seem to be running after me.'

'Yes! I found myself put to that necessity,' said Cedolf with emphasis. He stood swaying from the knees, very much in the right. 'I have something to give you from Jacob. He wrote particularly that it was to be delivered to you personally, and that no one should see. But that was the worst part. I've gone round with it on me for more than a fortnight, but no sooner had I caught sight of you than you disappeared again. I'm leaving soon too. Today I was sitting up with Klem the carpenter's family, and saw you going down here, but if I'd known I was going to frighten you out of your wits I'd have stayed where I was, and sent it back to Jacob – well, here you are, take it, now it's off my hands.'

Cedolf had taken a blue envelope with Jacob's handwriting

on it out of his inside pocket and handed it to Alberta. He took a deep breath, as if relieved of a heavy load.

Alberta might well feel a fool. 'Thank you,' she said meekly. 'Thank you very much, Kjeldsen' – She felt she ought to say a bit more and fastened on Jacob: 'You've just had a letter then?'

The situation was thoroughly embarrassing and beyond saving. And Cedolf was not quite himself any more, not just cheeky and self-assured. He had become more human, a big, injured boy. She wished she could put things right again.

'I told you, it was a fortnight ago,' answered Cedolf, a little absent-mindedly. 'Jacob's all right, they were lying in Bahia for coal. He's pleased with life. He's been lucky, has Jacob,' he continued conversationally, and suddenly seemed to have decided to take up the subject in all its ramifications.

But Alberta, who felt that this was bringing them closer together than she wished, asked no more. Besides, Cedolf was Jacob's evil genius. She prepared to take her leave coldly and politely.

As if Cedolf saw what she was thinking, he said: 'But you think me capable of anything. You thought I led Jacob astray.'

'You got him to go to Rivermouth and the Grand,' answered Alberta curtly. The whole thing must be brought to an end. She had not the slightest desire to discuss these matters with Cedolf any further. But right was right.

'To Rivermouth! And the Grand!' The same helpless expression she had once seen on Jacob's face came to Cedolf's for an instant. 'But where can we go? Can you tell me where we can go in this town?

'Besides, it might have been Cedolf Kjeldsen who held him back, when others wanted to offer Jacob drinks. That can happen too. He was inexperienced, was Jacob.'

Alberta started a little. Could it have happened that way? What did it matter, it wasn't seemly, this conversation with Cedolf on a quay. She brought the subject back to the letter, waving it a little. 'Thank you very much then, Kjeldsen. It was kind of you to come after me with it. I'll write and tell Jacob I've had it.'

Right through it all she had felt Cedolf's compelling power.

It was not simply that he was tall and handsome, he was almost *too* handsome, it was too much of a good thing. Rather it was something in the voice, a dark timbre it took on now and again. Or – God knows what it was. Perhaps it was only Alberta's own miserable nature.

A little reluctantly she extended her hand. She could hardly avoid it. She would go now, irrevocably: 'I wish you a good journey—'

But Cedolf held on to her hand: 'Yes, I'll soon be tossing on the briny again.'

'Yes, you will. Pleasant trip. And many thanks.' Alberta withdrew her hand.

'I expect I'll be leaving on the next boat for Hamburg.' Cedolf seemed to have something on his mind. He was uneasy, uneasy in his arms and his hands.

'I want you to believe that I've never wished you any harm,' he said suddenly.

'Of course I've never believed you have,' answered Alberta, her voice at once failing her. It was the dark timbre in Cedolf's—

'Jacob's told me what a fine girl you are. There aren't many like you.'

'Good-bye then, Kjeldsen, pleasant journey—'

'But it doesn't matter to Miss Selmer what Cedolf Kjeldsen says, I suppose.'

'I must go now, good-bye.'

And Alberta really did. If only she were out of the dimness here under the wharf, out in the light on the slope up to Strand Street. If only she were well away from here.

But Cedolf still had something on his mind: 'Fare you well.'

Alberta stopped. God knows why. She was somehow unable to go on. She was seized by inertness.

Then it happened.

As if guided by fate, by something inevitable, Cedolf moved nearer. And she was paralysed by it. All she saw were the beautiful, deep-set eyes, that came closer and closer, with something stiff and tense about them. Her hand was not free any more.

Then Cedolf's face was there, his mouth was on hers. 'I don't wish you any harm,' she heard him murmur, and in his voice was the same warm magic as in the spring, when he had said: 'Don't you be afraid.'

She sank back helplessly against the wall, and let Cedolf kiss her.

But when he tried to put his arm between her and the wall and draw her to him, she came to her senses, slipped out of his grasp, tore her hand out of his, and ran.

'Whatever is it?' exclaimed Jensine, as Alberta rushed through the kitchen.

'Nothing!'

Up in her room she tore off her hat, stood for a moment looking into her eyes in the mirror, blushed crimson, hid her face, and went and washed it and her hands.

She sat at the window. Her heart would not stop beating. It pounded as it did when she had run up the hills without stopping, as if it would knock her down. She sat staring out at nothing, feeling her eyes unnaturally large in her face. She went over to look at herself in the mirror again. A stranger was there. A new and unknown Alberta.

There was so much grown-ups and old people neither knew nor suspected. They went about so innocently, busy with this and that, thinking that was all there was to it. They knew nothing of what was insidious and dangerous, of what was coiling and twisting beyond all reason in hidden places.

Beyond all reason. For she would not, could not, live with imitation leather sofas and china dogs. She would die of it.

She hid her face again, aware of her own degradation.

'If only I'd gone to Røst,' she whispered, and repeated it mechanically several times with her thoughts elsewhere. 'Beda,' she whispered.

Then she remembered the letter, lying crumpled on the wash-stand. She had gone through town, through the kitchen, with it in her hand, quite openly, this secret document, a confidential missive from Jacob. Heaven knew what it might contain.

She tore open the envelope with trembling hands. In it lay two ten-*kroner* notes and a little piece of paper: 'Dear Alberta,

201

buy yourself something nice with this. Something you want and like. More later. I'm fine. Yours, Jacob.'

Alberta sat twisting and turning the little piece of paper. Then something was released in her heart, and she wept copiously over everything at once: the island of Røst, Beda, herself, our complex and erratic nature, and Jacob. Over life in general.

Alberta did not go out for two days. She found all kinds of excuses to keep to her room, and displayed an unusual amount of interest in the red and white tablecloth besides. Sometimes in this life one needs a refuge, a fortification to which to retire. Then one turns to whatever is available.

Now and again she glanced surreptitiously, searchingly and enquiringly at Mama. But when she surprised Mama looking back at her, surreptitiously, searchingly and enquiringly, Alberta disappeared from the sitting-room for good. Upstairs she sat for hours at a time inspecting herself in the mirror.

On the third day Jensine, who had come from the baker's, remarked: 'I heard Mrs. Kjeldsen saying to Mrs. Theodorsen that that fellow Cedolf went south today on the Hamburg boat.'

That afternoon Alberta hurried out along Rivermouth, restless from sitting indoors and from a suppressed need to be alone with life's problems under the open sky.

At Louisa-round-the-bend she almost ran full tilt into Mrs. Selmer and the Magistrate, walking peacefully down one of the cross-streets from Upper Town.

'Heaven preserve us, child, how you run. What's the matter?'

'Nothing,' answered Alberta, her heart sinking. In that respect she was unchanged.

'Well, I must go home, but you young things ought to take a walk in this fine weather,' said Mrs. Selmer, throwing them together. She looked preoccupied as she did so, as if thinking about something completely different, but she had a glint in her eye as if she was secretly a little amused, and Alberta noticed it.

'I'm going home too,' she said sulkily. Then she caught the Magistrate's eyes, full of unhappy astonishment. She remembered her intention to be kind. Besides, she already felt a little faint on account of her bad conscience.

'Well – yes, all right – I'd like to.'

And they wandered out of town along Rivermouth together.

*   *   *

Sounds travelled so strangely at Rivermouth and on the river during the autumn evenings. It was as if the thick darkness, black as velvet, carried them. Voices, the stroke of an oar and the creaking of rowlocks came clear and distinct across the water, as at no other time.

Gudrun, Christina and Alberta lowered their voices involuntarily and spoke softly, as they sat one evening at about ten o'clock in the Archdeacon's skiff, scarcely able to distinguish one another. Alberta and Gudrun were each carefully resting an oar; Christina was on her knees in the prow, on the look-out for posts and moorings lurking in the darkness. They were between the wharves in the old harbour and had happily avoided bumping into rowing boats and sailboats and the Russian ship, which was taking on fish from Badendück. Now they had to find their way to the Archdeacon's mooring innermost on the Kamke quay, which was an awkward manoeuvre, and walk along the pitch dark wharf among barrels and crates, the worst part of all. If only Beda had been with them. She was so brave.

Crash! They bumped into something big and black, that towered above them. Alberta fell backwards across the thwart and got her behind wet: 'You might have gone back for the scoop, Christina,' she whispered in annoyance. 'It was mean of you. What did we bump into?'

'It must be Badendück's steps, you're rowing too fast.'

'Nonsense, it's you who's not looking out.'

'Oh yes I am,' answered Christina angrily. 'I wish I'd left you behind on the other side – I wish I'd never taken you with me at all.'

'You needn't bother to take us with you another time, then you can sit all by yourself on the other side, poor thing. Who got the boat free again, you I suppose?'

They quarrelled volubly under their breath, and it did them good. The eeriness seemed kept at a distance. It lurked ready to pounce in here between the great wharves, about which so many tales were told.

For a couple of hours they had fought against the current swirling out of Rivermouth on the ebb tide. The cold fright that had crept over them when, laden with frozen cranberries, they had come down to the shore below the mountain and discovered the boat lying far up the shelving beach among the boulders, was still with them. The lengthy business of getting it down again, the tension as they rowed and rowed while nothing changed its position on land, while darkness fell and the lights were lit over in the town, still quivered in their remarks.

The Kamke quay was particularly sinister. Old Kamke's father was supposed to haunt it. None of them would admit they were thinking about him, but all three were doing so.

'As long as you know about it, Christina, we can leave the oars and everything in the boat until tomorrow. It'll make such a din if we take them all up, we might wake someone. Who knows what sort of people may be hanging about behind all the barrels further down the quay.'

'We *must* take them with us. I *daren't* go home without them,' whimpered Christina. 'And you'll be good enough to wait and help me,' she bullied. She was sitting for'ard, was responsible for everything, it made her fractious. It was well known that the Archdeaconry family was unreasonably pernickety about the boat. They would even unhook the rudder and take it home.

'I hope we don't meet Kwasnikow,' said Alberta in order to blunt her own fear. 'I'm thinking mostly of him.'

In her imagination she saw Mama waiting to write *finis* to the escapade, sitting upright with blank expression on a chair in the dining-room, the attitude Mrs. Selmer always adopted on occasions such as this. Nevertheless she was longing for the moment when the porch door would close behind her, and she was safe at home again.

There, they bumped into something else! 'What a fool you are, Christina, can't you look out?'

'*Look?* Did you say *look?*' Christina was about to say more. She began: 'If you think I'm—' then suddenly stopped, and all three sat quiet as mice, paralysed with fear. They had all heard it simultaneously, someone walking slowly along. One minute it sounded as if it were coming down the quay, the next as if it were going away.

'Oh God!' whispered Gudrun. 'Shhh!' pounced the others.

They scarcely dared breathe, and a wave of relief went through them when the footsteps seemed to fall away from each other and lose their rhythm. There were at least two of them. And they were people. Drunk and dangerous perhaps, but still people.

'My God, I thought it was Kamke,' exclaimed Gudrun.

'How stupid you are,' sneered the others. 'Imagine, Gudrun believes in old Kamke! Oh Gudrun, you are a joke.'

Now they could hear voices, the voices of two men, of a sudden violently raised and mingling in angry exchange.

'Oh, I hope they're not from the Russian ship,' whispered Christina, and a bitter feeling of helplessness crept into the other two.

Then the footsteps stopped. Quite clearly, spoken normally and very calmly, a sentence came through the darkness: 'Sir, you are a blackguard.'

'I beg your pardon?' came the answer, sharp and furious, considerably less calm.

'Irrevocably a blackguard,' repeated the first voice. 'It gives me great satisfaction to tell you so, and I will gladly repeat it in the presence of witnesses.'

The voices flowed together, the sharp, furious one in a confused torrent of words, the calm one in short, cutting phrases: 'Precisely – exactly – I agree with you entirely—'

'Damn you,' shouted the sharp voice, 'I repeat, I don't even know if I am responsible. I have considerable doubts, and with good reason—'

'The only responsibility you have now is to make yourself scarce,' answered the calm voice coldly. 'Now we've got you covered it's all we demand of you. You're finished in this town, Sir.'

'May I ask,' shouted the furious one, intending to continue with a long dissertation about having to answer for this and it would cost him dear. But he was hushed up: 'For goodness sake hush, man, don't scream like that – you'll make a scandal—'

The voices were lost in mumbling, the speakers moved away. And now it was clear that they were not on the Kamke quay at all, but on one further away.

The three in the boat sat in dead silence. Nobody wanted to be the first to speak. '*Haben Sie gehört*,' whispered Christina finally, as if it was necessary to fool listening ears.

Alberta and Gudrun attacked her together. 'You're not to go telling anyone about this, Christina, we're telling you now. So just you keep your mouth shut.'

'And why should *I* be the one to say anything?' asked Christina, insulted, and she may very well have been right. Perhaps she was no more of a tattler than most; but she was mistrusted on account of her notorious reputation for being a pattern of virtue, who liked to sit with her elders round the tea table and chat precociously. Over the years she had been suspected of various treacheries, without anyone being able to accuse her directly.

They brought the boat in and moored it, handed up the oars and rudder and left everything tidy. None of them was frightened any more. Each was wrapped in her own thoughts. Christina was speechless with affront, Gudrun and Alberta only exchanged words when necessary. All were bursting to discuss the incident, to find out what the others thought about it, but they felt embarrassed and no-one would begin. Besides, Christina had her insults to nurse. When she disappeared through the back gate of the Archdeaconry, laden with equipment from the boat and still speechless, the others relaxed. 'What do you think will happen, Alberta? You heard who they were?'

'Yes.'

'But he told him he ought to go away. He'd better make himself scarce, he said. Can you understand that?'

'No, it's frightfully odd.'

'Do you think it's true what they're saying, Alberta, that Beda's going to have a baby?'

'Don't be so silly! Who says that?'

'Oh, a lot of people. The maids at home. Olefine the dressmaker. They say so at school too.'

And it was not that Alberta had not heard it. But she had

rejected it, denied it consistently, as if things could be undone by keeping silent about them. 'That's just nonsense, surely?'

'But supposing it's true?'

'It can't be true.'

A window opened above them. Mrs. Selmer's voice came through the darkness: 'Is that you, Alberta? Heavens, my child, we're sick with anxiety. Where *have* you been? Hurry home, Gudrun, your mother's quite desperate.'

And Alberta and Gudrun went their several ways, heavy with the knowledge that Jaeger, the Recorder, had called Lett the dentist a blackguard on a deserted quay in River Street, where he had thought himself to be without witnesses.

*   *   *

See, how crisp and light the shadow of shoemaker Schoning's rowan had become. It was a round, gently swaying mass of shadow no longer, but a lattice-work of thin, blue branches, restlessly flickering over the pavement. Soon not a red leaf would be left on the tree. The clusters of berries swayed on the bare twigs, and the sky behind them was ice blue.

One morning there was newly fallen snow in the mountains. It lay half-way down them, and a raw cold, naked and biting, set in from above. It arrived in the night and dug its claws into Alberta, gripping her from behind between her shoulder blades and buckling her tightly into the old enforced position with her legs drawn up and her arms crossed over her breast, keeping her awake for hours. Now she wrapped herself in a nightgown again, shivering and quaking, with the prospect of her own greyish-violet winter face in the mirror.

Mrs. Selmer sat at the breakfast table with a shawl over her dressing-gown. She looked at Alberta resignedly as she handed her a cup of coffee, and according to established tradition Alberta sank conscientiously into the depths, flushed and quivering. Automatically she continued Mrs. Selmer's train of thought: 'I have so few pleasures in life. I don't think I should be deprived of seeing my only daughter looking a little attractive. But even that is denied me.'

Alberta sat at the little table where the mending basket stood – where the mending basket always stood – took a stocking and began to darn it. Frozen, she twined her legs round each other. Her fingers were dead and numb. If only the Magistrate had eaten, if only Mrs. Selmer had gone upstairs, so that she could get hold of the coffee pot.

And she ran up the hillsides. This year as last year.

On her birthday at the end of the month Alberta as usual received a potted plant from the Chief Clerk. There was nothing surprising about it. The Clerk had always been attentive in this way, both to Mrs. Selmer and Alberta. It was taken for what it was – a courtesy.

For two years it had been a pot of Michaelmas daisies. This year it was neither more nor less than the big blue hydrangea that had stood resplendent in the Sisters Kremer's window for several days, attracting attention and admiration. Mrs. Selmer had even asked about it the other day just to find out what it cost, and, believe it or not, it was ten *kroner*. For this reason she exclaimed from a full heart: 'Mr. Gronneberg must be mad, to go to such expense. It would have been quite sufficient to give less.'

Alberta was hostile towards the hydrangea from the very beginning. In any case she felt not the slightest sense of ownership towards these annual offerings. It was Mrs. Selmer who received them and put them in an advantageous position in the sitting-room, Mrs. Selmer who drew the attention of visitors to them and said: 'Isn't it lovely?' Alberta's was the blame when they lacked water and hers the unpleasant duty of thanking the Clerk, a duty she carried out as quickly and in as low a voice as possible, being supported by Mama, who always emphasized the excessive amiability of the enterprise.

This year the plant's dimensions, together with something indefinable that hung in the air, oppressed Alberta. Since it came into the house she had continually felt her heart thumping. It was as if it were held in a vice and were beating to free itself. She tried vainly to shake off this uneasiness. It occurred to her that Mama was emphasizing more strongly than usual that the plant was Alberta's. '*Your* hydrangea,' she would say, and she never tired of pointing out that a hydrangea at this time of year was something quite out of the ordinary, a work of art.

Alberta demonstratively held her tongue when its merits were under discussion, defending herself with her sole weapon – silence.

*　　*　　*

Mr. Selmer, Magistrate, and Mrs. Selmer.

It was written on a small, hard, unsealed envelope with a local postmark. Alberta peeped into it on her way home with the post.

She remained standing as if rooted to the spot, looking alternately down at the two cards it contained, and then straight in front of her. 'Oh!' she said. 'No!' she said. And the painful pressure in her breast suddenly increased, her heart pounded as if to free itself. She had a desire to hide the cards, to throw them away, but realized that it would be of little use. So she took them home.

On the one there stood: Beda Birgitte Buck. On the other: Adam Jaeger, Recorder.

'Nothing less than a blow in the face to all respectable people,' asserted the Governor's lady. 'We can assume that the child is that fellow Lett's, I suppose. And now we shall have the pleasure of seeing the worthy Beda amongst us as the Recorder's wife, we shall even be compelled to receive her in our homes. Just imagine it, picture the situation to yourselves. It will be far from pleasant, let me tell you. It's true they say the Recorder is thinking of applying for a transfer south, but that won't happen immediately. What? Could the child be his? Well, in that case all I have to say is what kind of morality is it that allows such a relationship with one man while spending day and night with the other. After all, they've been seen at nightfall all over the place, Beda and her dentist. I'm so glad now that we never set foot in his office, but kept to old Oyen, even if he is old-fashioned and it hurts. Yes, he *is* ham-fisted, but he's thorough, and you can't complain about his reputation.'

The Archdeacon's wife objected with crystal-clear eyes that

after all, for the Recorder's sake, one must – one could not very well do nothing. 'And besides, now Beda is marrying such a splendid man, perhaps – It's amazing what a difference a change of circumstances can make, Mrs. Lossius.'

'Naturally, one must do something. That's precisely what is so disagreeable. If I didn't have to, I shouldn't give it a thought.' The Govenor's lady was irritated over the matter, taking it as something of a personal affront, and bore contradiction with less patience than ever. As far as a change of circumstances went, she doubted whether anything would affect Beda. 'I am deeply distressed on the Recorder's account,' she announced in conclusion.

Mrs. Pram honestly thought that if Mr. Jaeger wanted to go off and get married in his old age, he could surely have found himself something better. 'We had given him up,' said Mrs. Pram. 'He had been ranked with the confirmed bachelors long ago. But just think, if only he had chosen Otilie Weyer for instance, what a joy for us all. They say she doted on him the first few years after he came here.'

Papa said: 'Ha-ha – the Recorder – ha-ha.' He laughed inwardly a little and looked at Mrs. Lossius, who also laughed inwardly, lifted her glass and said: 'Skaal, Mr. Magistrate!'

But Mrs. Selmer surprised them all. 'I can't be anything but sorry for Beda,' she said. 'The difference in their ages is great. I don't suppose it will be so easy for her.'

'Easy!' Mrs. Lossius had to repeat it, so indignant was she. 'So easy! May I ask why it should be easy? If it should turn out to be difficult, it's really only what Beda thoroughly deserves. For the Recorder's sake we must hope for the best, but otherwise—' Her lorgnette struck her left hand in a series of nervous little taps.

The general consensus of opinion amongst the ladies was that the Recorder was doing it out of chivalry, because he was so fearfully chivalrous. Mrs. Selmer was quite alone in declaring, mischievously and cryptically: 'What have I always said, you never know where you are with that man. He's an old slyboots, let me tell you.'

To be honest the town did not know what to make of it. Was

the child Lett's or Jaeger's? Was the Recorder taking Beda out of compassion or love? Was Beda taking the Recorder to save her skin, or was she in love with him? Did she start a relationship with him as soon as she had finished with Lett last summer, or had it begun before, or had there never been any such thing?

Lett the dentist had left, rumour had it, following a violent encounter with the Recorder on one of the quays, during which the two gentlemen were said to have exchanged insults and been finally reduced to fisticuffs, hitting each other with their sticks. When Alberta and Gudrun tackled Christina about these rumours, she said that by God she hadn't breathed a word. And perhaps it was so. Who could guarantee that nobody else had heard the two vociferous gentlemen that evening?

Olefine the dressmaker was significantly silent over her sewing machine, but Jensine seized every occasion to point out that many people had prophesied that Beda Buck would come to a bad end. 'And what can you expect of simple folk, when grand folk are no better than they should be? Anyway, we only have to wait and see whether it's a little Lett or a little Jaeger,' chuckled Jensine.

Mrs. Buck's closest acquaintance, the ladies Dorum, Kilde, Lebesby and Elmholz, insisted to all who would lend them an ear, that the Recorder had really loved Beda for two or three years, but had held back on account of the difference in their ages. But then this summer ... Then when he came and asked to have the wedding immediately, Mrs. Buck had said: 'But my dear Mr. Recorder, Beda has nothing. She scarcely owns anything but the clothes on her back.' To which the Recorder had replied that that was not what he was asking for.

At home Mrs. Selmer sat speculating over the affair with her knitting and her book. When for strategic reasons Alberta sat down beside her with her everlasting tablecloth, Mrs. Selmer would speculate aloud, holding her knitting up in front of her to cast off: 'This affair of Beda's is really a terrible business. I shan't tell you what is being said about her, Alberta, I only hope none of it gets to the ears of you young girls. She must know herself how matters stand. But if she was really fond of that fellow Lett, I cannot do otherwise than feel bitterly sorry for her, poor child, for in that case she has many a sad day in front of her. For my part I shall be as friendly as I can towards Beda – she may find she is in need of a little friendliness. You must sew her some little thing, Alberta.'

'Go up and congratulate her yourself, Alberta, she'll be so pleased, she's all alone at home,' was Mrs. Buck's reply to Alberta's careful: 'Congratulate Beda for me,' when they met a couple of days later outside Kilde's shop. And Alberta, who had thought of nothing but Beda since the cards arrived, went with beating heart.

Beda was sitting sewing on the couch. 'Is that you, Alberta? How nice of you to look in.' She put down her sewing, but did not get up. Her face when she lifted it was sunken round the eyes, patchy and brown, so changed that Alberta's heart sank.

'Congratulations, Beda,' she said, troubled, and extended her hand. 'It was quite a surprise.' She could hear how strange her voice sounded.

'Yes.' Beda smiled a little crookedly. 'I'm a little surprised myself. You never can tell, as they say. I expect it was the last thing you all expected in this town, that the Recorder would marry Beda Buck.'

Her tone was facetious. Nevertheless it dismayed Alberta. The whole thing dismayed her. She did not know whether Beda was happy or miserable, and it did not seem to matter. Reckless Beda, reckless with money, clothes and everything else, reckless with herself, the bold representative of defiance, now sat quiet and changed with her sewing, Nurse Jullum's certain prey. And she was to marry an old man, a man of over forty, a man like Papa, thought Alberta, although she knew the Recorder was considerably younger. In a short time, only a few months, it would be Beda the ladies would be discussing: 'How are things at the Recorder's? She should be near her time now.'

It was too outrageous, it was unbelievable, it must be possible to prevent it. Alberta wanted to take hold of Beda, to persuade her to back out in time, to make her see that it was insane. But something restrained her.

'I must be glad to be getting such a good husband,' said Beda quietly. She had taken up her sewing again.

'Is that for your trousseau?' asked Alberta for something to say.

'Yes, that's what it's supposed to be.'

There was a pause.

'He's so kind, Jaeger, I don't know how I shall ever be able to make it up to him—' Beda took up the conversation again. 'He wants to apply for a transfer south as soon as possible.' It was almost as if Beda was apologizing for herself.

'So I've heard.'

'Yes. He doesn't want me to stay here for the rest of my days. It's very kind of him. We're going abroad too, later on.'

'How marvellous!'

Was Beda really looking forward to the future with optimism, or was she simply bracing herself to meet it? It sounded to Alberta as if she were mechanically repeating something learned by heart.

'You're going to get married soon, I understand?'

'As soon as the banns have been called. That's why I'm so busy, as you see.' Beda held up her sewing in front of Alberta, and the same crooked little smile again came over her face. A completely strange, new smile, so unlike the old Beda. The wide mouth over the even teeth was no longer animated. It was closed and there was something secretive about it.

'What are they saying in town?' she asked. 'How about Mrs. Lossius, what does she have to say for herself?'

'They're surprised, of course.'

'Oh indeed? Well – they'd better prepare themselves for a few more surprises,' answered Beda curtly, and made no further comment on the subject. On the other hand she invited Alberta to visit her when they were married: 'We're not having a big wedding. It will be very quiet, but afterwards you must be one of the first to come and see us, and you will be very welcome.' She smiled again and extended her hand. Alberta could stand it no longer. Her mouth trembled and she failed to utter a sound.

'But Alberta, what's the matter, how silly you are—' Beda's own voice was trembling, nevertheless. Alberta, who turned away to dry her eyes, did not know whether it was laughter or tears. 'It's just that it's so strange that you're getting married,' she managed to say.

'You're right, it is strange. But I'm going to have such a kind husband. I couldn't have found one kinder.'

'No.'

And they had nothing more to say to each other. They stood shaking hands for a while, considerably embarrassed.

'Well, I just wanted to congratulate you.'

'Thank you for coming.'

Alberta left her. She saw Beda in the old days, following the Recorder through Upper Town, where he had then lived, tilting her shoulders a little, as he did, and singing 'Adam in Paradise'.

She saw Beda's pale, closed, distant face up on the bog some time ago, heard the Recorder's calm, cold words through the darkness that memorable evening: 'Sir, you are a blackguard' – and Lett's furious: 'Damn you, I don't even know if I'm responsible.'

She heard Mrs. Buck: 'You must let us use our heads a little.'

Then all else was pushed aside by Beda's face as it had looked that spring, in the short moment at the dance when she had laid her cheek against Lett's: the sweet, tender smile, the closed eyes, both as if spun together and entangled with the deep call, the strong, demanding sigh in Alberta's blood, her paralysis under Cedolf's kiss.

Life was a trap. Even Beda, frank, courageous Beda, was she not sitting there like a fly on flypaper, having, as far as one could see, kicked out and then given in?

*　　*　　*

That letter from Uncle the Colonel – had Mama left it lying on the sewing table, open, out of its envelope, on purpose?

There it was, anyhow, and Alberta found herself alone with it. It was folded over in the middle. On the part facing upwards she caught sight of her own name at the first glance.

She hesitated no longer, but leaned over and read:

'... and I understand to the full, my dear sister-in-law, your anxieties on Alberta's account. Lacking the opportunity, as you do, of giving her a more extensive education, it is reasonable that your mother's heart should turn in its anxiety to a good and suitable marriage as a solution – all the more reasonable when we consider that woman's natural place is and always will remain the home, whatever people may say. Within the four walls of a home your daughter will find the surest happiness. Now it is my impression that our dear Alberta is a thoroughly good, well brought-up young girl, with an excellent brain, but of a ... to be sure, loving and winning – but nevertheless modest appearance, together with a quiet and somewhat timid personality. In these circumstances I believe very little would be gained either for her or yourself by allowing her to spend a winter down here. Among the young ladies of this town, some of whom, I must admit, old man as I am, are unusually vivacious and beautiful, she would find it difficult to make any impression. You would also be compelled to put yourselves to quite disproportionate expense, in order that she might merely be enabled to present a tolerable appearance, as her birth demands and warrants. The expense of the carriage for our Lydia alone has been particularly heavy on my budget during the current winter; but since, by reason of various circumstances, and in spite of the fact that we ourselves have never been in a position to reciprocate adequately, she has been accepted in those circles which entertain a great deal down here, I decided I ought to sustain such expense. This has shown itself to have been entirely justified, since it was precisely in these circles that she met and became more closely acquainted with the exceedingly pleasant and sympathetic young man who is to become our son-in-law.

'The position is quite different for your Alberta, who, as you know, has grown up quite outside these circles. It would of course not be particularly easy for her to gain access to them. The fact that you yourself have celebrated triumphs both in the Association and in private salons would scarcely be sufficient in this case, nor would the fact that she was living with us. Your time down here was too brief, and it was too long ago. I am afraid that our dear Alberta, even if she paid the obligatory visits, would find herself leading a somewhat unheeded existence. Such is the world and the people in it. In addition, when present at such events to which she might have some expectation of being invited, she would in all probability, mainly on account of her lack of acquaintances, come to play the less amusing rôle of a wall-flower, a humiliation to which she should not be unnecessarily exposed. You know from your own experience, I am sure, my dear sister-in-law, what importance society attaches to external appearance. With an appearance and conduct such as yours, one could make an impression almost anywhere. All doors are open to the lady who is both beautiful and distinguished; she is welcome everywhere. Those less richly endowed on the other hand should rather seek happiness in quieter and more modest circumstances, and heaven forbid that it should be suggested that they hereby choose the worse part.

'But to be brief: you should look for a husband for our dear Alberta in the circumstances she knows and to which she is accustomed. There she will have every prospect of winning the respect and the love of a worthy and honourable young man. I understand that at the great trading posts up there in your Arctic regions there resides a veritable trading aristocracy (the so-called "lords of the headlands"), many of whom, it is said, keep quite impressive households under the circumstances, and whose sons are on no account to be despised as mates. Would it not be a task for your anxious mother's heart to bring it about that Alberta might one day sit secure and happy in the position of rightful lady of the manor on one of these aforementioned headlands? This is only a suggestion *en passant*; there are of course other prospects of meeting "the right person" up there. Many young men of excellent family apply to go north when they begin their careers, in fact, I hear that you already have an efficient and sympathetic young man in your employ. I assure you, a wise and tactful mother can do much in a matter such as this, I would even go so far as to say that it is a most important part of her duty.

'This is, my dear sister-in-law, the humble and well-meaning advice of an old man experienced in the ways of the world, in a matter that is of particular weight and import as much for you and my brother, as for your daughter.

Your ever devoted T.B.S.

P.S. The date of our Lydia's wedding has been somewhat advanced. It will now take place next month. My wife will write to you about this in more detail. She and Lydia send you most affectionate greetings.'

Alberta put back the letter as it was, went upstairs and sat by the window. For once she did not cry.

She sat, her blood running cold, imagining the small moves

being made backwards and forwards concerning her inconvenient self, with whom none of them really knew what to do. She sat for a long time, dazedly feeling something stiffen and remain in her face, feeling pain from the clenched hands in her lap. She hated them all.

'I'm glad I kissed Cedolf,' she said eventually through clenched teeth, 'Very glad, very glad. Come back Cedolf, and I'll kiss you again. As much as you like, as much as you like.'

* * *

The Clerk's hydrangea seemed as if it would never fade. The weeks went by, and all that happened was that its flowers assumed a semi-artificial, slightly desiccated appearance. 'By Jove,' said the Magistrate. 'Never seen a plant last so long.'

Alberta watered it reluctantly and insufficiently. She had an antipathy towards it. When, one day, she came too close to it, the smell of it, chilly and sickening, made her recoil. And it occurred to her that the hydrangea smelt of corpses. It smelt like old Mrs. Veum when she lay dead. The three clusters of flowers were three well-preserved relics. After that she avoided it when dusting and passed it by purposely with the watering can.

But Mrs. Selmer drew everyone's attention daily to the fact that it was wonderful how the hydrangea was lasting so long. She would notice that it lacked water, and advance with can upraised: 'Alberta, you've forgotten this poor plant of yours again, and here it is flowering for us so nicely. It's sad to see, my dear, that you have no feeling for this sort of thing.' Mrs. Selmer watered it thoroughly. 'But things will surely be different when you have your own home one of these days, if not before,' she said, sighing.

Then she would invite the Clerk to supper again, although he had been quite recently. 'It seems to me that he is getting more attached to us,' she would explain. 'I do think that's nice.'

Perhaps he was. He came when invited, at any rate, was more talkative, more outspoken, stayed late.

Alberta froze up, remained on her guard, and ignored all her former intentions to be kind. She perched on the edge of her chair more awkwardly than ever. If she met the Clerk's eye, she immediately looked away again. Under their shyness was there not something she had not seen before: tenacious, obtrusive determination, a kind of triumph? They defiled her. 'Leeches,' she thought. 'Leeches.'

The sum of her conversation was yes and no. She contributed absolutely nothing to these social occasions. Nevertheless, Mama had recently seemed to be eyeing her more hopefully and indulgently, even to the extent of treating her with a certain amount of deference. It increased her repugnance and uneasiness.

One day she met old Mrs. Weyer, leaning on Otilie's arm. Old Mrs. Weyer stopped and shouted: 'And what about the Recorder, eh! What about the Recorder!'

'Yes—'

'Well now, I hope we shall be hearing some more pleasant news soon. It won't be long now, I hear.'

And old Mrs. Weyer slapped Alberta hard on the shoulder several times: 'Yes-yes, yes-yes, a good husband, a good husband. Just wait, my child, you'll feel like a new woman after the first confinement. Confinements cleanse the body, let me tell you,' she shouted into Alberta's ear. Alberta shrank back, horrified.

'But Mama,' sighed Otilie unhappily. She whispered to Alberta: 'Poor Mama, she gets more forgetful every day. You mustn't mind what – she's getting you mixed up with someone else,' she said, attempting to gloss it over.

But Alberta rushed away as if pursued. It was no figment of her imagination. A horrible notion, a breath of nightmare, glimpsed far out on the edge of evil, uneasy dreams had suddenly taken shape and become real. Now it was going about freely, haunting the streets and the market place.

Was it not grinning at her from all the eyes she met?

She rushed home, and upstairs, to bury her head in the pillow. Something seemed to rise higher and higher about her, a revolting slime. She could no longer breathe—

That night she did not close her eyes. Her thoughts circled endlessly round one idea: to get away, free from it all.

There was an English ship anchored at the Klykken quay . . .

In her search for a hold, for a thread through the passing

days, something from the time when she worked regularly, when she went to school, Alberta had joined the gymnastic society. Her old gym costume still fitted her, the fee was a bagatelle. Mrs. Selmer, whose ways were past finding out, produced her objections in a tone of capitulation: the company was mixed, it would be most unpleasant to have to come home so late in the dark, she would have been pleased if Alberta indulged herself in the same sort of pleasures as Harriet, Christina and Gudrun, but good heavens . . .

Alberta had gone to Mr. Kirkeby the editor, who was the demonstrator, and joined the group. Now she went twice a week, enjoying the opportunity to move about freely and get warm.

She was in fact more at peace in certain respects. Mrs. Selmer did not sigh over her so much, and looked at her searchingly rather than with resignation. Alberta interpreted this in her own way and made use of it cautiously, with all her wits about her. But sometimes she would turn bold and abuse her position, as is only human. Did she not simply get to her feet one evening when the Clerk was there and announce that she was going to the gym? One chooses the lesser of two evils: to be an object of ill-concealed curiosity and banter was bad enough – to sit here with her parents and the Clerk was worse.

But it was a case of the biter bit. Just as Mrs. Selmer, her eyebrows raised, was about to express herself, the Clerk remarked obligingly that in that case it would be a pleasure to fetch Miss Selmer after the session.

'It's not necessary, thank you,' snapped Alberta.

But Mama cut the discussion short: 'Yes indeed, it's necessary, my dear. I am *so* grateful to Mr. Gronneberg. I always worry about your coming home. Thank you very much, Mr. Chief Clerk.'

Alberta left in a fury.

At ease in the stale, heavy air that remained thick in the gymnasium after the men's group, she wondered how she could get through this situation. To be met outside by the Chief Clerk, to be simply fetched, to be accompanied home in the sight of all, would be unbearable. She would run the risk of being congratulated in the street tomorrow by all and sundry.

She would have to go home early, find an excuse, steal a march on him. Sneak out during the next march, perhaps, as she went past the door.

At the bar Palmine Flor was just stepping out of the ranks and preparing to turn a somersault. She put her heels together at attention, threw back her shoulders, stuck out her breast, smiling and twinkling at Kirkeby from under her golden curls while she waited for the word of command. He was finding it difficult to keep a straight face and not smile back.

One – two—

Alberta suddenly put a hand to her heart and stood staring, holding her breath, her eyes distended. Something terrible was about to happen, something contrary to nature, to all instinct. And nobody seemed to notice. They were all standing at ease, chatting quietly. Nobody rushed up and tried to prevent—

She felt sick and closed her eyes. And it was done. Palmine went over the bar on her stomach. And Palmine was pregnant. It was when she had stood to attention that Alberta had realized it.

It was done. It was as if something soft and small and defenceless had been crushed and trampled on, just as when Ola Paradise in his drunkenness had dashed a blind, newborn kitten against the wall of Ovre the baker's shed. Everything stopped, you dared not breathe, not look, something moaned and whimpered deep inside you.

Involuntarily Alberta looked round her. First Beda, now Palmine. Were there more? It was an epidemic, it seemed unavoidable. That Palmine could do such a thing, that she could do such a thing.

Palmine could. She did not use gym shoes like the rest, but wore high-heeled, pointed dancing shoes. She swung herself through the apparatus, a little heavily, but with precision; made a tiger-leap over the horse, lay horizontally in the air with upswinging legs and thick stomach, sailed smiling down towards Kirkeby, who caught her in his outstretched arms and held her for a moment before putting her down. Kirkeby was the kind whose hands seemed to stick, reluctant to let go. They often wandered about a bit when they got the chance. He had a reputation for it.

'What's the matter?' asked Karla Schmitt suddenly, pushing past the others towards Alberta. 'Do you feel ill? You look as if you'd escaped from the graveyard.'

And Alberta gratefully put her hand in Karla's and allowed her to lead her out. For everything was floating round her, and she was sweating as if she were seasick. Crushed, she sank down on to the bench in the cloakroom, and Karla quickly moved away clothes to let her lie down, rolling up a coat to put under her head.

'Here you are,' said Karla, bringing water. 'You mustn't faint.'

Alberta swallowed a little water, squeezed Karla's hand, closed her eyes, and surrendered herself to her indisposition. When it was over and she could sit up again all the others were streaming out of the gym. She was doomed.

Outside stood the Clerk, polite, smiling, punctual, right under the lamp. He attracted attention, as she had expected. The small groups that passed turned to look at him and Alberta, buzzed, whispered, smiled.

Of a sudden all that Alberta had repressed during the previous months exploded. She did not attempt to hide her ill-temper, answering curtly and angrily, without looking in the Clerk's direction, walking ahead as if she were about to run away from him. In reply to one of his cautious remarks she stopped suddenly and stamped on the ground. The next moment she burst into dry, tearless sobs.

She heard him beside her, unhappy, obliging: 'Dear Miss Selmer, is it in any way my fault? Have I been so unfortunate as to hurt you? If so, it was entirely unintentional – I deeply deplore—'

'Yes, go on, deplore, deplore, deplore,' shouted Alberta scornfully. 'Go on, deplore.'

Then she controlled herself and managed to say: 'Forgive me – please forgive me – but everything is so loathsome—'

There was a pause.

'But it seemed to me that recently – Have I really not insulted you?' said the Clerk at length, hesitantly but with insistence.

'No, no. Only – don't send such large flowers – don't come and fetch me – don't come at all—'

There was another pause. The ground sunk beneath Alberta's feet. What had she said? Wasn't it too much, hadn't she gone too far? It had slipped out in a sudden flame of fresh irritation. Thoroughly unhappy she walked on, waiting for him to digest it.

'No, no,' he said quietly.

They had arrived at the Selmers' doorstep. Alberta extended her hand. She felt a certain warmth towards him: 'Thank you very much for seeing me home.'

'It has never been my intention to pester you, Miss Selmer.'

She met his eyes uncertainly in the lamplight. Was not that little look of triumph more cunning than ever? Was he not standing there safe and sound, while she—

But she was suddenly relieved that what had been said could not be taken back in any case.

'Good night, then.'

'Good night, good night.' He bowed, stood and waited while she went up the steps. As she closed the door behind her he turned and went. Alberta watched his back as it was swallowed up in the darkness and was seized with pity for it. It looked lonely. Poor fellow, if he really had believed that she, ugly and impossible as she was, could be had for the asking, there was nothing strange in that – on the contrary, he might well—

Alberta smiled to herself.

Mrs. Selmer was sitting in the dining-room with her keys and her book, ready to go upstairs. She had waited for Alberta, had sat up later than the Magistrate, contrary to her custom. A little tray with cakes and jam stood on the table. She pushed it across to Alberta and remained seated, talking in random.

Mama's mischievous searching expression was so distasteful to Alberta that she abandoned the idea of telling her she had felt ill. She tried to get down a little of the food and behave as if nothing was the matter. But she could not manage it, and put down her knife, just as the flush reached her face. There she sat, crimson and trembling.

'And did Mr. Gronneberg come to fetch you?' asked Mrs. Selmer.

'Yes – he came.'

'It was nice of him, don't you think?'

'Yes.'

'It seems to me he has become remarkably attentive this autumn.' Alberta looked up, on her guard, and trembled even more.

Mama smiled. 'Would you accept him?' she said.

Alberta felt herself turning white.

She rose and looked Mama straight in the eye. 'I would not accept him,' she said, her lips tight, yet with surprising clarity. And she walked past her out of the room.

*   *   *

Between seven and eight o'clock the traffic in Fjord Street was considerable. It was frosty and the autumn evening was dark. Under the eight arc-lamps the stream of humanity flowed quickly and smoothly, egged on by its awareness of the snow and the winter perhaps already lying in wait up in the mountains, perhaps ready to descend on the town that very night. People walked fast, talked loudly, inaugurated their new winter clothes upon the bare paving stones of summer, knowing that the snowstorm would soon tear and pull at their finery, making it dishevelled. Now was the time for display and gratification, for taking a few quick turns between Theodorsen the baker and Louisa-round-the-bend.

Harriet Pram and Dr. Mo had announced their engagement. They were walking arm-in-arm for the first time. Harriet was wearing a new boa, earrings, a veil and white gloves. Palmine and Lilly stopped and stared after her, scarcely able to believe their own eyes.

She was openly radiant. Her good evening was louder and more cheerful than ever, and her thanks when someone stopped to congratulate them were pearls of laughter ready waiting. Dr. Mo lifted his hat, embarrassed but smiling. He had a new stick with a silver handle.

A little way behind them came Gudrun arm-in-arm with Christina, who shrank and crumpled up and was no longer walking with Bergan. It had not come to anything between them, whatever the reason. Each was walking by himself again. Bergan was quite unchanged, but Christina was if possible even more modest than before.

Gudrun would stop people and say: 'Honestly, I'm going to accept the first person who proposes, with the exception of that fellow Stensett. If you only knew what fun it is to be engaged.'

Christina might make herself small, but was brave enough to joke about it. Perhaps she wanted it to be known that if she was walking alone, she was doing so of her own free will. Giggling, she asked whether Gudrun had forgotten the song: 'No, better say no, and show them the way to go; And then you'll avoid the infant's cry and a hullaba-loo-ba-lo.'

Gudrun assured her at the top of her voice that there might easily be an infant's cry just the same and a great deal more hullabaloo, and Christina said: 'Hush, don't be so silly.'

Papa and Alberta did not walk along Fjord Street as far as Louisa-round-the-bend and turn there like other people. They had their own route and turned down into River Street, which was very dark and deserted in the evenings.

Young Klykken's living-room windows shone red, and an edge of light round a blind showed where the Catholic priest had his office in the Badendück building. But the other old houses lay quite black, their dimensions unnaturally large. They were said to be haunted.

Papa and Alberta walked down to the Old Quay, stood still in the circle of light under the lamp, and looked out at the river, where the eddies moved cold and comfortless in the reflections from land. A fishing boat with red and green lights was drifting out on the current, and Papa conjectured that it was a Russian boat. 'Bound to be the one that's been tied up at the Kamke quay, loading dried fish.'

'Perhaps so,' answered Alberta.

They went down on to the New Quay, wandered out as far as the red light at the end of the breakwater, and Papa remarked: 'By Jove, I wonder how many more times we'll be able to walk out here this autumn. The snow may come before we can say Jack Robinson.'

'Yes,' answered Alberta.

'You're very quiet, my child. Is anything the matter?'

'No—'

'Cheer up, Alberta! No use being down-hearted. You're young,' added Papa, as if he meant: 'It's no problem for you.'

'It's awful to be young,' said Alberta, and held her breath for an instant. Was she on the verge of talking to Papa?

He came to a halt, shocked: 'Awful to be young? Stuff and nonsense, child, that's just a phrase you've picked up somewhere. You young things don't know how fortunate you are. To be young is *everything*, child. Wait until you're old.'

'Life's horrible,' said Alberta in repressed rebellion.

'Now listen to me, a young girl has no right to say life is horrible. Mercy on us! But it's these novels again, these damned problem novels. A lot of these muddled scribblers ought to be hanged, indeed they ought.'

They were silent for a while.

'I suppose we ought to go home,' said Alberta inertly.

'How right you are, by Jove, we must.' Papa pounded with his stick, and they went.

In Fjord Street they met Harriet Pram and Dr. Mo, who were still out.

'Extraordinarily pretty girl,' remarked Papa. 'And Doctor Mo is said to be a promising young doctor. Well, well, it must be gratifying for the Prams.'

A subdued light shone from the Recorder's living-room windows, probably from a table lamp. He and Beda had just returned from a short journey to the city where they had had a civil wedding. It had taken everyone by surprise. Neither of them had yet been seen in public.

Outside Kilde the watchmaker's there was a mob of street boys, country folk, youths from Rivermouth. Above them all could be seen Kwasnikow's fiery red hair and beard and Crazy-Philomena's flowery hat with the veil. The hat bobbed back and forth throughout the violent altercation that was taking place between herself and Kwasnikow.

He was drunk, and had the appearance of an ancient child,

225

blue-eyed and lisping. His nose and cheekbones looked like three roses painted on his face. In Russian, Swedish and Norwegian he defended himself against Philomena who, tiny and furious, hissed in his teeth.

Alberta suddenly caught sight of the Clerk among the spectators. He stood watching for a moment, then disappeared.

'Lousy Russian,' spat Philomena.

Kwasnikow took her by the shoulder, shook her backwards and forwards, and shouted threateningly: 'I give you payment for this, Philomena, I give you payment.'

The crowd yelled with glee. Someone shouted: 'Here's your topper, Kwasnikow!' The weather-beaten top hat, Kwasnikow's summer wear, inherited from Kamke, was planted on his head from behind. It was grey with dust and had a dent in the middle.

'What's going on?' asked Papa sharply.

'Kwasnikow wants to murder Philomena,' explained a boy, forgetting, as Kwasnikow seized Philomena again, all respect for the Magistrate, and shouting in ecstasy: 'That's the boy, chew her up, chew her up!'

'You rascal, I'll ask the police to take care of you. Where are they, in any case? It's too bad they're never on the spot when they're needed. Ah, there's Olsen. Let's get along then, Alberta. Excuse me, be so good as to let us pass—'

A way was made for Alberta and Papa. P.C. Olsen arrived at full speed with a stern face, shouting: 'Move along there!' to the crowd, which retreated, but immediately gathered again.

'That poor fellow Kwasnikow,' said Papa, completely forgetting the boy the police were to take care of. 'He hangs about here – but Alberta, wasn't that Gronneberg standing over in the corner by Kilde's?'

'Yes, I think so.'

'He disappeared so suddenly. How odd of him to leave like that, without speaking to us.'

'I don't suppose he saw us.'

'No, no, it's possible. But he seems somewhat changed these days. I'll wager there's something the matter. I should be sorry if—

'He's no Adonis,' said Papa, quite irrelevantly. 'But he's clever, and very useful to me. I should be sorry to lose him, by Jove.'

Mysterious words, that could be interpreted in more ways than one. Alberta glanced at Papa searchingly, but looked quickly away again. Papa was looking straight in front of him like the Sphinx.

Mrs. Selmer was sitting at the supper table gazing across it blankly. Her reply to their greeting could scarcely be heard, she hardly seemed to see them. They were late too, in addition to everything else.

The Magistrate tentatively began to converse about Jacob. Mrs. Selmer replied in the tone of voice that always spoiled everything. He muttered: 'Oh, so that's how it is, is it?' His hand shook.

Mrs. Selmer turned to Alberta. 'Did you see anything of the engaged couple?'

'Yes.'

'The Prams must be very gratified.'

'Yes.'

'A few people do have something to be pleased about. I met Mrs. Bremer today. She was so sanguine – the Headmaster has decided to apply for Kragero.'

'Really?' The Magistrate looked up with interest. 'Kragero! I'd have thought the position here was better.'

'Mr. Bremer says the children are stagnating here.'

'Stagnating!' Papa chewed over the word, and Alberta's heart shrank. 'Stagnating,' he repeated. 'That's a strong word, by Jove.

'Nonsense,' he suddenly decided, resolutely describing a circle in his porridge bowl with his spoon. 'Nonsense.' He muttered under his breath, and his hand shook. Jensine, who had just arrived with his fried egg, eyed him askance.

Mrs. Selmer stared resignedly into thin air, in silence, letting it be known by her expression that she would not deign to argue with unreason itself.

'How does Jensine put up with a family like ours?' thought Alberta. 'How can she stay here of her own accord, when she could be in all sorts of other places? She isn't a sister or a daughter of the house.'

Mrs. Selmer disappeared immediately after supper, retiring without a word. The Magistrate looked askance at the closed door over his pince-nez, remained seated until her footsteps reached the top of the stairs, rose, and went across to the sideboard. Alberta half rose in her chair, almost stood up, but it was no use. He filled his glass to the brim. 'Must have something to sleep on,' he explained.

When, a little later, Alberta put her arms round his neck to say good night, her face was suddenly wet with tears. Papa had never plagued her, he had always left her alone. He never sighed, but a certain tired expression in his eyes when he removed his pince-nez stabbed her like a painful stitch. Papa was one who had found more than his match in life, and never complained. She could rage at his closed door, clench her fist, call down God's curse on him, but an irreparable weakness and anxiety for him was there, always ready to flame up, beneath everything else in her heart. He was as men are, his worst enemy, and needed her there.

Alberta did something unusual. She kissed Papa twice. He looked up, surprised, saw her tears, and exclaimed: 'Good gracious, Alberta, a big girl like you? Whatever next, you crybaby!'

But he held her closely and kissed her emphatically back again. Altogether it was quite a little scene, without either of them knowing how it had really come about.

'Off to bed with you, child.' Papa pointed to his eternal pile of newspapers: 'I have a little reading to do.'

Alberta wandered upstairs and sobbed into her shawl until she was calm again. She remained sitting in the dark without attempting to light the lamp and go to bed. Her thoughts floated up from obscurity, the one evolving out of the other, falling away and making room for others, as thoughts do, while the restless little lump that was her heart moved painfully and irregularly; thoughts that had acquired something mechanical about them, a tendency to rise and spin in the same ambit as soon as she was alone, sending waves of blood up to her face, giving her a feeling of suffocation.

Now and again she mumbled words into the darkness: 'To be offered frugality in love, no insult is greater – none—

'—but the colliers will come and go, and I'll never have enough courage – Beda, yes, she could have done it. Now she sits sewing under the Recorder's lamp instead, knowing that the faces are pressed up against her window, tight as a shoal of fish—

'—and this is only the beginning.'

Alberta felt her face grow old and shrivelled at her own words. She was a shadow already, half old, distressing, comic. Something happened from year to year, suspicion became knowledge, bad dreams reality.

A weariness crept over her, more intense and pervasive than any she had known before. It sat in her back, sapping her strength. She sank down into it as if it were an abyss, sank inwards into gaping emptiness. It was as if she were sinking back into—

Did she not glimpse an endless, grey ocean, as light and colourless as a misty autumn day? Was it not in and behind all things – was it not that which one slipped into, became united with when death came?

Death?

Perhaps something scattered and finely dispersed is always lying in the mind, waiting for a long, quiet moment in which to flow together and condense. Something indefinable.

Alberta rose, drawing her shawl about her. One more nightmare had taken shape, one she had glimpsed farthest out on the edge of evil dreams. For days and nights she had suspected that it was moving towards her, and had wept with horror under the bedclothes. Now it was upon her, and she could not avoid it. To live with this deep weariness, this disgust for all existing possibilities, this endless oppressive greyness of everyday existence behind her and before, this fear of life – she could not bear it. But then she must do it – *must* – the sooner the better.

It was late. The final creak of the floor boards under Papa's heavy tread had died away long ago; it was a while since the church clock had struck its four slow quarter-strokes followed by eleven very fast strokes on the hour.

When she was out of the back door and the autumn darkness enclosed her, malevolent anxiety settled like a mask over her face, stiff and cold, yet burning and pounding painfully out through her ear lobes. Something knotted itself in the pit of her stomach as when, as a child, someone had done her an injustice. But just as she had occasionally, in spite of her fear, crossed Dorum's threshold, and Papa's, and contradicted Mama, so she took one step forward, then another. She walked across the yard and down to Flemming's quay as she used to walk through dark rooms when she was small; not too fast, struggling to keep calm as if to deceive watching eyes – half senseless with fright.

Now she could distinguish dark from dark. The piles of barrels and crates rose up threateningly on either side. The knot tightened in her stomach. Her body seemed to be dwindling and shrinking with agonizing fear.

At the same time everything was strangely unreal, as if she were already outside life, out in a world of shadows, where what she was doing was fated to take place in accordance with inexorable, cast-iron rules – one action inextricably linked to the next, dragging it after. First this, then this, and no way back.

She felt as if she were re-enacting something she had done once before in some obscure past, as if she were once again carrying out something difficult, sinister and inescapable.

She did not think, but she wept calmly, making no sound.

She was at the steps. It was low water and far down, a black, repellent abyss. As if remotely, from far away, she sensed that here it was shallow, with large boulders, she must go out in one of the boats; remotely too, she sensed her own horror. She found the boat chain, climbed down backwards, holding on to it—

Then she slipped on the smooth steps, hung by her arms on to the chain, clawed the air with her legs and found no foothold, while her blood ran cold from top to toe, and she wailed aloud in fear. Her skirts and legs were in the water. Her clothes absorbed it and she was dragged down by an icy and terrible gravity.

Shortly afterwards Alberta lay full length face downwards on the quay, clawing at the planks beneath her, breathless and whimpering with exertion and fright; no longer daring to move, or to believe that she was on dry land.

One thing was hers. Her bare life. It was hers still, hers – it throbbed and hammered through pulse and heart, quivering in every muscle. They had not succeeded in driving her into the sea, and never would. Something had been roused in her down there in the icy cold as it crept up round her body. It had been terror, violent beyond control, but it had also been something bright and hard, a raging refusal. It had been like touching bottom and being carried upwards again.

Below her the water slapped lightly against the stones. There it was again, that little swarming sound of activity and labour. The tide was coming in. In a kind of demented rapture she lay listening to the incoming tide and to her own throbbing blood.

Once Alberta was inside the back porch, enfolded in the little warmth that seemed to reside in the staircase when one came in from outside, she collapsed. Her legs gave way, gusts of heat and cold passed through her. A feverish shivering rose from her wet skirts. And the terror, which had lain in wait and seized her as she groped her way back up Flemming's quay, making her stumble and run in panic, still moved like puffs of wind over her body.

Voices had whispered behind her, hands had clutched her. – Miserable and idiotic, here she sat on the stairs. Only one thing was lacking – that she should meet Mama. Then her expedition would be described as it deserved, as foolery and showing off. And she would be utterly prostrated, for the laws of nature cannot be changed.

No matter. She had brought one thing back to the surface with her, life. Life, that at any time, even at its most wretched, bears every opportunity within it as does the dry, inconspicuous seed. No-one sees them. But they are there.

Alberta opened the kitchen door cautiously. Her wet skirts slapped heavily about her legs. Then a chill went through her once more and her heart stopped. For through the kitchen window and a window lying at an angle to it she saw a light. The person carrying it was shielding it with the other hand, and Alberta first saw only the light-encircled black hand, as it passed the opening between the curtains. Then the candle must have been put on a table, for the glow from it fell steadily and clearly on something white, moving between the table and the sideboard. And the whiteness was no ghost. It was Mrs. Selmer, Mama herself. Alberta felt rather than saw her.

She held her breath, and squeezed herself into the darkness between the kitchen cupboard and the wall, prepared for the worst.

But the candle remained in there, stationary. Alberta peered out. She saw Mama hold something up to the flame and inspect it, touching it with a finger as if making marks. It sparkled for a moment, opaque, golden, like a large, round topaz. It was the whisky decanter.

Mama put it down again. She remained standing above the table, leaning on her hands. Her face sagged as if her legs were failing her. The candlelight fell on it strongly, and Alberta could see her expression, an expression so empty, so tired, so bereft, that she herself seemed to shrivel too.

Mama stood thus for a second, perhaps two, perhaps longer. Time stood still while it lasted. Essential facts were revealed, a whole sequence of cause and effect was exposed. Mama's true face, moulded by life and the years, was in there by itself in the dark, as if the strife and turmoil of everyday had parted to let it be seen. Simultaneously, memories floated up from the deepest layers of Alberta's mind: memories of Mama's hands, cool and firm, good and safe about her head, of warm kisses from Mama's mouth, of tender smiles; memories of times long ago when everything had been different. And something that had frozen and died one evening in the dining-room put out fresh shoots in her mind.

Now the candle was being lifted, now it disappeared. Alberta heard a door, and the night settled down on everything.

When the church clock began its twelve strokes she found herself in Jacob's room, heaven knows why. From some sort of need to be with him for a while as best she could, from old

232

habit. For leaning her forehead against Jacob's window frame she had ridden out many an inner storm, found calm after many tears of distress.

His books still stood on the shelf. There were invincible ink blots left on the unpainted wooden table – they could be glimpsed even in the dark. And that indefinable smell of the wharves that Jacob had had in his everyday clothes and which had transferred itself to the rest of his belongings, to Mama's despair – did not a little of it still hang in the air?

When she had crept past the bedroom door a stripe below it and the rustle of a book had betrayed the fact that Mama was not asleep. Papa was snoring with a loud droning sound.

Alberta was back again. Back to it all, to all that was warped and desultory, to the lies and evasions and small, hidden irons in the fire, to humiliation and hopeless longing, to the grey road of uniform days.

To live in spite of it, to live on as best she could, with her two warring natures: one that willed, no-one knew how far – one that could let itself be bound any time and anywhere. To live and lie and listen her way forward, to seek haphazardly in her tomes, to wait and see—

Everything was unchanged and the same. But Alberta had been in touch with what lay beneath and behind ordinary existence.

Behind Mama's bitter little everyday face, behind her almost convulsive party face, a face which was the real one, and which was deathly tired and corroded by lonely anxiety—

Behind Papa's little catchword, 'Cheer up, back we go,' the set features of one without hope—

Beneath her own weariness and despondency a stubborn will to continue, a hungering uneasiness, that could only be quieted by life itself; that could intoxicate itself with small, fluttering verses on a clear evening in spring or a moonlit night in August, yet hankered restlessly and desperately for something else, something undreamt of, far distant and obscure.

Over it all flowed everyday existence, turbid and shallow, with many small backwaters and eddies—

People swarm about together. The one knows so little about the other.

233

It occurred to Alberta that ultimately Jacob was the only one who turned his true face out to the world, a face full of undaunted confidence in his own two strong arms.

The street lights had been extinguished a long time ago. The church clock shone alone, like a moon in the night sky. Alberta was still standing with her nose against the pane. Then she picked up her wet skirts, shuddered with cold, and went to her room.

Soon it would be another day.

AFTERWORD

by Linda Hunt

Reversing the old adage about a prophet not being honored in his own country, Cora Sandel's *Alberta Trilogy* has long been a classic in her native Norway but is nearly unknown in the English-speaking world, especially in the United States. *Alberta and Jacob, Alberta and Freedom*, and *Alberta Alone*, first published in 1926, 1931, and 1939 respectively, were not even translated into English until the first half of the nineteen-sixties when they appeared in England; a one-volume American edition (which contained all three novels under the misleading title of *Alberta Alone*) appeared in 1966 but drew few reviews, little attention, and soon fell out of print. A look at the *MLA Index* for the decade of the seventies shows that numerous critical articles on Sandel, and especially on the *Alberta* books, appeared in the Scandinavian languages but none in English. The card catalogue of the New York Public Library's main branch reveals no holdings in English on Cora Sandel.

For American readers, Ohio University Press in publishing the *Alberta Trilogy* is making an important contribution to what Germaine Greer has called "the rehabilitation of women's literary history." These three feminist novels are so good that along with hailing their recovery one cannot help but feel angry that we in the United States have had to wait so long for the opportunity to experience their excellence.

Alberta and Jacob (1926) is an evocation of one year in the life of a shy, repressed adolescent girl living with her family in a stuffy, provincial town in the most Northern part of Norway during the last years of the nineteenth century. Alberta Selmer's family and their neighbors could be characters out of Ibsen in their bourgeois concern for sexual respectability and the importance of keeping up the appearance of material prosperity. Alberta despairs at the prospect of a life like that of any of the women in her town. If spinsters, they are objects of pity and, actually, objectively quite "odd"; if

235

sexually rebellious, pregnancy tames them. Respectably married, their lives are bounded by food and servant worries, gynecological troubles, and envy of their neighbors. This grim destiny is appropriately emblemized for Alberta by the figure of Nurse Jellum the midwife who keeps reappearing throughout the novel (and indeed recurs in memory in the sequels), "with her terrible bag and her quiescent know-all smile."

Alberta's options are contrasted to that of her brother Jacob who functions as a foil lest we make the mistake of not recognizing that Alberta's troubles are related to gender. While his life in this environment is far from enviable, he is encouraged to stay in school (although he is a terrible student and she is an excellent one), and he is able to find some relief from the stultifying life of the family by carousing with a sailor friend and coming home late, sometimes drunk. His decision to go to sea is a calamity for his caste-conscious parents, but they accept the unavoidable and he makes his escape. Alberta cannot follow Jacob's example and simply leave or even plan eventually to leave because she has internalized the family's assumption that as a dutiful daughter she will sacrifice her own well-being to be a buffer between her wretchedly-married parents.

Sandel expertly uses the frozen landscape of this Arctic town and the frigid interior of the Selmer house as an externalization of Alberta's inner life. The strange, brief summer of Northern Norway with its twenty-four hours of daylight functions as a metaphor for the protagonist's first furtive recognition that there is a world outside of her experience which can offer light, warmth, and happiness.

Alberta and Freedom (1931) begins with its protagonist standing nude, in Paris, posing for an artist. Lest the reader think Alberta has found the freedom and warmth she longed for as a girl and which the title of this volume seems to promise, we are told immediately of the terrible vulnerability Alberta feels, of the physical and mental discomfort of standing in one position for so long, and, inevitably, of the cold-

236

ness of the studio. (External cold and heat are metaphors for Alberta's emotional condition throughout the trilogy.) The Norwegian young woman's parents had died, and she has at last been able to flee to the Bohemian fringe of Paris; it is the period before the first world war when the Left Bank became a symbol of youthful release from restrictive conventions, but, as this novel and its sequel show, the pursuit of freedom is not easy for a woman.

Alberta and Freedom is framed by images of a woman's physical vulnerability and susceptibility to bodily exploitation. The opening scene of Alberta posing, compelled to earn her bread by making a body into a commodity since she has been trained for no profession or occupation, is matched by the closing scene of the novel in which Alberta, unmarried and pregnant, wanders around an exhibition of "man-eating" tribes from Central Africa which has come to Paris. She comes upon a young "Negress" nursing a child; the African woman recognizes Alberta's condition and nods in delighted affinity. The experience releases in Alberta previously pent-up maternal emotions, and yet it is clear from the imagery that for Alberta, both she and the Black woman are, like animals, captives of their bodies, reduced to a bodily existence. The fact that the African mother is being exhibited to crowds for a price serves to underscore the theme of sexual exploitation.

Between the first and closing scenes we read of Alberta's life in Paris: perhaps the most striking thing about this life is its apparent purposelessness; she does make occasional undisciplined, almost furtive attempts to express herself creatively through writing, but it is impossible for her to take herself seriously enough to have genuine literary ambitions. She spends her time wandering around Paris half-starved—on the Metro, on foot, on trams—taking in the human drama all around her but always a stranger at the feast. Unwilling to accept any of the roles society has assigned to women, Alberta, at this stage, is a kind of Underground Woman, "an outlaw" as one character calls her. She is the

237

female counterpart to all those male anti-heroes of modern literature who define themselves in terms of their marginality. Alberta has no analysis of what is wrong with the position of women in society, but all of her instincts are to keep herself a marginal member. As the narrative voice tells us, "She still had only negative instincts just as when she was at home. They told her clearly what she did not want to do. . . . she was left free to reject what she did not want and without the slightest idea of what she should do with herself."

Sandel depicts the circle of Alberta's Montparnasse friends, men and women who have come there from all over the world to be artists. Alberta's closest friend is Liesel, a struggling painter who always spoils her paintings just when they are very good by putting a dab of color where it does not belong or painting in some lines that mar the overall design. Like Alberta but several steps ahead of her since at least she is able to define herself as an artist, Liesel cannot trust her inner vision. She succumbs to a young sculptor, and initially her love affair is joyous, a reproachment to Alberta's loneliness. But Elial, Liesel's lover, determines the conditions of their life together so that his work always takes precedence over hers. Sandel is certainly making a point about the obstacles to artistic success for women since none of the women in Alberta's and Liesel's Paris circle achieve artistic fulfillment, but both Elial and Sivert, Alberta's lover, become quite successful. The women painters as they get older are evoked as "trudging around Montparnasse. . . . they had wrinkles and untidy grey hair, and they dragged themselves around with large bags of brushes over one arm . . . fussing and wearisome, they filled the academies and life-classes . . . they lived on nothing, making tea with egg water. . . . "

In the final volume of this trilogy, *Alberta Alone* (1939), the protagonist's existence is much less marginal as a result of a marriage-like relationship and motherhood. Alberta has backed right into a life not too different from the one she

238

sought to escape. In this book Sandel shows that integration into society for women too often means oppressive burdens: Alberta is encumbered by the endless work and persistent worry that being a mother entails; weighted down by her lack of love for the father of her child, on whom she is financially dependent, and by her developing love for Pierre, another woman's husband. But the relationship with Pierre is different from either of her previous entanglements with men in that he encourages Alberta to take seriously the pile of papers in a folder that Sivert has always demeaningly referred to as her "scribbling." For the first time she begins to think in a positive way about what she might want to do with her life.

In the course of this third novel Alberta becomes increasingly aware that she must find a way to be financially self-sufficient. In the last scene she walks along a road in Norway carrying the completed novel in a suitcase, her aim publication and the beginning of an autonomous and purposeful existence. Because she has left the child behind, everything she sees along the road, a mother and a baby, mare and foal, seem to tell her she is at odds with nature. Sandel defines Alberta's emotional state at this juncture in her life by an image of external cold which by accretion through the three novels has become increasingly powerful: "the mist had risen now, there was clear visibility and it was cold. No arms around her anymore, not even those of a child; naked life as far as she could see, struggle for an impartial view."

Throughout these books Cora Sandel is a fine stylist with a keenly-observant eye and a good ear; she has been well-served by her translator. Sandel's mastery of precise detail and fresh imagery allows her to bring place and character to vivid realization, endowing both with the emotional meaning she seeks. Thus, the coffee pot in the chill, cluttered Victorian dining room in the Selmer home "stood there like a revelation, its brass well-polished, warming, steaming, aromatic . . a sun among dead worlds." Seen through the window of the office where she works, Beda Buck, the girlhood friend who is as free in spirit as Alberta is repressed, "shook her fist through the window at Alberta, because she was wandering about . . . while Beda had to sit indoors." In Paris the cafe awnings, the dry leaves in a hot summer square, the "rusty" voice of a night club singer, the shrouded shapes in a sculptor's studio, all suggest Alberta's melancholy at being alone in the nearly-deserted city in August. In Alberta's down-at-the-heels hotel room mice drown in the wash-bowl. As Alberta and Sivert become increasingly estranged, his eyes are "much too blue," his presence on several occasions experienced as "a wall." Sandel's ear for dialogue is equally evocative.

Moreover, these novels are structured in such a way that form imitates substance. Instead of chapters, we have a series of scenes separated by blank space or blank space with asterisks. Each time the scene changes the reader must struggle, without expository narration, to re-orient herself, to figure out where Alberta is, who the other characters are, what is happening or what the conversation is about. The effect, especially because Sandel's writing is so visual and reliant on dialogue, is almot cinematic. For example, in *Alberta and Freedom*, an early scene opens in a carefully-described studio in a Parisian hotel. Alberta is lying on a bed talking to Liesel whom we are meeting for the first time. The reader wonders: is this where Alberta lives in Paris? Who is this friend? (The room turns out to belong to Liesel.) In having to work out the situation, the reader is experiencing what Alberta continually goes through as she struggles to make sense of a world which is not welcoming and where nothing is easy for her. Like Alberta, the reader feels peripheral to the life which unfolds.

Sandel's skillful experimentation with formal innovation along with her command of language and the importance of her themes certainly should have ensured her an audience and a reputation outside her native Norway. The question remains: why were these novels not recognized for their quality earlier, at least in the sixties when the Elizabeth Rokken

240

translation appeared in England and America? An examination of the reviews from that time reveal some clues. It is apparent even from the positive reviews (and on the whole the novels were well-received) that the specifically female reality Cora Sandel mined, the answers she found to problems of plot and structure endemic to women's fiction, and her feminist themes made sufficient and appropriate appreciation unlikely in the first half of the sixties in England and America. The work done by feminist critics in the last decade has made Cora Sandel's achievement accessible to us in ways it simply was not earlier. (It would be fascinating to know what Scandinavian critics have been saying about her work all along.) The sixties' reviews also show the extent to which bias against feminism and even downright sexism was an obstacle to a fair literary assessment of Sandel's work.

In 1966 an American reviewer (a woman), writing for the *Saturday Review*, enthusiastically compares Alberta with Philip Carey, the protagonist of Somerset Maugham's *Of Human Bondage*. Like Carey, she says, Alberta emerges from a dreary small-town childhood into "pre-war Paris and the brief years of freedom, art, and love, no money, and infinite possibilities." Since this is not what happens at all, we can only assume that the reviewer processed what she read to suit her preconceptions about what the artistic life in Paris was like in those years, preconceptions that had been formed by reading both the literature and the literary mythology produced by men.

Sandel has written these books in part to show us that while Bohemian Paris may have been a moveable feast to male writers and painters, there was no way that Alberta and her friends could have had the same joyous experience. While they do possess talent, they lack the self-confidence, the money, and the freedom from both conventionality and heterosexuality that made it possible for some few women—the likes of Gertrude Stein and Natalie Barney—to establish a woman-loving artistic culture in Paris in this period. As Liesel says in a letter after she has returned home to her fam-

241

ily, "The artistic poverty-stricken life isn't much fun in the long run. The men can do it, but not us."

The reader today finds herself nodding, 'Yes, that's how it would have been for most women.' She is likely to think of Virginia Woolf's hypothetical story, in *A Room Of One's Own*, of what would have happened to Shakespeare's equally-talented sister (if he had had one), if she had tried to go to London to become a playwright. Shakespeare's sister, in pursuit of freedom, adventure, and creative fulfillment, falls victim to, among other things, her lack of control of her reproductive life—as do Alberta and Liesel. But back in 1966 when the *Saturday Review* piece on the Alberta books appeared, few people were reading *A Room Of One's Own*, and literary minds, even female ones, were not sensitized to the fact that reality gets dangerously distorted when we try to fit female experience into a framework of literary conventions made by and for men.

Almost all the reviews from the nineteen-sixties complain that in Sandel's trilogy "nothing happens." The reviewer of *Alberta & Freedom* in the *Times Literary Supplement* (July 26, 1963) asks, "But what about development, action, drama?" Because of the work of such feminist literary critics as Joanna Russ, Annis Pratt, Nancy Miller and Gubar and Gilbert, we understnd that Cora Sandel is avoiding the patriarchal plot-structures that have been recognized as a major obstacle to women writers seeking to express an authentic female point of view. Since women in stories inherited from the male literary tradition have limited alternatives regarding what they can do (fall in love and marry, fall in love and die), Sandel chooses plotlessness, but in doing so she is not choosing lack of form. Joanna Russ would describe the structure of the Alberta trilogy as "lyrical" in that images, events, passages and words are organized around an implicit emotional center, that center being Alberta Selmer's repressed soul and its yearning, as it gropes in the cold and damp of life, for freedom, warmth, and security. Virginia Woolf structures her novels along similar principles.

242

These three novels read together also have another kind of structure which comes from the working out of certain mythic patterns which feminist criticism such as Annis Pratt's *Archetypal Patterns in Women's Fiction* and Carol Pearson and Katherine Pope's *The Female Hero* show us are recurrent in fiction by women. Both of these recent studies stress the importance of the mother-daughter relationship, symbolized in Greek mythology by the story of Demeter, the goddess of the harvest, and her daughter Persephone who is stolen from her side. Just as in the myth the season of cold when nothing grows initiated by the ruptured relationship between mother and daughter can only end when the two are returned to each other, a female hero in fiction often requires reconciliation with her mother or a mother-figure in order to get in touch with her own power and achieve her creative potential.

Alberta's relationship with her mother is already deeply estranged when *Alberta and Jacob* opens. Mrs. Selmer, self-doubting and disappointed with her life, is incapable of nurturing a daughter. Although Alberta is so cold that her skin is perpetually blue, she has to sneak the hot cups of coffee she craves. At the breakfast table Alberta must help herself to food as surreptitiously as possible while Mrs. Selmer loads Jacob's plate with piles of cheese. Alberta's mother is similarly ungenerous on the level of emotions. She tells Alberta repeatedly that she is a disappointment because of her lack of beauty, her shyness, her inability to interest herself in domestic accomplishments, her inexplicable interest in reading "learned tomes," and her refusal to encourage the attentions of her father's clerk.

Mama's inability to provide warmth is largely responsible for Alberta's guilt-ridden and anxious personality; she is so constrained that she feels "she was without the use of speech, she would die of muteness." Always afraid of eliciting her mother's scorn or anger, Alberta can never feel relaxed in her mother's house.

Given the youthful Alberta's fear that she will "die of

243

muteness," we can understand why in later years her writing becomes the key to life for her. Given the lack of ease she feels in the house in which she spends her childhood, Alberta's discomfort in a series of dingy, even sordid hotel rooms and then in Sivert's crowded studio takes on greater poignancy. Even in a pleasant summer cottage in Brittany she is unable to enjoy the beauty of her surroundings because she is terrified that the sea air is dangerous to the health of her delicate little son. Alberta can never feel at home anywhere.

The inhospitability of her environment, wherever she is, is a factor in her failure to impose coherence on her manuscript. We see Alberta wrestling with her "muddle of scribbled papers" in poorly-lit hotel rooms and on the slopes near the beach in Brittany where she must "struggle . . . with the wind for control of her straying papers."

Towards the close of the last volume Alberta is sitting in a wood in rural Norway uncomfortably balancing her manuscript on her knees, desperate to finish, when she is discovered by an old woman with a "kind, wrinkled face tied up in a handkerchief." The woman, Lina, invites Alberta to see her house on a nearby farm. They go upstairs to a room where "the sun poured in on a large table standing between the windows . . . . There was simple furniture . . . Some dried wreaths above the sofa gave out a strong sweet scent. . . . Alberta had, without thinking, put her folder down on the table. There it lay as if it had come home. She almost felt at home herself." The farmwoman allows her to use the room to work on her manuscript, and in it, over the course of a beautiful Norwegian summer, she completes her novel.

Lina's psychic function is to be a surrogate mother to Alberta and, appearing just when the younger woman needs her most (exactly when Pope and Pearson, in their book on the archetypal "journey" of the female hero, say this figure appears), is able to heal the damage done by Alberta's actual mother who had functioned as a "captor." Lina's description fits that of the "wise old woman" whom Annis Pratt tells us is often in women's novels an archetypal guide for the soul as it pursues its spiritual quest. Lina is surrounded by plants and animals and, as the sweet-smelling wreaths in the room demonstrate, has a knowledge of herbs. Married, but very much her own woman, Lina provides a model of calm autonomy. Most important, she not only provides Alberta with the sanctuary in the form of a simple room which Pratt reminds us so many women characters need to get in touch with their power but, like any good mother, she affirms Alberta's gift by recognizing it: "I understand enough to see you're a kind of author too, it's just that you don't want anything to interfere." Again like an ideal mother, she compels Alberta to impose discipline on herself by telling her firmly she must vacate the room by the date summer visitors are due to arrive. In finding a spiritual mother who both nurtures and yet encourages separation, Alberta becomes capable of saving herself through mastery of language, overcoming the "muteness" which was her biological mother's inadvertent legacy.

Alberta can develop as a person only through the kind of inner, psychic experience that reconciliation with a mother figure represents. As the reviewer of *Alberta and Freedom* quoted before complains, she does not develop psychologically very much in the course of the novels. For example, when Jeanne, Pierre's wife, orders her to send him a telegraph terminating their relationship, she simply complies, as much a slave to an authoritative voice as when she was a child who had internalized her parents' values.

Reading Annis Pratt can help us to understand that Alberta fails to develop much psychologically until the very end not as a result of weakness in Sandel's narrative skill but for the same reasons that female heroes in general don't progress towards maturity through action in the social world. The female bildungsroman cannot demonstrate "*bildung*" in the way that male novels of development do because in patriarchal society adulthood for women means neither authority nor autonomy. Unlike the male hero who develops by achieving an adult social identity, for Alberta increasing

245

integration into society only means further entrapment. Like so many protagonists of women's fiction she can "break through" into true adulthood (as she is told to do in a very Jungian dream by the "young girlish figure" who is her guide) only by asocial moments of epiphany such as she experiences in her almost clandestine first visit to Lina's room.

Alberta's reconciliation with the symbolic good mother links the last volume with the bad-mother motif in the first book, *Alberta and Jacob*, providing unity to the trilogy as a whole. Since Lina is encountered in summer, and Mrs. Selmer tyrannizes over the adolescent Alberta predominantly in the dark, freezing depths of winter, it seems possible that Sandel may even have had the Demeter-Persephone myth consciously in mind. Certainly the extraordinary emphasis on the soul-withering Arctic cold in *Alberta and Jacob* suggests the endless winter that results, in the myth, from the rupture of mother and daughter.

Other criticisms of the *Alberta* books in the reviews from the sixties require no response but are interesting because of their naked anti-feminism and sexism. An unsigned review of *Alberta Alone* in the *Times Literary Supplement* (February 25, 1965) dismisses Sandel's concern for the emancipation of women as outdated and complains about the "female narcissism" in the book. This same reviewer finds the character of Alberta insufficiently deep to warrant her position as the center of interest in a trilogy, an opinion he is entitled to, but one is forced to think about his biases when he observes, "This is not *just* to say that women are less interesting than men, and that this is the flaw" [emphasis mine].

The resurrection of feminism in the years since the *Alberta Trilogy* was first published in English has encouraged literary minds both to develop the interpretative skills necessary to understand women's literature and to be on the alert for "lost" books by women. The appearance in America of these three novels by Cora Sandel should be regarded as an important event of literary archeology. However, literature by women has been retrieved in the past only to slip again into obscurity. It is important that people be told how good the novels in this series are and be urged to read them singly and/or as a unit; it is important that these novels be taught and written about. Readers are ultimately the ones who keep worthy "lost" books alive.